The Boomship Crisis

Written by Brady Gorrell
Edited by the Fulton Books copyediting team

Fulton Books, Inc.
Meadville, PA

Published by Fulton Books 2021

ISBN 978-1-63860-104-3 (paperback)
ISBN 978-1-63985-134-8 (hardcover)
ISBN 978-1-63860-105-0 (digital)

Printed in the United States of America

For Carrie, without whom this tale may have never existed

A man, skin wrinkly and tanned, was staring off at a decrepit building with his squinted brown eyes, causing them to wrinkle in the corners. He could have sworn he had been there before all this happened. Maybe not. The whole city used to look so different on every corner, but now it was all the same—muddled gray mixed with a splash of green foliage spreading across these vaguely remembered ruins. How long had it been since he had been back here? He guessed maybe around eight months. He wondered if the crops would come in well this fall. They seemed to be increasing in health each year.

He scratched his bare chin before rubbing his head of nearly silver hair sitting short, straight, stiff, and strong atop his head despite his age. He ran his hand down his long face, past his similarly long nose, to his narrow lips. He stretched his face downward. He was exhausted from his long walk into the city yesterday despite a night's rest. Surely he would find the old agricultural store soon. He would know the way back then and could make the trip home shorter than the squiggling path he had taken into it.

He reached back up his face to his slightly protruding ears to rub each of them. It took a lot for him to sunburn, but he was growing concerned with those ears. He dropped his arm back down to his side, slapping into the thigh of his hardy jeans. He looked down at his feet to stretch his neck and observed the condition of his stiff brown leather boots. He wondered if he would find any boots today. A good pair was getting hard to come by.

A drip of sweat ran down his nose and paused right on the end of it. He pulled up his plain white T-shirt and wiped his face with it to rid it of the droplet. He noticed that the veins in his bony but strong arms were protruding. He must be getting too hot.

The man ended his short break in the shade of an aggressively growing tree jutting out from the building behind him and started back down the littered street. He always liked that tree. It reminded him a lot of himself—born in a hard place, growing things to survive, and despite the odds, somehow finding a way out into the light and living to an old age. It seemed very fitting for him to be resting under it with its knotted bark and twisted trunk as the warm summer breeze blew through its branches.

He carefully scanned the area and walked across the street. It was so unfittingly quiet for an intersection of this size. A few vehicles sat dead on the streets, long ago stripped of parts and supplies. There was no point in searching anything on the streets anymore. They had all been picked clean like those vehicles. He hoped the agricultural store wasn't the same way.

He listened as the wind rustled through the leaves now climbing all over the remains of buildings. He wished he were up there to enjoy the breeze. A loud metallic bang interrupted his peace. He jumped, spooked by the sound, and dove in behind a nearby vehicle. Voices met his ear.

"Think you're going now?" asked a deeper male voice.

"Let me go!" pleaded a much smaller and younger one.

"Oh no! We have a feisty one. Who gave us this part of the city anyway?" complained a third voice in a nasally tone.

The deeper voice replied, "Doesn't matter. We got the boy. It is time to deal with him."

"Fine."

There was a session of clothes being yanked and grunting. The deeper voice chuckled. "Boy, he is a feisty one, isn't he?"

"Heh. Yeah. What are you gonna…" The nasally voice cut himself off. He started back in with a new topic. "Hey, what was that?" There was a pause. The nasally voice exclaimed a gasp. "It's that maroon guy and the dirty one! We gotta get 'em!"

The deeper one replied hastily, "Hey, we can't go now! What are we going to do with this kid?"

"I'm not a kid!" rebuked the younger voice. There was a muffled thump, and the younger voice grunted.

The nasally one continued the conversation as if nothing had happened. "I dunno, man! Just, uh, just throw him in that store we were headed into. It's in good shape, and there are bars on the window. He won't be going anywhere in there. We will come back for him later."

The deeper voice let a long breath out his nose. "Fine. Go after the other two. I will deal with the munchkin and join you." A set of footsteps ran off, and another session of grunts and the muffled sounds of clothes being dragged across the sidewalk ensued. The deeper voice grunted. There was a louder thump followed shortly by a brash squeak and a harsh metallic slam. A stern clack rang out, then a second set of heavier footsteps ran off.

The man stood from behind the vehicle. He shook his head as he watched the two scurry off down the street. He walked at his leisure to the store he had heard the door slam on. The man peeked around the edge through a set of vertically barred windows. A boy was inside, fixing his mess of brown hair. The boy muttered something. "Ugh. I really wish I could get a haircut."

The man coughed lightly to get his attention. The boy gasped and snapped his blue eyes up to reveal a slightly tanned face with a few freckles on the cheeks and a narrow, robust chin. He dove behind a crumbling counter with barstools attached to the creaky wooden floor in front of it. The man chuckled. "Don't worry, boy. I am not one of those Raiders." The boy remained hidden and silent.

The man continued. "Look, I saw those two buffoons lock you in here. I know they are coming back for you. I am willing to wager that you don't want them to find you when they come back." There was no sign of life inside the store. The man sighed. "All right, then. I guess I will just leave you in here." The man made an intentionally heavy footstep without turning around.

The boy's voice rang out. "Wait!" He peeked over the counter. "Why do you want to help me?"

The man smiled. "What do you mean?"

"Well, you have got to want something. Nobody helps others around here without benefitting themselves."

"That is your mistake. I am not from around here."

This perplexed the boy. "Where are you from, then?"

The man smiled once more. The boy knew he would receive no answer. The man leaned against the barred window. "I am willing to just let you out, but you seem uncomfortable with this idea. You might think it is a setup, or maybe you don't want to be indebted to me. Now I have no plans for either of those things, so I will give you a deal instead. Then you can hold your end and get out free." He eyed the boy, who seemed interested. He turned away to look down the street to relieve the tension. "Do you know where the old agricultural store is in this area?"

The boy thought this was a strange request. What could he need from there? There was not a plot of land in this entire city that was worth farming, besides maybe the sports stadium, but it was right in the middle of Raider territory. The man did say he was not from here, though. The boy had no choice anyway. He nodded. "Yeah."

The man nodded in return. "I will let you out of here, and then you take me to that farm store. Once we get there, you point me in the right direction to leave the city in the quickest way possible, and you are free to go."

The boy liked the sound of that, but he held a stern face anyway. "All right." He stood from behind the bar, dropping the shard of glass he had been hiding, and crossed the room to the door.

The man met him there. "It seems they have jammed the door with this metal pole through the bars of the door."

The boy nodded. "Yeah. That was lying on the ground right there. Think you can get it out?"

The man pulled on it with a grunt. "Yes. Stand back. It might be under a load." The boy took few steps back. The man yanked on the rod. It slipped out with a metallic ping as it struck the edge of the barred door. The man tossed the bar aside and started pulling on the door as it clanked across the sidewalk. He made no progress in opening it. He waved the boy over. "Hey. Come on. Help me get this open."

The boy crossed the room and pushed on the back of the barred door. The door groaned in response and shot open with a banging sound. He flew out of the doorway and rolled onto the concrete. He stood quickly and looked wildly around. The man was casually leaning against the freshly opening door. He squinted at the boy. "Are you going to dart?"

The boy relaxed and wiped his hands on the seat of his dark-blue jeans before adjusting his black shirt back down. "You were being honest."

The man tipped his head to the side and furrowed his brow. "What made you think I would lie?"

The boy was as equally confused as the man. "Everyone lies here. You really are not from around here."

The man shook his head. "I am not from here."

The boy looked down at the man's boots. "You must live somewhere nearby even if you are from outside the city, though. You didn't walk too far in boots like those."

The man looked down at his boots while chuckling at the falseness of that remark. He then looked over to the boy's old black canvas sneakers. "You are obviously a city dweller wearing sneakers like those."

The boy chuckled as he crossed over to the man. He was about a head shorter than him. "I suppose we are both guilty of judging by appearance."

The man grinned as he pointed to the pole on the ground. "Grab that and bring it over here." He started closing the door.

The boy retrieved the pole. "Why?"

"Because we are going to block this door up again to make it look like you are still here. Your friends will have a waste of time and a rude awakening when they get back." The boy smiled. After the two reapplied the jam to the door, they started down the street. The man began explaining his predicament. "Well, if you haven't caught on, I am looking for farming supplies, mainly tools for breaking ground. A have a lot of fields that haven't been tilled in years. They are essentially useless since they are so hard that I can't plant on them. I don't know how I am going to do it alone, but I am sure that I will at least need tools. The only place I know of left is the agriculture store here in the city."

He peeked down at the boy. "Maybe you would be interested in leaving the city and joining me. I have enough food for you and shelter. You seem to be having a hard time here with the Raiders."

The boy shook his head. "This is my home. I don't know how to leave it."

"Well, I could teach you."

The boy flattened his lips out as he pondered the idea. "I will have to think about it and let you know when we get to the store." The Young raised an eyebrow toward the man. "You sure are quick to trust someone."

The man chuckled. "I consider myself a good judge of character." The boy nodded more out of politeness than agreement.

*****

A young girl, somewhere in her early twenties, was crouching behind a metal crate, listening to the angry voices of nearby Raiders. They had been tailing her through the city for days. How long would it take for them to finally give up on her? What did they want with her anyway? She didn't know, but she wasn't willing to find out. Women in these parts are hard to come by. If they are like the others, she needs to stay as far away from them as she can.

She had tuned out the Raiders. They were just blabbering on about places she might have run off to, not knowing she was sitting right across the sloped parking garage floor from them. She wished they would just leave already. But a change of tone from the Raiders caught her attention.

A gravelly male voice spoke first. "Well, I reckon we have lost her."

A sleek, powerful, quick voice responded, "I dunno. She couldn't be far. We only just lost contact." The girl scoffed quietly from behind the crate.

The gravelly voice responded after a moment. "Come on. She is trapped in this garage anyway. All the buildings around this are collapsed in. There is only one entrance, and it is too high to jump off everywhere else. We can just camp right at the entrance and cut her off if she runs."

The other sighed. "Fine. I am getting hungry anyway. Do we still have any of that venison?"

There was a sound of shuffling shoes on the rough concrete surface. "Yeah, I think so. Let's go find out." The voices began to fade.

"All right, all right. I see you want to go. You know it isn't every day we find a woman out here."

"I am aware," stated the gravelly voice.

The other paused. "Ya know, I think you don't care about finding women anymore because you have your girl back home."

There was a quick session of shuffling sounds followed by the ruffling of clothes. The gravelly voice took a serious tone. "You had best keep quiet about that. You know what the boys would do to her if they find out about her. I ain't going to stand for it."

The other voice seemed panicked. "I know! Don't worry, man. It is all under wraps. Nobody knows."

"Good." There was a quick release of clothes. The footsteps continued away and around a corner, then became inaudible.

The girl sighed and flopped out onto the rough concrete surface. She stretched out and tugged down on the long sleeves of her well-fitted dark-green shirt. She pushed a wisp of brown hair away from her equally brown eyes and tucked it into the band holding her ponytail tight on the top her head. She sat back up and rose to her feet and adjusted her skintight black pants back down, which had ridden up from when she slid into hiding behind the crate.

She dusted them off, careful to avoid the completely black hatchet vertically strapped in a special loop in a narrow black belt as she got around to dusting her right thigh. After brushing off, she checked the hatchet for scrapes, fearing she had nicked it on the concrete. She was relieved to find only the thin silver glint on the end of the sharpened blade.

She ran her finger gently across the blade, which was pointing toward her back, and still found it to be sharp enough. She always kept the blade pointing backward like this, so if she sat down, crouched, or laid her hands on her lap, she would not have to worry about the blade cutting into her wrist. Besides, it had been there for so many years that she was used to avoiding it in that position.

She checked a green compass positioned on her right hip, just above the hatchet's head. She opened its lid, seeing if it still functioned. She did this check out of habit. It had never let her down. She flexed her strong legs and observed them visibly through the tight pants. She bent back down to retie her ugly gray sneakers. She missed her fancy old black stealth shoes. They were much more reliable than these. If only they hadn't fallen apart from the abuse she had put them through.

Her hands felt odd tying the laces. She had been wearing a pair of fingerless black gloves for years until just now, when she lost them to a doorway. The Raiders had tried to cut her off by slamming a door, which her hand was grabbing the edge of, and she was able to escape this pain by sliding her hands out of the gloves, letting the door that was pinching her hands shut the rest of the way and claim the gloves. Then she ran away. There was no way she was going back for them now. She would just have to get used to not having gloves.

She ended her quick check and switched to thinking about how she was going to escape these Raiders. They were right, there was only one way out. She could just camp here, but she was out of food. She would have to find food somehow. She leaned over a railing to check for any Raiders below her. Instead, she noticed a building at the bottom through a crack between the ramp up the parking garage and the next slightly sloping floor above it.

A faded sign read Vehicle Maintenance and Repair above a closed metal doorway. It was braced up against the wall of the building, but there was no garage door available. There must be one on the other side. If she could get through the metal door, she might be able to sneak out through the garage door. At the least, she could grab some tools to help her escape.

She checked the surrounding area once more and hopped over the railing. She hung from the crumbling concrete wall and dropped herself quietly onto the hood of an ancient, rusted vehicle. She slipped down off the right side of the vehicle and crouched in case she had been spotted. After another check, she sped out from behind the vehicle, staying as low as possible while headed down the ramp.

She rounded the corner and skittered to a stop. An entire floor of the parking garage had fallen in. She figured she could drop down just fine and then use the crumbled remains to get the rest of the way down to the building, but she definitely couldn't get back up without a ladder or some rope. She had no other choice. She lay on her stomach and lowered herself off the edge, allowing her arms to extend all the way out. She released the ledge and dropped down onto a busted large slab of concrete. It shifted slightly underneath her. She wobbled to regain her balance and began picking her way down to the building.

*****

"So what is your name?" the young boy asked.

The man said nothing. He looked right through the boy for a moment, causing the boy to shift nervously. His focus returned as he said, "I do not think we should share our real names. You know that as soon as your name gets out, people can run it through the systems or around people and find you all too easy."

The boy started to argue. "You are right, but don't you think it will be hard to call for each other if we need to?"

The man cocked his head and smiled slightly, showing a couple of teeth. He seemed to be staring off into the sky, blue and cloudless.

He nodded lightly, still looking at the sky. "Yeah, I suppose you're right. So I will tell you what"—he turned his head to look at the boy—"I will call you Young Boy, and you can call me Old Man. That way, the systems can't trace us since there are all kinds of boys and old men."

"I don't like being called Young Boy. That is so vague."

"Well, eh, that is the point." The man sighed. "How about just the Young, then?"

The boy paused and thought this over. The Young—he liked it. It had a nice ring to it, mostly because he wasn't getting called a boy. "Yeah, let's use that. Are you sure you are fine with Old Man?"

The Old Man chuckled. "Yes. I need to own up to my age anyway." He cracked a wide smile, and both of them laughed.

The boy refocused on the Old Man. "Why does it make a difference, then, the names? If we are going to call each other by the same two names, what does it matter if we use our real ones or a nickname?"

The Old Man snapped his eyes over to the boy's face. "You do not talk to many people, do you?" The boy shook his head. The Old Man continued. "Have you ever told anyone your name?" The boy shook his head again. The Old Man relaxed. "Good."

He started to look away but realized that he had not answered the boy's question. "Oh, and using a nickname prevents people from running your name through old security systems or searching programs. Some of these programs still exist here, although they are largely defunct. It also helps you conceal yourself from people who you do not want to know you well."

The Young did not reply. He was busy thinking the information over. The Old Man continued the thought. "The Raiders have access to your history if they know your name. It is all general stuff for the most part, like your last recorded height and weight, hair color, eye color, and so on. If they know that, so what? They still have to find you.

"Now the issue is, it also tells them who your family is. If you have any family members still alive, they can track them down and use them as bait to lure you into a trap. Then they might just kill you both. It is a brutal system of looting, so our best bet is to never say our names so they never have a lead on us of whatever information they have."

The Young nodded. He looked up to the Old Man's face. "What if you don't have any family left?"

The Old Man stopped walking for a moment. He hesitated. "Young, how old are you?"

The Young shook his head. "I don't think I should tell you."

The Old Man sighed. "Yeah. Can I at least get a decade? I could probably guess it by looking at you."

The Young nodded. "Guess."

"Early twenties."

"You said a decade, not five years."

"Fine, twenties."

The Young nodded. "Twenties. Eighties."

The Old Man seemed appalled. "What? Do I really look that old?" He scanned his tanned arms.

The Young chuckled. "No. I am just messing with you. You look like you are in your sixties."

The Old Man relaxed. "Oh. Yeah, sixties is right."

The Young was confused. "Why did you ask that?"

The Old Man snapped back to the previous conversation. "Oh, I was just curious, uh, when you had lost your family."

The Young looked up again. "Who says I have?"

The Old Man was swept by the awkwardness of the situation. "No one did, but I thought you had implied—"

"Don't worry about it," interrupted the Young.

The Old Man nodded and started walking again. "Well, to answer your question about not having family, they can still track your appearance and anything that was posted about you in about any newspaper. That means they might be able to predict more things about you, like if you won an archery competition, then they would know you are a good shot. Now in a city this big, the only newspapers you probably made it in were from the local districts, so they may not even have access to those."

The Young scoffed. "Thanks for the confidence in my popularity."

The Old Man looked back down at him. "I am just being realistic here."

The Young nodded. "I know. I am just giving you a hard time. Don't worry, I am fine with never using my real name." The two continued down the street.

*****

The girl had made her way down to the maintenance building. It had been a hairy trip down those teetering slabs of concrete, especially when she was trying to remain quiet. She crossed the last open area of concrete, populated only by the occasional Deep Blue Danderons, to the gray solid-metal door. She had heard that the head of those danderons were actually edible, but from her experience, they tasted rather nasty.

She pressed her hand up against the door. It opened just a crack before bumping into something. She pushed on it harder. Whatever was blocking the opposite side seemed to be light enough that she could shove it out of the way with the door. She set to work. The object on the other side made an extremely loud screeching sound as she pushed it. She panicked and continued pushing it. She would hide inside and barricade the door again.

The door abruptly shot open. She belly flopped onto the floor inside the building. An arm snatched her head. Before she could scream, a massive hand came down across her mouth. She wriggled and squirmed. She managed to kick the person holding her, but it seemed to have no effect. The person dragged her to her feet and pinned her face against the wall. She grunted through his hand.

A large voice pleaded behind her. "Please stop! There are Raiders outside. If you yell, you will kill us both." The hand forced her head around. She took in the sight of her attacker. He was a giant, maybe middle-aged. His arms bulged with muscle. They were riddled with cuts and scars. A particularly large diagonal cut crossed his left bicep. She followed his massive arm to the dull-gray T-shirt hugging his body tightly and tucked into his stiff, slightly worn blue jeans held up by a thick black belt, which had seen better days.

She continued down to the floor where she spotted the man's jeans hiding a pair of black leather-bound boots. They must have steel toes, as the toe of the boot was worn evenly in a curved shape instead of being crumbled in on itself. She swung her line of sight up to the man's face. He had a bold, clean-shaven square chin. His nose was large like the rest of him. He had a pair of thick, bushy dark-brown eyebrows that were borderline black against his white skin. His head was completely bald.

She met his pleading brown eyes. She relaxed. He released her head cautiously. She spun away from him and drew the hatchet. The man held his hands in the air as he apologized. "Sorry. You probably thought I was going to kill you."

She shook her head. "I thought you were going to do much worse than that." She tugged at her pants. The Mechanic had no response to this. She continued. "Why didn't you?"

The Mechanic was appalled. "Not all men are sex-hungry whores. That would only be the Raiders."

The girl raised an eyebrow. "Which you aren't?"

The man shook his head again. "No, I am not a Raider. In fact, those scum can stay as far away from me as they like." He crossed his arms.

She nodded and stowed the hatchet on her leg. "Are you sure this hatchet isn't persuading you?"

The man again shook his head. "I didn't even notice you had it at first." He lowered his hands. "Come on. We need out of this hall-way. It isn't safe." He jerked a large filing cabinet with a loud screech and shoved it up against the door. He pointed down the hall. The girl walked down it followed by the man. He started up a conversation. "I am impressed."

"By what?"

"By the fact that you could even move the cabinet back there. It was heavy."

"It wasn't easy. Did you rip it out from the door partway through?"

"I spotted you through the crack in the door. You definitely weren't a Raider, and you were making too much noise. I pulled it out of the way to get you in here faster. Take a left and go into that room across the shop. It is the safest place here."

She did as she was told. The man shut the door behind them and locked it. He slipped past the girl and leaned against the far wall. She seemed confused as to why he had pushed her toward the door. "I don't want you thinking I am trapping you in here. You can unlock that door and run whenever you like." She nodded.

He picked up a stiff plastic chair and placed it down facing the middle of the room. He waved her to it. She sat down. He took another plastic seat, which was already placed behind a rusty metal desk. He clasped his hands. "Why are you here?"

The girl shook her head. "I don't know. I have been running from the Raiders for weeks now. The last few days have been rough. I don't know what they want with me." The man raised a bushy eyebrow. He nodded down to her legs. She sighed and rolled her eyes. "Do you really think that is the whole reason?"

"It is certainly one of them. Women are scarce around here. How old are you?" The girl shot a warning glance at the man. He held up his hands. "I already told you, I am not like them. Besides, I am probably too old for you anyway."

She nodded. "Twenties. And age never seemed to stop the Raiders."

The man furrowed his brow and let out a long breath. He nodded down to her legs again. "That is definitely why they are after you. They must be getting pretty desperate to follow you for weeks on end."

"Yeah. I must be something special." The man was caught in a situation where no response was a good choice. He remained silent. The girl held her forehead. "I am sorry. I didn't mean to—"

"Don't worry about it," he interjected. She sighed. The man picked the conversation back up. "Earlier, I didn't mean why you are in the area. I meant why you are in my hiding place."

"Do you mean this building?"

"Yes."

"Oh. I was running from the Raiders."

The man waved her off. "That is obvious. What am I missing?"

She paused for a brief moment to collect her thoughts. "I thought there might be a second way out of the parking garage through this building. It said Vehicle Maintenance and Repair on the sign, but there was not a garage door to get the vehicle inside on the side I came in through, so it must have been on the other side. I thought I could just pass through here."

The man nodded. "What were you going to do after that?"

The girl hadn't thought about that. She sat back in the chair and ran her hand through her hair. She dropped her hand to her thigh with a slap. "I have no idea."

The man leaned forward. He was visibly considering something. "Do you like it in the city?"

The girl grew concerned. "Not really. I just don't have anywhere else to go."

"What if I told you that I learned the world outside of the city isn't completely destroyed like they told us?"

The girl grew perplexed. "What do you mean?"

The man scooted his chair an inch or so toward her and leaned in once more. "I overheard the Raiders talking about some business fellow. He was doing a deal with the outside world. What with, I have no idea. It doesn't matter. He is doing something with somebody from outside of the city."

The girl was unimpressed. "That is all you have to go on?" The man nodded. The girl shook her head. "I can't leave the city on that small of a lead."

The man sat back in the chair. "Look, I am leaving in the next hour out the same garage door you thought you were going to use. That garage door is very loud to open. That means I need you to stay here until we can both leave at once. From there, you can do whatever you want, but I am offering you a one-way trip out of the city. I know the route. I met a fellow down on his luck and gave him some food in return for directions out of the city."

"Is he a trusted source?"

"He says he has been here his whole life. Knows the city like the back of his hand."

She nodded, accepting this was likely true. "Do you have any tools in this place to build shelter with once we get out there?"

The man shook his head sharply. "No. This place must have been looted forever ago. I came in here searching for them. I planned on just getting outside and going from there."

The girl shook her head. There was a long pause. "Oh, hell, I have nowhere else to run to anyway." She leaned forward. "Call me the Survivalist."

The man smiled. "Call me the Mechanic."

*****

Meanwhile, the Young and the Old Man had finally arrived at the agriculture store. The Young pointed at the long, flat building. "That is it."

The Old Man followed his finger. "Welp, thank you for getting me here, then." He turned to look at the Young. "Are we good?"

"No. I haven't told you the way out."

The Old Man seemed impressed. "Ah, yes. You are one to keep your end of the deal, aren't you?"

The Young smiled. "Do you remember telling me earlier that you are a good judge of character?"

The Old Man furrowed his brow. "Yes."

"Well, you are. I am not here to screw you over."

The Old Man nodded. "What about these directions, then?" The Young hesitated. The Old Man pressured him. "You do have them?"

The Young rushed his response. "Yeah! Yeah, I have them. It's just…" The Young sighed. "You offered for me to come back to your farm. I have nothing left here. I have been scavenging to survive for ages now. I'm tired of it. Growing some crops really doesn't sound too bad." He looked up at the Old Man. "Can I come with you?"

The Old Man smiled. He rubbed the Young's messy hair. "Of course, you can."

The Young pushed the Old Man's hand away. "Please don't do that."

The Old Man chuckled. He swatted the Young's back lightly. "Come on. Let's go check for supplies here. Then you can guide me out."

*****

The Survivalist nodded to the Mechanic, who reached down and snatched the lip on the garage door and began pulling it upward. It groaned and strained on the rusted runners guiding the door in segments up vertically and around an arc and rested them horizontally against the ceiling. The Mechanic leaned around the corner. He waved the Survivalist out. He scurried off, leaving the garage door open. The Survivalist followed him out onto the street and into a nearby ally.

He vaulted a pile of wooden crates. This surprised the Survivalist as she hopped over them. He was quite the agile fellow for being as big as he was. She guessed it was because he was so strong instead of fat. His weight and size only gave him more power instead of hindering him. She was even having a hard time keeping up with him, although she didn't know the area or even where she was going.

The Mechanic stopped at the end of the ally. He motioned the Survivalist up to him. She leaned around the corner. The Mechanic gestured down the street. "Okay. Do you see that agriculture store?"

"Yeah? What about it?"

"The fellow I talked to before said to go past the agriculture store and keep going. Follow the path all the way out. Don't get off the road. It is the fastest way out now due to the damages to the other routes."

"Ah, so we just make a break for it here or what?"

The Mechanic shook his head. "It is far too long of a road to sprint the whole thing. We are going to have to take our time and hope we don't find any trouble."

She nodded. "All right. Let's go, then."

The Mechanic stepped around the corner and began casually strolling down the street. "Out of curiosity, how well can you fight?"

The Survivalist shrugged. "I try not to. When I have to, I usually hit and run."

"What if you just had to bare-knuckle and roll with it?"

"You mean stay in a fight? No, I probably would do well with anyone larger than me."

The Mechanic nodded. "What about with me?"

"Oh. I have no idea. You would probably end up doing most of the work, and I'll just be there to pick off the stragglers you toss over to me."

"So if I pummeled a guy, you would be able to take care of him the rest of the way?"

"Probably."

"Have you ever killed before?"

"Who hasn't?"

"But have you?"

The Survivalist paused. "Yes. I had to shiv a couple Raiders trying to, uh, get after me, if you know what I mean. It was not a pleasant experience. I had someone I used to see around tell me that I am cursed by my own good looks. What about you?"

The Mechanic lifted his eyebrows. "Too many. Raiders mostly. They gang up on me when I am alone to try and take me out because I killed a bunch of their guys once. I had no beef with them. They attacked me for loot. If they had just left me alone to begin with, I wouldn't be in a virtual gang war with them."

The Survivalist looked over to the Mechanic. "That is rough. How did you do it?"

He stared over hesitantly. She nodded and waved off the question. The Mechanic continued the conversation. "I do what I have to. You put it right—it was not an enjoyable experience."

*****

After scouring the entire property of the agricultural store, the Young and the Old Man came up with nothing. The Old Man led the Young out of the store, checked the area, and sat down on the curb. The Young smacked the Old Man's back. "Sorry, Old Man. I figured there would be something left in here. I should have known better. This whole area has been picked clean, but I never thought anyone had a need for agricultural supplies here in the city. There isn't a big enough plot of land anywhere to do it. People just farm on the rooftops and such for personal use, and even those get sacked and burned a lot."

The Old Man glanced over. "Any tool in there was probably looted and used in the Faction Wars."

The Young pressed his lips. "Do you mean as weapons?" The Old Man nodded while staring off past the Young. The Young furrowed his brow and looked down the street for a moment. Seeing nothing, he turned back to the Old Man. "That is brutal." The Old Man nodded again while continuing his gaze down the street. The Young turned and looked once more. "What are you looking at?"

The Old Man rested a hand on the Young's shoulder. He stood using the Young's shoulder as support and squinted down the street. The Young stood as well. Now that he had stood, he could see over a concrete barricade. The Old Man must have been just tall enough while sitting to see over it. There was a pair of Raiders at the far end of the street. A building had collapsed, spilling chunks of concrete over all of it. The Raiders were busy rummaging through the pile to find a way through. They seemed to be in a hurry.

The Young elbowed the Old Man gently. "What's got them going?"

The Old Man shrugged. "You live here. You tell me."

The Young shook his head. "I have no idea. They have their weapons drawn."

"You mean the pipe and the wooden plank?"

"Yeah."

"Those are considered weapons here?"

The Young looked up at the Old Man's confused face. "Old Man, everything is a weapon here. How long has it been since you have fought somebody?"

The Old Man replied under his breath, "Oh, about a day."

The Young didn't catch it. "What?"

"Nothing. Let's go figure out what these two are up to. Maybe they have supplies that we can use. At the minimum, we can let them do the work of digging us a way out. They are digging the same path we need to use, right?"

The Young nodded. "That is smart. Let them do the work, and then escape behind them."

"Good. Let's go." The two started down the street, staying close to the crumbling building walls.

*****

A fellow in black khakis ran his hands through his front and back pockets to stretch them back out. He hated it when they bunched up. He adjusted the smooth round lapels on his maroon overcoat and dusted off the exposed bit of his black shirt underneath it. He glanced down dismally at his black sneakers. If only his dress shoes were more fitted to surviving out here. He ran his hand through his brown hair, laying it back to reveal a sharp and healthy hairline, before allowing it to relax to slightly lift off his head.

He lowered his hand. On the way down, he spotted a spot of grime. He licked his finger on the opposite hand and rubbed it off to reveal his smooth white skin beneath it. A second man stood watching him nearby. He somewhat missed his old business suit, but he certainly preferred his current outfit over the constant maintenance the fellow across the room put into his. He couldn't resist the urge to scratch his own head while he watched the other.

He scratched his clean-shaven, pointed chin and then his rounder head above it. He quickly rubbed the dust out of his sharp, spiky black hair. He noticed the maroon fellow checking his overcoat for stains and remembered the few he had on his long-sleeved black dress shirt. He ran his hands along the barely noticeable vertical stripes embroidered into the fabric and tucked it into the narrow black belt holding up his gray jeans.

He looked down at his black sneakers, then at the maroon fellow's pair. Black sneakers were either popular, so there were many produced, or they were the least favorite and the last to be looted, as all he could find in the entire city were more of these similar black sneakers.

The maroon fellow glanced up as he finished dusting off. "Do you think we…" There was a massive crash outside. "Never mind." The man in maroon took off. The second man followed him. They ran down the street, away from a pile of collapsed building rubble.

Shouting could be heard behind them, along with the sounds of metal clanking and wood thunking. A more familiar voice yelled at them. "Radioman! Get in here!" The man in maroon paused in the street, and the man following him nearly plowed him over.

The man in maroon darted into an alley, following the familiar voice. He spoke aloud. "Hobo! Where are you?" An empty metal can clattered out onto the concrete. The man in maroon ran down the alley and located a narrow horizontal window at ground level. He crouched down and peered into the darkness inside.

The voice returned. "Come on! Get in here. It isn't safe out there!" A dirty white hand shot out and snagged the man in maroon's lapel. It retracted into the window, pulling the man with it. The man lay flat on his stomach and slipped through headfirst. A few grunts later, the shuffling sounds inside stopped. The voice returned. "Radioman! I haven't seen you in ages. I thought they got you."

The man in maroon, who had been called the Radioman, replied, "No, they did not capture me, Hobo, although they might have had you not warned me. But we can catch up later." The Radioman returned to the window and stuck an arm out. The other man, who was still outside, bent at the waist to follow it to the Radioman's dimly lit face. The Radioman greeted him. "Come on, Entrepreneur. Get in." The Entrepreneur lay on his stomach and slipped in feet first with assistance from the Radioman pulling on his pantleg. The Entrepreneur dropped the short distance to the floor.

The Hobo elbowed the Radioman. "Who is that?"

"That is the Entrepreneur."

"The one that has been trading with the outside?"

"Yes, that is the fellow."

The Entrepreneur was confused by all this. "Wait a minute. You know this guy, Radioman?"

The Radioman nodded in the dark. "Yes, I have for a short while now, just about as long as I have known you."

The Entrepreneur seemed taken back by this. He shook it off with a shake of his head. "All right, then. How do you know me, then, eh…"

"Hobo. Call me the Hobo. And all you need to know is, there is not much in this city that I don't see. I go unnoticed, but I listen to everything."

The Radioman tapped the Entrepreneur's shoulder. "You can trust him. He and I have a deal."

The Entrepreneur shrugged off the Radioman's hand. "Which is?"

"We both want out of the city. It is becoming far too dangerous here with the Raiders, and both he and I know it. He knows the way out, and I was able to get the radio frequencies of some old channels and figure out where they were headed. Most of the Raiders are on the far side of the city, searching for some large fellow and a girl. Now is our chance to escape."

"So why did you bring me?" questioned the Entrepreneur.

"I didn't want to leave you behind. I figured I could at least get you out of the city." The Entrepreneur had been through far too many scams to fall for that. He raised a questioning eyebrow. The

Radioman sighed. "I figured we may need a briber to get us past some Raiders if it came down to it."

"What do you have to bribe with?"

"Nothing. That is why I brought you. Maybe you could figure something out."

The Entrepreneur chuckled and held his forehead in the palm of his hand. "Well, tough luck. I can't pull off that much of a deal."

The Radioman sighed. "Are you still coming, then?"

The Entrepreneur grinned. "Ha! Of course, I am. I have been trying to get out of here for ages. The city's economy is dead, even for a dead economy. As you and your friend apparently know, I have been trying to trade with the outside."

"For what?"

"Passage out of here. Nobody is crazy enough to do it. It seems to me that you have just solved that issue for me."

The Radioman grinned. "Great! Let's…" There was a particularly loud session of crashing sounds followed by a voice.

"Hurry up, Old Man!"

"I am trying! Where are we going?"

"We were supposed to stay on that street, but there are too many Raiders!"

The Hobo retrieved a glass bottle from a nearby drinking bar. He fumbled past the barstool and tried to slip past the Entrepreneur to the window. The Entrepreneur interrogated the Hobo as he pushed him. "What are you doing, Hobo?"

The Hobo brushed him off. "I know that voice. Get out of the way." He shoved the Entrepreneur out of the way and chucked the bottle out the narrow window. It plinked once on the concrete before shattering.

The voice gasped. "Hobo?"

"Come on!"

There were footsteps shuffling about. The Young poked his head into the window. "Oh yes!" The Young slipped through the window with ease and landed softly on the damp floor. "Hobo, I will never get tired of you finding these hiding places. You know—eh, who are these two?"

The Hobo turned as if he had completely forgotten about the two behind him. "Oh. The closer one is the Entrepreneur, and the farther is the Radioman. Who is that one?" He pointed out the window to the Old Man.

"That is the Old Man. He, uh…" The Young realized the Old Man might not want them to know of the farmhouse.

The Old Man held out a hand into the window. "I told the boy—sorry, the Young—that he could come with me to a farmhouse I have outside the city if he would take me out."

The Hobo switched back to the Young. "Are you taking him out the route I gave you?"

"Yeah."

The Hobo stepped closer to the Young and lowered his voice. "I told you that was only for you."

The Young matched his tone. "I know, but I didn't have anywhere to go once I got out." He pointed out the window. "He gave me somewhere. It is the only chance I have. He is from outside the city."

The Hobo sighed in defeat. He stepped back and returned his voice to normal. "Fine. Is it just him?"

"Yeah."

"Get him in here."

The Young turned around and grabbed the Old Man's arm. He started guiding him in. The Old Man was a tad slower on getting through than the rest.

The Entrepreneur snagged the Hobo and the Radioman. He spoke quietly to them. "That guy is as old as dirt. He is going to slow us down. We cannot bring him."

The Hobo shook his head. "We can't leave him behind. He has a farmhouse we can use even if it is just a place to hide for the night."

The Radioman nodded. "We don't know how to get to it without him."

The Entrepreneur shook his head. "We don't even know that this farmhouse exists, assuming we even make it to it dragging him along."

The Hobo grabbed the Entrepreneur's arm. "We don't have a choice."

The Entrepreneur shook his hands angrily at the Hobo. "Did you tell anyone else about this route?"

The Hobo hesitated. The Entrepreneur stepped toward him. The Hobo held up a hand. "I told one other person. He is all the way across the city. He isn't going to be a problem."

The Entrepreneur was outraged. "Do you realize he could have sold us out?"

The Hobo stepped forward, toward the Entrepreneur. "He isn't going to be a problem, all right?"

The Entrepreneur was shocked by the harshness of the Hobo's tone. The message had gotten through. "Fine. We will bring the old guy."

The three turned to the Old Man, who held up his hand to stop them from talking. "My ears might be old, but they aren't that old. I heard everything. You can stay at the farmhouse if you can get me and the Young out of the city in one piece."

The Young was appalled. "I know the way out! We don't need them."

The Hobo butted in. "No, you do need us. The route I gave you is chock-full of Raiders by now based on how fast you ran in here. We are going to have to take a detour, which you don't know."

The Young leaned against a cold, slimy wall. He jumped off it in disgust. "All right." He looked at the slime on the wall. "Is it covered in this stuff?"

The Hobo grinned. "No. This way."

The Entrepreneur snapped his head over. "Wait. We are leaving now?"

"Yep. We have no time to lose. It is going to get dark soon."

The Radioman shrugged and started following the Hobo. The Young and the Old Man joined him. The Entrepreneur released a sharp breath, relaxed his shoulders with a frustrated shake of his head, and stepped through an ancient doorway on the far side of the room.

*****

The Survivalist bumped into the Mechanic. She had been ignoring her surroundings for the most part until now, as she had gotten lost in thought. The sudden bump into the Mechanic interrupted her trance. She looked around to catch up on what she was missing. It was incredibly dark in these old tunnels. She wondered how the Mechanic knew where he was going or if he did at all. She decided she would ask and find out. "Hey, Mechanic? Is this a good time to talk?"

The Mechanic nodded. "Sure. It seems pretty empty down here."

"Where exactly are we?"

The Mechanic hesitated. "I am not entirely sure, but I remember this line."

"This line?"

"Yeah. You know, the Magnitube lines."

"Like, the transportation train things?"

"Yes."

"I thought it was hazardous to touch anything on the floor of these due to the risk of electric shock."

The Mechanic laughed lightly. "No. They were required by law to tell people that after one fellow somehow managed to get shocked. It wasn't nearly strong enough to kill him. It merely stood his hair and gave him a good spook. These tubes are run entirely on magnetic fields. The only shock possible would be generated accidentally by the metal body of the transit vehicle passing quickly by another piece of conductive metal in the magnetic field.

"The magnetic field might temporarily align between the two to cause a minor jolt that would quickly zero out to the nearest ground. The fellow just happened to be holding the exact piece of metal that the effect grounded to, which in turn grounded to him to spread the charge and scared him."

The Survivalist honestly had no idea what the Mechanic was talking about, but she rolled with it. "So we are perfectly fine here?"

The Mechanic peeked back. "You didn't get any of that, did you?" The Survivalist had been caught. She shook her head. The Mechanic chuckled. "Yes, we are fine. There aren't even any trains to cause the spark."

"Oh, good. I thought these things had tracks on the ground?"

The Mechanic paused his walk. He turned to the Survivalist. "Did you not ever ride one of these?"

"Well, I did, but I didn't pay much attention, and I only rode them on special occasions. I never really had a need to ride one, as most everything we needed was right around home."

The Mechanic nodded. "Well, you are partially correct. A long time ago, these things used to be driven by wheels on tracks. Then they switched to magnetic hovering with guide rails, which is what you are thinking of, then they abandoned the rails altogether and just had a magnetically stable train floating in the middle of these tubes."

The Survivalist nodded. She was just happy to break the boredom of the walk. To keep the conversation going, she asked a question she figured the Mechanic could answer: "Did they ever have to work on it?"

"Well, rarely. There was no friction besides air resistance to cause wear on anything. The only problem was, the walls would become magnetized. Over time, they had to bring a special train through here to scramble the magnetic alignment of certain sections to keep it stable."

"How do the walls get magnetized? They aren't made of magnets."

"Well, yes, but the walls can get aligned still to be weakly magnetic as well. If you don't believe me, take out that compass on your hip and move around. It will point to the walls if they are still magnetized." The Survivalist grinned. She pulled the compass from her hip and held it flat. It swung over to the wall closest to her. "See? Try to move to the other wall." She crossed the tunnel. As she did, the needle on the compass teetered back and forth a bit before finally resting, pointed at the other wall.

"Huh."

The Mechanic grinned. "Come on. We can talk about this as we keep walking."

She jogged for a moment to catch up. "So this train was circular?"

"It was a hollow cylinder with smooth edges. It stayed very close to these walls all the time. The magnets were on the train itself. The magnets were so precise that they pulled the train in all radial directions at the same time, which was how it was able to hover in these tubes."

"It pulled on these metal walls?"

"Yes, all the time."

"How did it go?"

"What do you mean? How did it accelerate?"

"Yeah."

"That gets a bit more technical. I know they were somehow able to tilt some magnets and pull others away from the metal to cause a forward motion. They did the opposite to slow down and back up."

"Oh. That is cool."

The Mechanic was visibly excited. "I know! I wish I could have worked on them sometime."

"Why didn't you?"

The Mechanic's excitement left him. He sighed. "That is a long story."

The Survivalist was going to pry, but her shin drove into something hard. She winced. "Ah!"

The Mechanic turned back to look at her. "Are you all right?"

The Survivalist was rubbing her shin to ease the pain. "Yes. I thought you said this place didn't have rails in it?"

The Mechanic nodded. "They don't."

"Well, then what did I just hit with my leg?"

The Mechanic looked down and spotted the rail in the dark. "Oh. That is a rail. Wait. I thought these tubes only had rails…"

He trailed off for a moment and then looked up. "Oh, that's right. They had rails at the stations and removed the magnetic layer in the walls. They did this as one of the walls would be missing to allow the passengers on, and the train would fly right over into the remaining wall. What station are we at?"

The Survivalist shook her head. "How would I know? I just asked you where we were."

The Mechanic pointed up to a wide crack in the ceiling, which was the only light source in the tunnel. "Can you see that?"

"What?"

"That building. I recognize it. The agricultural store is just back the street. We were supposed to be on the surface past that agriculture place, but we missed our exit. We need to head out here."

"How do we get out?"

The Mechanic smiled. He pointed across the tunnel to a flat large concrete pad. The two clambered up onto the pad. The Mechanic pointed to a door lit dimly by daylight at the top of a flight of stairs. "We take the stairs out." He lightly tapped the Survivalist's back with his right hand, smiled at her, and started across another set of rails on the far side of the concrete pad. He waited at the stairs for the Survivalist to warily fumble her way past the rails and scale the edge of the pad attached to the stairs. The two hustled up the stairs toward daylight.

*****

"How long have we been down here? It is going to be dark outside, let alone in here," said the Young.

The Hobo shook his head. "We have been here for a few hours."

"Why can't we leave?"

"I already told you, we have to stay here until the streets clear a bit, and then we bolt."

"The Old Man says we won't make it back to the farmhouse before dark if we don't leave soon. You and I both know we don't want to be out in the city in the dark."

The Hobo turned to where he thought the Old Man was. He couldn't quite make anyone out for sure across the room. "Is that true, Old Man?"

The Old Man spoke from the Hobo's left. The Hobo had been looking at the wrong person. He snapped his head over to the correct person as the Old Man responded. "Yes. It will take us a couple hours at least to make it back even if you run and carry me."

"What about at your normal pace?"

"At a reasonable pace and a direct path, it would still take three hours. Unfortunately, the direct path is not an option due to our current position, so it is going to take around five hours."

"How far is it?"

"I would guess about thirty miles with the route we are taking."

The Hobo wheezed. "Thirty miles?"

"Yes. Just be happy you didn't just make the trip yesterday."

The Hobo rubbed his head. "You are sure you know where to go once we get out?"

"I am certain. I know my land."

The Hobo nodded. He held still for a moment. The room fell silent besides a faint rumble of a breeze gusting through the dark chamber. He started across the room. "Then we had best get going." He pulled himself up the damp concrete block he was leaning against to a decrepit doorway. He nudged the door. It didn't move. He forced it open, struggling to shove a soda machine out of the way in the process. He stopped once the door was wide enough to slip through and motioned the group to follow him. He turned sideway and waddled his way through the crack.

Once the group had all joined him on the other side, he motioned for them to stay quiet and forced the soda machine back into position, blocking the door. He crept up the stairs. Seeing no motion, he hopped through a broken window next to a closed door. The others followed suit. This brought them out into an old transit hub filled with decrepit stores and aging signs. None of the overhead lighting was active, leaving the whole place dark, except for a few large caved in holes dripping water in the ceiling. Voices suddenly rang out, and a figure stepped into view, facing away. The group froze.

"Hey, do you think this would be useful?" The figure speaking was a woman. Her voice echoed slightly on the walls. She was holding an electric power tool.

A much deeper and powerful voice spoke in return. "No. We don't have power to run it. Plus, the chuck is completely rusted through."

The girl sputtered and tossed the tool onto a pile nearby. She turned to rummage another stack. She snapped her line of sight directly toward the Hobo. She froze. The Hobo dove into hiding. A pair of feet rushed across the floor to the far side of the hall between the stores. "Mechanic? We aren't alone."

"What?"

The Hobo snapped a cautious glance to the Entrepreneur. The Entrepreneur caught the glance and grew concerned. The Hobo raised his hands into the air and stood from behind a toppled shelving unit strewn out onto the concrete path. The girl drew a hatchet from her leg.

The Hobo put both his hands directly in front of him, palm outward. "Wait! I know your friend. I ain't a Raider, and last time I checked, your friend wasn't either, which leads me to believe we are on the same side here." The girl peeked over her left, then resumed eye contact with the Hobo. The Mechanic stepped around a shelf. He squinted down the aisle. "Hello, Mechanic."

The Mechanic started down the aisle. He snatched the Hobo by his shirt and pulled him up. "Who are you?"

The Hobo chuckled. "I am just a guy down on his luck."

The Mechanic realized who he was holding. "Is that really you, Hobo?"

The Hobo tried to nod. He dropped the Hobo. The girl replaced her hatchet. The Hobo gestured to her while fixing his clothes. "Who is your friend here?"

The Mechanic turned to see the girl. "She calls herself the Survivalist. She was getting hounded by the Raiders. She is coming with me on a route out of the city."

The Hobo nodded. "I know. There has been a change of plans for you. You just don't know it yet. Come on out, guys." Nothing happened. He beckoned them again while turning around partially. "I am serious, people. Get out here."

The rest of the Hobo's crew stepped out from hiding. The Mechanic shook his head. "Wait. You aren't—"

"Yes, I am. They are too."

The Mechanic laughed. "I can't believe that. What did they do to you?"

"Nothing. We just came to an agreement." The Mechanic raised a doubtful eyebrow. The Hobo insisted. "I am serious! I am leaving, and so are they. Now do you want our help or what?"

The Mechanic sighed. "Yes."

The Hobo turned to the Old Man. "You have space for two more?"

The Old Man shrugged. "One of them might have to sleep on a couch. I assume they aren't comfortable sleeping together."

The Mechanic and the Survivalist stepped apart from each other. The Survivalist shook her head. "No. Yes. No. You are correct. We don't want any of that." The Mechanic nodded awkwardly.

The Old Man chuckled. "Well, what do we have to lose? Come along for the trip to the outside."

The Mechanic was not hasty to agree. "Wait. Where are we going?"

The Hobo looked back at the Old Man. "Are you fine with telling him? I trust him."

The Old Man answered, "I have a farmhouse that will provide us shelter for a bit. You can come with us there if you want. If you stay or not after that is your own call."

The Entrepreneur stepped in. "Hey! No. Wait a second. You can't just let people in without the agreement of the rest of us. Hobo, is this the third guy you said wouldn't be a problem?"

The Hobo sighed. "Yes, and that is still true. He won't cause any issues." The Hobo turned to address the group in general. The Entrepreneur was not satisfied with this response. He started to argue again but was promptly cut off by the Hobo, who snapped at him in an irritated voice. "He saved my life!" The group fell silent. "He just doesn't know it."

The Mechanic joined back in. "That is for sure. I don't recall ever saving your life."

The Hobo sighed. "You did it before the first time I introduced myself to you. You remember that poor fellow who was nearly starving not far from that parking garage shop you were holed up in? That was me. I was having a bad time. I was running from a bunch of Raiders after they had found a way into one of my hiding dens downtown where all my food was. I was trying to get away, then they saw you.

"For whatever reason, they went after you instead of me. Had they not, they would have pinned me down in an old grocery store with two exits, both easily guarded, and the store was looted. I wouldn't have lasted long. It was a last-ditch effort to get something to eat and hide at the same time. Apparently, that hole of yours worked well, because I saw you again later after leaving that grocery store. I felt like I needed to help you since you helped me even if you didn't know it. I didn't care if it was the last thing I got to do. Somebody should know what I learned even if I didn't make it. That was why I allowed you to find me.

"I gave you the most valuable information I had in secret gratitude, which was the way out of this city. I didn't expect you to be so kind as to give me food in return, which was also a much-needed lifesaver, so although I repaid you for saving my life from the Raiders as best I could, now I am in debt to you for saving me from starving. I am trying to make up the debt now by letting you come with me out of the city and guiding you out."

The Hobo turned back to face the group. "Okay. Now that the whole story is out there, does anyone have any problems with these two coming with us? I have somewhat known the Mechanic for a while now, at least long enough to know that he wouldn't bring a scoundrel with him and that he is handy with any tool in the world. Good enough?"

The group, stunned by the story, nodded nonchalantly in agreement. The Entrepreneur waved the Hobo off. "Fine. Whatever. I hope you people know what you are doing. I know a lot of untrustworthy people."

The Survivalist had a comment for that. "Sounds like you need better friends."

The Entrepreneur scoffed. "Yeah, sure. Like I need more people to deal with."

The Hobo turned to the Mechanic and the Survivalist. "Ignore him. You two are as trustworthy as they come." He focused on the Mechanic. "You in?"

The Mechanic looked over at the Survivalist. She nodded. He looked back at the Hobo. "We are in."

"Perfect."

The Old Man rejoined the conversation. "Do you have any tools from here we could use to fix up the farmhouse? It has a few leaks here and there and could use a general fixing up."

The Mechanic shrugged. "No. This place is sacked. We searched everywhere. The only tool we have is the Survivalist's hatchet that she just threatened the Hobo with."

The Hobo was quick to add, "And this tiny knife." He retrieved the small knife from his pocket and held it out toward the Old Man before continuing to talk. "The thing isn't even long enough to kill someone, though. Trust me, I tried. I doubt it will do us much good." The Old Man nodded.

The Radioman stepped into view. His maroon outfit caught the attention of the Survivalist and the Mechanic. "Hello. I figured, if we are going to be in cooperation for a period, we should introduce ourselves. I am the Radioman." He stuck out his hand. Neither of the two took it. He retracted it. "This is the Hobo, as you know. That is the Old Man. The grouchy one is the Entrepreneur. The boy is called the Young."

The Young, who had been silent this entire time as he stared at the Survivalist, at last broke his own silence with one word: "Hey." He waved shyly. The Survivalist met his eyes briefly before looking away. He shook his head and stepped back out of view.

The Mechanic spoke to the Hobo and the Radioman at the same time. "Look, we can talk more later. How far is it to this farmhouse?"

"The Old Man says thirty miles."

"Thirty?"

"That was what I said. Come on. We don't have time to waste." The Hobo tapped the Mechanic's arm as he brushed past him and started toward the shattered glass entrance to the store. "Come on. There is a shortcut through this building that can get us onto a safer street. I thought this was the best route, especially since it was underground, but being that you two found it without any help, I would say the safety of it has been changed." He vaulted through the window back into the store. The whole group followed his lead.

*****

As they stepped out into the light of day on the far side of the building, the group finally got a good look at the Hobo. He noticed them all looking and turned to accept his judgment. He cocked his head to the side and leaned on his right leg. His chin was covered in a black stubble that wrapped up and around his face, nearly reaching his ears. He had shaved off the sideburns. His nose was longer above his narrow lips. He reached up to pull off a faded-black winter hat and revealed a buzz cut of short, wiry black hair.

His tanned face swept across each group member as he squinted in the daylight. He was wearing a thin black hoodie with the sleeves pushed up that, at one point, might have displayed a concert or band name on it. The hoodie fitted him baggily, but he must enjoy the large size of it as it was obvious he had worn it for a long time. The hoodie's tattered bottom edge joined a pair of blue jeans. The jeans were heavily worn and would have been a brighter blue, but they were so stained by unknown substances that they remained a dark navy. A small cut had been gashed into the left thigh and then stitched up roughly. A short pocket knife was just poking out of his left pocket, hooked onto a belt loop by a clip on the back, that could be easily accessed at any time.

His shoes were substantially worn and nearly smoothed of any tread on the bottoms. He lowered his arm to his lean body as his eyes at last adjusted to the brightness of the outside. The motion drew attention to his well-toned arms. The group shifted to checking his condition. Despite his tattered appearance, the Hobo was in surprisingly good physical shape. A toothy grin revealed mostly white teeth. The stubble, although a bit sporadic on his face, was at least trimmed off, presumably with the knife. His hair stayed straight and stiff on his head due to how short it was. Although his arms and clothes were covered in grime, it was apparent that the Hobo had at least attempted to keep his hands and face clean.

The Hobo cut off the viewing session. "All right, I get it. I am dirty and could use a fresh set of clothes." He started to turn away but hesitated. He turned back. "Just know that I try, all right?" He sighed. "I know I look like a filthy hooligan, which might not be that far from the truth, but at least I am trying to get better."

The Radioman shook his head. "Hobo, you are fine the way you are. Social standards are overrated. I couldn't tell you how many times I have been judged for wearing my maroon outfit."

The Hobo stared blankly back at the Radioman. "I am not doing this for social standard. Those all went out the door a long time ago. I am doing it for myself. I know I can improve. These people might not." He waved his arm to sweep a gesture out to the whole group. He turned away and started down the street. "Come on. This is the way out now."

*****

The group had been walking for around two hours now without a single word. They all followed the Hobo as he picked his way across the shattered road surfaces, decrepit vehicles, and crumbling parts of buildings. He stopped for a moment in front of the group and scanned the area. Something caught his eye. He crossed the street quickly and returned with a folding ladder. He stood it upright next to a brick wall at the base of building, just below a large hole in the same wall.

He spoke the first words. "This is one of my old hiding dens. I abandoned it a few years back. It was too far out of the city. It should be safe in here. Let me check it out. Only come in if I throw something out. If I plead you to come in but don't throw anything, don't come. They have caught me and are using me for ransom to get to you. If you hear gunshots, turn and leave. Then you will be on your own."

He scaled the ladder and threw himself over the wall before anyone could protest him. The group stayed put. After about a minute, a rock flew out over the wall. It clacked across the pavement. "Hey! Come on in." The group huddled around the ladder and ascended it one at a time to hop the wall. The Mechanic came through last, landing heavily in a puddle on the floor after a good drop from the wall and splashing everyone.

The Hobo waved them along. "This way. If you want to talk, it should be safe here in this tunnel to do it." The Young sighed in relief. He had been itching to talk for a while now. He jogged up next to the Old Man and tried to think of something to talk about. The only thing he could think of were books. Old people liked books. He decided to try that.

"Have you ever read *The Angry Brantar*?"

The Old Man squinted, obviously trying to recall his memory. "Eh, maybe at some point. Why? Do you like that book?"

The Young rubbed his forehead. "No, but I had to read it in school, and I remember it being the most enjoyable thing that I was forced to read." The Old Man chuckled and shook his head. The Young continued on. "Come on, Old Man, I'm trying to start a conversation here. This walk is boring."

The Old Man stopped walking and looked at the Young. "Oh, really? The walk is boring to you? Well, I will have you know that I find walks quite enjoyable, and I still find this one in particular…a little lackluster." He continued walking as the Young grinned. He spoke once more. "So who read that to you anyway?"

The Young glanced up at the Old Man, who was prodding him on by raising his eyebrows. "How young do you think I am?"

The Old Man looked forward, observing the damp tunnel walls, seemingly taken aback slightly by the accusing tone of the question. The Young berated him with an explanation. "The Crisis only happened ten years ago. I was well old enough to be in school and be reading by then."

The Old Man cocked his head over, nodding as he thought about the timeline as well as his own age. He figured he wasn't getting a direct answer to his previous question about the book without an accidental argument, so he settled for the implied response that the Young had read it himself and asked another question. "What was that book about? Refresh me."

The Young's face grew perplexed. He slowed his walking pace a bit as he thought. His face lit up, and he trotted for a moment to catch back up. "I think it was about this brantar who was angry." He paused. "Imagine that. Totally not in the title or anything. Anyway, the brantar was angry because it thought society was treating it wrong. In reality, the brantar had been pampered its whole life, getting all sorts of fancy snacks and the wondrous tuse greens, but the people just now started treating it like every other brantar.

"The brantar took the lack of treats and suchlike as a sign that the people were mistreating it. All the other brantar told it that it was simply getting a taste of reality, but the brantar refused to believe that. It fussed and hissed, trying to get its old life back, until it eventually passed out from exhaustion while flying over town in a rant and fell to its death."

The Old Man paused, taking a quick look at the Young to be sure he wasn't fond of the book. Seeing the Young's perplexed face, he spoke. "I definitely haven't read that. That is a very strange story."

The Young nodded. "That was English class for you."

The Old Man snickered. "It does not make sense either. What is a brantar anyway? Or tuse greens?"

The Young shrugged. "I don't know. I guess it is a thing that could fly or something. Tuse greens must be some kind of flying animal food."

The Old Man seemed perplexed but intrigued enough. The Young paused briefly to let the Old Man speak. The Old Man took the opportunity. "Would a brantar not land before dying in flight from exhaustion?"

The Young scoffed. "Look, Old Man, I didn't write the book. I was forced to read it." He paused. "And it didn't die in flight. It passed out and fell to its death. So technically, it died by hitting the ground." The Young paused again, shaking his head in realization of how arbitrary this argument was, and added, "But of everything that class had us read—in fact, out of everything in school—that one will always stick out."

The Old Man was genuinely curious. "Why?"

The Young thought about this for a moment before replying. "Because it is the one thing that actually applies to my life now that I learned in school. Think about it. Every person in the world was just like that brantar before the Crisis. They had no idea how good they had it. And then the Crisis came along and set them all in a flutter. Many never had a chance, but those who lived had the opportunity to sit down and complain about losing everything until they died or went out into the world and accepted the fact that they were all just regular brantar. Now the only people who remain are all the regular brantar."

The Old Man said nothing. He could not argue that logic, but he was stunned that someone so young could make such a vastly accurate comparison, especially since the events happened at such a young age to him. The tunnel had nearly ended. The Young fell back, and everyone returned to silence.

*****

A few hours passed. The group had slipped through a hole in the final outskirt wall of the city and stepped out into the grassy plains and hard trees. They took a moment on the outside of the wall to regroup. The Old Man took a deep breath. He turned to the group, who seemed fascinated with their lively surroundings. He questioned the group. "How long has it been since you all have been outside the wall?"

The group exchanged knowing glances. The Hobo replied, "They never have. I haven't either." The Old Man was sent through a moment of realization. The Hobo shook his head. "Why would we have? We didn't even know anything was out here. Had it not been for the Entrepreneur's dealing with the outside getting leaked, we might have never known." The Hobo turned to the Entrepreneur and spoke to him directly. "How did you find the person on the outside anyway?"

The Entrepreneur seemed nervous to answer this. "I didn't. They found me." The Hobo spurred him on with a hand wave. The Entrepreneur shook his head. "It is best you don't know the rest." The Hobo gave up. The group wandered the nearby area for a bit, exploring the trees and feeling the thick grass. After the newness wore off, they continued their trek with the Old Man taking the point.

Another few hours passed before the Old Man abruptly left the path they were following. The group beat their way through a pile of brush along the edge of the path and followed the Old Man over a hill through the woods. The Old Man led them to a rotting wooden fence at the edge of the woods. He gasped. His face drained to a pale color. He had spotted something over the hill and rushed to the fence to lean on it. The group ran up beside him. A two-story old house was ablaze at the far side of the field. Men scurried around the outside, chanting and causing a ruckus. The Old Man's face drooped, then stiffened to anger. "Those Raiders have never been out this far. Never. They stay in the city. Why are they here?"

The Young pointed at the burning house. "Is that the farmhouse?"

The Old Man was boiling with rage. His whole body shook. He managed a nod. The Young turned his head to watch the flames. The Old Man slapped the wooden fence. It emitted a snapping sound. "That was all I had left! There was nothing they could have wanted there besides some food and beds. They could have just left my things alone out here. I wasn't bothering them. Instead, they burned it the instant they found it."

A rageful tear ran down the Old Man's cheek. "That was my family's house. I grew up there." He whimpered for a moment.

Nobody took their eyes off the orange flames. A dark-black smoke began rolling out of the upper-story windows. The Survivalist looked down at the field. "What about your crops?"

The Old Man shook his head. "They probably already looted and burned them. I didn't plant this field in front of us this year."

The Entrepreneur drew in a breath. The Hobo smacked the side of his head to shut him up before he even said anything. The Hobo whispered to him, "Now is not the time for any of your shit, Entrepreneur. This man has just lost everything. Now if you can get that through you thick skull, I would recommend you choose your next words carefully."

The Entrepreneur took the hint. He cleared his throat while rubbing his head. "Old Man, do you have anywhere else we can go? If it is fine with you and everyone else, I would like to keep moving before the Raiders spot us." The Entrepreneur gave a cautious glance to the Hobo. The Hobo nodded approvingly.

The Old Man sniffled. "Fol…" Something caught his voice. He cleared his throat. "Follow me. I have one spot we can check. It is a cave nearby here I used to hang out in as a kid. I suppose it is still there." He took one last look at his blazing beloved home. His face hardened. His voice took a darker tone. "I have one place I need to check on the way there." He started off to the right along the fence.

The group left the field with the farmhouse. They passed the last post of the fence. They crossed through a section of unmarked woods. They arrived at a small wooden shack still in the woods. It had ivy crawling all over it, ironically the same kind as the stuff back in the city. Moss covered every untouched surface. A small window still had glass in it, although it was dirty and foggy.

The Old Man held a finger to his lips. He motioned for the group to stay put by pointing at the ground. He slowly snuck up between the window and the only door on the structure. He placed his hands into a small pocket on the door, lodged it in place, and ripped the door open. The door careened outward around the hinge to the right and slammed into the outside wall. The Old Man swung around the left edge of the door and lunged inside with surprising agility.

The sounds of a few footsteps were muffled through the open doorway. A shadow passed by the milky window and back again. The Old Man stepped back out into the doorway and calmly waved the group over. They crossed the brushy edge and walked across the open area of the forest to the door of the shack. The Old Man spoke. "Just wait out there. I don't care if you see what is in here, but it is pretty small. It was only ever made to fit two people, three at the most."

Sporadic shuffling and banging sounds emitted from the shack. "Ah! There it is. Thank goodness." There was a final scooting sound followed by the sound of the Old Man stepping across the muddy wooden floor. "Here is what I was after." He tossed a backpack out onto the ground in front of the group. It was a dull-green color and rather sizable with holsters and straps on the side. It clanked as it sagged onto the ground. "Somebody pick that thing up. I would suggest someone strong. I surely can't hump that anymore."

The Survivalist caught his attention. "You can't what?"

"Hump the backpack." The Survivalist looked around to see if she was alone in the confusion. The Old Man chuckled. "I know what you are thinking. That isn't what I mean. To hump is to carry something around in a backpack."

The Survivalist looked down at the pack. "Oh. Why do they call it that?"

The Old Man smiled and raised his eyebrows. "You know, I haven't the foggiest idea." He swiveled and returned inside the shack, and there were more banging and clanging. The Old Man yelled out as he dug, "I have managed to make a mess out of something that was already a mess in here! This building was my hunting cabin. I haven't used it in years after getting the farm going. Deegos roam these woods. They are large, beastly animals. They have four hooved feet, which makes tracking them easy since they weigh so much and press far into the soil.

"Those feet also allow them to make high jumps. Most fences are a suggestion to them. The males have antlers in the fall, which they use to fight with, while the females remain without antlers all year. They don't like loud noises, which the city used to make, so they would always stay a certain radius away from the noise, which happens to be right here. There are farmlands all around us that left this one patch of forest here. The deegos use it as a place to bed and as a covered highway around the city.

"There is a creek just up ahead that acts as a bottleneck. They have to cross an open part in a field and jump a narrow part of the creek to get to the relatively safe woods on the far side. It was common to hunt there as they jumped across. The problem was always getting the deego back across the creek if it made it before it died. The creek may be easy for a deego of that size, but for a human, it can be quite a challenge."

The commotion in the shack halted. "Ah! There it is." The Old Man returned to the doorway holding a stiff black box by a handle on the middle of its side. He lowered it to the ground and snapped open two latches on the side closest him. He pulled open the lid, obscuring the group's view. The lid caught on something. He tried forcing it open. The lid snapped off its hinges and slapped onto the dirt. The Old Man winced, seemingly frustrated with his own actions, and stood with a rifle in his hands.

It was a long gun and apparently quite heavy. The Old Man continuously pointed the barrel at the ground as he pulled the blackened metal bolt on the side of the chamber open partially, spotted a round, and opened it the rest of the way. The brass-pointed round pinged out of the equally blackened chamber. He snatched it in the air and stuffed it in his pocket. He pressed a button on the front of a short magazine on the bottom and gave it a yank. It stuck. He smacked it gently with the palm of his hand and tried again. It slid out smoothly. He held up the magazine to count the bullets. He smiled.

"We have enough here to work with. I am going to get us something to eat. You all are more than welcome to stay put. I have confidence I will be able to get something quickly just over the ridge." He retrieved the bullet from his pocket and forced it into the blackened magazine before slapping it back into the flared magwell. He snapped the bolt back and drove it forward with a pair of weighty metal clunks.

He checked the iron sights away from the group. Lowering the gun, he ran his hand down the barrel to remove the thin layer of dust from it. His hands caught on a few specks of rust on the blackened metal barrel. He frowned as he scratched at the rust with his fingernail. He checked the wooden stock for cuts and dents, finding none.

He adjusted a shining small oval tag dangling from a red strip of fabric on the bottom of the wooden handguard and back toward the trigger housing. He held the tag in his hand, observing how it wasn't symmetrical, as part of it had been cut off in a smooth arc. He sighed softly. The Mechanic stepped forward and crouched next to the Old Man. "Where did you get this?"

The Old Man shook his head. His face was racked with an old remorse. The Mechanic nodded and began to stand. The Old Man smacked the Mechanic's leg. He crouched down again. "I got it from my father. He got it from his father. I don't know where it came from before that. It used to be too large of a caliber to hunt with at all until the Crisis allowed the rapid growth of the deego population around here to take effect. Before, they were hunted enough at younger ages to prevent them from getting very large. After, there were too many to manage and not enough people to hunt them. Now this is the only thing around that can even puncture their skin."

The Mechanic gently raised the cut tag up with a single finger. It appeared to have had something on it long ago. The Old Man smiled and took the tag. "It was a name, the name of the original owner. I never knew who it was. The tag was cut long before my time to show respect to the owner. They have moved on from this life to another. They no longer need this weapon, so if they choose to keep the tag on the weapon, their name is removed by cutting it off like that." He smiled at the Mechanic as he met his eyes. "Old traditions. Nothing more." He broke the eye contact and ran his hand down the barrel once more.

The Mechanic pointed to the red fabric. "Why red?"

The Old Man shook his head. "It was originally tied to a beaded chain of some sort. It rusted off. I think it was the source of the scratching that led to this rust anyway. I replaced it with this fabric when my dad gifted me the gun. It was the best thing I had access to at the time."

The Mechanic nodded and replied, "It must be good fabric to have lasted this long."

The Old Man nodded. "Like I said, it was the best I could get my hands on."

The Mechanic didn't reply immediately as he was thinking something over. He had to ask one more question. "Why does it sadden you like this to see it?"

The Old Man frowned. "This weapon has seen far more than hunting deer, especially in the Faction Wars. I swore I would never pick it up again except to clean it or to use it in times of desperation." The Mechanic realized what the Old Man meant.

The Hobo joined in from over at the group. "Will that thing even fire? It has some rust on it."

The Old Man nodded. "It will."

"How can you be sure?"

"I fired it in this condition not long ago."

"Did you hit your mark?"

The Old Man grimaced. "Yes." The Mechanic tried to heed off the Hobo. The Hobo didn't notice.

"What did you shoot? A deego like you said before?"

The Old Man stood. He set the butt of the gun on the ground and leaned it up against the rotting cabin wall. "No. It was a Raider scout. He found me while I was hunting not far from here. Now I had never seen a Raider out this far. That led me to three different situations. The first was, he was deserting his Raider group and looking for shelter, which I could provide. The second was, he had been exiled and needed help to get away, which I could give him directions for. The third was, he was a current Raider scouting the area.

"There was a two-thirds chance he was a good guy. I walked up to him, maybe thirty yards out, and called to him. The poor guy jumped and turned around. He looked like he had seen a ghost. I mean, I am getting old here, but I am not that old. I asked him if he needed any help. He didn't reply. He started to reach for his pistol on his hip. It was situation three. I swung this gun around and aimed it at the ground in his direction.

"I told him he could leave and forget he ever saw me and nothing would happen here. He drew the gun. I shot him. Out of all the things and people I have killed, that one hurt me. That man, he didn't even want to be out here. He was following his orders from some man he was more afraid of than the rifle in front of him."

The Hobo met the Old Man's sorrowed gaze. He questioned the Old Man in disbelief. "You shot someone with that?"

The Old Man nodded. "Blew a hole the size of your fist right in the middle of his forehead. You couldn't even see his eyes. He was wearing a military helmet." The Old Man squinted up at the Hobo. He was staring down at the gun. The Old Man retrieved it. "If it is fine with you all, I would prefer to keep ahold of this one myself. I don't want any of you firing it. It has done wicked, evil things. I would rather keep that force of suffering to myself." Nobody argued the request.

The Old Man lightened the mood. "That backpack has some tools in it. All of the containers are empty. Why don't you go up on the ridge and set up camp for the night? We will need a cooking fire for the deego."

The Entrepreneur looked around. "What deego?"

The Old Man smiled. "I will need your help in a bit, Mechanic." He turned and started off into the woods.

The Mechanic pointed up the hill. "Come on. Let's do as he asked."

*****

Not half an hour had passed before a massive gunshot erupted close by. The Mechanic stood, alarmed. He told the group to stay put and started down the hill toward the sound. A few minutes later, the Old Man returned with the Mechanic. Both of them were struggling to yank a deego up the hill. It was a truly brutish thing—taller than the Mechanic if it were still standing. It had long, bony legs. Its backbone could be seen visibly running down the top length of its body. Its shoulders bulged with strong muscles. It had a neck as big and round as the Mechanic's chest.

It was sporting a massive rack wider than both the Mechanic and the Old Man put together. A relatively small pocket of blood had formed just behind the shoulder. The Hobo went down to help them drag it. He turned and came right back up after meeting them. "Hey, Survivalist, get in that backpack and find that cooking pot. Fill it up with water and boil it on the fire. There is a creek down the hill that way." The Hobo pointed off to his right before turning and jogging back down the hill. "Oh, and leave your hatchet. We are going to need it."

The Survivalist drew the hatchet and laid it against the log she was sitting on. She snatched the backpack and unzipped it. She stood a moment later after finding a collapsible pot. She swung it and snapped it open. "Cool." She ran down over the hill.

The Old Man explained to the group that despite how hard it was to penetrate the skin of the deego, cutting it once it had been opened was surprisingly easy. It was hard to cut from the outside but easy from the inside. The meat was also very easy to remove for the same reason. The hard part was the ribs, which could not be broken without a special set of tools or excessive brute force. They would have to remove the organs with the ribs intact.

He set to work skinning and cleaning out the deego of its organs as he pointed to the back and ribs of the deer to show the only edible parts of this kind of deer. The rest, including the neck, rump, round, both sets of shanks and legs, and most of the shoulders, were inedible due to how tough they were. The ribs were best fresh and would be plenty enough to feed all of them today.

In this desperation, they could prepare the backstrap into jerky for later. He assured them the deego would not be wasted if they left the rest behind. The other animals with sharper teeth would quickly scavenge the rest, leaving nothing behind but the bones. With the help of both the Mechanic and the Young—the group had refused the Hobo due to his dirtiness—the Old Man made short work of the deego with the Survivalist's hatchet.

*****

After cleaning off down at a wide spot in the creek, returning the Survivalist's thoroughly cleaned hatchet, starting the fire, and boiling the water, the group sat down in a circle as they watched the fire slowly cook the venison. Darkness was setting in soon. They would have time to cook the deego, eat, and find a comfortable place to sleep before night.

Except for the subtle wind in the trees and the crackling of the fire, the area was in silence. The Old Man looked up at the group. He began speaking. "Well, it appears that we are going to be together for a while. I figured we had better get to know each other some. Now is as good a time as any." He looked at the group for approval.

"What about staying secret of each other? Is that not why we don't call each other by name?" asked the Mechanic.

The Old Man replied, "Yes, that was the plan. But the plans have been foiled since my farm got destroyed by those Raiders." The area returned to silence. The Old Man broke in once more. "I think we are going to be stuck with each other for a long time now. I figured we should get to know each other before something serious happens and we are unprepared to work together. Before long, we will already know too much about the recent past events of each other to remain separate anyway."

The group nodded. "Is everyone all right with sharing their history here tonight?" asked the Old Man. The group nodded once more. "All right, then. I will start," he proclaimed. The Old Man cleared his throat and took a moment to collect his thoughts. After a period of silence, he started. "Well, I was thinking about how far back we should go with this. I suppose we go all the way back." He hesitated for a moment to collect his thoughts.

"When I was a kid, I grew up on that farm with my parents. I went to school like every other kid. During the summers, I typically bailed golden alfens, a type of tall and hardy grass that gets its name from its color. However, we did it the classic way. I am old enough now to remember the beginning of the farming revolution. You see, they had come out with all sorts of new mega harvesters that could do our entire field at once. They also devised a new string of crops that could be grown in massive quantities on a tiny plot of land at accelerated rates without destroying the soil there.

"I never did figure out how those crops worked, but I do know they required extremely precise conditions to stay alive. Naturally, a few farms achieved these rigid requirements and took over the entire farming market, and the food supply nearly quadrupled. With so much food going around, a lot of farms actually closed down, especially the ones that tried to remain as traditional farmers like I was, as they had no plausible way to compete with this level of mass production.

"That led to a massive loss of farmers, most of which moved on to working on the new harvesting tech for the very people who ruined their livelihoods. But me and my family, we stuck it out. At first, we basically supplied food for ourselves and saved what credits we had. Traditional farming equipment prices fell quite a ways, meaning we could get away with staying at the old tech level for as long as there were still old tractors and such to be found.

"This went on for a few years. Then a big, haughty businessman came to the front door." He glanced over at the Entrepreneur, who was not at all offended and was instead nodding in agreement. "I was fully prepared to open the door and deny his requests to buy the farm, as we did around twice a week." The Entrepreneur smiled. "Then that fellow said something I hadn't heard in a long time. He said, 'Do you all still farm the correct way?' This obviously caught me off guard, so I kept the door open instead of slamming it shut.

"I asked him what he meant. He replied, 'I have been looking all over for somebody who still uses the traditional practices of farming. There is a whole market of people who are all looking for the freshness and flavor of the old way of farming.' Then the fellow paused. He was waiting with high anticipation for the answer to his question. I replied, 'Well, we do, in fact, use the traditional methods of farming. But what is this market of people you are talking about?' At that moment, a massive smile spread across that man's face. He immediately asked if he could come in, which I allowed, and we had a good, long talk over some aruze I brewed up for him."

The Old Man noticed the confusion among the group. "Aruze is a bitter drink made by boiling the golden alfens in a batch of water. It is an arousing drink that gives you a ton of energy if made properly. Now back to the story. He essentially told me that the new crops, the ones being mass-produced, had much less flavor than traditional farming did. He explained that a lot of very wealthy folks wanted to know what true flavor was, and they were looking to buy traditionally grown crops at the highest value. After he got done with his whole spiel, I looked up at him and said, 'Well, it's about time.'

"The man stood and extended his hand. He said, 'If you shake my hand, I will contact you about any opportunities I find. You don't bother trying to make more than you can. Instead, just sell what you don't need, and these people will pay you so many credits that you won't have to worry about savings for the rest of your life.' I hesitated in shaking his hand."

The Old Man took another glance at the Entrepreneur, who was waiting in utmost suspense, leaning so far forward that he was nearly falling over. "Well, I thought it over for a minute or so. He kept his hand outstretched the whole time. I asked him if I still retained every right and piece of property I had if I did not want to give it to him or anyone else affiliated with him. He nodded and raised his hand higher up. I took his deal and shook his hand." The Entrepreneur lurched backward, leaning against the rock he was against, rubbing his forehead. "You know, don't you, Entrepreneur?"

The Entrepreneur stopped rubbing his forehead and looked around at the group's redirected eyes. "I might. My guess is, that deal started out real sweet. You probably got loads of credits, which you saved in the banking system because you thought it would be a good idea to save your credits and then never have to work again after a while. That was a good idea at the time, by the way. Then the economy did its massive belly flop at the time of the Crisis and destroyed all your savings in some massive bank closure—not that you needed the credits afterward anyway since there was nowhere to spend them—so you continued farming just as you always had, except now you began looting things since credits didn't really exist anymore, along with the majority of the people you would buy your equipment from.

"You likely did that same thing all the way up until now, and you probably had to make a move anyway from your local area to the city since finding any good equipment now has got to be difficult." The Entrepreneur stopped and looked directly at the Old Man. The group swiveled back to him, waiting for his response.

"You got it all right, except you don't know of one thing. My mother passed away of old age before any of the Crisis ever happened. So she went out feeling great about life. My goal is to do the same." The whole group sat in silence, contemplating how profound that statement was. The Old Man pointlessly stirred the venison a little in an attempt to break the awkwardness.

After a good period of nothing but the noise of the crackling fire and sizzling meat, the Old Man broke in, "Yeah, anyway, let's move on to the next person. What about you, Young?"

The Young shied away. "Well, my life is a lot shorter than your story." He paused. The group gave him time. "I suppose my life before the Crisis is kind of hazy. I went to school like anyone else. I remember I was around ten years old at the time of the Crisis, but I don't remember much about it other than that pretty much everyone I knew died in some massive fire while we were inside the school.

"I was small enough that I could wiggle out a window, which my best friend actually shoved me out of against my will before we both roasted alive. He was too big to fit through. I assume he died there with the rest of them. He told me to never look back and regret this as he pushed me out. I regretted it anyway. I felt really sad for a long time. I felt guilty for living, I guess. But right after the burning, I didn't know what else to do besides move on with my life and be happy my friend was such a good person that he would think to save me. I figured school would just start up somewhere else and life would sort of continue on.

"That was when I discovered that the whole city was having these kinds of problems. My school was just the beginning. My mom had told me that canned stuff seemed to last a really long time compared to all the other foods one time, so I went to the supermarket and just took a whole bunch of the canned food in my backpack and a big cloth bag I found on the wall there. I went home to find everything but the basement of my house leveled to the ground. My parents were nowhere to be seen, but I figured they would come back home if they were all right.

"I tried calling them with my phone, but it was already having problems. My phone screen went bright white after a period of time and then shut off forever. Of the few things left intact, buried in the rubble of my house, the only thing working was the radio. I sat and listened to the radio, trying to figure out what was going on. One by one, the radio stations shut down. They were all blasting breaking news and talking about places I had never heard of.

"I didn't understand anything from them. It got down to where there was only one station left. Whoever that spokesman was, he was trying hard to explain in a comprehensible manner what had happened to the world. He was just about to make it through to where things would make sense when it cut off." The Radioman had perked up, but he said nothing, and his face dropped to deep confusion.

The Young did not continue on. He had noticed the Radioman. The Radioman spoke up.

"That was probably my radio station, the last one running. I made sure to keep it up as long as I could."

The Young stepped back for a moment. "You were the radioman from that station? Prove it."

The Radioman stood and cleared his throat. He spoke quickly and clearly. "It appears that the downtown area has received substantial damage. The integrity of the buildings appears to have dwindled in the last few hours, and the buildings may soon tumble down. The northern area seems to be unchanged in the last day. The—"

The Young cut him off. "All right. It was you. You are the person." He rubbed his forehead while visibly remembering a rush of his memory. The Radioman sat down again. The Young asked him a question. "What were you going to say then? When the station cut off?"

The Radioman crinkled his brow. "I believe it was something along the lines of the world being ruined. Truth be told, I didn't understand what was happening either. I was simply spreading what information I could obtain to at least attempt to protect and comfort the listening population as best I could."

The Young was not pleased with this answer, but he understood it was true. The Young continued. "A while after that radio station cut out, I sat in silence while taking stock of my canned food. About three weeks passed of me hiding in the basement, and I was beginning to run low on food and water. So I got up and took what little food I had left. At this point, I had gone through the grief of my parents likely being dead and the stress of figuring out what I was going to do next.

"I went to the supermarket to find it completely ransacked. I had no idea what else to do, so I started exploring the city. That was when I discovered all the other people for the first time. I was too small to fight, so I learned quickly to be extremely quiet. That led to good hiding skills. Then I got tired of waiting for good opportunities. I started taking risks and traveling in daytime.

"Over the years, I developed a skill of sneaking right past people without them ever seeing me. I developed my sneaky nature, although you all have never seen me sneak yet. I used those skills to slide through the city undetected and steal food from stashes. That pretty much brings us up to now." The Young goes silent. Nobody seems to want to pick up the conversation next.

After a while, the Entrepreneur spoke up. "I suppose this is as good a time as any for me to tell my story, but I am not sure if you all really want to hear it. I honestly had a pretty boring life to anyone who does not enjoy the art of making a deal." The Entrepreneur went silent. The group looked around at one another cautiously.

The Radioman finally spoke up, as he hated waiting awkwardly for replies. "What kind of deals?"

The Entrepreneur lit up. The Radioman looked at the group, both apologetic for instigating a potentially bad story and curious to hear it at the same time. The Entrepreneur started. "Well, on the surface, most deals are just a bunch of paperwork." He hesitated for a moment. "You know, I am on a tangent here, but I think it is really strange that the business world never got a new word for *paperwork*. I don't think I have seen a paper legal document in years, especially after the encryption process got down to the subatomic level, although people still write down their memories and make flyers on paper. So maybe..." He trailed off, picking up where he left off.

"Anyway, back to my story. The surface value of my life was boring. I worked at a joint called Allister Accounting as a sales rep. Yes, I know, that is already strange. Allister Accounting used to solely focus on the paperwork, but they had recently moved into the foreclosure business as well since they already knew the entire legal process of it. Anyway, I looked just like any other salesman, and I was just an ordinary salesman, for the most part.

"You see, I really didn't like working as a salesman. I had just gotten hired when the foreclosure salesman opportunity showed up, but being a salesman is boring. You don't focus on any one person. Chances are, you can always find at least one sucker wanting to buy an item no matter how bad of idea it is or how ugly it is. Instead, I wanted to be a deal-breaker.

"Deal-breakers are a critical role for high-end deals. You persuade one particular client to buy expensive foreclosure items. You give and push for their specific needs. It sounded wonderful to me, but like with most things in life, there was a catch. Now you see, the issue here is that the extremely high up deal-breakers are the only people to get the good positions at Allister Accounting—clean, good salesmanship with high prices and fantastically witty, convincing skills. It is a battle between a client who knows what they are buying and a deal-breaker who knows what he is selling.

"These are-hard fought sales and nearly as fun to watch as to perform if you know what to look for. The catch? Well, the new deal-breakers get the dirty jobs, the impossible jobs, the ones that will likely end in a massive failure. So it's a huge risk to get in on the deal-breaker side of sales. Now what did I do?"

He paused, and he glanced around, observing how he had captured his audience. "I did it. I took the risk. Like I said, I was not happy with my life at the time. I would never have been happy with my job. I didn't have a wife or kids to look after, so the jeopardy was all my own. I could lose it all or win big. Either way, to me, it was worth it. So I found a way in. They never did tell me the name of the deal-breaker who gave up the job, but whoever it was made a smart choice.

"I had to sell an entire crate of Crystobyte to the BureauRat." The Entrepreneur paused, scanning faces. "You all have no idea what either of those things are, do you?" The group shook their heads collectively. "All right. Crystobyte is the name of an extremely addictive drug. It was created by accident by a company called CrystoCode while trying to find a way to encode matter into a shape. They were using large hexagonal crystals and combining them with some very strange chemicals in hopes of getting a predictable change in the shape of the crystal, which would revolutionize shipping and manufacturing by allowing people to buy these generic crystals on a smaller scale and then simply adding a specific chemical to them to allow the crystal to form exactly what they want.

"It was a great idea in theory. However, they never did quite figure out how to get a reliable output from these crystals. They were about to give up due to lack of funds when somebody accidentally tried to encode too many bytes of data at once." The Entrepreneur paused again after seeing the confused faces. He lightly grasped his forehead and closed his eyes for a moment. Once he was done thinking, he continued speaking.

"All right, look, bytes used to refer to a quantity of data in computer programming exclusively. However, they had adapted the term to include the amount of crystal being changed since they were technically coding matter. So this fellow I was talking about accidentally changed too many bytes, as in too much crystal, at once in one of the final tests. They let the batch go as it was considered unsafe to interrupt this process of crystal encryption. To their surprise, the crystal actually formed a reliable material.

"Upon testing, the scientists in the lab became so intoxicated that they could not walk, communicate, or respond to any provocation. They nearly died. They later discovered that the scientists had all experienced an extremely high dosage of an unknown drug. Then with a lot more precaution, they found this stable crystal to be the source of the drug. Upon breaking it apart, the crystal pricked the skin and released the drug, even through the full bodysuits that the scientists were wearing. They also found it to be an extremely addictive substance with just the one exposure to the previous scientists resulting in them going through two years of full drug rehabilitation to get off the stuff.

"Luckily, the drug made them incredibly agreeable and passive once they came around again, so keeping them at bay wasn't a challenge as long as none of them came across the notion to go find the drug again, which changed their behavior to extremely hostile until they passed out to overexertion. So long story short, they accidentally made the most potent drug in history that caused sporadic and violent action to find more of the drug.

"Obviously, this stuff was immediately made illegal, and the government swept it under the rug so quickly that the news didn't even catch on." The Entrepreneur paused and glanced over at the Radioman. "Wouldn't you have loved an interview with me on your station?" The Radioman nodded his head. The Entrepreneur grinned as he continued on. "The government basically forced a foreclosure on false grounds and made CrystoCode essentially vanish from the market as if they had gone out of business like their trends showed they would have done anyway. So now—"

"Wait, so then how do you know all of this?" the Survivalist asked, interrupting the Entrepreneur.

The Entrepreneur responded, unshaken. "I was getting to that. Let me continue on." The Survivalist accepted the defeat as the Entrepreneur continued. "So where were we? Oh, the foreclosure, right. So the government apparently pawned the foreclosure to Allister Accounting thinking that the new foreclosure business would just do what they were told, and since they didn't know what they were doing, then they could slide the whole drug issue right over the company's head. That worked until the company came across this large, airtight crate of the Crystobyte in the foreclosure that the government had overlooked, and that led the company to the BureauRat." The Entrepreneur paused, once again gathering his thoughts.

"So the BureauRat is actually a person. He went by the name Austin Douglass. He was actually a bureaucrat in the government who used to perform well in his position, but that changed after the Crystobyte discovery. He basically turned his position into a cover job, as this guy just so happened to catch on via the government about the Crystobyte event that I just explained. Instead of sweeping it under the rug like the rest of the government, he used it to his advantage. He became a massive drug dealer for Crystobyte.

"At this point, he realized he could not stay in office and run this drug cartel at the same time, so he left and gave his position to a man who looked, acted, and sounded just like he used to under the same name of Austin Douglass with the deal that the impostor Austin

Douglass would get a good share of the profits from the Crystobyte, which was quite the sum of credits. He could get away with this since most politic events and meetings happened digitally anyway, and it was hard to tell specific features that couldn't be hidden with makeup and screen effects.

"The underground then renamed the original Austin as the BureauRat, a play on words. They did this to make it easier to define which Austin they were talking about. The BureauRat then went on to cause a borderline epidemic in the underground by giving free samples to the poor, who would inevitably do anything to get more, meaning he could use them however he wanted. Now my job was to sell Crystobyte to the man who basically ran the entire underground industry for it. This was where I got all this information from. Allister Accounting did not send me in blind."

He glanced over at the Survivalist, who appeared to understand suddenly, while he continued talking. "They told me all of this to at least give me a shot at making a deal. If I sold it, then I was granted the high position deal-breaker spot that I had always wanted. If I failed, they didn't tell me what would happen, but they let me know it would not be a fun time. I believed them, but I asked them why they wouldn't send someone more experienced. They would not answer that.

"Their empty response combined with such a high reward told me they were desperate, so I did it. I went and met the BureauRat. Well, sort of. I met a digital projection with a voice distortion that represented what might have been the BureauRat. Now here was where my deal-making skills really came into play. I sold the entire crate of Crystobyte to the BureauRat for twenty credits." He glanced at the Young and the Survivalist. "About enough to buy myself a single meal from the underground system or about half a meal aboveground. That leads to a question: Why did I sell it for such a low price?"

The group stared at him while they tried to connect the dots. The Entrepreneur waited while sporting a wide grin. "You all give up? All right. Earlier, when I made the deal with my company to sell the Crystobyte, they never specified how many credits I had to sell it for. They told me to sell it. I did. Now when I went back to Allister Accounting, I expected them to be angry. But instead, they were overjoyed that I had even managed to get rid of it without anyone knowing. I got promoted immediately and enjoyed my life as a deal-breaker for the next two years until the Crisis happened.

"After it went down, I basically hid with some friends in the company, pulling strings to get resources to survive. After a few years, our luck ran out, and I was forced to move on from them. Then I was greeted by a fellow who was trying to deal with outside the city. I told him that I was willing to set up a deal with him if he could get me out of the city. The Hobo found out about this, apparently spread part of this information to you already, and now here we are today."

The group sat in silence for a moment as they reeled in the line of events that had just been set before them. The Old Man finally broke the silence after several minutes of thought by removing the venison from the fire and dishing it out to the group. He also set the pot of water from earlier on the fire in place of the venison to boil it a second time.

After devouring the venison, the Mechanic spoke up. "Welp, I made short work of that venison. Thank you, Old Man." He nodded to the Old Man, who dipped his head and raised his hand slightly to show he appreciated the gesture without stopping his munching on the venison. The Mechanic continued. "Since you all are still eating, I will go ahead and tell my story." The Mechanic bolstered his jaw as he thought of his past. He started. "I suppose I should start with my career. My career was basically my life. I did have a wife, but she left me and took my kid with her. We just didn't get along about a lot of decisions, particularly ones about my job and living conditions."

The Mechanic paused. He was visibly straining to find a way to properly place his thoughts into words. "Look, I loved being a mechanic. I loved helping people fix the vehicles they loved, and I wanted more than anything to meet the requirements to get to work on the Boomships." The Survivalist perked up, seemingly wanting to say something, but remained silent. The Mechanic continued.

"However, to get this opportunity, I had to pass a rigorous examination, which consisted of physical skill as well as a knowledge test. My wife, she knew I was trying to do this and was supportive of it. So I went in to the testing center and sat down. They called me in eventually. The physical tests were always before the knowledge tests. They had me reweld and reinstall one of the engines, which was far more complicated than I had ever imagined, but I managed to fumble my way through it, and miraculously, it ran, although poorly, as I had not trained for this at all. But they passed me with a low score.

"Then I went into another room, which I will always remember as it was so white and eerily quiet. There was a man on a white stage with a black podium on one side of the room and another black podium lacking a stage across the room. I was instructed to go stand behind the shorter black podium. After I got there, the group closed the entrance door, and it was just me and the fellow on the stage podium.

"He began with the words, 'Welcome to the Knowledge Examination for Boomship Level Ability, or KEBLA. This test is taken orally. You must describe to the best of your ability what the problem is, how to fix it, and what potential dangers the fix may cause based on randomly selected indicators of problems.' I failed this part of the test horribly. I remember those instructions to this day, word for word, because I would take this test so many times later. I took it every week until the collapse.

"All I wanted was to be able to work on the Boomships. I knew I had the skill. After the first few tests, I figured out the processes behind the complexity of the engine and never had any trouble fixing it. But that knowledge test, they always had some strange question that never made complete sense. I could not describe to them the issue. I wished I could just show them by pointing at the engine that actually had this issue, but they would not allow this. I never managed to pass the exam.

"My wife eventually grew tired of trying to convince me of giving up. She became a nuisance to me, not because she was holding me back, which she wasn't, but because all she could ever talk about was that test and how it was eating up so much of my time when really it only took a couple hours every weekend. She grew increasingly frustrated with me for trying the test over and over. Eventually, she got tired of waiting for me to pass and filed for a divorce.

"Now this test was not the only frustration we had. It was simply the act that pulled the trigger. She obviously wasn't for me anyway if she couldn't support my goals or deal with not seeing me for those two hours a week. But my kid, my little girl, she took her from me. That little girl was the only other reason besides my own interest that I was trying to get this better job. I wanted to show her the world, give her any opportunity she wanted, and the way I could do that was by getting the great pay of working on Boomships, which again required I pass that test.

"My daughter somewhat understood this despite her young age. My wife, however, would never see it this way. Soon after the divorce happened, the collapse occurred. I don't know what happened to them. I tried calling them, but all the services were out already. I searched everywhere for them. I couldn't find them. I spent a good while wandering the city, looking for them, but eventually, I was forced to give up as the Faction Wars were getting too prominent in the area. So I went back to my garage, which was amazingly still somewhat intact, and began to search for ways to survive.

"I lasted a good while by looting nearby stores. My strength allowed me to get resources others couldn't access since I could move heavy things out of the way. Then I moved on to using my mechanical skills to open locked doors and rig up traps around me. That allowed me to make it for another good spell, but then the Raiders formed and were growing suspicious of the area as they noticed my changes. They began a large sweep of the entire area. I hid after being trapped in a parking garage. I was about to run out of food when the Survivalist came about, and we all know the rest until now." The Mechanic hung his head. He was obviously not sharing some details of the story, but nobody pressed him to share any further. A silence and stillness took over.

The Old Man again broke the stillness. He motioned for the Mechanic's backpack. The Mechanic peeked down at the pack, grabbed it with his massive hand, and began to throw it to the Old Man. He stopped halfway through the throw, stood, and walked over to the Old Man instead to hand it to him. The Old Man appeared thankful as he opened up the pack and retrieved a long, flat container. The container had a stiff mechanical seal on it, which the Old Man forced open. He took the boiling water pot from the fire and dumped part of the pot's water into the container. He set the rest of the water in the pot on a nearby rock to cool.

For the first time since they had gotten to camp, the Hobo spoke up. "I guess I am next. My life before the Crisis was not exactly wonderful. I ran the streets and scavenged for food. I had nowhere to go, and I couldn't find work anywhere that would accept me in those advancing times. I occasionally met up with a few other hobos like me just to talk and occasionally trade some things with each other. The majority of my life was like this.

"It all started when both my parents got killed trying to protect me from some rival gang who decided it was a good idea to rob what little we had. I ran off. They took the bodies of my parents with them. I obviously never saw them again. Since I had little to no education, I moved to the streets, looking for whatever low-end job I could get to feed myself with. The local baker had heard the news, and he took me in for a little while. He fed me there and gave me a few credits here and there to deliver something or run an errand. That was the best my life had been in a long time until he became worried that the gang, which he told me was called the Grunge, would kill him as well to get to me.

"Apparently, my parents had succeeded in taking some of their members with them to the grave, and they wanted revenge on me for it. Before he could get hurt, I ran off. I hoped he understood. After that, nobody wanted to help me. They all knew the risk. I moved on to other parts of the city, moving from place to place, and then the Crisis happened. I thought for sure I was going to die right then and there, but I didn't. I managed to get into a parking garage stairwell that saved my life.

"The whole rest of the area fell down around me. I think I am one of the only ones to live through it in that entire area. It took me around an entire day to dig my way back out of the rubble formed by that parking garage, even with the head start from going up the stairs a few floors. Then my life resumed as normal—scavenge for food, find shelter, hope for better times. The only difference was, now there was much less food to scavenge for since not a lot of new food was being made, and the large majority spoiled within three days of the Crisis.

"It turned out that being a hobo actually helped me. I knew where to scavenge, and that is the sole reason I am still alive here today." The Hobo paused for a moment. "I suppose that is really all I have to tell." The silence returned. The Old Man prodded the fire with a stick, causing it to crackle and pop.

After a good while, the Survivalist took in a deep breath. "I guess I will go next." The group adjusted their focus to the Survivalist. She waited for each person's attention and started in. "My life is similar to Young's. I went to school each day, and I came home each night. But really, the time I enjoyed out of each day was being at the park. To get home from the school, I used to go around the city streets, but I started taking a shortcut through the park one day. That turned into the best time of the day.

"It would only take me ten or fifteen minutes to cross the entire park, but I began staying there for thirty minutes to an hour each day. I think my parents caught on after a while, but they didn't mind, or at least they didn't stop me. Over time, I got more interested in nature. I liked the trees and how tall they were. I liked the ponds and little bridges. The only problem was, the park was largely neglected. I wondered if there was something that I could do to help out.

"A few days later, I found an info board with a message on it that explained that the park was looking for volunteers to help with fixing it. I looked over the requirements. I met them—they were pretty lenient—but I didn't know when I would have time to help.

As I turned around, a ranger asked me if I wanted to help. I jumped as I didn't know she was there. I replied by explaining that as much as I would like to help, I simply didn't know when I would have time to do it. I was at school all week, and my parents and I typically did things on the weekends.

"The ranger looked at me for a while. It was like she was sizing me up for a fight. I looked back at her. She was this tall and narrow lady dressed in a dark-green shirt, stiff boots with a pair of tan pants, and a rigid hat to match the pants on top of a head of vibrant red hair in a bun. Her skin was pale, and she had freckles on her cheeks. I was growing concerned about her just staring at me. I began to shuffle away.

"She noticed me leaving and quickly spoke up. She said, 'You are here every day after class for around an hour, right?' I hadn't thought about it for some time, but she was right, I was spending about an hour there each day. I nodded to her. She said, 'Well, then how about you just help me for that hour? Nothing more. If you need to leave early, you can, and I will meet you here each day.'

"I was thrilled. I nodded again, and she asked me if I wanted to start now. I hesitated. She understood, saying I should probably run the idea past my parents, so I went straight home and asked them. They were pleased that I was taking initiative on something. They could count this hour a day as volunteer work and boost my academic scholarship chances with it. I wasn't wanting to do it for school, but whatever they needed to think to let me do it was fine by me.

"From then on, I worked every weekday for an hour after school. I loved it. I became great friends with the ranger. I even got to stay the night in the park with her over the weekend a few times, and she taught me how to camp. Then the time came that my family was going to move. I was distraught. How could I ever make it to the park to help? We had already done so much, like fix the pathways, plant flowers, oil the doors, clean the facilities, and so much more. The park looked better than ever. More people were showing up to use it. It was finally taking off. I couldn't just abandon the ranger.

"I tried to argue this with my parents, but they insisted upon moving. On the day before we moved, I snuck out of the house and ran to the park. It was a Saturday. I wasn't sure the ranger would be there, but I found her tending the flowers we had planted. They were Tindertufts, a good-sized and bushy flower with bright-orange and burnt colors that make them look like they are burning when the wind shakes them. They had just bloomed in. She had taken off her hat to show that red hair. Some of the flowers matched her hair color.

"I told her about the move. She appeared sad, but she explained that she was more sad for me than for herself or the park. She understood that I loved being there. I remember clearly that her face lit up, and she ran into the building behind her briefly before returning with her hands behind her back. She made me promise that I would be careful with what she was about to give me. I agreed. She gave me my hatchet."

The Survivalist stopped. She looked down at the hatchet, running her finger along the back of it, feeling the flint strike affixed to it there that she used to start fires. She snapped back into reality. "She explained to me that this hatchet was everything I really needed if I ever needed to survive the woods. It could be a weapon, a fire starter, a way to make a shelter. But then she corrected herself by saying that there was one thing it couldn't do."

The Survivalist subconsciously tapped her hip. "She left again and returned with a small green box. I did not know what it was. She explained it to me. 'This box is called a compass. If you open the lid and hold it level, it will show you which way is north as long as there are not any large magnetic fields nearby. You can use it to navigate, something the hatchet cannot do.'

"She handed me the compass. I opened the lid and watched as the needle settled between the *E* and *S*. She grabbed my shoulders and turned me until the needle pointed to the *N*. 'You see? That is north. Now you know what direction you should be facing based off of that.' I smiled. I turned back around and gave her a long hug. Afterward, she stood and looked at me with a hopeful expression, which fell to concern when she saw me holding the items in my hands. She glanced down at her waist.

"I had never noticed, but she was wearing a thin black belt. She took the belt off and wrapped it around my waist, measuring me. She stood and motioned for the hatchet as she stood awkwardly and tugged on her pants, which were trying to fall to the gravel. I gave her the hatchet. She poked a hole in the belt with the corner of the blade and returned the hatchet to me. She crouched again and put the belt around my waist, using the hole she had just made to fix the buckle. Then she took the compass and stuck it on the belt."

The survivalist motioned toward the green compass on her right hip. "She took the hatchet and strapped it on my leg, instructing me to always keep the blade toward the back so that when I sat down, I wouldn't cut myself and if I ran, I wouldn't catch my hand on it. The ranger stood again, beaming with pride as she again pulled on her pants. She wished me the best, gave me one more short hug, and sent me on my way.

"I didn't think I would ever see her again. I didn't think I would ever see the park again. I don't know if either exists anymore. That is because we moved to the other side of the city. There was a park there too, but it was much smaller, and there were no rangers at it. It was managed by the city itself instead. I had to start taking the Magnitube to school for a brief period, which I hated and tried to avoid. I figured out it must have a magnetic field in it, as the compass would never work near it.

"We were not at the new house for a month when the Crisis happened. I was ridding the Magnitube home from school when the whole thing shut off. The tube-shaped deal we were in suddenly fell and landed on the floor. It slid to a stop, making this horrendous noise, and then all the doors opened on it. A red light flickered to life behind a sign that said Evacuate the Magnitube System Now. Everyone scrambled out of the train and followed the red signs to the nearest station. I followed them out and started home.

"Before I made it anywhere, a phone call came through on the watch that my mom made me wear. I answered it. Her holographic face came up. She seemed scared. Her voice shook. She asked if I was all right. I told her I was. She asked me where I was. I told her I didn't know but gave her some street names that I noticed were painted on the wall. She nodded and told me to find someplace to hide, someplace strong looking. I told her I would. I had a feeling something was wrong.

"She was busy moving about in the hologram frame, causing it to jostle and shake her image on my end. She seemed to be rushing away from something. I asked if I would ever go back home. She shook her head. I asked her if she could grab my hatchet and compass. She nodded, explained she already had them with her, and told me to find cover. She hid her face from the hologram, instead using the voice only option. Then I saw a sign for the old park. I told mom I was going there and that I would be inside the building at the center. She said that was wonderful, told me she loved me, and hung up in a hurry.

"I went over to the park, listening to the chaos around me. There were these deafening blasts of noise followed by a strong gust of wind once in a while. I went into the park. It had not changed much. The Tindertufts were still in bloom. I went to the center building and rapped on the door to see if the ranger was there. I found the door unlocked. That was strange. It was always locked. I peeked in the door, but no one was inside. I went in and sat down in the stairs. My school had taught me they were strong in bad events. I stayed there.

"My watch lost all signal and abruptly shut off. I took it off and laid it on a nearby wooden table. I never did like it. I always felt like it was recording everything I did. Eventually, after several hours of blasts and noise, my mom came through the door. She practically rammed it open with her shoulder. It scared me to death. She ran over and hugged me to calm me down. She immediately thrust the hatchet and compass into my hands. I asked her where Dad was. She explained he was just outside the park, trying to find a way out of the city. I nodded as I fixed the hatchet and compass to my belt.

"Looking back now, the weight of what she had said did not really strike me at the time with all the things that were going on. We were leaving the city. I had never done that before. But I was more focused on my mom. I could tell she was nervous about the hatchet, but she didn't take it back. We left the building. On the way out, I noticed that the Tindertufts had been smashed by a tree branch. I wondered where the ranger was. I hoped she was all right, but I knew better than to get my hopes up.

"We found my dad right outside the park, as my mom said. He quickly told us that all the public transportation had gone down and that this was all some big disaster. Then we all started running. I followed my parents through so much carnage. Entire buildings were missing. Materials lay all over the streets. There were a lot of dead people lying around.

"My mom tried to hide my eyes from the dead people, but there were too many. She gave up trying to block my vision after a while. They were slaughtered in a variety of ways—everything from being burned alive, to being severed somehow, and to being crushed by impact of rubble or other things. I wondered what caused so many of the buildings to collapse. What had that much force?

"We were almost out of the city, clear into the suburbs, when a loud noise came from above us. Before we could even look up, an explosion of some kind happened a few streets down. The blast sent me flying, even with it being that far off. I don't know what happened then. I blacked out. I woke up lying sideway on a reclining chair that had tipped over backward. My back hurt. I checked myself for injuries. I had a lot of cuts and some long glass shards sticking out of my left arm, but otherwise, I seemed all right.

"I plucked out the glass shards from my arm. They came out easy. They must have been those fancy injury-proof glass they had come out with for toddlers and workplaces. I stood and looked down at myself. I still had the hatchet and the compass on the belt, but my pants and shirt were destroyed. I went to the window and peeked out. Everything was quiet. Where were my parents? Where was anyone? I didn't know.

"I remember Dad saying something about getting out of the north end of the city. I looked at the compass. That was to the left, up the road. I scoured the house I had crash-landed in for food, coming up with a few cans of Toros, a kind of red meat, and left to head north in hopes of finding my parents. I came across a store on the way, which I looted for these clothes before continuing on for my parents. I never did find them.

"Luckily, I had some knowledge on how to survive and the tools to do it from the ranger. I owe my life today to her teachings, as those are how I have survived until now. After I ran out of food some week or so later, I still had not found my parents. I had no idea where they were, but I knew I needed food and a more secure sleeping situation. I went back into the city to find some supplies, like rope and tools to build a more permanent shelter, but that led me to getting chased by Raiders for weeks.

"I basically spent the next many years just running around in the city, looking for my parents and scavenging. Then a long time later, I ended up finding the Mechanic, and you all know the rest." The Survivalist went quiet. The silence of the woods took over once more. After a bit, she piped up again. "So what about you, Radioman? You are the last one. Why do you still wear that suit of yours? And how have you kept it so nice and intact over the years?"

The Radioman stood, dusting his maroon overcoat off as well as the black shirt underneath. "This coat has a much deeper meaning than strikes the eye. It is part of who I am now." The group remained silent, watchful eyes egging him on. "You see, I was not always as fortunate as I am now." He paused for a long moment while realizing the irony of that statement. He passed it off to continue his story.

"When I was a child still attending school, I was very economically destitute." He hesitated, glancing at the Hobo, who seemed minorly offended. "I am sorry, good fellow. With all due respect, I was not in nearly as tight a spot as you were, my friend, but I was also not able to go out and buy frivolous things of luxury." The Hobo smiled as he rested back, feeling happy to be understood for once.

"My mother was single. My father abandoned her long before I was born. I never knew my father, and I still don't, but this doesn't bother me, for I know how wonderful a job my mother did raising me despite her circumstances. She did everything she could for me. Then one day, I went to school. They announced picture day was approaching. I hated picture day. It was the day that the whole school mocked me for my appearance—more precisely, for my lack of any proper appearance.

"My mother could not afford to purchase me a new, fancy suit for each picture day as those smug faces' parents could. I understood that. I stood up for my mother when people tried to shun her in front of me. The principal had noticed this abuse over the years and called the whole group of these boys as well as myself in from class to the office. I had thought for sure I was in trouble. Instead, the principal reprimanded the boys for being so harsh to me and awarded me with a brand-new suit to take the school photos in.

"The suit was not of high quality—very rough around the lapels and made of a cheaper material of a matte color—but I did not care. It was my suit, and those fools had received proper justice. I went home that day in a rush of joy, eager to show my mother the suit and being extremely careful to get it home safely. I was successful, and when I showed my mother my sacred new article of apparel, she, too, became overjoyed. At long last, she could have a good photo of me from the school, something she had wished to provide me for years.

"She had me put it on, spin, and show her how it fitted. It did not fit me well. It hung loose on my shoulders and hung too far down my back, but she understood that I knew no different. She let me have my fun. I carefully placed the coat in my closet with the only hanger I had, which I had found on the ground nearby a dumpster up the street. It had been discarded due to the metallic hook disconnecting from the wooden frame. It simply needed to be screwed back in, which I performed to recreate a perfectly usable hanger, hoping one day I would have something to put on it. Now I had just that.

"That was a Friday. The next morning, I awoke and went over to look at the prized suit once more. Oh, how I wished to try it on and walk up the street before the throngs of the crowd came from the city to start the weekend. I put it on and snuck out the front door. I was walking up a slope in the street when I came across a tall curb in the sidewalk. I had jumped up this curb hundreds of times before but always in pants that had so many holes in them that they had grown flexible. The new pants on the suit were much more stiff, and they restricted the movement of my leg as I attempted to hop over the curb. I caught my toe on the edge.

"I began to fall, but after some flailing and teetering, I was able to stand upright. However, my knee felt wet. Upon inspection, I found a gaping hole in the right knee of my new pants as well as a bloody cut on my leg. I had scraped it off of the concrete ledge. No one was in the street yet, so to avoid staining the pants with blood, I immediately removed them, leaving me in only my boxers and the top half of the suit. I rushed back home while holding my leg with one hand to attempt to stop the bleeding, trying to figure out how I was going to prevent my mother's watchful eye from noticing my leg or the hole in the pants, but found my mother standing in the doorway.

"She had thought nothing of me trying out my suit, but she was concerned that I had walked home in my underpants with a bloody knee. She patched up the knee and looked at the hole in the pants. She did not seem angry. Instead, she left the room and returned with a wooden stool, which she placed by a table. She left and returned once more with a thimble, a large pile of scrap cloth, a spool of thread, and a sewing needle."

The Radioman stopped, noticing that the Survivalist wanted to speak. She took the opportunity. "So you learned to sew there, and that's how you keep your suit so nice now."

The Radioman smiled widely. "Precisely. However, there is more to the story. My mother was particularly strict. She did not let me leave the chair all weekend except for food, the occasional bathroom break, and bath time. I did not get to sleep in my typical quarters, instead falling asleep on the stool. All the while, I sat in my boxers, staring at a sewing kit and a hole in my pants. I sat there a whole day, realizing that my mother was serious and that as it was now Sunday, school would be starting again, and more importantly, the picture day would occur. So I set to work.

"I sewed the scraps together for practice, nearly creating a quilt by the time I was done, before I finally learned to sew with some respectable ability. I moved on to fixing the hole in the pants. I got down from the stool and handed the pants to my mother once the sewing was completed. She ignored the pants, first taking my hands and observing the many cuts and prods from the needle, proof I had done the work. Then she looked the pants over.

"She ran her hand over the minuscule seam in the knee. The sternness in her face melted. She grabbed me, giving me a long and warm hug before saying, 'You have a photo to be taken tomorrow.' I smiled and returned her hug. The next day, everyone except the group of insufferable boys in the corner complimented my suit. I had never been complimented besides by my own mother. It was wonderful. That day, I decided I would never wear anything less than a suit. I did not think I would stay true to that, but I was forced to.

"After school ended that year, I officially graduated with average grades and found work at a radio station. I became quite successful at it since I had many backstreet plugs from my impoverish status who always watched the events of the city. I would return the favor by getting attention drawn into the district. Improvements began to flow into impoverished neighborhoods, and with those improvements, I received a new position as the head radioman. The old one wanted to retire, and he wagered that a young boy like myself who had all the news at his fingertips was bound to be a better source than himself.

"I was thrilled. They gave me a work suit, but I declined, instead purchasing the very suit you set your eyes on today. I had risen from the ashes. What more appropriate color than maroon to represent the smoldering remains where I have my roots? I went on for many years as the Radioman. In fact, I went all the way up to the events of the Boomship Crisis, even announcing during it until the radio towers went out, and I was the last station—"

The Survivalist cut him off. "Wait. The what? I thought it was just a crisis in general, like some freak natural disaster. It has a name? You and the Mechanic both mentioned something called a Boomship. What are those?"

The Radioman stopped his grand retelling. His face dropped. "You don't know, do you? Neither you nor Young know?"

The Survivalist was beginning to speak when the Old Man quickly stood, pointing in the distance. "Talk about that later. We are soon to have unwanted visitors if we don't move." The group followed his finger out to see a pack of Raiders headed their way. "They saw the smoke from this fire. Put it out and pack your things. We are leaving right now."

"Now? It is nearly dark," said the Mechanic.

"Yes, now. There won't be anything but trouble if we stay." The Old Man grabbed the container and dumped the now cool water from inside it onto the fire, extinguishing it. He shook it and then began layering the cooked venison into it. He finished with the venison, snapped it shut, and hastily grabbed the pot from the rock with the remaining water. He fetched some metal bottles in the backpack, which now lay empty on the ground, and began filling the bottles with the water. The rest of the group quickly grabbed what they had and got ready to leave.

The oncoming crew of Raiders was growing ever closer, marching with purpose directly toward their location. The Survivalist was busy helping the Old Man fill the bottles with water. She asked him a question. "What do you think they want with us?"

The Old Man started to glance up at her but quickly readjusted his focus to the pot to avoid spilling the water. "I don't know that they want anything from us in particular. I think it is more along the lines of them taking an opportunity to steal from strangers."

The Survivalist nodded. Her face was tense and filled with worry. The Old Man poured the last bit of water into the last remaining bottle, leaving it about half full. The Survivalist spoke up to the group as she sealed the lid of the bottle. "All right, everyone. We have three and a half bottles of water for now. Don't waste any of it and make sure everyone gets their share." She noticed that the Old Man was shoving the bottles back into the backpack. "The bottles will be in the backpack, which will be with the Mechanic."

The Old Man handed her the backpack, which she quickly ran to the Mechanic. The Mechanic adjusted the straps to fit him as he put it on. The Hobo was busy scattering the firepit rocks. The Entrepreneur and the Radioman were spreading the embers. The Young was keeping watch of the oncoming group by standing on a large and smooth boulder. He turned and yelled to the group. "They are getting closer fast. We need to move and get quiet." He hopped off the boulder and started toward the group.

Everyone met up near the Old Man. The Old Man stood. "Does anyone have any ideas where we could go?" No one replied. The Old Man grimaced briefly. "All right, then. I have one location, but I haven't been there in years. I don't even know if it exists anymore. We go down over this hill and cross the creek at the bottom. The creek is not easy to get across, but if we manage it, then we can buy some time from the Raiders.

"After we get across, we are looking for a cave. It is not very large, but it should buy us some good cover and a place where we can ambush the Raiders if they follow us in. If all else fails, the cave is not long and has two entrances. I guess it is more of a natural tunnel. We can talk about where to go from there when things settle down. Does everyone understand?" The group nodded collectively. "Okay, then. Let's get moving."

The Old Man grabbed his rifle from a nearby rock and started down the hill with it. He was surprisingly agile for his age. The group followed close behind. They reached the creek a few minutes later. The Young had stayed back a bit to see what the Raiders did when they got to the camp. He popped out of the woods to see the group at the edge of the creek. He spoke up. "The Raiders have stopped to search the area around the camp. I don't think they saw us go down the hill and into the woods, but they definitely know we were camped out there. They won't be there long, though. I overheard one of them say that if they didn't find much, they would continue on to find where we had gone."

The Old Man looked at the creek. It was swelling with water. He spoke. "This creek is much larger than it once was. It has chewed away at its banks and widened. It is going to be a challenge to cross it. We don't have any other options, though." He handed the rifle to the Mechanic and asked, "You know how to use a gun?"

The Mechanic nodded and replied with, "I used to hunt, but I have never shot anyone."

The Old Man released the gun. "It is the same basic concept. Shoot for the lungs and heart. Hit the head if you have to and you trust your shot." The Old Man hesitated. "Just know that this thing kicks hard. It will blow whatever you hit to bits unless it has some thick hide on it. I know I said I didn't want anybody else shooting that, but I have no choice. Nobody else knows how to get to the cave. You stand the best chance of getting across quickly with how strong you are and the only one strong enough to handle the kick on that gun."

The Mechanic peered down at the weapon in his hands. "If it kicks that hard, how do you shoot it?" He looked back up at the Old Man.

The Old Man grinned. "Experience." He glanced at the rifle and then back up to the Mechanic's eyes. "Just be careful."

The Mechanic tightened his grip on the gun. "I don't know how similar hunting and killing people are, Old Man, but I will do my best if it comes to it."

The Old Man smacked the Mechanic's shoulder and shoved him toward the group. "You don't have to kill them. Just get shots close by to scare them. In fact, I recommend you don't kill them unless you have to. The Raiders don't take kindly to having one of their members killed anyway. You just cover the group as they cross. We will do our best, but I don't know that we can all get across before they find us."

The Old Man pointed toward another smooth gray boulder behind the Mechanic. The Mechanic walked past the group and crouched down behind the boulder. He checked the rifle for ammunition by removing the magazine, finding only one bullet. The Old Man reached into his pocket and threw a smooth brown sack to him. The Mechanic rubbed it between his fingers for a moment, feeling its odd flexibility and stretchy properties, then opened it to find more rifle bullets.

"That's all I've got. I unloaded the gun earlier to prevent any mishaps and left the one for emergencies. Chuck those in the mag and make them count." The Old Man looked at the group as he started toward the creek. "We have to wade in partway and then let the current take us downstream while we try to swim across. Don't go too far, though. If I remember right, there are a bunch of rocks down below a set of rapids that will grind you up." The Old Man began wading in. "Come on. We have no time to lose."

The Survivalist started to the creek, tucking her shirt and pushing up her long sleeves. She adjusted the belt as she started into the water. The Young followed her in next as he also tucked in his black shirt. The Hobo hopped into the water more abruptly and let out a small yelp to the temperature. The Entrepreneur sighed, glancing at his black dress shirt that had just been soaked by a splash from the Hobo, and stepped in next. The Radioman looked down at his nice black kakis and his maroon overcoat. He visibly winced as he witnessed the pants get soaked with water and grew noticeably distraught when the overcoat touched the water. It took all the Mechanic had to refrain from laughing.

Meanwhile, the Old Man had found a log and caught it. He dragged himself along its length to the steep bank. The Survivalist nabbed the same log but on the downstream side and hauled herself up on top the log. She shook her sleeves, shimmied along the log past the Old Man, and hopped onto the ground. She turned toward the Old Man to help him but noticed the Young clambering in the water. He was going to miss the log.

She looked at the Old Man, who shooed her away. The Young flopped past the log. She ran down the bank. "Young! Are you all right?"

The Young swirled around in the water to look at her. He spat a mouthful of water out. "Yeah! Can you get a"—he spat out another mouthful of water—"stick or someth…" His head went under a large wave in the rushing water. The Survivalist unstrapped the hatchet from her leg and whacked the nearest branch off a tree. It was a long and slender branch. It was smooth and bendy with healthy round leaves. She dropped the hatchet and ran after the Young, who was busy spitting more water.

She plunged the leafy end of the branch into the water. The Young flailed around, finally getting ahold of the branch after multiple swipes of his arms. The Survivalist swung him to shore. He grabbed onto a rock and hauled himself onto the ground. He coughed as he stood. "Get the others. They are doing worse than me. The bed of the creek sagged when you guys went across. It is deeper there now than expected." He went through another series of coughs and took off to pull up the Old Man, who was still hanging on to the log.

The Survivalist looked up the creek. She saw the Hobo clambering up the bank using a mess of tree roots. The Entrepreneur was floundering down the creek. His business shirt was clinging to his body. He did not appear to be able to swim well. The Survivalist preemptively stuck the branch into the water, awaiting the Entrepreneur to grab it. Instead, the Entrepreneur ducked his head underwater to avoid the branch. When he resurfaced, the Survivalist coldly scolded him. "Grab the branch! Don't dive under it!" The Entrepreneur lunged for the branch but missed by quite a distance. He narrowly missed a large rock.

The Survivalist continued her rant. "The drop is coming up! You have to get to shore!" She reached the branch out once more as she ran along the bank. The Entrepreneur swam toward the branch. Just then, an earsplitting crack filled the air. It was followed shortly by a whizzing noise passing by the Survivalist's left ear. She gasped and quickly glanced at the source of the noise. A much closer roaring blast came from across the creek. A large plumb of dust and debris appeared on the hillside down to the creek.

She gathered that the Mechanic must have returned cover fire for her. She searched the waters for the Entrepreneur. He was downstream from her, still floundering in the water. She sprinted toward him and plunged the branch into the water. The Entrepreneur bounced off a boulder as he grabbed the branch. He kept his grip.

The Survivalist's footing slipped. There was another bang in the distance followed quickly by a closer version. She began sliding across the bank, falling to her rear.

The Entrepreneur still had the branch in his hand, and his weight was pulling her to the water. She stood and dug her feet in. The Entrepreneur swam toward shore. Just as his right hand touched the bank, another bang came from afar. The Survivalist flinched in fear, but nothing hit her. She looked down at the Entrepreneur. He was clambering up the rocks above the drop. He waved his arm at her, motioning for her to leave him. She ran toward the forest. A nearby tree exploded its bark, followed by another bang. She ran into the woods and hid behind a tree. A closer bang reciprocated through the woods.

The Entrepreneur peeked up at the Survivalist. He had reached the top of the bank. His head disappeared. A decent-sized rock plopped onto the bank followed by the return of the Entrepreneur's head. He looked toward the gunfire. No noise occurred. He picked up the rock with both hands and threw it into the field. A puff of dirt flew up near it, and another bang blasted through the air. He quickly scrambled over the bank and ran across the opening. There was no closer bang.

The Entrepreneur dove headlong into a ditch near the Survivalist, where he stayed put. The Survivalist peeked around the tree. She spotted the Mechanic up the creek. He was pointing the chamber of the gun. He held the brown sack and crushed it in his hand. She realized he was out of ammo. She saw her hatchet at the edge of the woods and smacked the side of her leg where it was typically stowed, realizing she had dropped it in the rush earlier. The Young, the Old Man, and the Radioman were nowhere to be found. She had to do something.

She made a break for another nearby tree. There was another crack from far off, but nothing occurred around her. She broke off for another tree. She lay on the ground and wiggled her way down the length of a fallen log. She peered around the end. She spotted the Raider gunman. Other Raiders were beginning to descend on the Mechanic, who was cowering behind the boulder. The gunman appeared to be looking away, so she made a dash for the tree she had broken the branch off. The hatchet lay nearby on the ground.

She began to peek around the tree but stopped when she saw the Radioman frantically waving his arms from behind a different boulder. His coat and pants were still dripping with water. The Survivalist thought he must have made it across himself. How had he not been spotted in his maroon coat, though? He peered around the rock. He shook his head at the Survivalist. He peeked again. This time, he waved his arms and pointed toward the hatchet through the boulder it was behind.

The Survivalist lunged for the hatchet, retrieved it, and went back behind the tree. Another clap emitted from the far side of the creek. A yell caught her ear. She peeked around the tree. The Raiders had reached the Mechanic. He had knocked one of the Raiders far back the way he came. He was checking a pistol clip for ammunition. He clumsily put the clip back into the pistol and aimed it at the edge of the rock. The Raiders hesitated on the other side of the rock. The gunman's rifle was pointed right at the Mechanic's boulder.

Something else caught the Survivalist's eye. Her jaw dropped slightly. It was the Old Man. How had he gotten back across the creek? She watched as he slowly approached the gunman. He grabbed the gunman from behind. The Old Man took him behind the rock he was perched on. After a moment, he hopped up on the rock and scooped up the Raider's rifle. He immediately checked the chamber. He grimaced and scurried back down behind the rock. He appeared a moment later, roughly slamming the bolt of the gun in place and aiming it down at the Mechanic's rock.

A puff of smoke emitted from the end of the gun, quickly followed by another crack. One of the Raiders near the Mechanic fell over, clasping his left calf and dropping his pistol. The other three Raiders scrambled for cover, including the one the Mechanic had thrown. The Mechanic quickly stood from behind his boulder, snatched the dropped pistol from the ground, and pointed it toward the Raiders. The Old Man stepped out from cover. The Mechanic harshly yelled at the Raiders. "If any one of you moves, either this pistol or the rifle will blow your heads off. Drop your guns and knives on the ground."

Two of the Raiders did as they were told, the one with the injured leg shoved a large stick away from himself, and the other fiddled with his belt to drop a sheathed knife. One resisted. Another clap came from the rifle, and a puff of dust came very close to the resisting Raider's foot. The last Raider quickly tossed his pistol onto the ground and raised his hands. The Mechanic berated them. "Now if you want to leave here alive, go collect your friend on the ground and your buddy up the hill and leave. Don't bother trying to take your weapons with you."

The Raiders lowered their arms and went over to their fallen comrade. They scooped him up and carried him up the hill, all the while being followed by the Mechanic and traced by the Old Man's stolen rifle. The four Raiders disappeared behind the boulder where the Old Man was. The Old Man continued aiming for a bit. The Young appeared and scooped up the belt and the pistol. He observed the pistol curiously but otherwise avoided tampering with it.

The Old Man lowered the rifle and started down the hill. The Mechanic met the Young and took the knife and pistol. He tossed both of the pistols into his backpack and put the sheathed knife on his belt. The Old Man made it down to the group. The Mechanic handed him his rifle and took the stolen Raider's rifle in return. All three returned to the edge of the creek. The Survivalist cut off another longer branch and used it to transport the backpack across the creek dry by reaching across it. She used the same stick to help the Old Man and the Young across. The Young helped her get the Mechanic across. They left the clearing and dove into the woods for the cave.

They found the cave around thirty minutes later with the help of the Old Man's memory. By that point, the sun had nearly completely set. They did not set up another fire in case more Raiders came for revenge. For the first time since they left the creek, someone spoke. It was the Old Man. "Okay. That crossing was bad, but it could have gone worse. Nobody died, not even the Raiders. We just stole their guns and a knife."

The Entrepreneur spoke up. "You shot the one Raider's leg."

The Old Man sighed. "Yes, I did. I did it to scare the others. I could have killed him, though. He will likely heal the leg with the small round he was hit with. I got him with the stolen rifle, not my own. The Raiders likely stole medical supplies from me back at the farmhouse. They can use those to fix him up." There was a pause.

"So who gets the guns and the knife?" asked the Survivalist.

The Old Man shrugged. "Who can shoot or use the knife?" Nobody spoke. The Old Man continued. "Well, I vote that they stay in the backpack, then."

The Survivalist protested. "No way. Those guns could protect us if we ever get in another scrap like that. They have to be given out. We can't expect you and the Mechanic to protect us alone every time."

The Old Man nodded, considering that thought. "You are right. But if no one here can shoot, then no one needs the gun."

The Young spoke up. "I will take the knife. I know how to use it. I used one in the city for a while to open cans for food before the blade broke off."

The Old Man asked, "Any protests to that?" Nobody announced disagreement. The Old Man motioned to the Mechanic, who took the knife off his belt and tossed it in the sheathe to the Young. The Young put it on the belt loop of his jeans.

The Mechanic stated, "I will take a pistol. The rifle we got from the Raider is in very poor shape. The bolt and barrel are both rusted. The scope is cracked. I don't think it is even safe to use. I vote we leave it here in this cave and take the ammunition with us to use in the Old Man's rifle. I will take four of the seven pistol bullets. The second pistol with three bullets can go to whoever can shoot it."

The group agreed except for the Old Man. "The bullets from the Raider's rifle aren't of the correct caliber for mine. They are far too small. Taking the ammo won't do us any good. Just leave it behind along with the Raider's rifle. It is trashed anyway. I had to nearly break the bolt trying to get it to load a round. It is no wonder it was so long between each of their shots." There was another pause.

"I will take the second pistol." The group turned to look at the Hobo in the dim lighting. "I haven't told you all yet, but I have shot a pistol before, even at people. I had a hard time growing up. A gang tried to take me in out of pity, but it just ended in gunfire, so I gave the gun back and left. They gave me this knife instead to help me out." He held up the small pocketknife, but no one could make out what it looked like in the low light. "So yeah, I can take it if nobody else knows how to shoot it."

The Mechanic spoke again. "I think that is a great idea. If anybody opposes it, we can reconsider. But for now, I am handing the second pistol and the three bullets to the Hobo." No one disagreed. The Mechanic handed the gun over.

The Hobo held the gun in his hand and snapped it up to look down the sights out the entrance to the cave. "It is in decent shape," he said. There was a long pause.

The Entrepreneur picked up the conversation. "So, uh, where are we headed from here?" The group shuffled in the near dark to look at the Entrepreneur or at least in his direction.

The Mechanic answered. "What do you mean?"

"I don't know. Where are we going now? We can't stay here. The Raiders will find us and ransack our stuff again if we try to hole up here."

The Mechanic grunted. "He's right. We have some time thanks to how deep we made that creek crossing, but they will come for us again, especially since we let those Raiders live with an injured man."

The Old Man joined. "My knowledge is tapped. Your all's guess is as good mine."

The Survivalist added, "We certainly can't go back to the city. There are loads of Raiders there, more than we could ever handle. If the word gets out we took shots at them, then we are good as dead there."

The Hobo agreed. "Yeah, and there aren't any supplies left to scavenge out of there anyway."

There was a pause. The Young joined. "What about over the mountains?" The group paused in thought.

The Radioman sensed a confusion in the cave. "What about these mountains, Young?"

The Young lay flat on his back across the cold, smooth stone. "I saw a map once back in school. It showed a whole world out there past those mountains. Why can't we just go find somewhere new to stay? We can restart somewhere out there. Maybe it is better beyond here."

The Radioman answered, "We cannot travel out into the world. It is destroyed. I received incoming distress signals from all over the world—reports of thousands dying, entire landscapes ablaze, and more horrific things than one man could possibly cypher through and decode for an audience. There is no point or hope in traveling beyond the city outskirts around where the Old Man's farmhouse was located. Our plan is bust."

The Entrepreneur cleared his throat. The group interrupted themselves with silence. The Mechanic spoke up. "Entrepreneur, I know you were trading with outside the city. Who were you trading with?" The Entrepreneur shuffled in the dark. The Mechanic persisted. "Tell us, Entrepreneur." Silence. The Mechanic took a harsher tone. "Entrepreneur, this is no time for secrets and—"

"I know!" The Entrepreneur had at last responded. He cautiously approached his response. "I don't know who it was." A small sense of calamity rushed the cave. The Entrepreneur could feel the apprehension through the dark. "Listen, that is part of the deal. You don't know who you are talking to the entire time intentionally. That way, if the deal goes south, you both reserve the right to bail anonymously."

The Survivalist rejoined. "How do you talk with someone and not know who they are?"

"You send a trusted middle postman chain with sealed paper letters. In return for a safe and secure delivery, the middle postmen get a small portion of the deal from both sides for themselves. The middle man only delivers written messages but does not know what the message is himself and, as a result, only knows whom he got the letter from and whom he took it to. The less middle postmen, the better. Old-school technique."

The Survivalist was satisfied with that answer. The Mechanic was not. "Then you at least know where the other end of the deal is to get this middle postman to the other side?"

The Entrepreneur shook his head. "Nope. I never managed to get a deal to be accepted. Nobody ever started the deal."

The Mechanic smacked the rock floor. "Entrepreneur! What are you hiding from us?"

The Entrepreneur grew defensive. "Nothing!"

The Mechanic started to roll to his feet. "Now you listen here, Entrepreneur. You are going to tell us how this deal of yours would go down from start to finish if you don't want me to come over there and wring your neck."

The Entrepreneur understood. "All right. Listen, you don't start a deal directly with a person all that often. Instead, you mention that somebody, which may or may not be you, is looking to make a deal in general for something to someone you trust. You hand that person a sealed letter with a quick and vague description on the outside. If that person doesn't want it, they pass it on to someone they trust. This continues until they get a person who will take the deal, or it goes through so many iterations unaccepted that it fizzles out.

"If the deal is accepted, the letter is opened by the acceptor, and a response is written. The letter then goes back the same way it went out to the original source. If you word it right, nobody knows who is taking the deal or who started it. Nobody knows who the other end of the trade is, but both ends of the deal know they have somebody interested out there somewhere in the world. The acceptor picks a place and time that they will be making a drop. You show up some-time after that, collect the goods, and leave your end of the deal."

The Young sat up. "What if they don't deliver their part?"

"Then the deal is off. You keep your stuff and go home."

"What if you don't deliver your part but take theirs?"

"Now that would seem to be a problem, but everyone still alive knows better. If you do that, then the angry opposite end of the deal sends word back the line. They triangulate who the other side is, hunt them down, and typically kill them in some very brutal methods."

"Like what?"

"I once found a man with a six-foot shard of glass shoved through his stomach. They had obviously taken their time with him." That was more than the Young was looking for.

The Mechanic wasn't through yet. "What were you dealing for?"

The Entrepreneur chuckled. "What you all just gave me for free."

"Which is?"

"A safe passage out of the city. They could have whatever they wanted as long as I made it out unharmed."

"That seems like a pretty good deal."

"It may have been, but nobody in the city would leave, and nobody outside would come back."

"You knew there were people out here?"

"Vaguely. I knew they were outside of the city. That's it. It could have been the Old Man for all I knew."

The Old Man waved him off. "That wasn't me, that I know for sure."

The Mechanic pushed further. "Could you figure out where they were?"

"No, not now, not without going back into the city and looking for a guy who is probably dead by now if he didn't run from the city. As you know, the Raiders are taking over everything back there." The Mechanic laid his head back onto the rock with a sigh. He had been defeated. The Entrepreneur continued talking. "Although…"

The Mechanic sat back up. "Although?"

"I tried to make a deal with a fellow once, a year or so after the Crisis, for a box of ammunition. He told me to meet him halfway at the mountains."

The Mechanic grinned. "Which means there is something past the mountains?"

"No. I mean, there might have been something past the mountains at one point."

The Mechanic shook his head. "That is two leads, one from the Young and one from the Entrepreneur." He sighed. "Is everyone good with sticking together and trying to cross the mountains in search of a new, safer place with resources to live on?"

The Survivalist yawned. "Sure. Why not? Where else am I going to go? I am following you now, Mechanic."

The Young jumped in after her. "I will go too."

The Old Man nodded. "I will go if the Young does."

The Radioman chuckled. "I see no other alternatives."

The Hobo smiled. "I am coming with you all for the food at the least. That deego was good stuff."

The Entrepreneur smiled. "Yeah. That sounds nice. Let's do it."

The Mechanic smiled. "All right. It is settled. We head for the mountains in the morning. Everyone, get some shut-eye. The Raiders will likely be back in the morning. We need to get up early to get out of here before they find us." The group agreed and exchanged good nights. They all adjusted around in the dark until they found somewhere relatively comfortable on the cave floor and went to sleep.

*****

The next morning, the group woke up early. None of them had slept well. The Radioman was already up and looking out the entrance of the cave when the rest of the group got up. He enjoyed the mornings. It was something about how still everything was and how everything was just waiting to be woken up by the morning sun or maybe their favorite broadcasting channel. The Radioman redirected his attention from the forest to his overcoat and pants. They had gotten rather dirty during the creek crossing. His face brightened as he hatched an idea.

He checked to see if anyone else was awake. The Hobo had noticed him heading out and had rolled over to watch him. The Radioman spoke in a softer tone than normal to avoid waking the others but with the same quickness and somehow still retaining his everlasting zeal. "I am headed down to the creek to fix this dreadful apparel. I will be careful and keep a sharp eye out for any troublesome Raiders. If you here gunshots, know that those speeding bullets were directed toward me and that I will be headed directly back to this very cave."

The Hobo nodded. "All right. I will let everyone know if you don't get back by the time they wake up." The Radioman began striding through the forest toward the creek they had left. The Hobo grinned at the goofy man going to clean his clothes as his first thought in the morning as he rolled back over to get some more sleep.

The Radioman arrived back at the creek in only a short time. There were occasions when the Radioman did enjoy a leisurely stroll, but these were under the requirement that there was nothing to do at the destination. He stopped at the edge of the forest and observed the creek clearing. There was no one about. The Radioman did wonder if there was anyone behind the rocks on the ridges. Maybe they had fallen asleep there while watching for the group to return. Maybe this was all an elaborate ambush. But really, what were the chances of that?

He tried to reason with it so he could go wash his treasured clothes, but he knew all too well that this was a bad move. *How persistent are these Raiders, really?* he thought. He decided to do a test. He walked carefully back into the woods until he found a small rock. He figured he could throw it high into the air and see if anyone moved around to see where it had come from. Meanwhile, he would be safely hidden away behind a nearby large tree trunk. He wound up his arm and hurtled the rock high up past the trees. The rock arched downward as it reached its peak and came back down to the open clearing with a dull thud as it hit the ground.

The Radioman hid as planned. He scrutinized the opposite bank for movement. He was not surprised when nothing showed itself, but the rock had not made much of a commotion. It could have flown through the air completely unnoticed. So he grabbed a flat rock, this time lobbing it toward the creek in hopes of a loud splash. His hopes were realized as the rock made a loud smacking sound on the water. He crouched down and peeked around the tree. Nothing moved. He thought as he stood and began out into the field, *Ah, look at me out here playing pussyfoot with an open field that only contains a creek. How daft of me to even...*

His thoughts were frozen in place as he spotted a glint on his far right. He dove back behind the tree and adjusted himself to hide from the glint. He had seen something there. He knew it, but he had to be sure. He peered around the tree. He couldn't find anything. Far off in the distance, the glint happened again. He pulled his head back behind the tree. He waited a few moments and opted to check around the opposite side of the tree. This time, he spotted the source. It was a Raider with a rifle. The Raider was on his side of the creek, searching the clearing where the splash from the rock had occurred.

The Radioman pulled his head back behind the tree once more. *What am I going to do? There are surely more of them across the creek already if there is one posted there. I need to get back to the group and warn them. Maybe we can get going now in the early morning before the Raiders all wake up.* The Radioman checked the Raider again. The Raider was walking down the hill toward the creek. The Radioman realized he had a chance to make it out without being spotted. He started creeping back toward the forest he had come in through. If he could just make it back to the underbrush around twenty yards away, then he could easily escape the line of sight of the Raider.

He was about halfway across when the Raider made a long sweep with the rifle. The Radioman panicked and flopped down behind a fallen log. On his way down, he caught a branch and sent it swinging. He quickly shimmied along the ground to the end of the log to get away from the branch. He was only a quick jump across an open patch of ground to the underbrush, but the Raider had to have spotted the swinging branch. The Raider would be looking right at him if he made a break for it.

He did not dare peek around the end of the log. In fact, he tried nothing. He lay down perfectly still. Panic had struck him. He realized that he had dealt with panic every day at his radio station before the Crisis, but that was not a life-or-death situation. He lay there stiffened by fear. A noise caught his ear, a loud snap. The Radioman jumped at the sound. Was it a gunshot? No. It had sounded like a tree branch behind him. The Radioman twisted around to see where the noise had originated.

He spotted the Hobo hiding behind a boulder with half of a large stick in his hand. The Hobo was waving his arms frantically, signaling the Radioman to get out of the area. The Radioman rose to his feet, darted across the gap, and dove into the underbrush. He lay still for a moment before crawling out the other side of the bush he had landed in and working his way back toward the cave. After a moment, he turned and looked for the Hobo. He wasn't there. The Radioman immediately began a search for another rock. He found one and blindly launched it far across the forest. He heard it splash into the creek. *What a lucky throw!* he thought.

He heard a small rustle in a nearby bush. He froze. The Hobo popped his head out of a leafy bush. He whispered, "Thanks, Radioman. We need to leave. I came after you because I spotted a Raider on top of a far-off ridge right after you left. I started out, but I saw more closer by. I had a hard time getting here due to all of them. The group is awake, and they are heading around the hillside from the other entrance to the cave since there are so many more than we thought. We need to catch up to them and get out of here." The Radioman nodded. The two started off through the underbrush.

The Hobo waved the Radioman over after ducking behind a rock. The Radioman ducked down with him. The Hobo whispered, "Listen, Radioman. There are Raiders all over this place. We are going to have to sneak our way through as quietly as possible—no sounds, no distractions like your rock on the water. We are better off if these guys have no idea where we are headed."

The Radioman nodded. "I understand." The Hobo glanced down at the Radioman's maroon outfit. The Radioman shook his head. "I will be fine."

"You are sure?"

"If I am not, then I will be bait, and you can run off."

The Hobo widened his eyes with a slight head shake. "All right, then." He turned and peered around the rock. He lay flat on his stomach and parted a section of tall green grass sprouting from the edge of the rock. He held a hand palm out to keep the Radioman still. He turned his hand upward and curled it as he rose to a crouch and darted off. The Radioman rounded the stone and tailed him closely as low as he could. He expected to stop at some point, but the Hobo kept going in front of him. The Hobo was swiftly vaulting logs and hopping muddy sections.

The Radioman was trying his hardest to keep up. He was managing, but he feared going any faster for the noise. The Hobo abruptly dove flat and skidded to a stop in a section of grass off the right side of a narrow path. The Radioman lay flat where he was just off the left of the same path. The Hobo peeked out at something. He turned, spotted the Radioman, and waved him away as he rolled off into the brush.

The Radioman spun wildly. He noticed a log. He checked the path, seeing nothing. He stood to a crouch and dragged himself over the log, lying flat behind it on his back. There was a thump nearby. It was accompanied by a short, heavy grunt. Footsteps slowly approached. The grass rustled, then there was silence. The Radioman held his breath. The silence stayed. The Radioman began to wonder if he had been seen. No, there wouldn't be any of this waiting if he had been. What was the fellow waiting for, then? He had to get some information.

He picked himself up carefully from the dirt surface and scooted himself backward so that his head protruded out past the end of the log. A wad of roots blocked a clear line of sight, but he found the man. He was looking away, toward where the Hobo was. He took a step off the narrow path into the bushes. The Radioman panicked. This was his fault. He couldn't watch as the Hobo was found and given whatever punishment he would receive.

He looked around. There was a medium-size stick not far off. It looked rather stiff from the way it was lying across the dirt. He peeked at the man. The man had frozen just off the side of the trail as he scanned the grass beyond. The Radioman rolled over and scuttered over to the stick. He snatched it up and straightened to a sitting position behind a standing tree. There was a sound of cloth whooshing through the air. The Radioman took a deep breath. Just before he rounded the tree, a snapping sound came from the far side of the path. There was another whoosh.

The Radioman peeked around the tree. The man was turned from the waist up to look behind him. The Radioman swung around the tree and dashed the short distance toward the man, stick in hand raised behind him. He arrived at the man, twisted at his torso, grabbed the thicker bottom end of the stick with both hands, and started a long swing. The man caught on the commotion and turned back to figure out what it was. He found it quickly as the Radioman batted him directly across the bridge of his nose with the stick.

The rigid stick cracked but stayed together. The man grunted and fell backward. The Hobo appeared abruptly from the grass right next to the falling man, spooking the Radioman, and caught the man, laying him gently into the grass. The Hobo put his hand on the man's chest. He retracted it as he gave the Radioman an agitated look. The Radioman bent at the waist and gently hid the stick in the grass. The Radioman crouched low next to the Hobo and looked down at the man. The Hobo snatched the Radioman's hand and stuck it on the man's chest. The Radioman felt a heartbeat. The Hobo released the Radioman's hand and waved him on. He dragged the man's unconscious body into the grass. The two continued through the brush.

Not long after then, the two arrived back at the cave. There were Raiders swarming the entire thing. The Hobo pressed closer to the Radioman to whisper, "They must not have found them. Come on. They told me they were headed out the other side, and they would meet me at the highest place on the other side." The two slipped away.

After rounding the hillside, the two stopped once more to scout the area. The Radioman pointed over to an old building. "There. That is the highest place."

The Hobo looked over. "I thought they meant the highest natural place?"

"No, you said the highest place. That rooftop is the highest place." The Hobo didn't seem convinced. The Radioman tapped his arm. "If they aren't there, we can scout the area and see where they might have been from that rooftop." The Hobo grimaced at the idea but nodded. He took off with the Radioman on his heels.

The two arrived at the building. The Hobo leaned in through a crumbling stone doorway. He went inside. The Radioman stepped through to find the entire place covered in a leafy vine. Any small spot that wasn't coated in the crawling foliage was taken residence by a thick, soft nonvascular plant that resembled a lime pillow on the ground. The Hobo tested his weight on a flight of stairs off to the right of the Radioman. Satisfied, he waved the Radioman on. The Radioman took one last look around the room.

A television sat in the corner next to what appeared to be a holographic projector of some kind. The wooden frame of what must have been a glass table rested in the center of the room, glass shards still poking out, glittering around the corners. Part of a wooden chair sat tipped over nearby. If anything was on the walls, it was completely hidden by the vines.

There was a second door directly through the building from the one they had come through. The Radioman turned right to head up the stairs, instead spotting a cracked old countertop covered in a blackened growth of some kind. He could make out standard kitchen appliances—knobs on a stove, the handle of a fridge. All of it was corroded beyond repair. He started up the stairs.

The second floor was quite a contrast to the lively one below. The Radioman had picked his way up around the soft, fuzzy lime patches of plants growing on the stairs and rounded the overgrown banister to the left at the top in the corner of the room. The entire floor was blackened with burnt charcoals. Nothing was recognizable. Everything had blurred together into a massive black pile of ash.

He found the Hobo poking the ceiling with a blackened piece of wood. The Hobo glanced over. "They weren't here. There are no signs of them anywhere. I am going to try to get into this attic. They had this fancy metal drop-down stair installed, but it is entirely rusted through due to the fire that apparently burned this place up."

The Radioman somewhat ignored this remark. "Hey, Hobo, do you think that fellow back there—"

"He will be fine. You felt his heartbeat. A sore nose for sure. You knocked him clean out. You seem to have some experience with batting a guy's head. When was the last time you did it?"

The Radioman looked away. "It has been a long while."

The Hobo shrugged. "You did what you had to do, man." He stabbed the ceiling once more. It gave a little.

The Radioman, wishing to change the subject and partially regretting starting the previous short-lived conversation, crossed the room and found another charred wooden stick and prodded the ceiling. "It seems loose." The Hobo nodded. The Radioman continued. "Rust is not adding up. We should be able to break the rust off and get this open. It must be blocked from the far side."

The Hobo froze. He leaned in toward the Radioman to whisper. "Do you think someone is holed up in there?"

The Radioman had the uncomfortable realization that the two of them might be intruding on an occupied residency. He shook his head and poked the ceiling again. It wiggled. The Radioman whispered back. "I don't think the ceiling has enough structural integrity to support the weight of a person." The Hobo lit up. He pointed at the Radioman with a grin. He ran down the stairs.

A moment later, the Hobo returned with a large stone. He brushed past the Radioman, who turned to watch, and hurled the stone into the ceiling. The door bounced upward around an inch and shut once more. A small dent had formed where the stone struck the metal door. "It is blocked." He retrieved the stone and stepped back once. He hit the ceiling right next to the metal ceiling hatch. To the surprise of both of the men, the rock sailed right through the ceiling. It landed with a thump on the other side of the ceiling above them. The Hobo passed the Radioman and disappeared down the stairs again.

He returned with the wooden frame of the glass table. He took the charred piece of wood from earlier and dragged it along the frame, breaking off the remaining glass shards. Tossing the stick aside, he carefully stood on the table, one foot on the edge of each bar running the length of it. He was able to just reach the ceiling. He pulled on it, yanking a large chunk of it down. He observed it as he handed it to the Radioman. "Hmm. Nice material. If only it weren't rotting away from fire damage."

The Radioman laid it aside. The Hobo reached up to an exposed crossbeam in the ceiling and pulled himself up. He grunted. "Gimme a boost." The Radioman stood below the Hobo and picked up his feet. He shoved the table out of the way with his hip and tossed the Hobo into the ceiling. The Hobo shuffled for a moment. His movement stopped. His voice was muffled through the ceiling. "Oh, shit."

The Radioman peered upward through the hole. "What is the matter?"

"There is a dead guy in here. Or maybe a dead girl. I don't know. It is a skeleton." There was a brief period of thumping and shuffling. "There is a note here. Should I read it?"

The Radioman shrugged. "Why not?"

"All right, then." The Hobo cleared his throat. "'To whoever finds this note, I have been hiding in here for the last few hours. Someone is outside my house, raiding everything. I do not know why. My only guess is, it has something to do with the crazy events the news has been talking about.'" The Hobo coughed. "Sorry. It is really dusty up here." He continued reading after a short pause. "There is a gap in this note. There is another paragraph below it. The handwriting is sloppier on the second paragraph, like it was rushed. It reads like this:

"'The man outside the house has come in. I have been hiding in the attic to avoid being found. He seems to know I am here somewhere as he has searched this whole place over for me. I want this on record so I can report him. I haven't gotten a clear look at him.' There is another gap here. The third part is really difficult to make out. I'll do my best.

"'The man has brake…' No, sorry. 'The man has broken the majority of my property. I can hear him smashing it all up. I thought about coming downstairs, but he already tried to get into the attic. I blocked it off with a few heavy boxes.'" The Hobo paused. "Heh. Yeah, heavy metal crates right over there. Boxes is a bit of an understatement, really." There was another pause. "'He isn't getting in here anytime soon, but I can't get back out. The air is getting smoky in here. It smells like a fire.'" The Hobo paused. "Hey, uh, the rest of this is just pleading for life in a blind panic. I can't even read the most of it. He or she apparently spent the last minute or so of his or her life writing this. It is like they just gave up."

The Radioman shook his head. "That is rough. You think that happened right after the Crisis?"

The Hobo laughed. "More like during the Crisis. They didn't call it by name."

"Right."

"Well, the smoke got them. These bones aren't burnt, and this corner the skeleton is in isn't charred either. They suffocated." He paused before continuing. "The smoke may have killed that person, but I think it is going to help us."

"What do you mean?"

"The ceiling up here is damaged pretty badly. I think the smoke did it."

The Radioman shook his head. "It was likely the heat from the fire, the same heat that stripped the coating off the metal and allowed the hatch to rust."

"Oh yeah. You are probably right. Well, I am going to give it a good kick here and see if I can break through it." There was an audible thump with a cracking sound. Another thump came through with a much louder cracking sound. There was the sound of movement on the ceiling and then the sound of wood snapping. "I'm through."

"Wonderful. Go out and see if you can find the group. We need to go."

"All right." After a short bit, a pair of feet landed back on the ceiling. The Radioman shrugged. "Anything of interest?"

The Hobo nodded. "I found the Entrepreneur. He was lying right out in the shortest patch of grass in the entire area. Gotta be him." The Radioman smiled. The Hobo waved him on. "I also saw the mountains. They are a good way off. It will take us all day to get there. Come on. Let's get to them before we lose more daylight."

*****

The Survivalist tapped the Old Man's shoulders. He stopped leading the group forward and braced up behind a tree. He turned and silently motioned for her to tell him what she needed to with a nod of his head. She pointed to the right out into the field. The Old Man leaned around the tree. Four Raiders were prowling their way across. The Old Man looked back at the group and motioned for them to get down as he crouched. The Raiders seemed to be methodically picking their way across the grass. They were spread out to cover the entire area. Each one was armed with a rifle.

The Old Man checked the chamber of his own and realized it was still empty from yesterday's creek crossing ordeal. He grimaced and snapped the bolt shut. He shook his head to the group. The group switched to scanning the area. Nowhere seemed good to run. They had lost track of the mountains in the rush away from the cave. Anyone could guess which way was correct.

A small rustle froze the group in place. After a moment, they turned toward the noise. The rustling repeated. The Mechanic crept over toward the edge of the bushes. He ripped them open. The Hobo jumped backward. The Mechanic realized he had made quite a large sound. In a panic, he released the bush and dove into it with the Hobo. The two of them lay there for a moment. No sounds were heard. The Mechanic adjusted a short distance over, away from the Hobo. He whispered, "Hobo, where is the Radioman? Did you get him out?"

"Yeah. He is just back behind me in the grass. I told him to wait and cross after I made it to you."

The Mechanic relaxed. "Good. I thought we had lost him."

"Do you care about him or something?" The Mechanic was honestly unsure how to answer this immediately. The Hobo smiled. "No worries. I am just pulling your leg." He shuffled forward a bit past the slightly annoyed Mechanic. He gradually parted the bush and peeked out. He scurried off to the same tree the Mechanic had left. The Mechanic heard another faint rustle. He looked back into the brush.

The Radioman was wiggling his way through, picking the branches off his coat as he went. He looked up after removing a thorn from his wrist. He noticed the Mechanic and visibly jumped from being spooked. "Ah, Mechanic, you startled me. Have you seen where the Hobo is?"

The Mechanic smiled. "I just saw him. He is out with the group. There are four Raiders patrolling the field."

"Oh. Do we have a plan?"

"We don't know where the mountains are. We need to know so that we can plan a route out of here."

"Well, then, you are in luck. The mountains are off to the left of this field. We can hug this hill around to the left and then head straight up out of the hollow. The Hobo went up on the roof of the building over there and located them along with the Entrepreneur."

The Mechanic chuckled. "He is a horrible hider."

The Radioman snickered. "I know."

"Why were you in the building?"

"You said the highest place. That building is the highest place."

"I meant the highest natural place." The Radioman scoffed, realizing the Hobo was right. "Let's go tell the group about the mountains." The two shuffled to the edge of the bush. They waited a moment before sneaking out together. The Mechanic started by checking in on the Raiders. They were a good way off to the left now. The Mechanic turned to the group and started a discreet conversation. "The Hobo and the Radioman found the mountains. They are to the left. We just can't see them over this hill. We need to find a way past these guys without drawing attention to ourselves."

The Survivalist checked the surroundings. "There have to be more than just four of these guys. We saw a whole army of them when we left the cave."

The Young nodded. "There are more for sure."

The Mechanic caught the two of them. "But there are only four here. We only need to worry about those four if we don't get caught." This the three could agree on.

The Young replied, "Well, then, what is the plan?"

The Old Man answered, "I say we hug the left side and hope they don't see us in the brush."

The Young hastily shook his head. "No, it won't work."

The Mechanic looked over. "And why not?"

The Young pointed along the edge of the field. "Those are all thin, woody plants." The group exchanged confused glances. The Young continued. "Thin, woody plants swing a lot if you bump them. With all of us, we might as well be shaking this entire tree and hoping to not be seen. We are better off crossing the field behind the Raiders and getting up over the far hillside. They already searched the area. Why would they look back?"

The group exchanged another round of glances. The Survivalist nodded. "He is right, crossing would be safer. If we get scared halfway across, we can always fall flat into the tall grass. Look at that stuff. It is waist high on the Raiders." The group took a quick peek at the Raiders and returned to one another. The group seemed to be in a hesitant nonverbal agreement. The Young grinned, checked around the tree, and went out. The group panicked for a moment as they rotated around their hiding trees to watch.

The Young gracefully hopped across the field, never faltering, and stopped on the far side behind a stone. Despite the distance, the group could still make out his smirk. The Survivalist dove out next, crossing slightly slower than the Young but unseen. The rest of the group opted to go all at once. They slipped out from behind the trees and started across the field. Their collective noise must have caught the attention of the Raiders as they began to turn around. The entire group fell flat and motionless. They waited.

The Hobo looked toward the stone. Neither the Young nor the Survivalist were anywhere to be seen. Where had they gone? He didn't dare check the Raiders for fear of being seen. The Hobo searched the stone again. He nearly gave up when he spotted a small speck of motion. He focused in, adjusting a blade of the thick grass out of the way. It was a hand, held palm out and unmoving. It started beckoning. The Hobo popped his head out of the grass and found the Raiders looking away. He rose to a low position and started across the field. He heard the small noises of the group behind him. He arrived at the stone and slid in behind it. There was a dugout behind it. The stone must have slipped down the hill a bit to create the hole. He hunkered down against the far side to make room for more arrivals.

The Survivalist had her hand held out, motionless. She waited for a good period. The Young spoke to her in a hushed tone. "Not yet. They are confused. One of them is arguing with another." There was a pause. "The one arguing seems to have lost. They are headed off again, but one is looking back still periodically. He is on to us. It is going to have to be quick. Now! Go!"

The Survivalist beckoned with her hand. The Hobo heard the sounds of footsteps approaching. The Mechanic, the Entrepreneur, and the Radioman poured into the hole. They squished over to make more space. The Young scowled at them and scolded with the same hushed tone. "Quiet! They might here us." He hid behind the stone. A moment later, he peeked out again. "Who is left?"

The Survivalist replied, "The Old Man."

"Is that it?"

"Yeah."

"How close?"

"Not very. Maybe three-fourths of the way."

The Young shook his head once. "Great. Hold on." The wind rustled in the trees and through the grass. A stronger gust picked up and dissipated. The Young lit up. "That's it." He hid behind the rock and looked over at the Survivalist. "When that wind blows hard, get ready to signal him over. The wind will cover his sounds." She nodded. He checked around the rock. The wind started to pick up. "No. Wait. He is looking." A pause. "Now!"

The Survivalist furiously beckoned and leaned around the stone. Sloppy footsteps could be heard approaching. The Young began to panic. "Hurry up!" The Survivalist took a serious face toward the Old Man. He hastened his pace. The Young hid behind the stone. "Bail! Tell him to stop." The Young turned to see the Old Man panting at the bottom of the dugout. The Young released a long breath. "You people scare me with this stuff." He slouched down next to the Old Man.

The Radioman pointed to the spot they had come from. "I hate to be a bother, but there are reinforcements on the way."

The Hobo looked up. "What?" He peeked around the stone. "Oh, shit." He scurried over to the other side of the stone. "Come on. This way before they find us. We are just going over the hill. It should be safe over there to run." He dashed up and over the hill. The group followed him.

They met for a brief moment on the far side as the Hobo pointed out the peaks of the snowy mountains far off. They were cut off by the sound of footsteps approaching. The Hobo guided them across a short distance to a river. There was no way across. He pointed to a small stone building alongside the river and a wooded forest. The group sped over to it and tried the wooden door. It was jammed. The Mechanic pushed the group out of the way and rammed it open inward. The group slipped inside, and the Mechanic slapped the door shut. The Hobo braced it with a nearby green metal cabinet.

The group calmed their breathing and listened for anyone on the outside. No noises found their ears. The Entrepreneur broke the silence. "Hey, guys, I think we just found our ticket out of here." The group turned to the center. A makeshift raft comprised of cut logs strapped together with old green-and-blue ratchets floated in a pool of water in the center of the room. A rudder had been fashioned out of half of a hinged door and a metal pole driven through the top of it. They had walked into an old boathouse.

The Old Man approached the raft. "Whose is this?"

The Entrepreneur shook his head. "Doesn't matter. We need it more than whoever built it right now. Get on." He stepped onto the large raft. The group piled on behind him. It held their collective weight above the water. The Mechanic found a chain and yanked it. A metal door groaned open. He pulled it up just far enough to get the raft through and had the group lay flat on it. The current of the clean river soon found the side of the raft and took it. The group remained silent as they were carried swiftly away from the fields.

*****

After riding the raft toward the mountains for about half an hour, the group finally felt comfortable enough to speak. The Hobo pointed downstream. "There they are, the mountains." The group turned to follow his guiding finger. The mountains were sharp massive gray landforms. Snow crested the tops of each peak and sometimes connected between two of them. Trees dotted the sides toward the top and turned into a dense covering as they progressed downward. A few boulder fields were sprawled out in some steep crevices. A bright-blue sky was dotted with a sparse covering of high, thin clouds. The whole scene was mirrored on the smooth, wide river below.

The Entrepreneur spoke. "How are we going to get over that?"

The Radioman peeked over. "I don't know. It was your idea to steal the raft and get closer to them. You tell us."

The Entrepreneur defended himself. "No, it was my idea to steal the raft and get away from the Raiders. I would say that part worked out well. It was everyone's agreed idea to try and cross these mountains." This the Radioman could not argue.

The Young looked back at the group from his perch on the front of the raft. "How long do you think it will take to get there?"

The Mechanic answered from his position at the rudder. "Well, based on how much progress we have made and assuming this river runs to the base of those mountains, I would say we will be there before dark sets in tonight."

The Old Man evaluated the guess. "We are moving pretty quickly. This is far faster than walking, even for all you young people."

The Hobo sat up from his uncomfortable position, sprawled across the damp logs. "How much food do we have left?"

The Old Man answered, "Enough for a few main meals. None for snacking. We will eat after a while." The Hobo groaned. The group returned to silence.

*****

After a few hours of lying around on the raft, the group started another conversation, beginning with the Old Man. "There they are. Mechanic, pull us over to those berries if you can." The Mechanic guided the raft to the right bank and let it run aground just below the royal-purple berries on the bush. The Old Man stepped off and onto the bank and plucked one of the berries. He sniffed it and smiled. "This is the one."

The group stared at it. The Hobo spoke for the group. "What is it?"

"A berry."

The Hobo grinned. "What kind of berry?"

"A perkly berry."

"Perky?"

"No, perkly. There is an *L* in there."

The Hobo stood and crossed the raft to the bush. He plucked one of the soft round berries and observed the jade stem and prickly small leaf. "Is it edible?"

The Old Man smiled. "Oh yes. They are ripe this time of year." He snatched the berry from the Hobo's hand. "Go fetch the pot from the backpack." The Hobo turned, somewhat excited to eat, and rushed over to the backpack. He unzipped it and retrieved the flattened collapsible pot, pushed it open, and returned to the Old Man. The Old Man plopped a few of the berries into the pot. He had removed the stems and leaves. "These berries go a long way. Only a handful of them are needed."

A few minutes passed as the Old Man plucked his choice of berries. He left for a moment and returned with a small river stone. He dropped it into the pot. "You don't want this juice on your skin. It will stain you purple for ages." He pressed down on the rock. The berries emitted a strange popping sound followed by a squishy splat. The Old Man worked the stone through the berries for a minute or so before carefully removing the stone and holding it up for the group.

He carried it to the edge of the raft, dunked it in the river to wash off the leftover juice, and pulled it back up onto the raft. The bottom of the stone was stained entirely dark purple. "It even stains the rocks. I have no idea how it does it." He set the rock on the floor near the Young. The Young picked it up. "Don't touch the purple," the Old Man warned.

The Young had his fill and passed it over to the Survivalist. As the group observed the stone, the Old Man was busy ripping twigs from the bush. He broke them into several small pieces and tossed them into the pot. The stone had made its way around the group. The Old Man pointed at it. The Entrepreneur, who had it last, handed it to him. He dropped the rock purple side down into the pot and smashed the sticks. The sticks oddly collapsed under the weight and turned into a sort of pulp.

The Old Man removed the rock, again washing it off in the river and plopping it on the surface of the raft. He retrieved a longer stick he had held back and stirred the mix. He looked in the pot while pressing his lips. He retrieved a few leaves from the bush and tossed them in. Again, he pressed the substance with the rock, washed it off, and stirred. He peeked in the pot once more and smiled. He turned back to the bush and stepped off the raft. He looked up at the Survivalist. "Bring you hatchet over here."

She stood and met the Old Man at the bush. The Old Man dug a small hole at the base of the bush, revealing a starchy white root. "Cut that white part off." She retrieved her hatchet from its holster on her leg. She smacked the root. It cut easily. She replaced the hatchet. The Old Man yanked the root from the ground and washed it in the river. He tossed the entire foot-long root into the pot, bending it so it would fit. He took the rock and unsurprisingly smashed the root to a pulp.

This time, he cast the stone off into the creek and stirred the mix a little with the stick. The stick bent noticeably, as the consistency of the mix had thickened to a higher viscosity. The Old Man removed the stirring stick, flipped it to the clean end, and poked the now sticky substance with it. He removed it. The stick came out clean and unstained. The Old Man smiled. He went back to the bush and beckoned the Survivalist over. She again retrieved the hatchet from her leg and whacked off another foot-long root.

The Old Man pulled it up and laid it straight across the ground. "Cut that into seven pieces, one for each of us." The Survivalist did her best to keep the pieces of equal length. The Old Man picked up one of the pieces and dipped it into the pot. He gathered up a large clump of the purple goop on the end of the fuzzy white root. He bit a piece of the mess off. He grinned, closed his eyes, and let out a long breath through his nose as he chewed.

The Survivalist had a perplexed look on her face. She picked up a piece of the root, scooped some of the goop, and ate a bite herself. She winced. It was a powerful, tangy flavor that relaxed into a starchy, heavy, dry flavor. It had a strange, stringy texture. She liked it. Her smiled convinced the rest of the group. They dove in and tried the mix, cleaning the pot out by the end of the meal.

The Old Man had finished his piece. "This will feed us for the rest of the afternoon. It is an amazing carbohydrate. Really sticks to your ribs."

The Young checked his fingers. They were still normal, not purple. "How come the purple stain isn't on my fingers?"

The Old Man chuckled. "The branches and leaves nullify the dye. They prevent it from sticking to anything. That is why the whole bush isn't purple. The root acts as a conglomerate adherence. It sticks everything together. The part of the root I didn't mash in is basically acting as an edible spoon. It is called Perkly Berry Root Mush. You have to be careful, though. No more than what I gave you. The berries are a natural laxative." The Old Man chuckled as he remembered something.

The Young nodded. "Who taught you to make that?"

The Old Man frowned slightly. "My dad did when I was just a young toddler. I have been making it every summer for my whole life."

The Young noticed the Old Man's long face. He tried to make him feel better. "Do you miss your dad?" The Old Man nodded. The Young continued. "What happened to him?" The Old Man shook his head. The Young understood. "Too far?"

The Old Man nodded. "Too far."

After finishing up the meal, the Mechanic and the Entrepreneur shoved the raft off and clambered on. The entire group traveled downstream for many more hours, pointing at features along the way and enjoying the view. The mountains grew ever closer. The raft was approaching a large bend in the river. The Mechanic guided the raft over to the right bank nearest the mountains. The group lazily looked back at him from the positions of comfort they had found. The Mechanic explained his actions.

"I have been watching the river for a while now. We are slowly headed away from the mountains. There is no way the river crosses those mountains. I think this bend in the river is going to take us farther away. Do you think we should get off here and head toward the mountains on foot? It is going to get dark soon anyway. We need to find a camp and eat dinner."

The Old Man nodded. "I suppose we should. Is everyone else good with that?"

The group agreed in general. They all groaned and stretched as they sat up. The Young chuckled. "This wooden raft doesn't make a very good bed anyway." The group hopped off the raft and pulled it ashore together.

The Survivalist pointed at the straps holding the raft together. "Do you think we could take those straps?"

The Mechanic shook his head. "No. They are rusted clear through. They have been stuck there for ages. We would have to cut them to get them off, and then they would be worthless. Besides, we don't know what is in these woods. We may need a fast ride out of here." The Survivalist nodded. The group started a slow walk into the woods, leaving the raft behind.

A ways into the woods, the group found an opening in the forest to set up camp. They started in on the work but stopped after hearing a commotion not far off. The Radioman questioned the group. "Where did that come from?"

The Hobo pointed. "Over that way. I think we should investigate."

A gunshot blasted through the area, spooking the group. The Survivalist looked over at the Hobo. "You sure about that?"

The Hobo nodded. "Even if they do have a gun, we need to see who they are. They may be people like us. If they aren't, we need to leave anyway." The group couldn't argue. They gathered their things and started toward the noise. Not half a mile into the woods, the group could hear incomprehensible voices. There was a loud screeching sound followed by a heavy slam. The group followed the sound. They found a bloody pool on the ground with a pile of field dressings. The Old Man observed the steaming remains. "It was a deego. They dragged it off this way."

They followed the Old Man to a path. They followed the path a short distance to a clearing. A large gray stone wall stood intact and proud with a manned gateway. More of the fuzzy lime plant the Radioman had seen earlier in the house dotted the wall here and there. Armed men stood watch. A building sat behind the wall, seemingly flush up against the bottom of the skyrocketing mountains. The group slipped into a patch of bushes.

The Entrepreneur spoke first. "What have we run in on?"

The Mechanic replied, "It is some kind of stronghold."

The Radioman seemed puzzled. "What would they be guarding?"

The Old Man pointed up the steep mountains. "The only low pass in this entire part of the mountain range. It is a bottleneck."

The Survivalist looked up at the mountains. She saw a large, flat spot crossing over the mountain. It looked almost unnatural, as if something was once there but had since been reclaimed by nature. She shook her head. "I don't know, guys. I don't even think we can scale that. It would be nearly impossible to get up it." Nobody argued that.

The Hobo sighed. "What about the men? Are they Raiders?"

The Young peered out from the bush. "Ah, no." His voice jumped in surprise. "They are dressed way too cleanly for that. They must have some kind of settlement behind that thing."

The Old Man raised an eyebrow. "Do you think they are friendly?"

The Entrepreneur answered, "Judging by all the guns and men watching, I would say no." The group fell silent for a moment.

The Old Man shrugged. "We don't have any other way over these mountains, right? Did you see anything else while you used the rudder, Mechanic?"

The Mechanic shook his head. "I didn't even see this pass. The mountains all looked to be about the same height, except for some peaks here and there. I would say this is our best shot over the mountains and away from the Raiders."

The group paused to look at the mountains. The Young shook his head. "There is no way. We can't make that."

The Old Man pressed his lips. "How about we go find out if there is a way over? I am sure these people have some information inside."

The Survivalist responded, "There is no way we can sneak past them. There are far too many."

The Old Man shook his head in exhaustion. "Who says we are sneaking?" He got up, leaving his rifle flat on the ground, and hobbled out of the bush, limping obviously on his left leg and not swinging his right arm as far as his left.

The Survivalist tried to argue his actions, but the Old Man was surprisingly swift at getting out of the bush. If she called him back now, she would blow her own and potentially the whole group's cover. "Oh no. What has that crazy old man planned now?" she whispered. Meanwhile, the Old Man had hobbled about three-fourths of the way across the open pad toward a guard without being seen. He paused for a moment, watching the guard's head carefully and making sure none of the others spotted him.

Three or four seconds passed. The Old Man began to glance back at the group in the bush. He cracked a smile but quickly wiped it off, turned back from his half glance, and recomposed his feeble position as the guard turned his head. The guard jumped noticeably when he found the Old Man. He immediately pulled out a pistol and aimed it directly at the Old Man. "Do not approach!" he yelled.

The Old Man stood unshaken but maintained his acting pose. He asked in a particularly hoarse voice, "Please. I am just an old man. That gun isn't necessary, is it?"

The guard hesitated. He lowered the pistol to the ground but kept it ready. "What is your business, old man?"

The Old Man croaked on. "I just need through this mountain range. You can check me for arms and other weapons. I don't have any. I overheard your guards through the trees, and I am curious if you could take me in for the night and show me a way through the mountains." The guard shook his head in disbelief. Before the guard could speak, the Old Man continued. "Look, eh, I am not asking for much, just a safe place to sleep for tonight only and maybe a glance at a map so I can find my way over these mountains. It is getting dark soon. I don't want to be caught out here."

The Guard continued to say nothing. The two stood in silence for a period. The guard broke the silence. "Back up." The Old Man began to speak but was cut off promptly by the guard. "Look, I need you to back up so that I can safely get on my radio and ask for permission to enter you. If you do not back up, I will have to shoot you." He raised the gun once more. The Old Man hesitated. The guard flicked the barrel of the pistol, indicating for him to move back. The Old Man gave in and took a few steps back. "To the edge of the gravel." The Old Man did as he was told, but he never broke eye contact with the guard.

The Survivalist whispered to the group in the bush, "He is keeping eye contact so that the guard has less of a chance to notice us in this bush. Brilliant."

The Old Man stopped at the edge of the gravel. The guard murmured into a radio. There was a scratchy response, to which the guard replied with another murmur. A bang emitted from the metal door behind the guard, and a second, nearly identical guard stepped halfway out, spoke briefly with the first guard, who nodded in response, and then walked back in, leaving the door cracked open.

The first guard flicked the gun to the door. "Come on. Through the door, old man. We can't take any chances with unknown outsiders. You are going to have to go through the whole procedure." The Old Man did as he was told, continuing his false limp. He never turned to look at the bush. He went inside the door. The guard did not follow him in, instead remaining outside and slamming the door shut behind the Old Man. Another loud clunk from the door and the whole area returned to only the noise of the forest behind the group.

"Now what do we do?" asked the Entrepreneur.

The Survivalist motioned for him to quiet down. "We wait. We have no idea what his plans are. He will probably try to get us all inside the base there." The group fell silent.

Meanwhile, the Old Man was getting scanned top to bottom by three different guards. He was still holding his decrepit pose and wincing whenever they touched his leg to give off the impression that it was injured. The guards were surprisingly gentle with him. He spoke up. "You know, when you led me in here and I saw these fellows, I was wondering if they were going to rough me up. But they are being quite careful with me here. I appreciate that."

He was talking to a man up on a small balcony. The man replied with a deep, thick voice. "No worries, old man. You are obviously not armed. Had you been armed, things would have been more to your previous expectations." The Old Man nodded, unsure how to respond. The guards finished the search, and one of them motioned for him to follow him through another door on the opposite wall from the one he came in through.

The Old Man noticed a draft. It was getting stronger as they walked down the hall that the doorway led to. There were multiple pockets lining the walls, seemingly all leading upward. "What are all these holes?"

The guard stopped walking. The Old Man nearly ran into him. "Listen, I can't explain anything to you. You should remain silent and…" His voice trailed off, getting quieter with each word. The guard peered behind him. The door was out of sight. He turned to face the Old Man. "I am not supposed to tell you anything. If they find out I did, it will be bad news for both of us."

He hesitated. "I can't explain why I can't tell you either. That would be too much. You would give it away for sure. But you will figure it all out soon enough." Unsure how to respond, the Old Man remained silent. A quiet took the hallway, all except for a faint whistling noise. The Guard continued his whisper. "You hear that?"

The Old Man might not be able to see as well as he used to, but his hearing was still impeccable. "Yes. Is it wind?"

"Yes. All these holes are actually pipes. We are using an airflow tubing technique to remove CO_2 and stir the air around. It gets musty down here."

"Down where?"

The guard started walking again. "You'll see. Keep walking."

There was a long walk. The Old Man couldn't help but notice that they seemed to be going steadily down the farther they went. It was only a slight angle, but over time, that depth would add up. The temperature was dropping lower. The vents were making a louder noise when he passed them. "How much farther is it to wherever we are going?"

The guard pointed to the end of the hall. "Just up there."

The Old Man couldn't see anything but a wall at the end of the hall. It was getting very dark. Before, some of the holes had been letting in stray light from the outside, but it must have been getting dark on the surface as it was getting dimmer in the hallway. "Where are we going?"

"You said you needed a path over the mountains, right?"

The Old Man nodded. "Yes."

"Well, this is the way through them. Getting over the top is very difficult."

The Old Man couldn't help his curiosity. Why was the guard being so nice and answering his questions? He decided to ask. "So why are you being so friendly? I do truly appreciate it and all, but the outside world does not treat me nearly as kindly."

The guard had to think this question over for a moment. He replied with, "During our checkup upstairs, we identified that you had no weaponry on you. This indicated to us that you meant no harm. You walked up to an armed gateway with nothing to defend yourself with. A council in another room deduced you were, in fact, just an old man looking for a way through the mountains. Since our policy here is to help those in need instead of sending them packing, I was instructed to guide you, as I am now, and answer any questions you might have so that you don't feel in danger."

That last word caught the Old Man's ear. He picked up that this answer was well-rehearsed, as if the guard had said it many times over and was simply regurgitating it to him. The Old Man had to pry. He spoke. "Well, am I in danger? Be honest with me."

The guard took a quick peek at the Old Man. "Firstly, I have been and will always be perfectly honest with you. Second, no, you are not in any danger besides slipping on the floor here."

The Old Man pried further. "So your society does not have any weapons in this tunnel?"

The guard proudly stated, "No. No firearms of any kind are allowed here, excluding a few guards like myself."

The Old Man thought his next question over and worded it very carefully. "So you all don't even allow the transfer of weapons through here, even in a controlled manner? You would make the weapons cross over the mountains?"

The guard smiled. "Well, if there were still a way over the mountains intact, then yes, weapons would be allowed over the top. However, the Crisis destroyed so much of the infrastructure aboveground that the mountains are now impassible. The remaining roads were abandoned shortly after. This tunnel is the only way through." The Old Man nodded and stopped asking questions. He feared that he had already gone too far, but the guard still seemed happy to answer his questions.

The two arrived at the end of the tunnel. There was a steeper slope than before, down into a large pit. It went up again on the other side to the same height it was before. The guard noticed the Old Man's confusion. "That is a water trap. If it rains very hard at all, that tunnel will flood to the point it is basically a small creek. This pit typically holds enough water that it can drain out at a respectable speed via the drain at the left and right centers. Watch your step. This thing can get slippery with plant growths sometimes."

The guard slid a little on the surface as he spoke. The Old Man had to ask questions. "How far underground are we? And where does the water drain to if we are already underground?"

The guard beckoned him up the other side of the pit. As he traversed the pit, the guard spoke. "I am actually not sure how far underground we are myself. As for the water, it all gets drained to a massive central lake."

"An underground lake?"

"Actually, yes. I have been told it is actually some sort of aquifer that had eroded away and then fell into a sinkhole that formed under it. The water all drained down into the new sinkhole and exposed the cave around it, which is made of a much denser conglomerate. The result is an underground lake that we call the Lake of Underground. I don't think anyone has ever figured out what eroded the sinkhole to begin with, though some theorize that a creature ate the rock as it has a high concentration of natural salts, but what could possibly survive on just salt like that?"

The Old Man didn't know either. "Do you believe that?"

The guard shook his head. "No. That is only an old folktale."

The Old Man asked more. "So are we going to this underground lake?"

"Actually, no. You are going to the city around it."

"What?" There was no response. They had reached a large metal door. The guard went over and pushed down on a lever. It didn't budge. He put his whole body weight on it to no avail. He waved the Old Man over. He started pushing again as the Old Man assisted him.

"When this releases, it's going to lurch and make a loud noise. Don't be alarmed."

They grunted against the lever. "This lever is rusted shut," stated the Old Man.

"No, not shut. It is rusted, though. This entrance hardly ever gets used. We only defend that outpost you found to make sure nobody sneaks in that way. The water in that pit that you crossed splashes up here and sits on this lever when nobody is around to use it. The result is the..." The lever suddenly dropped out from under the both of them, groaning loudly and stopping with a sudden metallic squeak.

The Old Man stood and straightened out his back, wincing slightly, although he wasn't acting this time. He had wrenched his back when the lever gave way. The guard ignored the Old Man's trouble and went over to a large rod welded to the door. He gave it a good yank before sighing and putting his back into it. The door made a sudden popping noise. It cracked open, then drastically picked up speed until it caught on a large chain. A blast of air nearly knocked the Old Man off his feet. "What was that?"

"The wind? Oh. This door acts as an airlock and a water lock. Nothing goes in, and nothing goes out, unless you open it, of course. The air gets a certain flow on the other side of this door after a bit, and when you open the door, it disturbs that flow and redirects it all at once through the doorway. Once it balances out, the wind stops."

The Old Man glanced at the heavy chain above his head, linked to the top-left corner of the door. "I assume the door took somebody out once, and that is why the chain is there?"

"You nailed it. The fellow lived, but it severely fractured his left shoulder and broke his leg in multiple places. I had to drag him into the city to get help. It wasn't a pleasant experience for either one of us. When he got better, he welded that chain onto the door so that it couldn't smash anyone without breaking through the chain first." The Old Man nodded. "All right. Come on through." The Old Man crossed through the gateway and watched as the guard tripped a lever. The chain grew taut once more and slammed the door shut with a mighty clang.

"The one benefit of that wind is, it pushes so hard that it can lift a counterweight on the other end of this chain. The counterweight flies up this vertical column here and hits the top of it, which is what catches the door. When the wind stops, the counterweight sits on a spring-loaded ledge, which I just released by pulling the lever there. The weight falls and provides enough force to shut the door and reapply the seal from the tunnel. Another genius design that fellow from before came up with while he was healing.

"He couldn't move very far, so thinking about improvements down here, became a big priority for him. He ended up making quite a few improvements around here. It's just a shame some of them are hardly ever used, such as this door. We called him Mike. Anyway, take a look at this." They had been traversing a flight of stone stairs for a bit. They spilled down onto a balcony overlooking an open area. The Old Man went over to take a look off the balcony. "Welcome to the City of Underground, the only town that we think exists completely underground with no need for outside trade with the rest of the world."

The cave was massive, maybe five or six miles across. It was toweringly tall with massive stalactites on the ceiling. The majority of the area directly off the balcony was the underground lake the guard had explained. Around two miles of water later, the city shot up from the cave floor. It was entirely constructed out of stone materials of every sort and color. There were five-story buildings in places. Surfaces glittered and reflected light. There were fields down near the lake, planted in a green plant that the Old Man was not familiar with. There were lights everywhere, casting massive shadows on the walls of the cave.

"How do you all have electricity down here?"

"Geothermal. There is a volcanic hotspot on the left side in the far corner of the cave. That is why there are no buildings there except the one. That one is a massive power plant. Keeps the volcanic heat from cooking us alive in this cave while producing the power we can use. I do not know any more about that plant, though."

"That thing looks like it would produce far more power than you need. Where does the unused electricity go?"

"A massive ground cable at the end of all of the connections leads far off to some safe ground location, I believe. I guess it just gets wasted. A lot of those lights do turn off for around six hours at night, but a few never turn off, so the cave is always partially lit, just enough to see."

The Old Man stared in awe at the sight before him. The group had to see this, but how was he going to get them in? The guard broke the silence after a few minutes of the Old Man looking over the cave. "All right. I have to go back up to my post at the watch building. You see that pathway down there? Just follow it, and it will loop you right around the edge of the lake counterclockwise. It is a long walk, though, and it gets pretty dark there since there are no lights installed."

The guard walked over to a shelf built into the cave wall and retrieved a box. He opened it and retrieved a large metallic stick. He twisted a smooth ring on the center of it, and a massive flood of light emitted from the top end. "This is a Lightstaff. Use it like a walking stick, and shine it when you can't see. It has a long battery life, so don't worry about running out of light. We have had them last up to a month of continuous use at a time." He shut the light off and gave it to the Old Man.

It must have been nearly four feet long. The Old Man again thought that this explanation seemed rehearsed. He peeked up at the guard quizzically. "Go on and try it out," the guard advised. The Old Man swung the top of the stick down. It was amazingly light for its size. He looked at the black metallic body of the device as he searched for a way to turn it on, starting where the guard had moved the ring. He located the sleek ring on the center with indentations just big enough to grip.

He gripped the ring and tried to turn it clockwise. It wouldn't budge, so he gave it a ninety-degrees-counterclockwise twist. The staff vibrated slightly and shot out a beam of light from the end of the staff. The Old Man watched as all the rocks sparkled on the wall. The guard smiled. "It's always fun to see people use that for the first time."

The Old Man swung the staff around. "How are you supposed to use it as a light and a staff at the same time? Like, the thing is always pointing straight up into the air when you poke the end of it into the ground."

The guard grew perplexed at that question. "You don't. It is just a light on a stick. You carry it horizontally if you want to look around and vertically if you want to use it as a cane." The Old Man looked down at the staff. Something about that did not seem correct. Why did this thing last this long and had not been scrapped for parts if it was so inconvenient to use? He didn't bother asking.

The guard continued. "If you are hungry, there will be little gardens along the way that you are allowed to eat anything from. Some have little stoves and cots. Just be sure that you leave a note or some sign to show you were there so that the Weekly Checkup team can restock it." The Old Man nodded. "All right, then, good luck!" His voice suddenly took a much deeper and serious tone. "Don't lose the staff." After a moment of intense staring, he turned and started back to the door.

"Wait! You said this was the way through the mountain," shouted the Old Man as the guard began fiddling with the door.

"Oh. Sorry. It is. There is an exit on the far side of the city. You can't miss it. Just go around the lake and into the city, and someone will direct you to it."

The Old Man looked back at the city. He turned to face the guard again to ask him for some more specific instruction, but the guard had already disappeared. "All right. Thank you!" There was no reply.

"Psst!"

What was that? the Old Man thought. He glanced around.

"Hey!" a voice said softly but with urgency. The Old Man saw something move behind a rock. He held the rod stiff at its center and walked toward the rock. "Old Man, it's me!"

The Old Man stopped. "Young?"

The Young stepped out from behind the rock. The Old Man briefly shined the light on the Young but quickly swung it away in case the guard was watching. "Yeah! I followed you in."

"How did you get past the guards and all of the doors?"

"Uh, it's a long story. Look, I don't think there is any other way past this mountain range than through this place, but they won't let us bring our weapons in, and you know it. Also, is your leg hurt?"

The Old Man didn't answer immediately as his head was still reeling from analyzing how the Young had managed to follow them so quietly. "What? Oh, no. I was fooling that guard into thinking I was a frail person in case he got any bright ideas. I wouldn't have done it if I had known how far we were going." The Young chuckled. The Old Man continued talking.

"Anyway, I have no idea how you managed to follow us all the way in here, but you are correct. The guard was actually very helpful, and he explained that although routes did exist at one point over the top of the mountains, they were destroyed in the Crisis or otherwise abandoned. I got the feeling that he wasn't even supposed to tell me half the stuff he did..." The Old Man stopped. He wanted to explain more, but there wasn't enough time. "We can catch up later. For now, you are sure as well that there is no other way for the group to go?"

"Yes. I found a map of the surface on the way in. It showed a huge mountain range much steeper than we could ever cross. There was some road over the mountains at one point, but it was crossed out like it doesn't exist anymore. There is another entrance to this cave on the other side of the mountains. We could find it and get out the other side. Otherwise, there is no path through the mountains that the map shows."

The Old Man glanced at the guard, who was still fiddling with the door lever on the tunnel side of the door. "Go! Follow that guard back outside and tell the others all this information. The door doesn't have a lever on this side to open it back up. You can still make it before it shuts."

The Young turned to look. The guard had shoved the rusty lever, and the door began to close. The Young glanced back at the Old Man's Lightstaff. "What is that?"

The Old Man didn't have time to explain. He spat out, "It's basically a big, fancy light. Now go! Don't miss your chance!" The Young nodded and began toward the door, silent on his feet. "Wait!" The Young turned. "Above all, keep the group and yourself safe even if it means losing the weapons." The Young hesitated. The Old Man continued. "I know, the Raiders or whatever else might sack us all on the other side of the mountains, but that's only a chance, and the guards here will likely kill you if they figure out you have smuggled weapons inside here. I don't think these people are as nice as they try to appear. If it is not worth the risk to the group, then don't bring them. Just let the group decided what to do."

The Young nodded as he said, "I will meet you here in the afternoon tomorrow. It might take me awhile to get the whole group in."

The Old Man returned the nod. "The guard mentioned that they turn the lights off and on when it is dark outside, so I will be able to tell generally when you should be here. If you don't show up, I will come back out to the surface tomorrow night."

The Young nodded once more and took off toward the door in a full sprint. He expertly slipped behind the guard through the doorway. The door shut loudly, and the Old Man was left alone in the dark with his Lightstaff beaming down the trail.

*****

Meanwhile, the group had abandoned the hiding bush and had gone out a ways into the woods to avoid being spotted. They set up a simple camp consisting only of a branch lean-to and a small ring of rocks for a fire, although it was warm enough out that they did not start the fire for fear of the smoke giving them away like before. They slept in the small forest opening overnight. The group was scattered about the camp after finding the lean-to crowded with as many people as they had in it.

They were instead lying on the brown needles from the trees that covered the forest floor, sitting braced up against the trunk of the trees, or in the Survivalist's case, lying along a large, wide limb up in a tree. The group had questioned the Survivalist about sleeping in trees before. She had explained that she often would sleep on a branch with no rope keeping her tied to it, as she was now, and insisted upon doing so. They had collectively given up and let her do it.

The early morning sun had just started lighting the sky. A beam fell across the Survivalist's face. She stirred, opened her eyes, and quickly scanned the camp. The Radioman asked her in delight, "How do you manage to do such wonderful things as sleeping on a branch?" This spooked the Survivalist. He continued. "You are completely asleep, and you never seem to even come close to falling off."

She glanced at him in confusion. "Why are you up so early?" She realized that was a poor question. He was a radioman. He was always up early. The Radioman caught her minor embarrassment and ignored the question. The Survivalist replied to the Radioman's question. "I used to sleep in them as a kid," she said through a yawn.

He asked, "Have you ever fallen out while performing your daring slumber?"

She replied, "Of course. I broke a rib once by falling out. I landed right on an exposed tree root. After that, I guess my body learned its lesson, and I have not fallen out since."

The Radioman nodded, and the Hobo, who had also just awoken, commented, "I bet that one hurt." The conversation ended.

The Radioman got up and walked off toward the woods. "I will return momentarily," he stated as he left.

The Hobo sat up, rubbed his eyes, and looked over at the Radioman leaving. "I am going to go for a walk with him. I want to see what he does in the morning." He got up and started after the Radioman.

*****

Some time passed. The forest noise droned on, already starting even in the early morning, but they were interrupted by a snapping sound. The Survivalist immediately sat up and turned to hold the trunk of the tree, barely moving the branch she was on in the process. Neither the Mechanic nor the Entrepreneur showed any signs of being awake up the hill. The Survivalist dropped down from the tree, landing on the soft needles with an incredibly inaudible thud behind a boulder. She peeked between the boulder and the tree trunk, scanning the forest for any signs of movement. Nothing.

She hopped the boulder and quickly padded across the opening to a fallen log, which she lay down behind. There was another snap, this time just over the log. She crawled to the end of the log and looked around it. There was nothing there. The Survivalist's face dropped to confusion. There was sound of shoes scraping on a rock, this time behind her. She whipped her head to see a branch wiggle above the boulder she had hid behind. She waited, watching closely. Nothing moved.

She stood and started silently crossing the needles toward the boulder. A stick flew out from behind the boulder, poking the Survivalist on her stomach and falling to the forest floor. She winced in surprise more than pain, glanced at her stomach and the stick, and then ran to the boulder, leaning over it. Nothing was there. Suddenly, a small whoosh occurred behind her. Before she could move, a loud smack filled the air. She winched at a pain in her rear end, drawing in a quick breath.

A snicker of laughter caught her ear, trailed by short scuttering noises of needles being moved. She pivoted but saw no one. The Survivalist thought, *Someone just spanked my ass and got away before I could spot them. Who is it?* She proceeded to slowly walk toward the source of the scuttering from before, being extremely vigilant for any noise or motion. She noticed a footprint of a shoe on the ground. She bent at the waist to observe it. Suddenly, another pain struck her posterior, deep and stinging, paired with another outrageous smacking noise.

She straightened, holding the side of her posterior in one hand, her face red with anger, embarrassment, but also admiration for whoever had managed getting away with spanking her twice now without her spotting them. She adjusted the hand over to her hip, feeling the corner of the hatchet, leaning on one leg as she scanned the forest. As she adjusted her tight pants back down to their proper position, she came up with an idea. She walked over to a rock down the hill, a ways from the camp. It was oddly shaped so that there was a ledge protruding from the ground about two feet.

She lay on the ground and shimmied into the crack. The back of the hatchet caught the rock above, making an odd metallic scrape. Perfect, an accidental noise. She deliberately left her posterior just outside of the rock and pretended to be observing the woods while hiding. There was a small scurrying noise, but nothing more. She relaxed her posterior and allowed her stomach to drop to the ground. This had to look real. A tremendous clap filled the air as a burning sensation spread across her whole posterior. She winced hard, gasping in air due to the shock and being caught off guard by how quickly the spanker had found her, but she quickly lunged backward, flailing her arms, and caught an arm not her own.

The arm tried to escape. She rolled over under the rock and braced her legs against it. A short yelp came from above her as she used the leverage of being under the rock to her advantage, dragging the arm to her. The arm suddenly gave way, and an upside-down face peeked under the rock. The face did not remain long as it dodged her punch. It returned with a large grin and raised eyebrows. The arm had stopped resisting. She drew her arm back but hesitated.

"Hello, Survivalist," said the Young. The Survivalist scoffed and bashed the Young's nose. She released his arm and wiggled out from under the rock. She stood to see him rubbing his nose. "Good punch," he said, checking for a nosebleed.

She tried to be mad, but her curiosity got the better of her. "How did you manage to spank me twice without me seeing you?"

"I am sneaky, and I spanked you three times, not two," he replied, shrugging. She was not impressed by the answer. He continued. "You are easy to mislead because you are so sensitive to your environment. Any little thing can set you on investigation, focusing in on that one position. If one makes a noise somewhere intentionally to draw your attention and then remains silent afterward, then you don't bother to check your surroundings much, making it easy to sneak up on you and still get away."

This answer she was appeased with. "Fair" was the only reply she gave. She started walking away to get the crew.

"You aren't mad?" he asked.

The Survivalist thought this over. In reality, she wasn't angry at all, but she felt like she should be furious. Had she actually enjoyed herself in this game despite its strange nature? No, surely not. She replied, "Of course, I am mad, but you already know why. Come on. You don't look like a morning person, so you must know something, and you might as well tell it to the whole group at once." She started up the hill. The Young hesitated. He was slightly taken aback but still did not regret his decisions. The Survivalist turned partially around. "Plus, I nailed a hard punch on you." This the Young could agree with wholly. His nose hurt. He started running to catch up with the Survivalist. The Survivalist noticed him approaching. "So what gave you the bright idea to spank me anyway? Why not just pester me by throwing sticks like you started with or something?"

The Young look over at her. "Those pants did the convincing."

She looked down at her skintight pants. She flexed her legs. Her muscles did show through well. "I guess I can't fault you for that."

The Young laughed but quickly caught himself due to the risk of being punched again. He spoke. "Plus the challenge of doing it. I wasn't sure if I could get away quickly enough while staying quiet. I wanted to show you that I can be sneaky if I want to be. What better way to get you to remember that than humiliating you a little?"

For some reason, the Survivalist found this humorous, resulting in a wide smile, which she quickly attempted to cover with an agitated face. "That is true. I will never forget it now." A momentary pause of silence interrupted the conversation as they reentered camp.

"Where is everyone?" asked the Young.

"Well, the Mechanic and the Entrepreneur are both still asleep in the bed of needles over there. The Hobo and the Radioman both went for a walk. They said they would return soon. Where were you last night?"

"I was following the Old Man like I said I was going to. When I came back out, it was dark, and I couldn't find you guys, so I slept by the hiding bush near the entrance."

"You what?" the Survivalist asked, shocked.

"Which part are you asking about, following the Old Man past an entire squad of guards or sleeping in the hideout bush? Oh, forget it. There the other two are now." The Young pointed through the forest to see the Hobo and the Radioman laughing together. The Hobo wrapped his arm around the Radioman, who at first seemed fine with the gesture but soon changed his mind and politely slid away from the Hobo. The Hobo took no offense, seeming to understand he had given the Radioman a discomfort, and continued talking.

"Those two seem to get along well," said the Survivalist as she rubbed her posterior, which was still stinging from the last spank. The Young, still walking behind her, glanced awkwardly at her. Her face grew defensive. "You put some heat on that last spank."

"Sorry. I got carried away. I just find it strange that you seem to be handling that fine."

The Survivalist had a brief second of panic before immediately recollecting herself and stating, "Look, it already happened. It's over. Can we just move on?" The Young shrunk away. She wondered if she had hurt his feelings. She changed the subject as the Radioman and the Hobo approached.

"So where is the Old Man?" asked the Hobo.

The Young lit up. "Oh! That is what I need to tell you all about. Go wake up the other two over there."

The Hobo went over and shook the Entrepreneur awake, who looked around curiously before quickly standing and brushing the brown needles off his clothes. The Hobo tried the same with the Mechanic, but he remained fast asleep. The Hobo stood and gently kicked the Mechanic's ribs. The Mechanic took a broad swing with his arm, nearly catching the Hobo's foot, but stopped once he saw who it was. He sat up, saw the Young motioning him over, and stood to come see what was going on.

The Young started in on the events of last night. He explained the long tunnel, the City of Underground, the issue with there being no route over the mountains, a weapons search at the entrance, and a weapons ban on the inside. He suggested they find a way to smuggle the weapons through the city and out the other entrance or to abandon the weapons here.

The Hobo started up first. "I don't know about you all, but I don't think abandoning these weapons is a good idea. If anything, we can stash them away if we think we are going to get caught." The Mechanic nodded while pointing at the Hobo.

The Survivalist spoke next. "I don't think we should leave them either. We might need them on the other side of the mountains or in the mountains by the sound of how much the Old Man trusts these people."

The Radioman countered with, "If we do get caught, though, then things will quickly be headed south. Why don't we just do as the people ask here?"

The Entrepreneur nodded while stating, "Yeah. I don't see these people as the type to be negotiated with."

The group all turned to the Young. The Mechanic stated the deal. "What do you think, Young? It is currently three votes for and two votes against. What did the Old Man say?"

The Young swept his gaze across the group. "The Old Man left it to us to decide. He didn't have time to think it over. All he said was for us to be careful and abandon the weapons if we think it would be too risky. However, I know another way inside. It's the same route I used to bypass the guards and follow the Old Man with. I think we should do it."

The Mechanic shrugged. He boomed, "All right, then, it is settled—four votes for and two votes against with one indifferent vote. We go for it. Do you have a plan, Young?" The Young nodded. The crew devised a plan as they munched on the rations from the Mechanic's backpack that the Old Man had persevered from the deego earlier. They tore the lean-to shelter apart and scattered the rocks from the unused firepit. Then they all loaded up with their gear and left the camp for the gateway.

They all regrouped by the same bush as before. The Young whispered to the group, "All right. Everyone knows the plan, right?" They all nodded. "Okay, then. Wish me luck." He stood up and wandered out into the field. He crossed the entire gravel pad without being spotted by a single guard.

"How is he so stealthy?" asked the Mechanic.

"I don't know, but he is stealthy, isn't he?" replied the Survivalist, carefully rubbing her still painful rear end while avoiding being caught in the act by the group.

The Young glanced back at the bush and gave a thumbs-up. He worked his way back and forth along the wall, searching it for something. He stopped and observed a small cut in the wall. After sticking his foot into the cut and testing his weight on it, he lunged upward and just barely caught the lip of the wall with his fingers.

He struggled to pull himself up, taking quite a while to get himself on the top of the wall, where he lay flat and scanned the inside. He looked back at the group and pointed at the ground directly below where he was lying. "That is the signal. Get ready to run across the field, Radioman," reported the Survivalist.

The Radioman wiggled to the front of the group. "Are you sure the fine plan we have previously devised is still safe to operate now that we have observed the wall once more?"

"Yes, Radioman. Just get ready to run."

The Radioman timidly peeked his head around the end of the bush. The Young immediately pointed to him, holding up three fingers, then only two, then one and then motioned the Radioman across the field. The Radioman hesitated, but the Mechanic shoved him into the field. The Radioman ran for all he was worth, his maroon coat bouncing slightly as he traversed the gravel.

He touched the wall below the Young, who had his pointer finger on his lips to signal him to be quiet. The Radioman held still. The Young slowly turned his head, then quickly snapped it back and lurched his hand down. The Radioman grabbed it. "Put your foot in that crack and boost yourself over. Don't slow down when you get to the top. Go straight behind the crates when you get on the inside."

The Radioman did as he was told, being careful to remain as silent as he could be. He straddled the wall and hopped off the other side. It was a farther drop than he thought, and he landed with a loud thud, falling into the dirt behind the crates. The Young cringed, but no one appeared to hear the noise. The Young looked back at the bush, holding out three fingers once more.

The Entrepreneur was up next. He made it across without error. The Hobo took his time crossing. He picked key hiding spots and waited for another signal from the Young. After four rounds of hiding, the Hobo grabbed on to the Young's hand and boosted himself over. The Mechanic was nearly caught for being so slow while running across the field since he was carrying the backpack with the Old Man's rifle.

The Mechanic tossed the rifle and the backpack up to the Young, who dropped them each in turn down to the Hobo. The Mechanic waited at the base of the wall. The Survivalist had already safely crossed the field when the Young motioned for her to go. She motioned for the Mechanic to start over the wall.

The Young took the Mechanic's hand and gave him a weak anchor point. The Survivalist pushed on the Mechanic's back. The Mechanic suddenly made a lunge for the wall, nearly towing the Young off the wall in the process but managing to get a hand on the ledge. From here, he towed himself over the wall, hung from the ledge on the other side for a moment, and dropped on the ground with a heavy plop.

The Young whispered, "It is a good thing you are tall, Mechanic. We would have never gotten you over." The Mechanic smiled while snatching up the backpack and rifle again and flexed his arms before heading off to hide. Now it was time for the Survivalist to climb. She held up her hand to be pulled over, looked down to set her foot in the crack, and looked back up to see the Young suddenly dropping off the wall toward her and placing his hand over her mouth.

She looked at him with piercing anger in her eyes but stopped squirming when she saw the desperation on his face. A voice on the top of the wall broke the silence. "Did you hear something too?"

A faint, distant voice replied, "No. What did you hear?"

The closer voice answered, "I don't know. It sounded like something fell off this wall earlier, but I don't see anyone over here."

The farther voice responded, "I think you are losing it, man. That wall is far too tall and smooth for someone to scale."

There was a pause. "Yeah. Maybe you are right."

Footsteps slowly faded out of hearing. The Young released his grip on the Survivalist. "I am sorry. You would have blown our cover."

"Just boost me up."

The Young turned to the wall. "All right," he murmured. He had helped the rest of the group from the top of the wall. He couldn't risk getting up on the wall with the slow methods he used the first time due to the watchful new eyes above. He would have to get her over quickly from the ground and have her figure out a way to get him over from the other side.

"If I get you over, you are going to have to find a way to get me over as well. If I try to get up there now, I will be spotted since it takes me so long." She nodded. He scooted closer, grabbed the Survivalist by her waist, bellied up against her, and braced to pick her up.

"Uh, can you just boost me by my foot?"

The Young awkwardly released the Survivalist and crouched, cupping his hands and motioning for her foot. She stepped into the crack of the wall, pushed herself upward, set her opposite foot in his hands, and jumped to the ledge. Her hand came nowhere close to the top of the wall, as the Young's arms had given way. She landed softly on the ground at the bottom of the wall.

"Look, I can't get enough leverage to pick you up by your foot so that you can reach the top of the wall. You are going to have to let me boost you up by your waist so I can be in a more upright position when you need the boost. That way, I have enough strength to get you over. Is that all right?"

The Survivalist hesitated. The Young glanced up the wall. He got closer and whispered into her ear, "If you are worried about the others seeing me hold you somehow, they can't see you over the wall. I don't know why you are so skittish about being picked up, especially with how well you handled being spanked earlier, but you are the last person on this side, and I promise I won't make you uncomfortable."

The Survivalist glanced up the wall, sizing it up. "Fine. Let's just do it." The Young wrapped his arms around her waist once more. He braced to pick her up. "Wait." He stopped. "Please be gentle. And no tricks."

"Why would I do that here? What we did before was for fun in a safe location. I am just trying to get you over this wall before we get—"

"Okay. You are right. Just do it."

The Young adjusted his grip and lifted her quickly. He felt like he had nearly dropped her on the way up. She weighed much less than he had anticipated, especially after trying to boost her from her foot earlier. He held her up to the wall, letting her sit on his shoulders. Meanwhile, the Survivalist was thrilled. She did not think she would enjoy being picked up, but the Young was so strong and confident with his grip.

She felt very tall. She looked around and enjoyed the feeling. After a bit of time, she felt the Young's head shift between her legs and looked down to see him peeking up at her. She remembered that she was supposed to be climbing over the wall. She reached up, but her hands were still about a foot from reaching the top. "I still can't reach it," she said.

The Young paused. He let out a quick burst of air and bounced her to adjust his grip. "Can I touch your ass?"

"What?"

The Young sputtered under the effort. "I need to touch your ass so I can boost you the last bit, but I don't want to make you uncomfortable." He grunted.

She relaxed. "Oh." The Survivalist tugged the waist of her pants up. Feeling more prepared, she responded, "Yes. Just push me over." The Young released her waist and palmed her posterior from behind his head while being especially careful not to grab it. The Survivalist tensed, awaiting the lift, and said, "Watch the hatchet." The Young adjusted the grip of his right hand away from the blade and tossed her up to the ledge. She caught it, surprised by how quickly the Young had thrown her with his thinner arms. Then she slid over the wall and landed softly on the other side while being careful not to drag the hatchet.

The others had moved across the area to a large pallet of rusty barrels to create more space for her landing and to hide from the guard. Hopefully, they did not overhear the conversation over the wall. She began looking for something to get the Young over with. She located a rope, checked the guards, who were looking at something on the other end of the wall, and darted across to get it. After returning with the rope, she threw the end of it up the wall, but it failed to crest the top.

She looked around for something with decent weight. She found an old metallic hook of some sort and quickly tied it to the end of the rope. At one point, the hook must have been painted yellow, but most of the paint had chipped off, revealing the dull gray color underneath. Using the weight of the hook, she swung the rope over the wall. The rope immediately grew taut, pulling her across the dirt a bit toward the wall. She braced against the wall.

A few seconds later, the Young told her to relax and dropped down with the hook of the rope in his hand. Flawless. The two sat against the wall for a moment. The Young elbowed the Survivalist. "Smart thinking with the rope and hook."

"Thanks."

The two got up and searched the area. There were no guards to be found. The group motioned them over. The Survivalist looped the rope around her hands and tied it to herself like a sash, traveling the length of it from her right shoulder, down to her front, to her left hip, around the back, and back up to the shoulder until the rope ran out, letting the hook dangle just above her hip on the left side. The Young began talking.

"Earlier, after I told the Survivalist I was going to follow the Old Man and when you all were watching him talk to the entrance guard, I hid in a corner until things calmed down. I found that spot on the wall and used it to get over. I stayed hidden in this area for a while until I got a general idea of where I could go. I think the guards believe there is only one way into the tunnel, and it's through that door the Old Man went through.

"But there will be guards manning the door inside there that we can't sneak past, although the guards apparently don't scout the area very much. When I got over this wall the first time, I explored this complex a little since nobody was roaming around. I found that map of the mountains and routes I told you about on a table up the stairs there."

He paused while pointing through a doorway across the repurposed courtyard they were crouching in, directing the group to a flight of stairs headed upward. "I tried to find some other things but opted with not taking anything, as I did not want them to ever know I was there. There wasn't anything of value besides the map anyway. So I came back down the stairs and started searching for a way into wherever the Old Man had gone. That led me to just around the corner."

He paused again, this time pointing at the door and motioning to the right. "There is a grate covering a large vent with a small piece of blue fabric tied to it. That grate was loose when I touched it, and I was able to wiggle it out of position. I went into the vent and put the grate back on the wall behind me. I followed the voices of the Old Man and the guards he was talking to until I saw him through a second grate in a room full of guards searching him. I took a right, and there was a drop in the vent. It goes straight down and then bends at a ninety-degree angle to a grate that makes the floor of the tunnel.

"I had a hard time, but I was able to slide down the vent and get to the third grate. I expected the grate to be stiffly held in place, but it popped right off when I shoved on it. Someone has rigged the grates to make it easy to get in and out of the tunnel system without getting checked by the guards. By the time I had figured out how to get down the vent, the Old Man and the guard were far ahead of me. It took me a good while to catch up to them, but luckily, there really are not any places to go but straight down the tunnel.

"I found the Old Man and the guard struggling with some large lever until a door opened, which I snuck in through right behind the guard. There, I waited for an opportunity to talk to the Old Man behind a big rock. When the guard finally left, I ran out and told the Old Man about the map. He told me to come get you guys and to make a plan for the weapons. So here we are." Everyone nodded.

The Entrepreneur spoke quietly. "So you said you struggled with the vertical drop in the vent, but you are small and agile. How are we going to get down it, especially the Mechanic?"

The Young looked over at the Survivalist. "We can use her rope." The group collectively looked at the Survivalist. She gripped the rope on her shoulder, looking carefully at each member of the group in return.

The group waited for the guards to look away and scurried to the doorway as a group. They rounded the corner to the right, and with the help of the Young, they located the loose grate. The Young went first to guide the group. The Survivalist went in next with the rope and hook. The rest of the group funneled in behind them with the Mechanic squeezing in last and putting the grate back on. The Mechanic filled the vent, touching both walls with his shoulders. He was still able to slide through as long as the vent didn't get any narrower.

The Young led the group through the vents to the vertical drop. He wiggled his way down the vertical drop and looked up at the Survivalist. She removed the rope from around her and dropped down the loose end. She passed the hook back the line to the Mechanic. He wedged his shoulders into the sides of the vent and stiffened his arms so that the rope wouldn't move as the group used it to descend the vent.

The Survivalist grabbed onto the middle of the rope and worked her way down the drop with it. She slid past the Young, a tight squeeze, and made room for the Hobo to come next. The Radioman followed up next, being careful not to touch the dusty walls with his coat on the way down, and the Entrepreneur came down right after. The only person left was the Mechanic.

The group had opted to just let the Mechanic figure it out when he got here. They didn't even know if he would fit inside the vent. However, wedging his arms in the vent to hold the rope had given the Mechanic an idea. He dropped the hook down to the Entrepreneur, who handed it off to the Survivalist, and she collected the rope back around herself like before. He also removed the rifle and backpack, wiggled the pair of items past himself with some effort, and dropped them down to the Hobo.

The Mechanic sat on the edge of the drop, dangling his feet, and wedged his forearm and shoulders into the sides of the vent. He thrust his waist forward into the drop, but he did not fall. He was supported by his shoulders. He gently relaxed the pressure on his arms and tried to keep his grunting quiet as he slid slowly down the vent by using the friction on his arms as a break. When he reached the bottom, his face had turned a ripe shade of red from the exertion. His feet touched the bottom of the vent, and he immediately relaxed his arms. He cringed as he worked his arms about to relieve them.

The Hobo returned the rifle and backpack to the Mechanic. The group watched him pant. He waved them on while shrugging on the backpack. The Young pushed his way up past the group, led them around another corner, and pointed to a grate on the roof of the vent. He motioned for them to stay put by pointing at the floor. He wiggled over to the grate and crouched beneath it. He used the back of his head and shoulder to pop the grate up from the floor.

He peeked around, then hopped out of the vent and onto the cold floor of the tunnel and motioned the group out. One by one, the group spilled out of the vent and onto the floor, panting lightly, except for the Mechanic, who was breathing laboriously. The Young replaced the grate and motioned down the tunnel with a short grunt. The group stood and started walking.

By the time the group had reached the airlock door, they had recovered their breath. The Mechanic went over to the lever and gave it a great shove. The Young moved everyone out of the way as the large door rushed open and caught the chain. He led them all through. This left the Mechanic on the far side of the door. They had to close the entrance, but there was only the one lever on the tunnel side.

After some debate, the Young managed to move the lever and dashed through the doorway before it closed on him. After that close call, the group and the weapons were in. They all walked down to the balcony to take in the beauty of the City of Underground. The Entrepreneur redirected his sight down the line to the Young. "So where is the Old Man?"

*****

The Old Man woke up. He blinked his eyes. *Why can't I see?* he thought. A wave of remembrance struck him. He rolled over, flopping his left hand around in the dark for the Lightstaff. He grew worried for a moment before his hand caught the end of it. He tugged on it to pull it to himself, found the ring thanks to the finger indentations, and flicked it on. The light blasted across the floor of the small stone building and reflected across the dull gray wall. He hadn't noticed how smooth it was before taking his nap.

Wait. How long did I sleep? Did I miss the group? Have they made it in safe? He sat up too quickly. His head spun as he tried to stand, but he managed to stay upright by leaning on the staff. The staff suddenly vibrated. The Old Man looked down slightly at it. He had placed the light facedown on the ground so that it was now pitch-black again. He flipped the staff. The staff jumbled around for a moment before blasting another brilliant beam of light straight to the ceiling. A thought ran across the Old Man's mind. He spoke aloud. "How am I supposed to use this as a staff if it is always pointed straight in the air?"

The staff shuddered again, and a small dome formed on top of the staff. It must have had a mirror in it, as it reflected the light directly where he was looking. He turned the staff to see out the doorway but was surprised to see it rotate to stay aimed at the wall. He glanced at the darkness where the doorway should have been but did not turn his head. The light remained steady. He started to speak but stopped. This was ridiculous. He was going to try to talk to a metal pole.

Something made him want to try, though. He couldn't resist. He had to try. He started in timidly as if he was going to be made fun of. "Hey. Over there. The doorway." The staff shook violently for a brief period before snapping the beam of light to the doorway, casting a beam of light out onto the small garden outside. The Old Man was astonished. He looked around to see if it moved. Nothing happened. He grew curious. How smart was this thing? Could he give it vague instructions?

"What is over there in the darkness?" He pointed slightly with his hand. Surely this simple stick wouldn't understand that. The Lightstaff shuddered, more gently this time, and snapped the beam over to the exact position he had gestured to. The Old Man nearly fell over in surprise. The staff wiggled slightly to support his weight. He wondered how much he could do with this thing. He pointed to the floor just in front of him. The beam made a small vibration, caught for a moment, and then snapped into where he was pointing.

Could it find things? "Where is the group?" The Lightstaff shuddered, but the light remained still. Maybe that was too much to ask for. He knew there was a mushroom outside. He had spotted it glowing last night while walking around the lake. It was just outside the building. "Where is the mushroom from last night?" The Lighstaff shuddered again and started to turn but stopped. "Where is the cot I slept in last night?" The Lightstaff immediately changed direction to point right at his chest. The Old Man stepped aside to see the light shining on the cot.

The cone of light had widened in shape to include the whole cot. It was a simple stone structure with some form of woven fabric strewn across it. No wonder his back was sore. But why had the staff been able to find that but not the other things? The group might be too far away, but the glowing blue-green mushroom was right outside and in sight from where he was currently standing.

He pointed to the mushroom. The light snapped around, making a metallic squeaking noise, and illuminated the mushroom. The mushroom was actually a very white color now that a light was on it. *How strange,* thought the Old Man. He came up with an idea. He pointed to the floor, half expecting the light to not track his point, and was again surprised to see the light follow it. He then asked, "Where is the mushroom?" The light snapped up to the glowing mushroom once more and revealed its whiteness. Was that it? Did the light have to see what he asked in the beam before it could locate it? He wanted to experiment more.

He stepped behind the wall of the building so that there was no direct line of sight with the mushroom and directed the light to the floor with a point of his finger. "Where is the mushroom?" The light snapped over to the wall where the mushroom would have been but then immediately returned to the floor where he had pointed before. So the light had to be able to find the object in a direct line of sight as well.

He took off one of his shoes, pointed at it to get the light to see it, then pointed at the wall nearby. He kicked the shoes across the room. "Where is the shoe?" The light shot to where the shoe had been but returned to the wall when it was unable to locate it. "Ah. The Lightstaff can only locate things it has seen recently that have not moved and that are in a direct line of sight."

He motioned his hand toward the general direction of the shoe. The light made a broad sweep with another squeak. "Wait. That was different." He stopped his hand and closed his fingers and his thumb to make a pointing motion. The light narrowed. He opened his hand. The light widened into a cone. He spread his fingers and relaxed his hand. The light flooded the entire other half of the small building. The Old Man then hesitated. Was the staff reading his mind or simply noticing his gestures? He thought, *Where is the doorway?* The light remained flooding the entire wall. "Oh, thank goodness. That would have been so odd."

He started toward the door and nearly ran into the side of it when the staff did not change direction. "How do I get this thing to look in the direction I am going?" He thought about this for a moment before realizing he could probably just ask it to. "Can you show the way of where I am going?" The staff shuddered and pointed forward. The Old Man rocked back on his heels in delight.

He moved the staff back slightly, and the head swiveled completely backward, following his motion. The Old Man settled back forward in confusion, and the staff whipped the light back around. He wondered, "Can I tune it to what I want?" He decided it was worth a shot. "No, no, don't be that, eh, sensitive about it. I will move very deliberately in the direction I need to see in or point at something like I have been." The Lightstaff shuddered slightly.

He took a step backward. The light didn't move. He turned and walked back into the building. Then the light turned and showed him where he was walking. "Perfect." The Lightstaff pulsed gently in his hand for a moment. He retrieved his shoes and set the staff up against the wall. He bent to put the shoe on but found himself out of the light, and he couldn't see well enough. He started to move forward, but the Lightstaff suddenly made a whirring noise and shot off the wall, stopping perfectly vertical and holding itself there while adjusting the light to shine directly down at the Old Man's socked foot.

The Old Man looked up at it, half in fear and half in amazement. He put the shoes on and began to reach for it. Another whirring noise and the staff threw itself into his grasp. He grasped it and began to stand. The staff droned for a moment and assisted him up onto his feet. The Old Man smiled. "I could get used to this." The staff pulsed once more. He started out the door, but he had one last thing to try.

"Can you answer yes or no questions?" The staff didn't react. "All right. Point left for no and right for yes. Do you know where a tree is nearby?" The staff remained still. He realized that the staff might not have any idea what a tree was down in the City of Underground. "Okay. The same thing—left for no, right for yes. Do you know where a nearby mushroom is?" The staff shook and pointed at the glowing mushroom, ignoring the yes or no response prompts. *I will take that as it can't answer questions,* he thought.

He went back outside and looked at the garden. It was full of these glowing shrooms. He was hungry. Were these things edible? He wasn't sure, so he continued around the side of the building. Suddenly, the light of the city came into view. He had slept, but the city lights were on, so it must have been daytime outside. He didn't think it was the afternoon yet. Could he ask the staff what time it was? "What time is it?" he asked. The staff vibrated, seemed to get caught in a bind of some kind, and then shot to the right with such force that the staff nearly flew out of the Old Man's hand.

The staff whirred and straightened itself to support the Old Man and to become vertical once more. It swiveled slowly until it found the flat wall of the building, where it adjusted the cone of light to make a circle on the wall. A thin piece of metal poked out in front of the light from the staff, casting a shadow on the wall from the bottom of the circle of light to its center. The staff then lurched, wrenching itself free of the Old Man's hand, and fell to the floor while maintaining the projection on the wall.

It buzzed loudly and then popped up off the floor, pivoting on the top end of the staff where the light was, supporting itself with a narrow wing of metal, maybe a foot long, opening like a door hinged on the bottom of the staff. The staff lifted itself slowly with the wing and then froze. The Old Man looked back at the circle. The piece of metal was pointing up and to the left. It looked like a clock in a way with twelve little ticks around the end. It seemed to be pointing to nine.

"It is nine in the morning?" The staff buzzed, then it fell to the floor with a clang, made a bunch of commotion, buzzed again, repeated the same flopping commotion, rolled over, then whirred and righted itself into the Old Man's hand. "Amazing." The staff pulsed. The Old Man's stomach growled. "Can you find me something safe to eat?" The staff didn't move. "Not that smart, eh?"

The staff vibrated strongly, but not in a way that convinced him that it had understood. The Old Man went over and grabbed a large and healthy mushroom from the garden. It had a smooth and glowing large umbrella-shaped blue-green dome supported by a thick, glowing stem of a bright shade of green. It was around a foot tall and eight inches in diameter. The stem itself must have been a full two or three inches thick. He noticed that the other shrooms around had a bluer-colored stem and were smaller.

He tugged the whole green-stemmed mushroom, root and all, out of the rocks without much effort. He took it inside to a stove he noticed in the corner last night and set the mushroom on top of it. He opened the furnace below the stove, and a thin book fell out. The Old Man picked up the book as the light adjusted to focus on it. "*How to Cook a Mushroom for Beginners,*" the Old Man read aloud. The Old Man shrugged and opened the cover. "'Chapter 1: Cooking Asexual Moonshrooms. Dish One: Moonshroom Stew.' This must be it. 'Start by obtaining a large moonshroom with a bright-green stem.' Oh, well, that was lucky."

*****

Meanwhile, the group had started down the trail around the lake after the Young explained where he had seen the Old Man start off to as he left. The group started down the dark path beside the lake. The Survivalist noticed the Hobo stumbling over a rock in the dark. She spoke up. "How did the Old Man ever get through this in the dark?"

The Young looked up, or at least in her general direction, before realizing he couldn't see her in the dark. "He didn't move through the dark. He had a big stick with a light shining out of the end of it. He must have used it to find his way around." The Young continued picking his way across the wet rocks as he spoke more. "I looked for another one where the guard had picked one up, but I think the Old Man got the last one."

"Of course, he did," replied the Survivalist from the dark behind the group.

The Radioman's clean voice broke in. "I think you two under-estimate the strength of the Old Man. He knows a thing or two that you might not. He makes up for his lack of physical strength with wit and planning."

The Mechanic stated, "I am not so sure about that, Radioman. You can get a long way with wit, but sometimes, raw strength and agi…" He cut himself off. There was a thud and then a loud splash. The group stopped. "I am all right. A rock gave way under my weight. Anyway, raw strength and agility are what you need to complete the task at hand." The Mechanic waited and anticipated someone making fun of him for the irony of pointing out agility as he nearly fell in the lake. To his surprise, no one said anything. However, he could feel the Survivalist staring at him, even through the darkness.

The Entrepreneur broke in for the first time in a while. "My question is why these rocks are so slippery and damp. Does the lake have tide cycles even though it is underground?" The group was silent. The clatter of loose stones was the only noise filling the void. They had lost direct eyesight of the city.

The Young spoke. "Actually, yes, there are tides underground, just like there are in the oceans. It just typically takes a lot of water, and it usually doesn't move the water up and down this much. My guess based on the stuff I learned while following the Old Man and the guard is, the city uses the water from this lake for all sorts of stuff. That drains the lake out as we see here. Then when it rains on the surface, a whole bunch of the ground water ends up here again to refill the lake."

The Mechanic caught an idea. "The lake probably has a dam or valve somewhere that releases water way down into the ground or a pump that moves it away. Otherwise, this whole place would flood full of water over time since the water doesn't evaporate quickly due to the lack of sunlight in here."

The Young continued. "The guard said something about a geo-thermal power plant in the corner. Those make steam, right? Do you think they use it to dispose of the excess water by piping out the steam?"

The Mechanic nodded, but no one could see it. He spoke up. "Yeah. I think you might be on to something there." The group went silent once more as they picked their way across the rocks.

*****

The group had been picking their way across the stones for around half an hour. Suddenly, a beam of light came flying across the stone-filled basin they were on the edge of in a fast sweeping motion. "What was that?" asked the Hobo.

"That must have been one of those lights like the Old Man had," stated the Young.

"Do you think it is him?" pursued the Radioman.

The Young replied again. "Maybe, but I don't know if there are others out here. I remember something about a weekly crew that comes around to check out the path or something. If it is one of those guys, I think we should steer clear of the light since we aren't really in here under proper procedure."

Another beam swept back across the opening. The Hobo excitedly dove behind a boulder to avoid it. The rest of the group hunkered down. "Get behind something, guys! Come on!" He urged. The group found some hiding places. The Hobo inquired, "How far is it to where the light is coming from?"

The Mechanic peeked around the boulder he was behind. "Too far to run and make it quietly."

The Entrepreneur startled the Survivalist as he began speaking right next to her. "Somebody check and see if it is the Old Man."

The Mechanic leaned around his hiding spot. There was a pause. "That's the Old Man, all right."

"How can you tell?" asked the Survivalist.

The Mechanic smiled. "He is having way too much fun with a light to have used it a lot before. We are safe to cross the field. Let's go. We have an old man to catch up with." The Mechanic started picking his way across the open rock basin.

*****

The Old Man had cooked himself a meal from the mushroom using the cookbook and a few ingredients stashed around the building and the furnace. It had turned the mushroom into a sort of mushy soup. It certainly had a strangely mushy texture, although the book had warned him not to cook it too long to maintain a more crisp and flavorful stew. Overall, it really wasn't bad.

The Old Man rather enjoyed his own cooking. It had been a long time since he got to use a formal kitchen, if you could call a dark building with a stove and furnace combo a kitchen. However, he was now very thirsty. He had experimented with some cooking salt in the stew and found the salt to be extremely concentrated to the point that it robbed his mouth of any saliva. He sat for a while until boredom overcame him. He wondered where the group was. Maybe he could see them if he used the Lightstaff.

He went outside and made a broad swing across a stone field he had traversed before. He didn't see anything. He made another sweep. Nothing. He sighed and turned to shine the light against the wall. It still amazed him how brightly the rocks shimmered in the light. He swung the light all around with subtle hand gestures and points. The rocks sparkled brilliantly. It looked like the stars on a clear night.

Something caught the Old Man's ear. It was only there for a moment, but there had not been a noise not produced by him since he arrived at the building. What had caused it? Another sound arrived. His ear twisted slightly to hear it. He turned and directed the light across the field. There was another noise—no, multiple noises. The Old Man retreated to the edge of the building. He swept the light again. Nothing. He came up with an idea.

He shut the light off entirely by moving his left hand, palm down, horizontal and performing a quick cutting motion from his chest outward. He pointed in the direction the noise had come from. He then turned his left hand palm up, balling it up into a fist as it rotated. Just as his hand reached the palm-up position, he abruptly opened his fist to a flat hand and elevated it slightly. The Lightstaff blasted into a beam.

In the end of the beam was a large person. The person stood still, shielding its eyes from the light with its hands. It had huge, burly hands. The Old Man thought that it had to be the Mechanic. Nobody else around had hands that big. The Lightstaff suddenly cut out. The Old Man looked down at it in surprise. The staff then whirred softly and lunged forward, pulling the Old Man off balance. It positioned into a crevice to support the Old Man and then tossed him gently through the doorway of the building.

He dropped the staff and fell onto the cot. The staff righted itself, emitted a rather loud mechanical squeak once, and then fell over with a clang. It whirred quietly and rolled across the floor to the end of the cot. The Old Man sat up, very disoriented. Outside, the footsteps and shifting rock noises were getting closer. He started up. The Staff lightly slapped his leg, throwing him off balance and causing him to tumble back down on the cot. He grumpily reached for the staff in the dark. It whirred and shot up into his hand.

He began standing. The staff stopped resisting but did not assist the Old Man as he stood. The Old Man motioned with his hand to turn the light on. The Lightstaff did not respond. He repeated the motion. Nothing. The Old Man ran his hand up the staff until he located the ring. He snapped it counterclockwise and brought the beam to life. It was pointing straight in the air. The staff had reversed itself back to when the Old Man had found it. It was just a stiff staff and a light again.

A footstep occurred outside his door. The Old Man pan- icked and aimed the beam out the doorway. There, he spotted the Survivalist peeking over a stone. He relaxed. "Survivalist, it is me, the Old Man! Do you have the others with you?"

The Survivalist stood from behind the stone and stepped over it. She started toward the building. "Yeah. They are all right here. Are you having fun with your light?"

The Old Man shook his head. "I was. I don't know what got into it. As soon as you all came along and it spotted the Mechanic, it…" He trailed off. A realization had struck him. He restarted. "Look, this staff is, eh, not what you think. I mean, it works as a staff, but it's way better. It…it understands what I need and…" The Old Man struggled to find a good way to describe the staff. He gave up in exasperation. "Oh, just hold on. I think I need to convince this thing you all are friendly."

The Survivalist's face dropped to a judgmental disbelief. "You need to convince a staff with a light on it that we are friendly? Has the darkness gotten to you or something? Did you eat some of these mushr—"

The Old Man cut her off. "Yes! Just…hold on. Let me work." He noticed how strange this appeared. Oh well. He needed to show the group. He started in timidly. "Hey, uh, Lightstaff, these people are friends of mine. They aren't going to do anything to me." The staff did nothing. The Old Man looked nervously at the group, barely illuminated by some stray light from the staff. He came up with another idea. "They aren't going to hurt you either. I trust them."

The staff vibrated slightly. It adjusted his hand slightly toward the group. The Old Man adjusted the beam down to the group. The staff snapped over to the leftmost person, the Entrepreneur, and focused the beam on him. "Uh, that is the Entrepreneur." The Staff snapped over to the next person, the Hobo. "That's the Hobo." The staff proceeded along, sweeping until it found each person and waiting for the Old Man to identify them.

When it got over to the Young and identified him, the Old Man swung the staff up and stated, "All right. That is everyone." The staff shuddered before jolting out of the Old Man's hand and spinning its way into the middle of the group. It stood straight vertical, whirring softly, and directed the light down across itself. The Old Man assumed this was supposed to be an introduction.

"That is the Lightstaff. It has a mind of its own, sort of. It only recognizes hand motions and a few voice commands. For example, where is the cot?" The staff whipped the light up and beamed into the doorway of the building. "Where is the Mechanic?" The light swung around once more and adjusted the beam to illuminate all of the Mechanic. The Old Man motioned the Young to go behind a nearby rock. The Young caught on and did so. "Where is the Young?" The light snapped over to where the Young was standing, scanned the area, then returned to the Mechanic. "You see, it can find things it has spotted before, but only if they have not moved and the Lightstaff has a direct line of sight."

The group stared in shock. The Old Man proceeded to show off the clock feature and the assisted walking features and how it could lunge around to get to him. He also explained the things the guard had told him of the city, that the staff had opened itself up to him only as he walked along in the dark, and that he had decided to sleep in this little building when the lights over the city went out to simulate the nighttime.

He then tried handing the staff to the Young, who was curious to hold it. The staff shook and jolted around to dodge the Young's grasp. It flipped across the area and landed near the Old Man, where he caught it. The Old Man looked the staff over, perplexed. He tried every member in the group, but the staff refused to be touched by anyone but the Old Man. The Hobo remarked, "I guess the staff is yours to have, then. It doesn't like us."

The Old Man shrugged wistfully and straightened his posture. He replied, "I suppose so. I wonder why that is." No one answered him. After the short introduction, the Old Man asked if the group was hungry. They were, so he went in and cooked a large pot of the moonshroom stew. The stew received heavy resistance at first, but a few spoonsful of it convinced them of the meal.

While the group ate, the Old Man used the staff to drag the Mechanic's backpack over. He quickly inserted the thin cookbook inside it and replaced the backpack where it was before anyone noticed. He noticed that the deego rations were gone. The group must have eaten them overnight. The group finished the meal, thanked the Old Man for cooking it, and started outside once more. The darkness caught them off guard once more since the building had been illuminated by the staff.

The Old Man followed them out and started talking. "I would take some of these shrooms with us, but the book said not to. They apparently explode into thousands of slightly toxic spores a few hours after death unless they are properly cooked. They likely won't harm you any besides inducing a coughing fit, but we can't take any chances." The Old Man stopped as his face lit up. He remembered something.

He swiveled on his heels and strolled back into the building. There, he grabbed a pencil from the counter and held it to a piece of paper. How long had it been since he last wrote something down? It had to have been quite a long time. His hand hovered over the scrap of paper as he thought. He started writing the message. *I took a few shrooms from the garden outside and used some small amounts of the spices, mainly the salt. Thanks for the meal and place to sleep.*

The Old Man reviewed his note. He noticed that his handwriting had grown atrocious—not that it was ever good to begin with. He sighed, opened the furnace door, which was now cold from lack of use, and pinned the paper note in the crack between the door and the frame. The off-white paper clashed with the black furnace. He returned outside. "I was told by the guard to leave a note if I used something. That way, some Weekly Checkup team could restock it. Who knows if that will ever happen, though? Anyway, don't worry, I didn't say anything about you all being here. I assume you all found a way in besides the front gate since you still have the weapons."

"Yeah. I will explain that on the way," stated the Young. A moment of idle silence overtook the group.

"So where to now?" asked the Hobo.

The Old Man gestured off to his right. "I guess we continue on around the left side of the lake like we have been. Maybe the path will get better as we go," he replied.

The Mechanic scoffed. "I sure hope so. These slippery rocks are hard for someone of my size to stand on." The group chuckled and sorted themselves out in a line behind the Old Man as he used the staff to begin picking his way across the stone field.

The group was making noticeably faster time now that they had the light. Being able to see the stones made all the difference. The Young explained the events of getting inside the gates to the Old Man as they went. The Old Man explained the power plant on the far edge of the city the best he could. There was a period of silence before the Radioman spoke up. "This wondrous geothermal power plant you describe, are we going right past it on our trek around the lake?"

The Old Man had not thought of this. He paused for a moment, as did everyone else, as he had directed the light away from the path. "I suppose so. I do not see any other way around the lake and the building, for it is up against the water. It is strange that we will be going right around to where a volcanic activity is, but what else are we going to do?"

The group returned to silence. The Old Man swung the light back onto the path with a lazy flick of his hand. The Young spoke up. "Do they not have a boat down here?"

The Mechanic replied promptly. "I wondered the same but came to the conclusion that they probably never go out on the water. They have no reason to. It is not like they could enjoy the sunny afternoon down here, and fish probably don't exist in the lake."

"So what do they eat if not fish?"

The group pondered this over. The Old man broke in. "Well, I noticed that they have some crops growing down by the lake under artificial light. I would like to know how that works. We know for a fact they can farm and eat the moonshrooms."

"Yes, but none of those is really meat. Don't you need to eat meat to survive?" rebutted the Young.

The Old Man cocked his head over on the left side slightly. "Actually, no, you don't. However, you are right in that they need a source of protein. I don't know how else they would get it besides a meat source down here." The Mechanic noisily stumbled over a rock. He grumbled meaninglessly.

The Survivalist was busy thinking. She was buzzing with excitement. "What do you think the city will be like?"

The Old Man turned quickly. The light remained focused on the path. He spoke with a soft urgency. "For you and the group, it is going to be a lot of hiding. No one can know any of you are here. I am the only person they know about. If they find you, they will eventually figure out that you all smuggled yourselves in somehow. That will lead to them finding the weapons, and then...who knows?"

The Survivalist's face dropped. She ran her hand along the rope across her chest subconsciously. "We could hide and run at the first opportunity."

The Old Man raised his eyebrows. He had caught on to the Survivalist's secret wish to explore the city. "And if they find you?"

"We come out but stash the weapons."

"They might throw you out, and then the weapons will be stuck inside here."

"Well, then, we will run away with the weapons."

"You seem to forget we are in an enclosed cave underground that we are unfamiliar with." The Survivalist sank back. She knew he was right. The Old Man continued. "You see? I am sorry, but you all have to hide. It is the only way through. Seeing the city as a tourist or something just isn't possible."

The Young noticed the Survivalist being upset. He started speaking without knowing where he was going with the sentence to avoid losing the conversation. "What if we, uh, don't go in as tourists?"

The Old Man changed his stature to face the Young. "What do you mean?"

The Young grew diffident. "I don't know. Like, maybe we stay hidden, but you go explore and bring something to us." With a quick glance, the Young saw that the Survivalist perked up. He returned his view back to the Old Man's humoring face. The Young emboldened himself. "You said it yourself, the people here are expecting you." He struggled to find a reasoning behind the idea. He worked his hands through the air, trying to start another sentence.

The Radioman chuckled smoothly and grandly spoke. "Oh, maybe you can find some valuable information. You have already spoken with the guard and gotten more information than any of us."

The Entrepreneur broke in as well with his stiff and grungy voice. "Yeah, and maybe you can find a good deal for some goods. Who knows what they have down here? You already have a fancy flashlight that is more advanced than anything we own. Can you imagine what might be here?"

The Mechanic furthered the idea. "There might be wonderful tools down here of that capability. Who knows what we could use them for?"

There was a pause. The Old Man seemed firm on his ideas. The Hobo chose his words carefully. "Old Man, I understand you want us safe. I will tell you what, if we promise to stay hidden at all times, will you at least see what the city is like and maybe look around? I don't know that we can miss this opportunity to supply ourselves."

The Old Man's face gave slightly toward consideration. The Hobo pressed on. "Look, I will personally make sure they don't get into trouble. You know I survived before and after the Crisis on the streets and in the shadows. I will be able to get them around without being caught. I know what to look for. If it comes down to it, you can create a distraction, and I can get everyone to a safe place to stay until things calm down."

The Old Man lost his defenses. He sighed. "All right. I am clearly outnumbered. I will go into the city and look for any opportunities for us as long as you all promise to stick with Hobo and do as he says." The group agreed collectively.

The Young noticed a flaw in the plan. "Old Man, you left something out. I mentioned that you might bring something back to us."

The Old Man hesitated, glanced around the room at the approving faces, and nodded. "I will search for something for you all to see." He turned and started walking again. The Young took a deep breath and nervously peeked over at the Survivalist. She was beaming with excitement again. He exhaled quietly as he relaxed and began walking over the rocks with the group.

*****

The group continued around the lake. After several hours of picking their way across the dark landscape, they finally arrived at a smooth, paved path. The Old Man, very tuckered at this point, stated, "Walking on that makes you really appreciate pavement." The group collectively laughed.

The Radioman smiled widely. "I am unsure if you would have succeeded had it not been for the staff in your hand."

The Old Man smiled back. "You are right. I probably wouldn't have made it. It was a lifesaver." The Lightstaff pulsed in the Old Man's hand. The group returned back to laborious breathing.

A short bit of pavement walking later and the group found themselves approaching a large stone wall. A muffled rumbling noise was emitting from it. Inside was a tall and dull multiple-story building. The wall was much taller than the one the group had climbed over outside, and it surrounded the entire building and a small flat area around it. Tall lamps lined the pathway. The Old Man shut the light on the staff off. The Hobo asked, "You all think that is the power plant?"

The Old Man responded after a deep breath. "I would say so." He took in another heavy gasp of air. "It matches the description from the guard"—another breath—"large and by itself." He panted as he contemplated his age. He used to recover quicker from physical exertion. Maybe he had overdone it with the new power of the Lightstaff in his hand.

The Mechanic, breathing smoothly, took over for the Old Man. "The lights are also running above us. They have to be getting electricity from somewhere."

"So when do we start hiding and working through the shadows as the Hobo said?" questioned the Survivalist.

The Radioman pointed his hand up the path, his maroon coat catching the light. "I would say we begin that endeavor right now." The group refocused on the path. A large group of people was walking toward them, all dressed in working clothes and protective headgear. Some were carrying something shiny and silver.

The group looked at the Hobo, who spoke quickly. "All right. You all follow me. We need to hide behind this building." There was a small outbuilding nearby. The door on it had a simplistic yellow lightning bolt and a red triangle with an exclamation point painted on it. The Old Man continued up the path. The Lightstaff stopped adjusting to support his weight.

The group took their position on the far side of the outbuilding. The Hobo peeked around the edge. The workers had reached the Old Man. Many of them nodded as they passed. One stopped. The two moved off the path a short way to let the rest of the workers past. The silver items the workers were carrying were full bodysuits with clear masks on the head. The Hobo thought they must have been for extreme temperatures in the power plant or something. The worker, not dressed in the silver outfit and instead in overalls and boots, took off his yellow protective helmet.

The Hobo saw the worker's mouth begin moving and strained his hearing. He could barely make out the conversation. "Are you a new guy passing through?" The Old Man nodded. "Oh. Well, then, I must be the first person you have met in here besides one of the guards. I could tell you were the outsider based on your skin tan." The Hobo peeked at the worker. He was incredibly pale compared to the Old Man. "Anyway, welcome to the City of Underground, or should I say the outskirts of it. The rest of the city is just up the path there."

The worker paused, seeming to await the Old Man to say something in return. The Old Man did not speak. The worker grew concerned. "I understand you probably just went through the guard gates a little while ago. Those guys make it out like they are going to kill you or something if you do something bad while you are here. Well, I can personally tell you that as long as you don't bring in any weapons or do something blatantly stupid, then things will be just fine."

The Old Man looked up at him. "I hear people say that a lot. Do you mind telling me why weapons are prohibited?" The Hobo smiled at the Old Man's false personality.

"We have been having problems with outsiders recently. They try to come in here and hold us up. The guards typically handle them on the surface, or at least that is what they say. As you have probably noticed, we do not really have anywhere to run off to down here, so getting looted is incredibly easy for armed men. No weapons means no clear advantage and a high probability that you don't want to do any harm."

The Old Man nodded again. "Is it all right if I stay here for a night? I told the guard I just needed to pass through, but I am very tired. I am just an old man after all, and getting around that rocky lakeside was quite a challenge for me."

The worker grinned widely. "Of course it is fine that you stay. The guards don't mind if you do. Nobody ever leaves here anyway, as

I am sure you know." The Old Man nodded one more time. He had no idea what the man was referring to about not leaving. He wanted to ask more, but he did not want to test his luck. The worker clicked his cheek. "All right, then. I need to head in to work. I hope you have a good time in the city. If you need some pay, this power plant always has work available." The worker replaced his helmet atop his head and continued with a final wave. The worker turned right off the main path and wiggled along another to a door on the stone wall. There, the worker entered a code on the door, opened it, and walked in with the door closing behind him.

After a bit, the Old Man was sure the path had been emptied of other people. He motioned toward the Hobo. "Did you hear all that, Hobo?"

The Hobo nodded. "Let's get going. It sounds like you need to go find some information."

The Old Man relaxed as the staff began adjusting itself once more and started toward the city down the center of the path. The group followed behind him, following the Hobo's lead of staying close to the large stone wall for cover from anyone potentially looking out from the taller sections of the power plant.

The Old Man led the group into the city, and the Hobo immediately led the group into a nearby alleyway and began herding them through the backstreets. The Old Man held a steady pace. Once in a while, he would pause at an intersection. There, he would wait for a moment, taking in the view, and drop a very subtle motion with his left hand. The Hobo would promptly usher the group across the street on the signal. They had devised this strategy on a whim by the Old Man for a more controlled city traverse.

At an intersection in the street, the Hobo managed to get close enough to talk to the Old Man without breaking cover. "Hey, Old Man," he whispered. The Old Man raised his eyebrow in acknowledgment that he had her the Hobo. The Hobo continued. "I thought I was supposed to be taking the group to a hiding place while you explored the city."

The Old Man casually turned around and stepped into the alleyway, groping his pocket as if in search of something. Just as soon as he cleared the street, he dropped the act with his hand in the pocket and relaxed. He nodded. "That was the plan. I just don't know where to hide you all yet. What that worker back there said has me concerned. He said people don't ever leave this place. I think we have trapped ourselves in here."

The Hobo shook his head. "No. The Young said he saw another way out of here."

The Old Man raised his eyebrows. "Yes, but who knows if we can get out that way? That worker said they had guards on the surface fending off outsiders. They might not let us through."

The group suddenly fell silent. A common thought had rushed across all of them. The Survivalist brought it up. "Do you...do you think the outsiders are actually Raiders? As in there are Raiders on the far side of the mountains?"

The group didn't respond for a moment. The Hobo broke the silence. "We don't have a choice in the matter anyway. We can't go back the way we came in, as the door can't be opened from this side. I think we can all agree that something is going on here and that we shouldn't hang around to find out what it is."

The Radioman seemed perplexed. He replied, "I agree. I am gathering a strange sensation that all of these people are scared to talk. Sometimes, back home, when I was interviewing, people would get very defensive and dodge subjects deliberately to avoid talking about them. These people, the way they act, has me thinking they are scared of something or someone."

The Hobo nodded in agreement. "Yeah. There also hasn't been a single person on the streets since we saw all of those workers before. It is as if everyone runs on the same schedule."

The Old Man joined back in. "You are right. With that in mind, we had better get moving. We don't know when they will all come pouring back out of that place. We can talk more later once we find someplace safer." He turned to head back out but twisted his neck around to talk over his shoulder. "Keep hidden. No need to take chances." He looked forward as he stepped back out onto the street, again pulling an act to look like he was replacing an object into his pocket. The Hobo scanned the group and twitched his head toward a narrow alleyway parallel to the street. The group filed into the alley behind him.

As they worked their way across the city, the group took in the sights to see. The city was wonderfully detailed. The entire place had been carved out of various stones with the finest precision. The buildings had a surprising variety of colors, textures, and structures. The lack of weather erosion must have led to many abilities of crafts-manship. The Old Man stopped in an empty intersection and took a broad sweep of the area. There was a building with a smooth gray texture that had little blue stripes layered up the sides. The corners were fashioned to be large square blocks.

A building next to it was a grainy cream color with swirled brown sections. Another was a tall and narrow structure comprised of a sparkling silver material, likely a mineral found on stones. He found that building rather tacky. One was a rust-colored building with a short, squatty square shape. Almost every single building had slate roofing. Not one of them had a chimney.

One surprising feature was the existence of glass windows. Almost every building was equipped with glass panes. One building off to his right stood tall and proud with full walls of glass win-dows. A building up the street had a near mirror finish on the outside turned a dark gray by the reflection of the neighboring building. This created an odd question: Why do you need glass windows and roofs if you live underground? Why not just an open-air building to have some privacy? Things must usually be much livelier than the current emptiness of the area to require windows to dull the noise. Things must get a lot of viewing, especially for the amount of attention to the appearance of some buildings.

Every door was immaculately detailed with thick and heavy stone doorways covered in colorful, sparkling swirls and engraved patterns. Another thing that the Old Man noticed was the diversity of how complete each building appeared. Some looked like they had been there for hundreds of years, just as they were, with fully completed roofs and splendid attention to cleanliness. Other buildings seemed to have seen better days but from sheer usage.

Only things like the stairs being cracked and the foundation being rough were evident. There were no signs of blatant neglect. Some buildings looked like they were not even finished but were being used regardless. All of them varied in bulky and excessively strong architecture that the Old Man had never seen before.

Things were going smoothly. It was surprisingly easy to get through the streets. Still, nobody was there. They must have lucked out on the timing of when everyone went to work. But then the city changed. It switched from the grand architecture to a colorful splash. The buildings changed to vibrant shades of luminescent paint that changed shades depending on how you looked at it. The first building on his left changed chromatically from gray to blue and then ended in a forest green.

Some glittered and sparkled. Neon signs littered the streets, moving about in an eerily quiet manner while advertising clothing stores, grungy food stops, or an electrical supply store. Some had flashing large arrows, open signs that had spinning rings of color, or a neon man observing his neon suit in a neon mirror. However, the more the Old Man looked, the more he realized the true intent of this part of town. The smaller, more hidden neon signs told the tale.

They displayed cigars smoking upward in jumpy frames, orange booze bottles snapping back and forth, taverns' names, dive bars with signs pointing down the stairs, a dazzling-pink exotic dancing sign with a neon outline of a woman sitting down with her palms on the ground behind her while she raised and lowered a high heel, and a flickering motel sign directly beside the neon woman so run-down that only Mot remained. There was also something in a foreign language that the Old Man was unfamiliar with, a normal stationary sign with a light underneath it facing up to illuminate the words Grub and Drinks, and a few music notes stuck to a wall of a standard gray block building. It was a strange clash of culture—the erotic and tacky colors of lustrous paint and neon placed jarringly with the grunge and dirt of the city.

The Old Man started walking again. He had caught himself standing still and staring at this odd part of town. The Old Man made a quick glance around for the group. He could not find them anywhere. He continued on down the street in hopes that while he had stood around, they had made forward progress without him. Far down the street, the Old Man spotted a person. He couldn't make out who it was, but it didn't look like anyone from the group.

He continued at his own pace. The staff stiffed as he approached the stranger's location. The stranger was dressed in a ragged suit, satin black in color with subtle vertical gray pinstripes, and wearing shades that were likely useless in the low light. The only reason he was visible was the blasting reflection of his pale skin under a light. He was standing still, smoking a large cigar, staring across the walkway at the Old Man. The Old Man refused any eye contact. He did not want a conversation.

Just as he was about to pass by, the stranger stepped out into the walkway and cut off his path. He reeked of a sweet-smelling cigar smoke. He removed the shades and the cigar. He cocked his head as he looked the Old Man over. "Hey there, outsider." His voice was gruff and disturbed, likely from years of smoking. The Old Man looked up in defeat. "Your suntan is a dead giveaway." The Old Man glanced down at the back of his hands. "You care for a game of cards, Suntan?"

The stranger held his left hand out toward a dull-black building constructed of heavy one-foot-by-three-feet wide blocks. The Old Man looked over at the structure, then back at the stranger. He shook his head as he stepped around the stranger. The stranger sidestepped to cut him off once more. "Oh, come on, Suntan. There is nobody here this time of day. You can see that just by looking around. We need a player to fill the table." The stranger cracked a toothy grin. His teeth were chipped and yellowed. Something about those teeth made the Old Man realize what he had walked into.

The stranger was going to harass him until he went inside. The Old Man thought it over for a bit. He could fight the stranger and likely win, especially with the staff, but he feared the group would come out of hiding behind him to assist and blow their own cover. The stranger was quicker than him. If the stranger got away, the whole area would know about the group before they could escape. He also wondered about procrastinating until someone else came by or the stranger got angry, but this likely wouldn't work either since he hadn't seen anyone in ages besides this stranger, and the stranger would soon resort to aggressive tactics judging by his impatient, nervous shifting.

He realized he was likely being watched from the black building. The Old Man saw no other options, and he was out of time to think. He started toward the black building without a word. The stranger's face lifted from borderline threatening impatience to a cooperative businessman in the blink of an eye. "Oh, ho! Good choice, my friend. We will get some cards in your hand as soon as possible."

The stranger started to wrap his arm around the Old Man's shoulder to guide him inside. The Old Man poked the stranger's hand with the top of the staff before it could touch him. The stranger took the hint surprisingly well and kept his distance. He transitioned instead to tapping the cigar to rid it of the ashes. They reached the dark wooden door, and the stranger thumped it a few times with his fist. A slat on the door opened. A pair of eyes nearly covered in bushy black eyebrows peeked out, hesitating on the Old Man, and disappeared after noticing the stranger.

There was a thunk, and the door swung open with a squeak. The stranger showed another toothy grin. "Welcome to the Cave Dweller Cardhouse, Suntan." The Old Man kept his silent state. As he stepped through the doorway, he remembered something he should have considered before. He didn't know how to play cards. He whipped a hopeless glance out the doorway before the heavy door slammed shut and a large board was replaced to hold it.

Meanwhile, the Hobo had been watching the whole event. He had not realized that the Radioman had moved up right next to him to watch as well. The Radioman practically whispered directly into the Hobo's ear. "Does the Old Man know how to play cards?"

The Hobo nearly shed his skin. The Radioman had scared him. He went through a short phase of anger before calming down and quietly replying, "I don't know." He looked past the Radioman to the rest of the group. "Can the Old Man play cards?" Nobody responded definitively. The group shuffled their way up to hear the conversation better, except for the Mechanic, who was uncomfortably squatted behind a short dumpster with the backpack and the Old Man's rifle, scared to move.

The Young joined in. "I don't think he can. He doesn't seem like the kind of guy to be able to play."

The Survivalist started in. "You never know with the Old Man, though. He did get in here by approaching an armed security gate without any weapons. Who would have thought he would do that?"

The Entrepreneur spoke. "Yes, but he knew what he was up against there and had the choice of walking away. He had no time to plan here and nowhere to go. He might not want to be there."

The group continued to haggle, but the Radioman was paying no attention. He was keeping track of the stranger, who had just cracked a very toothy smile. The Radioman began to stand, but the Hobo quickly grabbed his shoulder and held him down. The group stopped the conversation to see what the matter was. The Hobo looked out to the Old Man. He was headed inside with the stranger. The Hobo peeked over at the Radioman. The Radioman was glaring at the Old Man and the stranger. His face remained calm, but his eyes raged. He stared unblinking, piercing right through the two men headed toward the black building.

The Hobo shook the Radioman gently to no effect. "Hey, Radioman! You all right?" The Radioman wasn't budging. The orange neon light from the cigar store reflected off his unwavering eyes, making them look like they were burning in their sockets. The Hobo looked back at the Old Man. He was headed through the doorway. The stranger's arm was outstretched to show him in, and his head was looking past the Old Man through the doorway.

The Hobo saw the Old Man make a sharp glance back out into the street. He knew immediately. He grabbed onto the Radioman. "Radioman, you can't go in! You have to stay here!" The Radioman continued his stare down, ripped the Hobo's hands off his shoulders, and promptly started across the street toward the black building, striding with purpose to the doorway. The Hobo turned to the group. "Something is wrong. The Radioman knows it. I don't think all of us combined could have stopped him. We have to stay here, though. We can't risk anything more."

He turned back to peek out to the street. The Radioman had already made it to the door but was not entering it. He was instead waiting very stiffly outside the edge of the doorframe. After just a few moments, the Radioman stepped quickly in front of the door, swiveled on his heels, switched his composition to his typical proud self, and knocked loudly on the door.

The Radioman stood in wait. On the outside, he was calm, even charming. Oh, but on the inside, he was seething. His head felt like he had just retracted it from a furnace. He struggled for a moment to take a normal breath instead of an amplified inhale. He recomposed himself despite already doing so once. He checked his maroon coat for dust and brushed off what he could.

The noise inside the building had stopped. He waited for the slat to slide open. There was a tap of metal, and the slat shot open. The Radioman smiled widely. "Hello there, my fine fellow! I am here to…" The bushy eyebrows started away from the slat opening. The Radioman raised his voice. "To play cards at the true gambling house." The slat was halfway shut but hesitated. It slid open once more. The eyebrows returned. The Radioman suppressed a smile. "I have heard this is the place to be for real card play. If I am mistaken, I will try a different establishment—"

A deep and gruff voice cut him off with a thick accent. "No, you are at the right place." The slat shut with a loud clack. There was a thunk, and the door swung open. The Radioman stepped through the doorway without hesitation. Eyebrows deliberately slammed the door shut behind him and replaced the wooden beam. The Radioman peeked back at the door in reaction to the loud slam. Before he could get a good look, he noticed the rest of the room staring at him, likely Eyebrows's intentions.

He snapped into position and stated, "I am here to play cards. I have heard this is the place to be. Is there a seat open at an active table?" The crowd continued watching him for a moment but lost interest once they had taken in the maroon coat and returned to their previous occupation. A single man stood, dressed in a black vest with an equally black tie and a white undershirt. He had tucked the white shirt into his long black pants. He was sporting greasy, smooth black hair and a wide black mustache curled up at the ends slightly. The Radioman wondered why everything to do with this place was colored in black as the man approached him.

He stood in front of the Radioman for a moment, sizing him up. He spoke in a nasally accent. "I am the dealer here, the only dealer. This is my establishment. If you want to play, you will have to wait your turn. The fellow over there took the last open seat." The dealer pointed over to the Old Man, who was blatantly staring at the Radioman in both confusion and curiosity.

The Radioman cracked a smile and chuckled. "Oh, I do not think it will be a problem. I am sure he won't mind if I sit in for him."

The dealer's composition flickered. He did not like being tested. He decided on humoring this strange maroon fellow and turned to look at the Old Man. The Old Man still had not spoken a word since he met the stranger, and he did not break the silence. After a moment, the dealer turned back to the Radioman. "It appears to me that he seems rather content where he is." He awaited the Radioman's response.

Little did the dealer know that the Radioman had gathered everything he needed to know in that short moment when all eyes were off him and on the Old Man. Just as soon as the dealer had broken eye contact, the Radioman had scanned the entire room for clues. The floor was made of a dark-brown wood with thick grain polished heavily but obviously worn over time. He was currently standing on a small raised platform that made a sort of entryway. The platform was surrounded with a smooth brass handrail supported by an equally dark shade of wood post except for a gap where a flight of stairs dropped down to the main floor, also the dark wood.

This level made up the majority of the rest of the room, excluding a lounge area and bar on the far side of the room lit with blue lighting and the bright pit in the center of the room housing a card table. He searched the pit but found the Old Man sitting there in blasting white lights that illuminated the immaculate green felt card table and the much gruffer men sitting on the stools around it, awaiting the dealer's return. He snapped over to the lounge and bar. It was up on an elevated platform and most entirely a shade of dark blue due to the lighting. The bar stood out starkly as it was the only place with colored lighting in the entire area.

There were some people sitting mindlessly at the bar and one fellow lounging on a reclining chair. The Radioman paused his scan on the reclining chair. He noticed a young boy filling a glass on a table right next to the recliner. The man in the recliner took a sip of the glass. As soon as he returned it to the table, the boy began refilling the small sip the man had taken. The boy stood very stiffly as if he was bound to that specific spot with foot-long chains. His face was tense. The blue lighting made it hard to see for sure, but the Radioman caught a glimpse of a scar across the boy's face from his right cheek, across his nose, and to just below his left eye. The boy had been struck with something recently as a bruise occupied the right side of his face, discolored strangely by the blue light.

The Radioman noticed the dealer turning back around and snapped himself back into the act. The dealer stated that the Old Man seemed rather content. The Radioman thought fast on his feet. He hesitated for a moment, but it worked out in his favor. He motioned for the dealer to come closer. He leaned slightly and whispered in the dealer's ear. "He is mine."

The dealer stepped back and gestured to the Old Man. The Radioman nodded. The dealer raised an eyebrow and turned to the table. "Hey, Suntan, are you serving this maroon fellow over here?" The Old Man tensed and looked up at the Radioman once more.

The Radioman made a faint smile with the corner of his mouth. The Old Man suppressed his own smile and nodded. The dealer pursued with another question. "Do you want to give up your seat at the table to him, then? He wants to play, but I told him you already had the last seat."

The Old Man stood hastily from the table and backed away from it, out from under the white overhead lighting and into the shadowed edges of the pit. The dealer turned back to the Radioman. "All right, then. The seat is yours. We are going to play a few rounds of Decker. No bets to start. You know how to play Decker?"

The Radioman nodded. "I have played a few hands in my time."

"Great. Come on over." The dealer began to reach for the Radioman's shoulder to guide him over, but a sharp look from the Radioman made him think otherwise. He swiveled around and led the way at a distance. The dealer dropped down into the pit and motioned for the Old Man to leave the area. The Old Man stepped out of the pit and traveled over to a chair in a dark corner where he sat down.

The Radioman noticed a pile of chips discarded on a tall round table nearby. He realized he did not have any cash to bet with, and he knew better than to sit down at the table without having credits to bet even if the table was starting with no bets. He scanned the room to look for people watching him but was surprised to find everyone looking toward the blue lounge and bar. Standing behind the bar was a worker that the Radioman had not spotted before.

It was a woman, the first one he had seen since the group arrived down in the City of Underground. She must have just come out of the back room via the dark doorway behind the bar. She was facing away, toward a wall of bottles, presumably alcohol, skimpily dressed in a revealing brown undercut bra with silver trim along the top ridges that stretched with a thick strap in an X across her back to an equally thick strap that wrapped around at a horizontal support, leading around to meet her breasts. The only other thing covering her alabaster skin, which was currently completely blue in the lighting, on her thin and slightly bowed body was a long, straight section of brunette hair stretching down to the middle of her back, stained black by the blue lights, leaving the rest of her skin exposed down as far as the bar she was standing behind.

The Radioman wondered for a moment if she was wearing anything at all below the height of the bar. She turned briefly to reveal a sharp chin on the bottom of a long face partially hidden by her hair. She held a labeled bottle out to a man at the bar, leaning forward over the edge slightly. The Radioman couldn't help but notice she was rather gifted on the front side, which explained the need for the thicker straps on the back, and that she wasn't necessarily afraid of people looking at her. She turned back to the wall of colorful bottles and began searching for a different selection after a man at the bar declined the one she had chosen a moment before.

As the Radioman slipped past the table, he dropped the chips silently into his left hand and stashed them inside his coat pocket. He had managed to do this completely unseen thanks to the blue beauty behind the bar. The woman began to turn around to face the table, and everyone broke the line of sight to avoid being caught staring. The Radioman stepped into the white light, his maroon coat gleaming a redder shade than normal in the harsh light. He took the open seat at the left point of the pentagon-shaped table with the dealer to his left on the flat bottom side.

Five other people sat at the table. Two were on the angled piece directly to his right. They were both in work jeans and faint blue long-sleeved shirts. One had a black stain on the left sleeve. Both of them needed a shave and a good sleep. Another pair sat on the sloped piece across the table from himself. The right one was in a black bomber jacket while the left was in a clean green tweed jacket and an equally green pub cap. They both seemed to be tired of waiting for the dealer.

The last person was seated on the narrow side of the pentagon directly across and parallel to the Radioman's seat. This fellow caught the Radioman's attention. He was wearing a charcoal pinstripe suit with sharp, pointed lapels, a notch at the neck, with a stark-white shirt featuring a tight color and a satin black tie that matched his slick, short hair. He had a black pocket square tucked neatly to form a short rectangle. Both of the buttons on his coat were fastened, which bothered the Radioman slightly. The man was sitting with his hands in his flapped pockets, awaiting the game, leaning back on the stool slightly, watching the dealer shuffle the two decks of cards together.

The man across from him in the charcoal suit broke out of his deep thought and glanced over at the Radioman. He looked away for a moment but returned for a second for a more thorough examination. The Radioman noticed he was looking at his maroon coat. The charcoal suit man spoke up for the first time since the Radioman had entered. His voice was deep, gruff, but oddly polite and charming in a way. "Who are you?"

The Radioman didn't even answer for a moment. He was blown away by the blunt statement, as he was expecting an eloquent conversation. The Radioman snapped back into reality and answered the question. "It is not important who I am. I don't need to know who you are either. All that you need to know is, I am here to play cards."

The man blinked at the Radioman. He clearly wasn't impressed by the obvious question dodge. He replied with, "All right. People here call me Charcoal." The Radioman stared blankly. Charcoal sat back in his chair, minorly bewildered, and looked over at the blue lounge. The Radioman followed his gaze over to the woman once more. Charcoal turned back to the table, and the Radioman snapped back to the card game.

The dealer had finished shuffling the cards and was currently dealing out each player their eight cards. The dealer cleared his throat. "All right, everyone. The game is about to begin. We are playing Decker at the table. No bets for a while since it has been a while since we last ran a game of Decker." The table said nothing in return. This did not faze the dealer. He did not expect any replies. He finished dealing out the eight cards.

The Radioman picked up his hand. It was a decent start—three sevens and two queens. He gathered his memory of the game. This game went on for five rounds before everyone held. The dealer ended up winning the round with two streaks of four. The Radioman cracked a smile, but it quickly dwindled. He had missed playing cards, but all he was doing here now was making a good enough appearance to leave and take the Old Man with him without seeming too suspicious.

The table went through two more games of Decker before the table grew bored. Charcoal started in with his bluntness once more. "Dealer, this card game is boring without bets. Can't we start up the betting already?"

The dealer scowled at Charcoal for trying to run his table, but he asked the group, "Is everyone fine with betting?" The whole table nodded except for the Radioman. The Radioman was not worried about the betting. He was more concerned with getting out of the game. But he knew that just as soon as betting started, then he would have to stay put. They would replace him with the Old Man if he left, and judging by the Old Man's reactions to plays during the last few games, he knew the Old Man had no idea how to play cards, let alone Decker for bets. The Radioman had to stay. There was nothing else he could do.

The dealer announced, "The minimum bet in this cardhouse today is two chips. Please begin using hand signals to prevent unnecessary interventions. To clarify for our new guest, tap the table for a card, wave for a hold, and place the cards on the table—facedown, of course—for a fold."

There were two more games, both of them going six rounds with the man in green winning one low-betting round and the other to the blue shirt man with the black stain. The Radioman realized that he had luckily gotten away with nobody questioning where he had gotten his chips even though he had never cashed in for them. He also realized that the only way he was going to get this table to stop playing anytime soon was to force an ending.

There was only one way in Decker to force the table to stop playing: go all in. This worked by assuring that at least one member of the group would stand and leave the table to cash in for more chips or to leave the cardhouse. The Radioman only had one issue with this: He lacked the number of chips likely needed to instigate an all in. An all in was only started if everyone agreed on the bets at hand as equal, and with the meager stack of chips the Radioman had left, this equal decision would never happen. This left the Radioman with only one option.

The Radioman played another round, playing more seriously. He won the game. This caught the table off guard. They noticed that the Radioman actually did know something about this game. They all leaned forward in their seats. The Radioman turned back to look at the Old Man in the corner. He thought about winking, but Eyebrows, the doorman, was looking right at him. So instead, he turned back to the table without a single indication of his plans.

A new game began. The Radioman won again with a streak of seven. The majority of the group were shocked by the Radioman's luck, but Charcoal and the dealer remained unfazed. The Radioman had found his true opponents. The Radioman started in another round, betting higher than the minimum and dragging the entire table to betting up with him. The man in green folded first, as he was running low on funds. The Radioman had no need to do so. In fact, his hand was a rather shabby set of three on the fifth round in, and he considered folding, but he drew again anyway with an even higher bet when his turn came around to force the table to bet once more.

Everyone, including the dealer, folded except for Charcoal. The Radioman knew by the wince on Charcoal's cheek at his last draw that he, too, had a bad hand. The question was, who had the worse one? The Radioman drew again to start the sixth round with the same bet as before. Charcoal held his hand and matched the Radioman's bet. The two both held on round seven.

The table command was spoken. The Radioman dropped his cards to the table to reveal his pitiful set of three number four cards. Charcoal laughed as he placed his cards down to reveal a streak of three, just shy of the Radioman's hand. The Radioman chuckled as he began his statement. "I thought you had me for sure on that one."

Charcoal shook his head in disagreement. "I figured you had me. I was hoping to force you to bail out, but it appears we had the same tactics."

The dealer collected the cards and shuffled once more. Charcoal stared over at the Radioman's decent pile of chips. The Radioman saw his opportunity in the greedy glint of Charcoal's eye. The Radioman peeked over at the dealer, who was busy eyeballing the Old Man. The game began. The Radioman picked up his card. For the first time in months, he had a difficult time holding his face steady. He had been dealt a streak of six spades. All he needed was an ace and seven of spades, and he would get a Great 8 Streak, the absolute best hand in the game. It was only rivaled by another identical Great 8 Streak in spades as well, which was possible due to the fact that two decks were used.

The Radioman had only gotten the Great 8 Streak once before—in fact, before the Crisis—but he was certain it had been given to him by the dealer of that pre-Crisis match intentionally to assure he won the round in hopes of a larger tip since the Radioman was having a rather lousy day of cards at the time. The Radioman forced his nerves to settle out. He realized his and the Old Man's escape method.

A few rounds went past. The Radioman had placed a chip higher than the minimum each round. He wanted to remain conservative for the first few rounds to make a better impression later with a more threatening pile of chip since Charcoal still had many more chips than he did. Round seven began. The Radioman tapped the table and bet. The dealer tossed over a card. He flipped it over. He nearly lost his composition by having an incredible urge to dance around the room. He had drawn the seven of spades.

He had two rounds to find an ace of spades, and the dealer's deck was running shorter. He discarded a worthless three of clubs onto the table. The table took their turns normally until it got to Charcoal. He smiled grimly. "I will bet one hundred chips this round on a draw." Gasps filled the room. The dealer hesitated to deal the card. "Come on, dealer. Give it to me. This game is getting boring." The dealer placed the card. Charcoal snatched it off the green felt and quickly discarded another. He leaned back in his chair with his arms crossed.

The dealer hesitated to choose an action. The whole room went silent. The dealer nodded and began speaking. "I will remain in the game on one condition." Murmurs spread across the room. People began lining the railing around the pit. Charcoal leaned forward once more. "This maroon fellow has to stay in the game."

Charcoal scoffed. "He doesn't even have the hundred chips to bet for one round in his whole pile."

The dealer glared at Charcoal. "You are right, but he does have Suntan over there." He motioned to the Old Man.

The Radioman's heart skipped a beat. He was unaware that betting beyond the chips at the table was fair game. He thought swiftly, drawing a blank on any response. He opted for a question instead. "Why do you request I bet my servant? What interest could you possibly have in an old man?"

The dealer raised his eyebrows. "Well, he is an outsider, isn't he?"

More murmurs ran through the bar. The Radioman allowed himself to smile and raise his own eyebrows. "Yes, he is." This drew extensive murmurs throughout the bar. The Radioman looked around the room. Not a single person in there had a suntan. Every last one of them was a pasty white. He remembered the guards earlier and how difficult it was to get inside the tunnel. How did that relate to now?

It hit him. Those guards were not primarily keeping people out; they were keeping them in as the Old Man had suggested. They didn't allow weapons in so they would have an easier time keeping the population down here at bay. He ran out of time to think as the murmurs died down and decided to press on. "In fact, he is my own informant of the outside world."

A borderline uproar swept the room. The dealer held up his hand. The whole room went silent. "Prove it," the dealer stated boldly.

The Radioman turned to the Old Man and waved him over. "Come on over and tell the group about your staff." The Old Man did not want this. The staff had hidden its functions for a reason. He was not going to explain the functions of the staff to the very people whom the staff hid from. The Radioman sensed the continued panic emitting off the Old Man and rephrased the question. "Where did you get that staff?"

The Old Man caught on. He relaxed slightly and cleared his throat, and for the first time since getting caught by the stranger, he spoke. "It was given to me by the guards on the outside gates to assist me walking across the boulder fields around the lake to this city."

The crowd erupted in chatter. The dealer silenced them with another hand raise. "What temperature is it outside?"

The Old Man shrugged. "I do not know the exact temperature. Last time I was outside, it was rather warm out."

The dealer grew curious. "There is no snow on the ground, then?"

The Old Man grew genuinely perplexed. "No. It is well above freezing. I was comfortable in the clothes I have now."

The dealer held up his hand before the crowd started back in to keep them at bay. "Maroon, if this is legitimate, I am fine with betting the one hundred chips for the outsider and his information."

The Radioman turned to the Old Man. The Old Man flicked his eyes to the left, past the dealer. The Radioman followed his line. The dealer had a large wagon containing a crate filled with complex parts. The Radioman leaned forward to get a better view. "Would you be so kind as to inform me of the contents of that in the crate behind you, dealer?"

The dealer looked over his shoulder at the crate. "Parts."

"What kind of parts?"

The dealer hesitated. "Robotic parts."

The Old Man made a sudden strange movement. It was as if he had nearly dropped the staff. He straightened and held his back like he had twisted something. The Radioman figured it out. The staff knew something that only the dealer knew as well. "Dealer, would those robotic parts happen to be, oh, valuable?"

The dealer was visibly perspiring, the beads of sweat glinting brightly on his forehead. "Yes, they are extremely valuable."

The Radioman saw an opportunity. He cocked his head to the side and again raised his eyebrows. "Are they valuable to you or in economic value? I still do not think they are worth the valuableness of this information from my friend here. Do you? They are not even assembled and may not function at all."

The dealer began to wither under the pressure of the crowd. "No, I don't think they are worth as much. What more do you want me to bet?"

The Radioman looked over at the bar. The woman had stepped out from behind the side of the bar. Her lower half could now be seen strutting a thick hipster bikini bottom, equally as brown as the top, tied with a large bow on her right hip with the two long ribbons about an inch wide hanging down freely at knee length. A two-inch-tall brass band was fitted tightly high on her left thigh.

A heavy chain was attached to the band. The chain was stretched tight as she tried to go around the end of the bar to see the table pit better. She was wearing dark-brown summer wedges strapped up to the ankle with a lattice. She was braced up against the corner of the bar with her left hip, a disgruntled and beaten look on her face. She had cuts on her left thigh where the band would fit. She needed sleep. She seemed miserable in her beauty.

The Radioman redirected his attention to the dealer. "I want you to bet her as well."

The dealer pointed at the woman, who had immediately perked up to her falsely positive posture before being caught. The dealer chuckled nervously. "You want me to bet the bar girl?"

The Radioman nodded. "Yes. It is only fair—a person for a person and information that interests you for the wagon of parts that interests me."

The dealer shook his head. "She is all I have left after betting the parts besides the establishment itself."

The Radioman pushed further. "Well, then, it appears we have an all-in situation."

Shrieks of excitement ran through the crowd around the pit. The dealer let them go for a bit. He was obviously running the odds.

The Radioman knew he couldn't pass this chance up, although he did wonder why they did not know about the outside world. The dealer cringed and hit his palm on the edge of the table. "Deal."

The crowd reached a high crescendo of yelling and howling. Charcoal, having peered once more back at the woman at the bar, shoved his massive pile of chips in. "I'm in. I will bet my entire pile to compensate for the parts and the girl." The crowd was in an uproar. The Radioman glanced over at the woman. She was straining the chain and leaning as far out as she could to see. A wink of hope ran across her face as she noticed the Radioman looking at her.

The Radioman pointed at her to give her a warning to straighten up. Once she had taken the hint and returned to her position, he said, "Go unchain her. Let her see the outcome of the last round." The dealer appeared appalled that the Radioman had ordered him at his own table. The Radioman held up his hand, palm out, to signify that he had not intended any offense. "I figured it is only fair for the person whose fate is at hand to be able to see the outcome in person, is all. My servant behind me can see the dealings. It is only fair she does as well."

The dealer held strong for a moment but abruptly gave and waved his hand above his head. Eyebrows walked over with a set of keys, fiddled with something behind the counter, gently took her hand, and guided her through the crowd to the pit while assuring nobody touched her. The woman followed carefully behind, keeping distance from the brute towing her along but also close enough that nobody dared bother her. They reached the inside of the crowd, and Eyebrows pushed her gently into the pit where she cowered into the corner opposite of the Old Man.

The crowd was ecstatic. The dealer tried multiple times to silence them, but it wasn't until the big brute Eyebrows threatened them with a few steps toward the crowd that they quieted down. The dealer took in a deep breath. "Let round eight begin."

The dealer looked over at the Radioman. He was up first, as usual, in the seat to the right of the dealer. The Radioman tapped the table. The dealer tossed him a card. He laid his hand on it gently, looked around the room at the captivated crowd, and flipped it up into his hand. It was a nine of spades. The Radioman quickly retrieved the old nine of spades and discarded it, making no progress on his fanaticized Great 8 Streak but at least not losing anything either. Surely his hand would be good enough anyway.

The dealer moved on to Charcoal, who quickly tapped the table, picked the card up with no emotional flicker, discarded quickly, and turned his gaze to the dealer. The dealer also drew a card. He hesitated but placed a different card on the table. The last round had been complete. The dealer straightened in his chair. He drew in a breath. "Rank." The Radioman was alarmed. This meant that a pick was available. He had not realized that the pick was allowed on an all-in round.

The Radioman hastily tapped the table and announced, "Pick." The dealer looked up in surprise at the Radioman. The crowd murmured about quietly. Charcoal, however, restrained. He appeared content with his hand. The dealer fanned his cards facedown near the felt table. The Radioman recalled that he got his choice on an unknown card from the dealer's hand with the cost of having to discard before he drew it. He discarded the junk three of clubs onto the table. The crowd watched the Radioman in suspense. The Radioman thought his choice over. He needed an ace of spades. The Radioman thought, *If I had an ace of spades, where in my hand would I put it?*

He allowed a smile to penetrate his stone face as reached up and took the dealer's rightmost card. The dealer slid it across the felt to himself. The Radioman did not bother flipping the card into his hand, instead holding it facedown on the table. The dealer scanned the table as he replaced the card from the top of the deck, sighing. The dealer's risk of losing a needed card to an opponent for the chance of one last draw off the deck had not paid off. Nobody moved. "Table."

The crowd leaned over the railing as they pried for a look at the hand. On the table rested two streaks, one of length four with the four to seven of hearts and the other of length three with the five to seven of spades and an extra worthless ace of hearts. Charcoal laughed deeply. "You came close." Charcoal was right. Had the dealer's drawn card during the pick been a four or eight of spades, he would have had two streaks of four, a highly ranked hand.

The dealer sneered in response to Charcoal. Charcoal revealed next. He laid them faceup one at a time—a three of hearts, a three of diamonds, a second three of diamonds, and a three of clubs. Three, three, three, three. Each three resulted in a louder murmur from the crowd above, starting small and ending in a triumphant applause. Charcoal grinned and leaned back in the chair, soaking up the praise of the crowd. Eight threes. No wonder he had not gone for a pick. He already had what he needed.

Charcoal laughed at the dealer, pointed at him while shaking his head in false disapproval, and reached out to begin raking in the chips. The dealer grabbed his outstretched arm. "You have forgotten about the last man at the table." Charcoal dropped his grin. He followed the eyes of the dealer to see the Radioman still holding his cards facedown. The Radioman knew the stakes. He either flipped his hand over to reveal the ace of spades and achieve the infamous Great 8 Streak, or he failed and the Old Man, the bartending woman, the massive pile of chips, and the wagon of parts were all lost.

He took in a sharp breath and shut his eyes. The whole room went silent. He flexed his wrist, feeling the felt drag the bottom of the card, listening to the soft scratchy noise it produced. He opened his eyes and tipped his head down to see the card. His eyes grew wide. He froze. *No. It can't be true,* he thought.

The crowd remained so quiet that they could hear the Radioman's increased breathing. They watched as blood flushed his face. The Radioman slowly pivoted his arm at the elbow until his hand reached the table. He dropped the cards from his grasp and retracted his shaking hand to the end of the table. The seven spades sat on the table. Seven, eight, nine, ten, jack, queen, king, and the ace of spades.

The crowd roared in disbelief. Yelling spread throughout the crowd. People began exchanging chips of their own in heated side bets. The crowd must have bet on the winner. The dealer silenced them with the use of a persuasive movement from Eyebrows. He spoke, his voice shaking and uncertain. "A Great 8 Streak of spades, the best hand in the game. And yet you drew the last ace from my own hand." He stood from the table and stepped away, motioning the pile of chips to the Radioman. "Well-played, Maroon. It has been a pleasure playing with you."

Meanwhile, Charcoal had caught on to the fact that he had just lost with an impeccable hand. He lunged forward to see the cards better. After confirming what he thought he had seen, he glared up at the Radioman. "Cheat!" The crowd went silent once more.

The dealer cocked his head. "You think he is a cheat?"

Charcoal broke his glare to the Radioman to look the dealer. "I don't think so. I know so."

"On what grounds?"

"He has slipped cards with sleight of hand."

The dealer did not seem convinced. "Are you telling me that I would not have noticed a sleight of hand at my own card table in my own cardhouse?"

Charcoal realized his mistake, but the damage had been done. He pressed on. "Yes. You do not think it is suspicious that this fellow has never been here a day in his life, and he walks in the front door and wins the highest value pot we have ever had in this establishment?"

The dealer looked over at the Radioman. "Can you protest that?"

The Radioman stood from his chair. "Certainly. Charcoal, I had no way of performing a sleight of hand. My hands remained on my cards or the table for the entire duration of the game." He paused. He walked over to Charcoal's end of the table and looked at his cards—all eight threes. The Radioman looked up at Charcoal. He spread a wide smile and raised an eyebrow. "In fact, I think you are the cheat, Charcoal."

The crowd gasped. Charcoal began across the room, rambling nonsense. The Radioman held up his hand at arm's length. "Save your breath, Charcoal. Do you agree that you got all eight of your threes without cheating?"

"Obviously, yes." The Radioman gestured to the discard pile. "Then can you explain why there is another three of clubs, the third on the table, inside the discard pile?" Charcoal did not respond. The Radioman revealed an evil grin. The dealer promptly snatched up the discard pile and located the three in question. He held it up for the crowd to see. Whispers ran the crowd.

Charcoal spoke in protest. "Did you discard the three?"

The Radioman nodded. "Yes."

Charcoal regained his posture. "Then you must have planted the three to frame me. You—"

He was cut off by the dealer. "I am afraid not. There is a second three in this discard pile that I put there. Either way, you are busted, Charcoal."

The Radioman smirked at Charcoal. "Search him."

Eyebrows lurched across the room and grabbed hold of Charcoal. Charcoal tried to resist but quickly stopped when he realized it was futile. He ran his hands through Charcoal's coat. Suddenly, a card fell to the floor. The whole room froze as it fluttered down. There was a pause while all observed the card at Charcoal's feet. Eyebrows stripped Charcoal of his coat and flipped it upside-down. A whole flock of cards fell to the ground in a loose pile. Eyebrows released a low, grumbling chuckle. He spoke deeply. "Busted."

He then turned to the Radioman. The Radioman held up his arms. Eyebrows searched him everywhere but in his underwear. The Radioman tried to relax, but that was difficult to do when someone was digging in his trousers. "He's clean."

The dealer walked over to Charcoal. "Well, well, well. It appears we have found the cheat. You know the rules, Charcoal. Don't come back." Eyebrows snatched Charcoal's arm and began dragging him toward the door.

The Radioman spoke. "Hold on a moment." He walked over to Charcoal, looking him up and down. "Do you know what charcoal does when in the hot seat?"

Charcoal glared at the Radioman but did not respond. "It goes up in smoke." Charcoal spat at the Radioman and missed. Eyebrows knocked him off his feet and threw him across the floor to the door. Charcoal stood to speak, but before he could get anything out, Eyebrows had removed the door latch and swung the door open. Eyebrows stiffly shoved Charcoal out the doorway, swung the door quickly, stopped just before it slammed, closed it gently, and replaced the latch. He turned and leaned up against the door.

The dealer approached the Radioman. "Congratulations, Maroon. The loot is yours." The Radioman hesitated. The dealer shook his head. "We have been thinking that fellow has been cheating for years. You just caught him in the act and called him out. For that, I owe you anyway. Take the pot, the parts, and the girl. You have earned them all twice over."

The Radioman looked over at the woman. She was still cowering in the corner, visibly concerned now that the game had ended. The Radioman walked over to her. She squeezed further into the corner. The Radioman touched her shoulder lightly. She flinched. "Come on. Let's get you out of here." The woman turned her head sharply to the Radioman's face. She froze. Something the Radioman had said had shocked her to the point of distress. A tear ran down her cheek, past the corner of her parted lips. The Radioman grew concerned. She relaxed as her eyes grew confused. The Radioman looked at the Old Man and waved him over to help collect the winnings. He then turned to the dealer. "May I cash out the chips?"

*****

Once the dealer had cashed the Radioman out for his credits, he started back over to the table. The Radioman caught his arm and spoke to him quietly. "I want to thank you for a wonderful time today. I was not expecting to have so much fun."

The dealer smiled uncomfortably. "I am glad you had fun."

The Radioman sensed that the dealer had found this remark awkward. "I am sorry. What I am truly asking is if you want me to spread the word of this place or if you are happy where it is."

The dealer turned to fully face the Radioman. He sighed and leaned on a nearby brass railing. "Honestly, I like this place how it is. I would love it if some new people like you came in once in a while, provided they aren't like you and sweep the whole house of chips among other things." He gestured at the bartender woman, who was speaking with Eyebrows. They both hesitated, then chuckled lightly.

"But in all seriousness, I cannot keep up the business at this rate. It is not your fault. I take into account losing the whole bet like this at the table. My issue is the upkeep. This place used to be a lot more glossy, if you know what I mean. I feel like I have let it go. If I don't reinvest soon, I do not know how I will keep it running."

The dealer stared off into space. The Radioman looked around. He did not see anything wrong. "Dealer, I hope you do not misunderstand, but I believe your establishment is doing just fine. Look at all the patrons in here. They seem to be having a grand time."

The dealer flipped back into reality. "Yes, they are having a good time. That is what made me realize that I am struggling. You are the first interesting thing to happen here in a few months. For that, I cannot have any regrets. Take your winnings and run. I do not expect you will ever come back. You seem to be the drifting type, or at least you are looking for something."

The dealer paused. He took a step toward the Radioman. "Now look. As you know, dealing cards is my business, which has nothing to do with whatever you are doing. But between you indirectly reminding me to reinvest in this place, giving the locals and myself a good time, and finally ridding me of that nuisance named Charcoal, I feel like I still owe you something more than just your winnings. Everybody always gets their winnings. I need to give you something extra under the table. Now I can't just give away my only remaining possessions here, but I can answer any questions you might have. Maybe I can help you out in this way."

The Radioman gazed around the room. He could not think of anything to ask that would not blow his act of being a local. He searched for a question until his vision landed on his winnings wagon. He carefully worded his question. "The parts you gave me, if I were to assemble them, what should I be expecting?"

The dealer pursed his lips in thought. "Look, all I know for sure about those parts is that they are of high value. I have had them checked. They are genuine robotic parts, pre-collapse tech. Apparently, nobody can make these parts anymore due to the extreme temperatures during manufacture or something. However, my guy couldn't tell what they would be if assembled. He is not that great at constructing the parts, only digging up their value."

The Radioman nodded. He had come up with another question. "Do you know the whereabouts of a millinery?"

The dealer furrowed his brow. "A what?"

"A millinery." The dealer remained perplexed. "Maybe you are more familiar with a haberdashery?"

The dealer laughed. "Hey, I deal cards for a living here. I am good with probabilities, not speeches."

The Radioman smiled and let out a short sigh. "I am looking for a place where I can buy clothing, specifically for the woman."

The dealer grew perplexed once more. "Well, there is only the one clothing store down the road, and they sell protective clothing for workers, but as you know, we are all men down here. Getting women's clothing is going to be difficult. You will have to get it like you got your suit."

The Radioman did not know about any of this. He could not ask without blowing the cover. He played along. "Where did you find her anyway? Why hasn't she been removed?" This was a wild guess from the Radioman. He was hoping that the vague sentence was enough to keep the dealer talking and get more information.

"We found her here. Actually, the doorman found her. The doorman felt bad for her running in hiding on the streets, so he took her in here. She worked in the back for a while until the word got out to the patrons here. I made it very clear that the woman could work here if they all promised to keep it a secret. They all agreed, mostly because they liked the looks of her, and she could make a mean Shroomshine."

The Radioman acted like he knew what that was. The Radioman pried more. "So why did you bet her?"

The dealer cracked a wide grin. "I am a betting man at heart. She is quite a liability anyway, and you asked for her." The Radioman could understand this. The dealer continued. "That was also why we had her chained up. We did not want her running out into the streets and getting caught." The Radioman did not understand that. He stopped asking questions. The dealer shrugged happily. "Welp, I need to get back to the table. There are new players from the crowd you drew in." He extended his hand. "You are always welcome back."

The Radioman took his hand firmly and shook it. Before the Radioman let go, he leaned in very close to the dealer and whispered to him. "The world is still out there, you know. Don't forget about it." He leaned away from the dealer and nodded toward the Old Man. The dealer peeked back at the Radioman, understanding the reference, took one last long look at him, nodded with genuine appreciation, released his grip, turned, and strutted back to the table. "Who is ready for some Decker?" he exclaimed while holding both arms outward in front of and above his body. The crowd exclaimed excitement, and people started down into the pit to fill the table.

The Radioman started toward the door. On his way, he took a slight detour to the table he had walked past on the way in. There, he quickly removed an entire handful of chips he had kept in his pocket and placed them on the table. "I have repaid what I have borrowed with interest," he murmured to the thin air behind the table. He started up to the door, where the woman was standing. She was having a quiet conversation with Eyebrows. The Radioman caught the tail end of the conversation as he walked over. Eyebrows was talking first. "You do?"

"I don't know. I will have to go with them. I have been pawned off."

"You don't have to go."

"It is my only chance."

Eyebrows noticed the Radioman approaching. "I did not mean to intrude."

Eyebrows shook his head. "We were just saying goodbye."

The Radioman looked over at the woman. He caught her gaze. She wished for something. He looked back to Eyebrows. "Is the old fellow outside?"

"Yes."

"Good. I will be outside talking to him. You two finish up and then allow her to meet me outside to depart."

The both of them relaxed slightly. The Radioman snatched the prized wagon handle and towed it out through the door as Eyebrows held it open. The door closed softly behind him. He sat down next to the Old Man, up against the wall, and rubbed his forehead with his hand. The Old Man said nothing as he watched the Radioman deflate into exhaustion. They sat there for a few moments until the woman came out, rubbing her thigh where the band had been. "All good?" asked the Radioman.

"Yes," replied the woman. This was the first time the Radioman and the Old Man had heard her voice at full speaking volume. It was smooth and rich.

"All right, then. Let's get going." The Old Man stood and started around the corner, heading toward the same direction he was going before the stranger had stopped him. The Radioman was busy fiddling with the handle on the wagon as the Old Man rounded the corner. Just as soon as the Old Man was out of sight, the woman snapped her sight down to the Radioman.

She strutted over, the heels of her shoes clacking on the rock surface. She stopped just behind the Radioman. He looked over his shoulder at her. She bent at the waist and grabbed his stomach, pulling him to his feet. The Radioman dropped the handle gently to the ground and turned to face her as he stood. The woman pushed him, nearly knocking him over. He tumbled into a secluded cubby on the wall behind him. The woman stepped in after him, placing her hands on either of his cheeks.

She tipped his head and lurched forward, kissing him quickly. Meanwhile, the Radioman was very perplexed but also starstruck by being kissed by this beautiful woman he had just met. He did not know what to do in this current situation. He broke up the kiss. "That was a bit forward, wasn't it?"

The woman smirked. "Yes. It was more of a thank-you."

"For what?"

"For getting me out of that damned cardhouse." The woman pushed forward once more, sitting the Radioman down on a ledge, straddling his right knee, and reaching for his coat button while dragging the ribbons on the bikini along with her.

The Radioman pushed her away. "I appreciate the thought, but I am afraid you are unaware that we may have an audience." The woman stood sharply. She looked down at her clothing, still the brown bra and bikini combo, and turned shyly to see if anyone was behind her. After not seeing anyone, she turned back to the Radioman. "The audience may not want to be seen. I will explain later. For now, we need to find you some clothing, and you need to explain some things." The woman nodded, adjusting her bra back into a comfortable position, as she had let it slip in the moment.

The two stepped back out of the cubby, and the woman handed the Radioman the handle of the robotic parts wagon. They both took strides to catch up with the Old Man. The Old Man spoke up while taking the handle of the wagon. "So do you know where a clothing store is?"

The Radioman broke in. "I heard there was only one in town, and it only sells men's clothing."

The Old Man looked over at the woman. "Well, I mean, I am not complaining here, but I figured we should get her something to wear. Are you comfortable in that?"

The woman looked over at the Old Man. "Yes. I have gotten used to it. The shoes are what are uncomfortable."

The Old Man shrugged. "Take 'em off. We don't mind."

The woman stopped and stood in awe as if that had never occurred to her. She bent down, cautiously untied the straps, and slid her foot from the shoe. The skin on her foot was indented to match the tight bands of the shoes. She rubbed her foot, and the indentations began to fade. She winced as she set her foot down on the cold rock.

"How long has it been since you took those off?" questioned the Old Man.

The woman frowned. "I don't remember the last time I had them off." She wiggled her feet and stretched her toes.

"What about your clothes?"

"I get a clean bra and bikini once a day. They force me to change into a new one, whether I want to or not." She paused, noticing a subtle confusion. "The bikini slips right over the shoe. That was how I kept them on." The confusion dwindled. "They say it keeps the look and feel of the cardhouse fresh when I change each day. But this particular set is luckily one of my favorites to wear as it is the most comfortable. It provides plenty of support."

"So what did they make you do in there?"

The woman went silent. The Old Man broke the silence. "I am sorry. I didn't—"

"No, it is fine. I am just not ready to talk about my past at the moment." The Radioman nodded, unsure of where to take the conversation now. The woman sighed and shook her head. She glanced up, meeting the Radioman's gaze. She melted. "I will never be ready to talk about it. I might as well just get it over with." She rubbed her forehead. "They made me bartend among other things. That wasn't the bad part, though. They…they never did anything to me." She struggled to continue.

"They just never let me out. I was always in that bar. This is the first time I have been outside in weeks. The only other time was for a few moments when a man decided he was going to shoot his shot, and things got uncomfortable. As you know, I am the only woman that I know of down here. There are a lot of men. They are all pretty lonely." She stopped for a moment. "They took me outside while the man was dealt with."

She cut herself off. She was obviously hiding something. The Radioman gently touched her shoulder, making sure to keep his distance. "If there is anything that we should know about this place or anywhere else to keep you safe, then you need to let us know. We are here to help you. If you need anything, just ask. You don't have to tell us your story if you don't want to."

The woman seemed pleased by this, but not in a way that led the Radioman to believe that he had comforted her. She shuffled away a short distance. "I understand."

The Radioman nodded in response. He began to turn away to walk the road some more but hesitated and turned back. "We are going to see the rest of our group. They are passing through, like me. They won't bother you if you do not want to speak to them." The woman began walking, prodding the Radioman to continue moving. The Radioman looked over at the Old Man and cocked his head as a signal to start walking. The Old Man tugged on the wagon handle to get it moving and followed along.

A short time later, the Hobo popped his head around a corner, scaring the woman. He stared blatantly at the woman for a moment before the Radioman flicked his forehead. He winced silently and backed up around the corner, motioning to the woman and raising an eyebrow. The Radioman stepped around the corner, out of sight of the woman, and shook his head vigorously while scolding the Hobo with his eyes. The Hobo raised his hands and began walking down an alleyway toward the lake. The Old Man and the woman followed while the wagon rattled loudly down the uneven path.

The group of four then came up on a narrow pathway down over the stone face. After the Hobo had scanned the area, he motioned them along and followed the winding path down over the face to a dark cubby. He motioned with his left hand as he shimmied into a smooth horizontal crack in the face of stone. He had to lay on his stomach and wiggle in by pushing with his feet. The Old Man dropped the handle of the cart on the ground, stepped forward, and peeked into the gap. "It is pitch-black in there," he reported to the Radioman.

A familiar voice echoed out. "It is much larger once you get inside. The tunnel bends to the right. There are lights in here."

The Radioman recognized the Mechanic's voice. "Mechanic? How did you fit through this gap?"

There was a short chuckle from younger voices followed by a short pause. "It wasn't easy. Just get in here."

The Old Man peeked back at the Radioman. They exchanged shrugs, and the Old Man slid into the crack. He slowly wormed into the crack until he completely disappeared. The Old Man's voice echoed out. "All right. It is clear."

The Radioman looked over at the woman, expecting her to resist. To his surprise, she was already walking toward the crack. She threw her summer wedges, which she had been carrying ever since taking them off before, into the dark crevice and clambered in. She was surprisingly quick to get through the tunnel. She jumped and let out a short yelp as her bare stomach touched the cold stone surface. She smiled lightly and peered back at the Radioman. "That's cold!" she exclaimed. The Radioman was starstruck by that smile. He had not seen her smile yet. It was wonderful.

As she disappeared, the Old Man explained, "We have a guest. Make sure to keep her comfortable."

The Radioman started toward the crack but was caught by the handle of the wagon. He stood straight. He was caught with the realization that he would not be able to fit the cart through the crack. He stooped once more and spoke into the darkness. "What about the cart?"

There was a pause. "How much is in it?"

The Radioman peeked back at the cart. "It is full, but there are numerous pieces of rather good size. Maybe I can pass them in?"

The Old Man responded, "All right. Pass in the goods. Do you have my staff out there?"

The Radioman stood once more and peered back at the wagon. The staff was placed up against once side of the wagon, pinned in with various parts. "Yes."

"Pass it in first. We could use the light in here." A shuffling sound came from within the darkness. The Radioman attempted to grab the staff and poke it into the gap. It suddenly ripped forward into the dark without him ever touching it. The Radioman retracted his hand in surprise. The Old Man's voice met his ear. "Thanks." There was a finger-snapping noise. "That's better. Where is the first part?"

The Radioman unloaded the parts from the wagon to the Old Man. The Radioman began to wonder how much space there actually was in this cubby. He informed the Old Man that he had given him everything but the wagon and asked for the backpack to put all the credits from the cardhouse inside of. He pushed the backpack back into the crevice and waited a moment for it to disappear. He stashed the wagon up against the rock face and slid into the gap. He wiggled in and made the right bend to spot a light at the end of the tunnel. He shimmied to the end and poked his arms out. A massive hand grabbed his arm and dragged him out of the tunnel. "Hello there, Radioman," said the Mechanic with a wide smile.

The Radioman smiled in return. "Hello, Mechanic. Hello, everyone." He brushed off his coat as he sat up. "So what do we have here?" The Mechanic stepped aside, revealing a large square room. Rusted piping lined the far wall, riddled with holes. The left wall was comprised of brick, chipping at the corners and covered in a blackish slime. The right wall was made of the same stone as the tunnel. The floor was textured with hundreds of small square stone tiles. "What is this place?"

The Mechanic shrugged. "More like what was it. My best guess is, this used to be a station of some kind that got abandoned. A set of pipes must have run out the crevice we came in, which might be why it is so straight with one bend in it." He brushed past the Radioman and pointed at a small circle on the wall. It was once a gauge of some kind, but the glass had been shattered, and the dial in it was unreadable. "I think this was a pressure valve. Maybe this was a water pumping station, which would explain why it is so close to the lake."

The Radioman nodded. He turned to face the rest of the group, who had collected against the right stone wall, except for the woman. The woman was across the room, examining the slime. The Radioman couldn't help but chuckle. The Survivalist had her head against the wall, eyes closed, presumably taking a nap. The rest of the masculine line was entranced by the woman. The Radioman stepped into the field of view, breaking the spell, and began speaking. "I suppose I have some explaining to do."

The Old Man stood. "I suppose I do as well." The Old Man began, explaining how he did not see any other choice but to go into the building. The stranger was not going to let him pass, and he feared he would be harmed if he walked away. He then passed off to the Radioman, who explained the betting and card game and how he had won it all. This led him to explaining the woman. He quickly explained how he had bet to try to get her out of the bar as she seemed miserable.

The woman stood, finally prying her eyes from the slime. "You are correct, I was miserable. But you all have no idea what this place is, do you?" The group remained silent. "The City of Underground? You don't know anything about it?" Nobody replied. The woman sighed. She stiffened her jaw. "If I tell you this story and anyone finds out, they will kill me and you all both. If I don't tell you the story, then you may never get out of here alive, especially with the guns you are toting.

"It is not my problem that you all are stuck in here even though you don't know it yet. However, your maroon friend here just gave me the opportunity I have been waiting years for. I have to repay him somehow. Risking my own life here is the only thing I can do to repay the debt." She stopped while she collected her thoughts. "If anyone asks, you did not get this information from me. Agreed?" The group nodded. "I need a verbal conformation."

The group collectively agreed, including the Survivalist, who had awaken a few moments ago after hearing an unfamiliar voice. The woman furrowed her brow. "I suppose I should start with a name, but you all seem to go by an alias. I won't ask why, but I will conform. Call me the Bartender." She paused while thinking that name over. She shrugged after failing to come up with anything better.

"As your friend in maroon here, whom I have gathered to be called the Radioman, has likely begun to figure out at this point, this cave is not as friendly as it might seem. Life is harsh down here. The whole city is an analogy in itself. On the surface, it looks to be nothing more than a mountain. However, if you dig a little deeper, you find entire populations.

"This is the same with the people. On the surface, they are all friendly and cooperative. However, deeper down, everyone here is looking for a way out. Now we all know of two exits, one of which your friend the Radioman here came in through if his tale was true." She looked over at the Radioman.

He quickly butted in. "That is true. We did come in from the far side of the lake."

She waited for him to buckle under the pressure of her stare. He didn't falter. She seemed appeased. "All right, then. So you did. What about the rest of you? Judging by the backpack and guns sitting around it, I am assuming you all are not down here legally."

The Young spoke. "We came in around the guards."

The Bartender whipped her piercing vision over to the Young. The Young responded with a sudden awareness that he might have made a mistake. The Bartender took a shuffling step forward. "How?"

The Young peeked around the room. No one seemed concerned about this situation. He guessed it was all right to tell her. "There was a grate loose on a wall. We snuck in through the vents after climbing over the stone wall."

The Bartender showed disbelief. She turned to scan the room. "You got past the guards? There is…" She took a quick inhale as a sharp clap filled the room. She snapped her gaze behind her to find nothing but the wall where the Young was before.

A voice came from where she was just looking as she spoke. "I might be more stealthy than you think." The woman snapped back around, following the voice, to see an empty space between her and the group. There was a snap of fingers behind her. She turned again, this time spotting the Young propped up against the wall where he had started. The Bartender adjusted her bikini bottom back into place as she glared at the Young. The Young cut her off by holding up his hand before she could begin. "It is nothing personal. I just find that to be very convincing."

The Survivalist cracked a smile. The Bartender realized she had just received proof of his skill. She tried to relax but remained visibly angry. "Let's assume you are slick enough to get through. What about the rest of you? Surely not all of you are this quiet."

The Young spoke up once more as he crossed the room to be with the group. "They aren't. I went in to make sure it was safe and then guided them across with hand signals."

The Bartender relaxed. "And you were able to fit in the vents?"

The Young shrugged. "Yeah."

The Bartender looked over to the Mechanic. "You fitted in a ventilation duct?"

The Mechanic smiled. "It was not a pleasant time." The Bartender waited for a clearer answer. The Mechanic pointed to the tunnel into the room. "I got through that tunnel, didn't I?"

The Bartender grew surprised before falling into thought. After a pause, she spoke once more. "Did you take a ventilation duct all the way in here?"

The Old Man spoke up. "Hey, lady, if you are just fishing for answers to get yourself out of here, you can forget it. Remember that the Radioman over there just got you out of a situation that you were likely never getting out of otherwise. Why don't you finish what you were going to tell us before we go answering all your questions?"

The Bartender stiffened. She backed into the far side of the room. After a moment, she nodded. "The people down here are all looking for a way out. Like I said, we know of two exits—the one you all apparently came in across the lake and the other just up the road from this end of the city.

"The one across the lake has never worked as an escape route. The only reason you would ever be over there is to leave the city. It is too obvious. The second entrance close to us now is heavily guarded on both the surface as well as underground all the time. It never stops. They just change out men. That entrance is about as long as the one you came in on as well, meaning we can't just sprint through the whole thing."

The Bartender stopped noticing that the Mechanic had a question. The Mechanic took the opportunity. "Why are they guarded? Can't you all just leave anytime?"

The Bartender smirked. "Of course not. We are held down here like criminals." She frowned as they remained confused. "There is a man keeping us trapped down here. We call him the Prospector for the lack of his real name. You likely haven't ever seen him, as he typically roams the nearby surface grounds, living a sun-filled life. We do not know why he won't let us leave, but we do know he is searching for something. He couldn't find it.

"For some reason, he was convinced that the thing he wanted was here underground, in this ancient aquifer. He hired a team to dig the two entrances we now have and to force a sinkhole that would drain the water and result in the lake. That was where the population of the city as well as I came into play. I personally came down in hopes of finding a working man to support my family. We were rather poor, and working as a woman was not socially acceptable in my old community.

"Anyway, digging the tunnels was a success. However, he never found the thing he was looking for or, at least, was not satisfied. He pushed his mining crew to the limits. They tried to quit. As they left the site, the man went insane. He had anticipated their resistance and hired a small army of guards. They herded the majority of the miners back down into the aquifer and told them to get busy building a civilization or die. They were never leaving this place until they found this mysterious thing that the Prospector was looking for. I was stuck down here with them.

"Only a select few people whom the Prospector could trust were allowed to know what the thing actually was. If they ever told anyone what it was without the consent of the Prospector, both the teller and the listener were executed on the spot. There were three groups killed for this reason that I know of, but the details here are not important.

"Once the trapped people, including myself, began to starve, we discovered you could eat the shrooms down here, hence began civilization. Many years later, the teams of engineers, miners, and other technical-savvy people used the tools at their disposal that were supposed to be used for mining to collect materials and build the City of Underground you know today.

"People got to the point that they stopped digging for the mysterious item the Prospector wanted. They would often break things as a way to get new materials from the Prospector, who yet again never came down here and simply approved the equipment. That was how things like the geothermal power plant, the lighting, and even the neon on some of the signs got constructed.

"They leeched the parts off the equipment to do it and got away with it by saying it was there to enhance the mining process, and it indirectly did help by allowing for electric drilling instead of the use of fume-producing fuels. The Prospector then realized that women were not helping the fake mining effort. Instead of letting the women out, the sick bastard had any one of them discovered to be affecting the working life of a mining man exiled, which is to say that virtually all women were executed in the first day regardless of being affiliated with a man or not.

"Rumors spread that he had said something about the risk of opening the gates being too high to let the women out since the men could riot out of the gates behind them. I hid for weeks until they finally gave up on executing the rest of the resisting women, figuring they had driven us out or starved us anyway, although the rule was still in place. I was still in danger, and I was looking for a way to hide. That was when the huge bouncer that the Radioman met, the one with the bushy eyebrows, got ahold of me and took me to the dealer. At first, he tried to strike a corrupt deal with me to work for food. I knew how to get my own food at this point. I did not need him. Then he resorted to threatening to tell the guards that he had me if I ever acted out, which worked for a while, but then he realized that men really liked looking at me, especially with the shortage of women around.

"He used me as a way to bait men into his cardhouse, forcing every person to swear to my secrecy, which they all happily did to continue seeing me. This led me to be a valuable piece of property to him, so he lost the ability to call the guards to have me killed. He instead chained me to that bar to work as the bartender. Luckily, no man was ever allowed to touch me, as he discovered my value would go down drastically if I was ever discovered to be in an affair with a man. And naturally, that could never happen if he wanted to remain profitable. However, dressing me up in this outfit was still on the table."

She ran her hand along the length of the ribbon draping down the side of her leg from the bikini bottom. "I figured I would spend the rest of my life like that. I could get out of the cardhouse somehow, but then the guards would have killed me on sight. After a long while, I figured so many people had visited the cardhouse and saw me that it didn't really matter if I was outside anymore. If people were going to tell the guards about me, they already would have done it. That left me with one issue.

"I had nowhere to run from the dealer. I am stuck in this cave like you all are now. He was bound to hunt me down eventually even if I got out of the cardhouse. That left me to staying in that bar, delivering drinks to lusty men, until your friend the Radioman walked in." She pointed over at the Radioman.

"I figured the Radioman was going to be just like everyone else, just here looking for cards and instead found a woman, but he showed a different interest in me. He wanted to help me. That makes him different from everyone else here. He wasn't out to exploit me like the others. For better or worse, he—and apparently, all of you—still has hopes of getting out of here." The Bartender went silent.

The Survivalist was first up. "How do you know all of this?"

The Bartender raised an eyebrow. "I spent a long time running and listening. You have to be keen to the events around you when you are running for your life. Even after I got stuck in the cardhouse, I could still listen in on conversations the men were having and get some idea of what was happening." This appeased the Survivalist.

The Old Man spoke up. "How many years ago was that? When the Prospector trapped you all?"

The Bartender thought it over. "I am not sure. For a long while, we had no way of knowing the time. None of our devices worked down here due to a strange magnetic field. It must be over ten years at least with our current approximations."

The Old Man squinted. "Do you know about the Crisis, then?"

The Bartender turned to face the Old Man. "The what?"

The Old Man stared in shock. "You have no idea that the outside world is completely changed? Forever gone from what it was?"

The Bartender chuckled. "You are surely joking."

The Old Man shook his head. "The entire world you knew outside is gone. The people you knew are likely dead. The places you knew have probably been either ransacked, destroyed, reclaimed by nature, or some combination of the three."

The Bartender chuckled more awkwardly, but her laughing dwindled slowly as it was replaced by a grim realization. She scanned the face of each person for validity of the statement. She started in very quietly. "You are serious?"

The Old Man nodded. "Wish I weren't."

The woman took a step back. "Everything is gone?"

The Radioman stepped forward. He explained. "Yes. There are still some ruins of cities and some old buildings, but civilization as you knew it is gone." The Bartender ran through a series of emotions. She appeared near to crying. The Radioman walked across the room and gently grabbed her by the shoulders. The Bartender started to resist, but her defenses melted when she saw it was the Radioman. The Radioman hugged her gently. The Bartender did nothing. She did not cry or speak or move. She did not even hug the Radioman back. She simply stared off blankly over the Radioman's shoulder at the wall with her arms limp at her sides.

The Radioman spoke as he hugged her. "There is still a whole world out there. It is just completely different from what you left." He paused as she continued sobbing. He tried attempting to comfort her. "This is probably a lot for you to handle, but you seem to have accepted this information without much explanation. Has someone told you about this before?"

The Bartender drew in a breath. "Yes, but they were from inside here. Nobody believed them. We just thought it was all a rumor to try to keep us pinned down in here. I know you all are from the outside, so now I know what they said is true."

The Bartender coughed gently. The Radioman's face grew concerned. "Are you all right?"

The Bartender pushed the Radioman away. "Yes." She recomposed herself. "I just had hopes that it was all false information. I had so much I wanted to do when we got out. I wanted to see my family again, but I haven't seen them in so long, and I have changed so much in this cave that I doubt they would recognize me." The Bartender began to trail off once more.

The Radioman wanted to ask about her family and why they weren't down here with her, but he decided against it on the terms that it might be too much for her to handle. He glanced sadly at the group, motioning with his hand in a cutting motion to tell them to stop asking questions, and caught her attention. "How about we focus on how we can all get out of this place? That seems to be the priority at hand. Once we are out, we can worry about what to do next."

The Bartender coughed once more and shook her head. "I don't know that there is a way out."

Everyone fell silent. The Radioman walked back over to the group. He prodded the conversation along. "While I was playing cards, I realized that the guards here are not primarily keeping people out. They are keeping you all in here. This would be why they do not allow weapons to be brought in, as it would give the people inside an advantage in escape. I figured they let people like us in to see if we will work and then kill us if we don't. Is all of this correct?"

The Bartender nodded. "This is how they collect new people. It is a shame that they let in someone as old as you, though." She nodded toward the Old Man.

The Old Man grew disgruntled. "I still have some life in me, thank you. No need to bury me before I am dead." The Bartender didn't know how to respond to this. She stood idle for a moment.

The Radioman asked another question. "Do you think we could sneak out of the entrance here?"

The Bartender slid away from the group. "No. The guards are too stiff in their posts, and the door is alarmed."

The Entrepreneur stepped forward, spooking the woman. She had not noticed him standing silently against the wall. He held up his hands to show he meant no threat while asking his question. "Do these guards get paid?"

The Bartender showed a perplexed face as a reaction to the sudden change of topic. "I suppose so."

"They are paid in credits?"

The Bartender nodded. "I think so."

"How much are they paid?"

The Bartender cracked a smile. "Not enough. They hate their jobs, but it is all they can get. Nobody in this city will hire them. They are like traitors."

The Entrepreneur displayed a wide grin. "So they might be, oh, bribable?"

The Bartender cocked her head to the side. "What are you getting at?"

The Entrepreneur stepped into the brighter middle of the room. "Well, the way I see it, the Radioman has just won quite a sum of credits at the cardhouse along with you and the parts we have piled up over there. We could use those credits to bribe the guards, couldn't we?"

The Bartender turned to fully face the Entrepreneur. "It would take quite a talker to bribe the guards."

"But it is still on the table?"

The Bartender straightened her head and raised her chin. "I suppose so."

The Entrepreneur adjusted his weight forward on his toes, toward the woman. "Then we shouldn't have any issues." He set his weight back onto his feet.

The woman placed her left hand on her hip and pointed at the Entrepreneur with her right. She appeared amused. "You are going to bribe the guards to get them to let you out? Don't you think that other people down here have tried that already?"

The Entrepreneur smiled. "Sure. They tried. However, those guards have never met me."

The woman raised an eyebrow. The Entrepreneur crossed his arms. The woman shook her head. "Normally, I would advise against this, but you are so cocky that failing here might do you good. I'd like to see you try."

The Entrepreneur laughed. "You underestimate me." He turned to the group. "Does that sound like a plan to you all?"

The Old Man spoke up. "I suppose we can't use it outside anyway. We might as well use it to bribe the guards."

The Mechanic nodded. "I would also like to keep the backpack as empty as possible. We do not need to be carrying extra weight. The credits in the backpack are taking up a lot of space."

The group went silent. The Radioman picked up the conversation. "So we are in agreement?"

"No, not yet. How is the Entrepreneur going to be seen by the guards? Won't they know he isn't here legally?" asked the Survivalist.

The Bartender laughed. Once her laughter dwindled off, she stated, "They don't check if you are here legally. What are those guards going to do even if they find out you are here illegally? They are just going to keep you in here. The only thing that would lead to a threat is them seeing me, that girl over there, or any of your weapons." Nobody could argue that. "Just walk in like you live here. The Radioman did just fine with it."

The Entrepreneur nodded. "Are there any details I should know about how people sell things down here?" The Bartender looked over at the Entrepreneur, prodding for details. He continued. "Dealing? Favors? Illegal item trading? Haggling?"

The Bartender lit up with understanding. "Dealing, yes. Do not do any of the rest. You are already pushing your luck by trying to buy out a guard."

The Entrepreneur nodded. The room fell silent. The Old Man clapped his hands. "All right! Let's do it." He walked to the center of the room, bent, picked up the staff, which had been lighting the room, and started to the gap.

The Radioman made a note. "Do not forget, we must find Bartender some clothes. You do want clothes, right, Bartender?"

The Bartender smiled. "Have the women on the surface lost their love of clothes shopping?"

The Survivalist answered, "Yes."

The Bartender tucked in her chin, obviously taken aback by the realization. She broke her own awkward situation. "Under the assumption I should have them, yes, I would like some clothes."

The Survivalist spoke again. "Good. Your skin would likely burn without it."

The whole room paused for a moment. The Hobo spoke up. "Do you think that is going to be a problem? Her skin getting sunburned? She has not been outside in ages."

The Young replied, "Does getting sunburned matter on how long you have been out of the sun beforehand?"

"I think people with darker skin tend to get a sunburn slower. If that is true, then she will burn before any of us due to her light skin," said the Mechanic.

The Bartender seemed a bit uncomfortable in the current situation. She shuffled about the floor, trying to look useful as the group gathered their things. The Radioman peeked over at the Bartender. "Do you know of a place to get clothing? I cannot recall if you told me or not."

The woman shook her head. "No. The only store mentioned was the one up the street, and it only sells men's clothes. After all, the women got…removed."

The group looked around at one another, waiting for someone to speak. "Well, I suppose we at least go look there for something. Even men's clothing would be better than nothing," stated the Radioman. The Bartender did not seem thrilled.

The group passed their things back out of the crevice and loaded the robotic parts back into the wagon. The Old Man walked out onto the empty street and waved the group on. The group followed the Hobo along the shadows. The Old Man peeked back once in a while to receive directions from the woman, who remembered most of the streets from her days of hiding. The Old Man located the clothing store and walked up to the front door. It was dark inside but for a lantern.

He tried the door and was surprised to find it open. He peeked inside but found nobody. A sign was sitting on the counter: "Take what you need and leave the credits on the table." Below the boldly scrawled letters, in a smaller print, read, "Remember, there are only so many places to run in this cave." The Old Man looked back out to the street and spotted the group. He scanned the area carefully. After finding nobody, he pointed to the woman and motioned her over.

The Hobo said something to her, and she ran quickly across the street. The Old Man held the door open for her as she scurried inside. He held his hand out to tell the Hobo to stay put. The Hobo responded with a quick wave. The Old Man went inside and closed the door. "Well, I suppose this is going to be a lot easier since you can try on the clothes."

The Bartender pinched a pair of jeans on a shelf. "I suppose so."

"Where are all the people?"

"They are all either working in the mines where the power plant is or hiding to act like they are working. Remember, anyone caught out this time of day is likely to be questioned by guards."

"Where are all the guards?"

"They typically don't patrol this part of town. They focus more on the areas around the power plant." She stood from looking at some jeans near the floor on a shelf and looked at the Old Man. "When did you guys get here anyway?"

The Old Man shrugged. "Yesterday, I suppose. It is hard to tell down here."

The woman smiled. "No. I meant what time."

The Old Man raised his hands palms up. "How would I know?"

"What was going on when you walked into town? Was it empty like it is now, or were people out and about?"

The Old Man remembered that all the workers had been headed into the power plant. "There were a bunch of people headed into the power plant."

The woman chuckled. "You got lucky. That is one of the only times the guards allow people to roam for a bit. The guards and workers both can talk and catch up with each other. A bit later, it was probably completely empty again." The Old Man nodded. The woman shook her head. "You are very lucky to have not been caught by the guards around the power plant by crossing the area on the only time in the day it is accepted."

The Old Man did not know the significance of the statement. "I did not see a single guard."

"That is because they look just like regular people. They blend in undercover to avoid getting harassed all of the time. The only exceptions are the guards obviously holding the main entrance gates to the city." The Old Man didn't respond. A moment later, the woman pulled out a pair of jeans from the shelf. "What about these?" She held them up to herself. They seemed to be a proper length, but the waistline was far too large.

"They look wonderful."

The woman peeked up at the Old Man. "You never looked."

The Old Man shook his head. "No. I don't need to. My answer would be the same no matter what you wear." The woman seemed caught between accepting this as a compliment and detecting that the Old Man was avoiding an argument. The Old Man detected a disturbance himself. "I know better than to tell a woman she looks bad."

This the Bartender could not argue with. She looked down and nodded once. She looked back up. "Seriously, what do you think?"

The Old Man crossed his arms and raised an eyebrow. The woman scoffed and turned away. A voice came from behind her. "They look fine, but the waistline will never fit."

She turned to see the Radioman closing the entrance door. She sneered at the Old Man and gestured to the Radioman. "See? He gives me an honest answer."

The Old Man furrowed his brow. "I did too," he murmured quietly.

The Bartender tossed the pants onto the shelf and began searching for more. The Radioman looked over to the Old Man. "I figured you would need a form of payment." He held up his hand, palm up, exposing a small pile of dull silver coins. The Old Man took one. He had not taken the time to observe one of the coins yet. He walked over to a gas lantern that had been quietly and dimly lighting the room.

The lamp was a heavy short boxy black metallic thing. On one side, three flaps were positioned horizontally so that they did not obstruct the light but for a few narrow strips of shade. He located a moving part on one of the sides near the bottom, a short crank, and gave it a spin. The lantern shifted, flipping the three shades shut. He reversed directions on the crank. All four sides of the lantern flipped open with three horizontal shades that were previously blocking the light. The room grew noticeably brighter, but it was still dreary.

The Old Man fumbled around once more until he found a knob on the exact opposite side as the crank. He twisted it gently. The knob refused to move for a moment before squeaking and twisting abruptly. The unflickering small flame shaped like a teardrop inside the lantern nearly doubled in size, spooking the Old Man as he twisted the knob back a bit to reduce the flame. He turned his head to find the room much better lit. "Sensitive knob." The other two smiled.

He looked back at the lantern and held up the coin. It was about an inch in diameter with a rounded rim around the outside edges. The coin had plain a design of a moonshroom on it on one side. The other side was more detailed. It showed a sharp upward point comprised of two lines. Under the point, there were multiple rectangles with small indentations near a smooth circle. The Old Man gathered that this must be a simplistic depiction of the City of Underground. He ran his finger around the smooth edge of the coin before turning back to the other two in the room.

The Bartender had already found another pair of pants. She was holding them up to herself, and the Radioman was judging. This pair got denied. She went back to searching. Multiple pairs of pants later, the Bartender found a pair of jeans that would fit her waist but were too short for her. She tried them on anyway by pulling them over her bikini. "What about these?"

The Radioman answered, "They fit your waist well, but they are entirely too short."

The Bartender glanced down at her legs. The pants only reached about halfway down her calves. "Is there a sewing kit in here?" she asked.

The Radioman perked slightly. "You know how to sew?"

"No, but I figured it would be a start."

"I know how to sew."

The Bartender stopped and stared. "You know how to sew?" The Radioman nodded. The Bartender seemed on the verge of debate but let out a short sigh. "All right. I believe you." The Radioman glanced over at the Old Man in surprise. The Radioman swiveled back and began looking for a sewing kit. The Old Man stood idle for a moment before starting his own search. "Ah! I found a needle!" exclaimed the Bartender. She stood from behind the register counter and held it out triumphantly.

"Is there any thread?" asked the Radioman.

The Bartender glanced down and nabbed a black spool. "Yes."

"Perfect. Let me have it and the needle." The Bartender handed it to the Radioman once he crossed the room. The Old Man carried the lantern over and placed it on the register counter. The Radioman grabbed the nearby pants. "Can you put these back on?" The Bartender took the jeans and slid them on, stuffing the long bow on the bikini inside the leg. The Radioman walked around the counter. "Do you want me to take the slack out of the cuffs? The rest seems to fit well enough."

The Bartender replied, "Yes. I think you can make these a nice mid length." The Radioman held up the needle to the Bartender's leg. She jumped away. "You aren't going to sew with these on me, are you?"

The Radioman angled his head up from his crouched position. "Of course not. I said I was only marking the place to sew." He motioned her back over. She complied. He gently threaded the needle through the fabric once and held on to the string. "All right. Now I need you to take the jeans off so that I can sew them. Careful to not break the thread."

The Bartender removed the jeans and gave them to the Radioman. The Radioman took a stool from behind the counter and sat down near the lantern. The Old Man spoke up. "How long will this take?"

"Fifteen to thirty minutes."

"Is it all right if I bring the group in? They are probably wondering what is going on."

"Sure." The Old Man walked to the door and then outside to go get the group.

The Bartender reached out and grabbed the Radioman's left hand. He froze, trying not to prick her with the needle. "We do not have an audience now, Radioman." The Radioman peeked up at the Bartender. She placed her other hand on his cheek and twisted his head to face her. She leaned forward and kissed him. The Radioman remained stiff while blindly trying to find a place to put the needle. He found a spot and reached over to hold her.

A voice came from outside. The Radioman pushed the Bartender away instead. She stood, realizing the group was about to walk in, and walked around to the far side of the counter. The Radioman floundered for the needle and began sewing once more. The Young stepped through the door. "It is dark in here." The Old Man followed with the Survivalist, the Hobo, and the Entrepreneur close behind.

There was a rattling, and the wagon was pushed through the doorway by the Mechanic.

The Young looked over at the Radioman as he struggled to see the needle. "Why don't you guys just use the staff to light up the room?" The Old Man looked over with a perplexed face, which he switched to realization, and then shook the staff in his hand a bit. It made a buzzing sound, and a beam of light shot out. It was blisteringly bright compared to the dark room.

The Old Man squinted and waved his arm across the room. The light spread to fill the whole room. He walked out into the center of the room and held it out in front of himself. He dropped it. The staff caught itself with a whirring noise and stood straight. The Old Man went to lean on a post. The Bartender spoke. "Why did we not think to do that?" She shook her head and turned off the lantern.

The Old Man shrugged. "I guess old habits are hard to kill."

The Radioman asked, "Are those scissors?"

The Survivalist picked them up, as she was nearest. "Yes, but not sewing scissors."

The Radioman shrugged. "They will work. Bring them over."

After a bit, the Radioman called the Bartender over. She put on the sewed jeans. They fitted her perfectly. "They feel like they were made for me," she stated.

The Radioman smiled. "That is because they were." He pointed the scissors at her. The jeans hugged the Bartender tightly all the way down to her calves. The dark-blue jeans clashed abruptly with her bright skin. She looked strange in the jeans and only her brown bra on the top half. The Radioman spoke up. "Go on now. Find a shirt to match."

The Bartender pranced barefoot across the stone floor to the shirts and began digging through them. After a few attempts, she found a gray shirt that was the correct length, but her breasts stretched the chest to the point that the bottom hung out from her stomach. The Radioman took the shirt. "This might take a bit. All I had to do to the jeans was stitch the leggings off shorter and bring in around the knees. This is going to require an entire restructure.

These threads look machined—far too even for a needle and sewing by hand. Are we sure there is not a sewing machine somewhere?"

The group went on the hunt for a sewing machine. After a bit, the Hobo spoke up. "Over here. There is a secret compartment with the sewing room." The group gathered around the wall behind the register. A narrow door was open that blended in with the wall. "I used to go in these sometimes to hide from people back in the city. The baker I was with showed me his."

The Radioman stepped inside. The room was almost completely filled with a massive device full of needs and threads. The Radioman glanced back at the group. "I will be honest. I have no idea how this thing works. I will figure it out." He stepped inside with the shirt.

After a few minutes of loud clanging and mechanical oscillating noises, the Radioman thoroughly hacked his way through the first shirt and had to get another similar shirt to patch the final product with. He finally called the Bartender over as he stepped out of the room. "That machine is wonderful, a dream to use once I figured it out. I wish I could take it with me."

The Bartender held up her arms as the Radioman slid the shirt down over her. The Radioman stopped after getting the shirt going and let her finish putting it on. She turned to the group. The shirt was stunning. It fitted tightly to her body. The collar had been converted to a pointed V shape instead of round, which allowed the chest of the shirt to conform to her shape. The sleeves had been cut to fit her arms but now only reached about halfway down her forearm.

The Radioman pointed to her stomach and ran his hands flat down to his waist. The Bartender tucked in the shirt. The shirt hugged up against her stomach and held her back. The group stared. The Survivalist was the first to speak. "Geesh, Radioman, do you want to sew me some clothes too?" The Bartender ran her hand through her long brunette hair and struck a pose. The Radioman stood proud. He could care less about the clothing. He was proud for the Bartender. She was enjoying herself. What a relief it was to see her have some fun.

The Mechanic broke in. "I don't want to ruin your fun, but you need to get some shoes."

The Bartender looked around the room. "What for?"

The Mechanic chuckled. "The outside world is a lot less smooth than the rock you have been walking on."

The Bartender seemed perplexed. "They do not have women's shoes."

She looked at the Radioman. He shrugged. "I don't think I can sew a shoe." She deflated.

The group pondered for a solution. The Entrepreneur snapped his fingers. "Is there a cobbler down here?"

"A what?" asked the Bartender.

"A cobbler." The Bartender didn't reply. "You know, a place that repairs and sells custom shoes?"

The Bartender thought this over. "Actually, I think there is. A fellow a while back at the bar talked about how much he liked his custom work boots. But I know it only sells men's shoes."

The Old Man chuckled. "What size are your feet?" The Bartender did not understand. The Old Man pushed off the post and went over to the counter. "All right, everyone. Get over here and take off your shoes. Except you, Survivalist. You can keep your shoes on. I suppose you can sit out too, Mechanic." The group came over. The Old Man lowered himself to the floor and sat down. "Everyone put their feet out like this. Come on. Get in a circle." The group complied. "Now whose feet are the closest to her feet?"

The group observed their feet. The group focused on the Young. The Young shook his head. "I am not going to go buy women's shoes."

The Old Man smiled. "You won't be buying women's shoes."

*****

After calculating up the price of the clothes they had gotten using a chart on the wall and leaving the credits on the table as requested, the Hobo sealed up the secret compartment room with the sewing machine. The group made their way through the city with the guidance of the Hobo, rough directions from the Bartender, and scouting work from the Old Man. They found the cobbler. A white neon sign spelled The Cave Cobbler in neat and uniform font. The Old Man walked up to the door. It was open. He walked inside.

A voice immediately greeted him in. "Hello there, sir! Welcome to The Cave Cobbler. What are you in need of today?"

The Old Man looked over to find a middle-aged man in a black vest and a white undershirt greeting him. The Old Man was caught off guard by the man's thick curled black mustache as he stepped through the door. "Well, actually, I am not needing anything. You see, I have a son, and he needs shoes that are built tough. They need to last him a long time for a lot of walking. But he also has some rather, oh, strange feet. I was curious if you all could try to help him out."

The vested man considered the idea. "I think we can do just that. When can he be in?"

"Right now."

"Oh! Well, then, show him in if you please."

The Old Man nodded and stepped back out the doorway. He motioned to a corner where the group was hiding. Nothing happened for a moment. Then the Young flew out into the street obviously by being shoved by the Mechanic. He paused for a moment to remove the sheathed knife and tossed it back behind the corner. He walked begrudgingly across the street and up the short steps to the door. "You owe me for this."

"I owe you nothing. The Bartender owes you for this." The Young shook his head. The two stepped inside.

The man in the store greeted the Young similarly to the Old Man. "Hello there! This fellow here has informed me you are in need of a particular kind of shoe designed to fit your foot."

The Young took a moment to take in the man's mustache before answering. "Uh, yes, I need a custom-fit shoe."

The man took no time to point out he had noticed them staring at his mustache. He motioned with a broad sweeping motion and an extended hand for the Young to walk through a nearby doorway. "Right this way, then. I will size up your foot for trial." The Young walked through the doorway. He peeked back and flicked his eyes toward a nearby chair. The Old Man took the hint and did not follow the Young and the man. Instead, he looked over at the chair.

It was made of some brown synthetic material that the Old Man guessed was trying to convey the idea of an animal hide. There was a small wooden table adjacent to the chair. The Old Man pondered, *Strange. The chair and table are made of things found on the surface.* The Old Man walked over to the chair and propped the staff, which had gone inactive upon seeing the unfamiliar man running the store, up against the smooth stone wall behind the chair. A lantern shined brightly overhead to light the room with its flaps fully open.

The Old Man ran his hand along the wooden table and recoiled in surprise. The table was made of stone. It was just detailed very finely to appear like a piece of wooden furniture. The Old Man took a closer look at the table. He noticed a drawer. Curious to see if the drawer actually worked or if it was a prop, he pulled on the smooth knob making its handle. To his surprise, the door slid open with a rough skitter.

Inside the drawer was a book made of the same material as the chair. It was tied shut with a quick bow using some kind of thick, stiff string. The Old Man realized he had not seen a true book in ages. He peeked over his shoulder to see if the other two had left the room. They had. He snatched up the book and turned to take a seat in the chair, half expecting it to be stone as well. The chair was quite springy but comfortable enough. He fiddled with the bow, making sure he knew how to tie it properly before opening it. A pair of voices floated out of the other room.

"Now you can call me Cobbler. That is what everyone in town calls me."

"All right, then, Cobbler. Where do we start?"

"Have you ever purchased shoes before?"

"It has been quite a long time, but I have."

"What about buying custom-made shoes?"

"No, I have never had custom shoes."

"Ah! Well, you are in for a treat, then. I will have you fixed up shortly." There was a pause. "You have a smaller foot than most people I size." Another pause. "Give me just a moment, please. I will return with some basic shoes to try on to get an idea of what kind you like." The noise of shoes clacking across a stone floor followed by a short squeak of a door hinge emitted from the doorway.

Meanwhile, the Old Man had figured out the knot and had untied it. He cracked the book open. He was greeted by the smell of old pages. Something slid partway out of a page in the book. It was a piece of paper, much newer than the book pages. The Old Man opened the book to the page. The piece of paper had some scrawled handwriting on it in a black ink. Some of the lines were smeared.

Far exit: Never an op———
Close Ex———: ———bility
Guards dislike night shift.
What's ——— ——— ——— ther side?

The rest of the note turned into a black smudge, and then the page ended with a torn bottom. The Old Man pondered on what this note meant. He carefully replaced the note and flipped back to the front page. It was a title page. It read, "The Accounts of The Cave Cobbler."

The Old Man turned the page. The next page was a list of items, presumably the things purchased on one side and things sold on the other, with a number next to each entry. The Old Man skimmed the page and found nothing of interest. He flipped through several more pages of similar contents. As he flipped through, another piece of paper poked out. He read it as well.

Shift Changes:
——— to Day
Day to D———
Dusk to Night

Night to Dawn—Brief Op——

The door squeaked once more. The Old Man peeked over the book. He could see the Young's shadow on the floor through the doorway. He listened for a conversation.

"How does this one fit you?"

"Not very well. It feels wrong on the toes."

"I see. How about these?"

The Old Man watched the Young's shadow bend over, remove a pair of shoes, and put on another pair. The shadow winced. "No. These are too loose on my feet."

"I figured they would be. Try these, then."

The shadow performed another shoe swap. "These fit pretty well."

"Good! What in particular could be improved?"

There was silence. The shadow shifted on its feet. "The sides need to be a little tighter on the heel and wider on the toes."

"Are you sure? They seem rather fitting already."

"Yes." There was silence. "Maybe also provide a little more arch in the foot."

"With all due respect, your feet are suited to the arch in this shoe. I would advise against increasing the arch."

The shadow held out a hand. "I know what you are thinking. Trust me. I know my feet. They are odd compared to the normal person's foot."

Cobbler stammered. "I…oh yes, you are right. I will alter a pair of shoes for you to try." There was a scraping sound of shoes.

"Cobbler?"

"Yes?"

"Could you also make the shoes more visually appealing?"

"Certainly! How would you like them?"

There was a pause. "A darker brown with tight laces."

There was a long pause, followed by a sigh from Cobbler. "Sir, I do not mean to offend you, but it appears to me that you might be asking for a woman's shoe."

The shadow turned to face the voice. It grew exasperated. "How am I supposed to help the fact that my feet are much like a woman's? I came to this shop in hopes that it would be different and that we would avoid this issue, yet—"

The Young's voice was cut off by Cobbler's. "I am sorry. I did not mean to offend you. I was merely intending to point out that a woman's shoe may fit your specifications better. The woman's shoe is only the base. I am fully capable of creating a shoe for your, eh, manly foot by using the woman's base to allow the shoe to fit you better. Nobody will know the difference besides you and me."

The shadow relaxed. "That is fine. I am sorry. It is just that I have been searching for so long, and no one has been able to serve me. I assumed you were the same."

"Quite the contrary. I will be back in a few minutes with a rough cut. I do not currently have any women's shoe bases in stock. There are no women here, after all." The shadow nodded. The door squeaked once more. A silence took the room.

The Old Man went back to scouring the book for details. He flipped through more pages of the book in search of notes. He found one. It was a short note, only one line in length: "Check at lights out for openings." The Old Man needed more information. He flipped through more pages until he found a thin scrap of wrinkled paper. The ink had been written in a hurry. "Night gd. maybe leave early."

The Old Man looked up from the book. The Young's shadow had moved closer to the door. The shadow was waving its hand. It paused after a moment and pointed into the room. Then it went back to waving. A noise came from the right of the Old Man, the opposite direction of the shadow. The Old Man swiveled over to locate the source of the noise.

There was a door to his right. Loud scraping sounds of shoes on stone were getting closer. The Old Man snapped back to the shadow hand, which was pointing at the door and shaking. The Old Man looked back at the book. He skipped all the pages clear to the back of the book. He flipped back a few pages. A note appeared. He hastily grabbed it and read it: "Alarm on door. Disable how?" A different ink below the first line read, "Hack door alarm. Need tech——." The note was smeared off.

The staff on the wall behind the Old Man jiggled. It emitted a whisper of a whir and shot out a thin beam of light onto the note. The Old Man followed the beam. It highlighted the word *tech* with a narrow rectangle. The shoes were getting closer. The Old Man flipped the note over. On the back, there was another scribbled message: "Guards punish bribes."

The staff stiffened and set against the wall once more. The Old Man quickly replaced the note, slapped the book shut, and began retying the bow. There was a loud step. Something struck the door from the other side. The door didn't budge. There was a muffled voice through the door followed by a pinging noise of a metallic object. The Old Man finished the bow and tossed the book into the table drawer. He slid the drawer close and leaned back in the chair. There was a heavy click from the door, and it swung open.

The Old Man shut his eyes and laid his head back on the top of the chair. The Old Man listened as a man walked through the door. He picked his head back up and opened his eyes. "Pardon me, sir. I did not mean to disturb your nap. That chair is rather comfortable, isn't it?"

The Old Man glanced down to see a gold-colored key in Cobbler's hand. Cobbler quickly stashed the key on a ring with two other keys, both silver, one short and the other the same length as the golden one. "Yes, it is comfortable."

Cobbler smiled. "I would tell you to continue napping, but the shoes are nearly complete."

The Old Man sat forward in the chair. "How are they done so quickly?"

"I have my own techniques and a wonderful machine I built myself to make it much easier." The Old Man questioned this statement, but after seeing the sewing machine the Radioman had used, he opted to not argue it. Cobbler took a few strides across the room and went back in with the Young. The Young's shadow hand had stopped wiggling. "Try these on if you will."

After a pause, the Young replied, "These are perfect, except they are black."

"I did not have any dark-brown material in stock. It will be quite some time before I can get more. I went ahead and substituted in the black in hopes that you would accept it."

"Oh. I suppose it will work, then."

"Please allow me to add the finishing touches to the shoe if you are satisfied with how they fit your feet." The shadow quickly removed its shoes. "This will only take but a moment. I have a machine that can do this in under a minute."

The Old Man reached over to the drawer and tugged the handle. The drawer didn't budge. The Old Man took a closer look at the knob. There was a keyhole in it. It must have latched when he slammed it shut and locked the drawer. The Old Man stood. He collected his staff from the wall. He walked across the room to the register and fished out some credits from his pockets.

There were around thirty seconds of noise from a fast machine and then silence. Cobbler spoke up. "How does this look?"

"It is nearly perfect, but can I get the laces in a tight strap instead of the bow?"

"Certainly. You simply attach the straps differently. Are you satisfied with the shoe?"

"Of course!"

"Wonderful. Please follow me to the register for payment when you are ready."

Cobbler walked into the room to see the Old Man leaning on the counter already. The Old Man spoke up. "I will be paying for the shoes."

Cobbler nodded awkwardly. "If I may say, between you and me, the fellow in the other room has quite an odd taste in shoes. It is as if he wants his shoes to be…very feminine. One is certainly entitled to wear whatever shoe pleases them, but this is the first time this has occurred in my shop." Cobbler caught himself. "I am sorry. You likely do not appreciate my explanation of my rude thoughts."

The Old Man had no response to give. He handed Cobbler a handful of credits. Cobbler counted them up. He tapped the counter. The Old Man rolled his eyes and placed another handful on the table. Cobbler slid a few coins back and smiled. "Thank you for your payment." The Young walked through the door carrying the new shoes. Cobbler glanced over. "Do you not enjoy wearing your shoes?"

The Young paused for a moment while trying to figure out what Cobbler meant. He snapped back into the act. "Oh! The shoes. I do enjoy wearing them, but they are so new and nice. I don't want to wear them out before I need to, so I figured I would wear my old shoes until I have to use these ones."

Cobbler paused with a skeptical glance but continued on merrily as ever upon seeing the Young's falsely relaxed face. Cobbler turned away to face a table where he fiddled with a registry of some kind. The Young caught the Old Man's attention and prodded his finger to the exit. The Old Man cleared his throat. "Are we all set?"

Cobbler turned back from the registry "Oh! Yes. You are free to leave or stay if you wish." He turned back to the registry. The Old Man shrugged and walked to the door and stepped out. After a moment, he waved his hand, and the Young followed him out the door.

The Old Man and the Young found the group in a small cutout of a building in a nearby alleyway. "How did that go?" inquired the Hobo.

The Old Man shrugged and started to speak, but the Young cut in abruptly. "It was terrible. That man silently judged me for getting these shoes the entire time I was in there."

The Old Man twisted his head over to look at the Young as he leaned against the stone alley wall. "I didn't think it was that bad."

The Young's eyes flared in anger. "That is because you got to sit on a comfy chair in the other room from that man."

"That chair was a bit springy." The Young threw his hands in the air. The Old Man smiled. "It is over with now. Relax." The Young settled to a low boil. The Old Man reached for the shoes in the Young's hand. The Young handed them to him. The Old Man turned to the Bartender and outstretched the shoes to her. "Here you are, Bartender, new shoes fresh from the angry one's hands."

The Bartender took the shoes and slid them on. The Young chuckled. "No, don't put those on without socks. They will rub your feet raw."

The Bartender removed the shoe. "I don't have any socks."

"Way ahead of you." The Young reached into his pocket and revealed a wad of short black socks. He tossed them over to the Bartender, who caught them. "Before you ask, I did steal them. They were sitting on the table, and when Cobbler left the room, I swiped them. It was compensation for the man's judgment." The Old Man placed his palm on his forehead.

The Bartender crouched, put the socks on, and slid on the shoes. She remained idle for a moment, in thought. "Hold on. It has been a long time since I have needed to tie my shoes." She grabbed the laces and tried a knot. It fell through. She tried again with slow hand motions. This time, she managed a loose knot that somewhat resembled a proper shoe tie. She paused, seemed satisfied, and stood.

The group remained staring at her horrid knot. She awkwardly shifted her weight. The Mechanic fell to a knee and grabbed the laces, untying her knot and quickly knotting it once more. This knot fitted neatly on the shoe and held her foot tightly. "How did you do that so quickly?" asked the Bartender.

The Mechanic was visibly baffled by the question. "I have done it for years like everyone else here." The Bartender nodded and tugged on the empty belt loops on her jeans. The Mechanic spoke once more. "How do you like them?"

The Bartender swiveled on her feet and rolled her ankles. "They fit very well. And they are so flexible!" She rolled up into her toes while watching the shoe bend.

The Survivalist chuckled. "I take it that it has been a while since you have worn something resembling a walking shoe."

The Bartender looked up with a wide grin. "Yes!"

The Survivalist laughed. "Those shoes look very close to a pair I used to have. I loved those shoes. I figure you will enjoy those the same." The Bartender was busy hopping up and down.

After letting the newness of sneakers wear off for the Bartender, the Old Man caught the group's attention. "I have been thinking some things over. I found a book inside The Cave Cobbler. Firstly, it is amazing to me that a hard copy of a book still exists. The book was filled with a bunch of old sales records from the store, but it also had stray tears of paper tossed in it.

"I think the fellow running the shop is trying to find a way out of the City of Underground, much like we are. The notes mentioned that the door is alarmed like the Bartender said and that the guards have shift changes at certain times in the day. They also mentioned the guards having repercussions in place for bribing." He looked over to the Bartender.

She cowered away. "I was going to tell you all when you got back with the shoes."

The group surrounded the Bartender. Before things got out of hand, the Old Man continued speaking. "Hold on. There is more. Between the night shift and dawn, the guards apparently leave shift early on a regular basis, as they hate being there for the night shift. That gives us a potential window of escape, but we still need to get past the alarm on the door. That was when I found a note that said it could be hacked and something about needing technology." He paused to look down the alleyway at the cart of robotic parts. The group followed his gaze.

The Mechanic started in. "Are you suggesting we repair a robot that we have no idea the original purpose of with no instructions and use it to hack an alarmed door?"

The Old Man nodded. "It is all we have. If we fix it, maybe it can at least provide us with some more information." The Old Man tapped the Bartender's shoulder. "If you are able to guide us to somewhere where we might find tools to fix a robot, then we can forgive your acts. It is a harsh world. People do what they have to."

The Bartender thought this over. She had no choice. "I remember people from the power plant talking about all sorts of tools, but going in there would never work. It is too heavily guarded."

The group spread out to give the Bartender space as the Young perked up. "How many guards are there?"

The Bartender shook her head. "Too many." The group exchanged glances. The Young smiled. "Surely you people are not thinking of sneaking into the most heavily guarded section in all of town."

The Survivalist chuckled. "Of course we are."

The Bartender searched the group for any signs of disagreement. None was found. She returned to the Young. "So you think you are sneaky?"

The Young chuckled. "Do I need to remind you?" He made a spanking motion with his hand.

The Bartender stiffened. "No, that will not be necessary." She hesitated. "I know the power plant is on the far side of the cave, but I have no idea how to get in."

The Young waved his arm. "Lead on."

The Bartender sighed and pointed out into the street. The Old Man strolled out as he checked to signal the Hobo. The Bartender motioned toward the Old Man. "Why do you always send out the Old Man first?"

The Mechanic answered, "He is the only one who is technically down here legally. We figured he can talk his way out of getting seen by saying he is new down here."

"That makes sense, but nobody is going to be on the streets right now except some patrols up near the power plant."

The Mechanic grew puzzled. "Why is no one ever out now?"

The Bartender peeked over. "They are all working in the power plant or hiding. The shops out here are typically side jobs with the exception of places holding lots of credits already, like the Cave Dweller Cardhouse. I was amazed the shoemaker was in his shop earlier. He must have something he really cares about in there."

The Survivalist joined in. "Why does everyone work at the power plant?"

The Bartender shrugged. "It is a requirement by the Prospector. In order to keep the city alive, nearly everyone must be inside that power plant to keep it running."

The Survivalist continued on. "What happens if the plant shuts down?"

"We don't know exactly. All we know for sure is, it keep the vital systems running, which are keeping us alive. I hear things like the carbon dioxide scrubbers, the oxygen pumps, and the farming lights are all tied into that power plant. If it goes down, we go down with it.

"However, there would be a gap in between the cave running out of resources and the plant shutting down. Occasionally, the plant is shut down intentionally to make repairs, and the city is ran with a backup generator on a highly reduced power grid. I have no way of knowing what would happen if the entire system went dark."

"It doesn't sound like a good idea to find out."

"No, it is not." The Bartender went quiet. The Hobo made a motion, and the group scurried across the street to another hiding place in another alleyway. The Bartender was now positioned near the Mechanic and the Young. She gently hit the Young's arm. "What do you plan to do at this power plant?"

The Young shrugged. "Get the tools we need and get out."

The Bartender was not satisfied. "No, I mean, how do you actually plan to do it?"

"I don't know. I will have to look at the area and figure it out as I go."

She frowned. "That is not a good plan."

The Young raised an eyebrow. "Look, I got in, out, and back in this cave on the far side undetected. I will be fine."

The Bartender glanced back at the Mechanic. He nodded, confirming the Young's statement. She resumed the conversation. "The door on that side was not alarmed?"

The Young came to the realization that it hadn't been. "No. It was just a loud old door."

"I could have gone out that way without tripping the alarm?"

"No. Earlier, I had to go back through the door as soon as I came in to avoid being locked in here. There is no way back out that side without it being opened from the outside. The guard opened it, let the Old Man in, and closed it behind him when he left."

The Hobo signaled again, and the group moved forward and into a stairwell diving into the sidewalk. The Bartender stuck with the Young. The Hobo caught her attention. "Which way at this intersection?"

"I think you need to go left. I am honestly not sure here." The Hobo nodded and began signaling to the Old Man. The Bartender resumed the conversation with the Young. "What is on the outside of the door?"

The Young shrugged. "There are a lot of Raiders and some forests with creeks. If you go far enough, you can find the city."

"What are Raiders?"

"They are people. They joined together in an attempt to survive by looting...and other things. We left the city to get away from the looting and to find some better place to be."

The Bartender smirked. "Well, you haven't found your refuge yet. What is this city you are talking about?"

The Young's face fell stagnant for a moment before jumping back to life. "Oh, sorry. This whole group is from near the city besides you. It is actually called Capital City."

"Why do they call it that?"

"It originally governed this entire area. Haven't you heard of it?"

The Bartender shook her head. "No. I grew up in the mountains above this cave until we came in here. It was isolated up there. We had our own way of life."

"You were able to get up the mountains? We assumed those were impassable."

The Bartender struck a solemn note for a moment, seemingly remembering a harsh thought. "They likely are now by the sound of things. There used to be a road up over the mountains. Sometimes, things were delivered up to us on that path, or we sent things out. It must be completely destroyed for you all to be here instead. It would have been obvious."

The Young replied, "I found a map with the road crossed out. I figured it was gone. Looking back, we still had to get the Old Man anyway, and this was a way through." The two fell silent, leaving the whole group in the quiet. The Hobo motioned, and the group crossed the street to a corner of a building. The Hobo peeked around to the left to spot the Old Man.

Many hiding places and signals later, the group arrived in sight of the power plant. The Bartender guided them around a street above the power plant in an attempt to see over the wall. They stopped at a perch on the cave wall to devise a plan. The Old Man started the conversation. "Mechanic, are you familiar with the parts of the robot?"

The Mechanic shook his head. "I am not familiar at all."

The Old Man grimaced. "Can you take a guess at what tools you might need?"

The Mechanic looked back at the cart he had been towing. "Eh, I would need a welding kit at least—and a whole pile of jumping wires." He paused as he rummaged through the cart. "Jeez, look at all these wires. Wait. These are all…" He trailed off while he continued his observation. A moment later, he turned back to the group.

"All of the individual components are here, excluding a few jumping wires. At least nothing is severed or torn out. It is like the thing just fell apart. No, it seems it was deliberately disassembled for it to be in this good of shape. I have no idea how to reassemble it, but there are only so many options with the plugs remaining. I can probably guess until I get it right with a little logic of where cables are running. I guess all I really need is a Scorch Torch to fuse the wiring and some joints."

The group stared blankly. The Mechanic explained, "It is a handheld device that emits a large and extremely hot flame. It is great for cutting and adhering things. It is typically a red-ribbed cylinder with a directional nozzle on the top."

The Young nodded. "So that is it?"

The Mechanic nodded. "As far as I know."

"All right, then. How am I going to get inside?"

The group turned to adjust the focus on the walls of the power plant. A pause ensued as the group observed the rectangular wall around the plant. The power plant itself was set into the cave wall. The Hobo pointed at the wall. "The wall leads all the way to the edge of the cave. There is not a back side. That narrows us down to three walls to work with."

The Bartender shook her head. "The power plant is set back into the cave wall. The far wall from us is very short. We only have about two walls to work with."

The Survivalist pointed at the wall closest to them and then at the wall parallel to the lake. "We were on that path on the way in. We hid behind that small building." She pointed to the outbuilding with the triangular warning sign from before across the paved pathway around the outside of the wall.

The Entrepreneur jumped in. "I believe that leaves us with one option, then. We already know that the pathway near the wall is out in the open, and there is nothing to scale the wall with there. We have to use the wall closest to us."

There was another pause. The Radioman spoke. "What about the corner closest to the cave wall?"

The Young adjusted to peek around the boulder he was behind. "If I could get a boost, then I might be able to scale the rock face next to it. Even if I could, I do not know how I would get back across the wall without help."

The Mechanic gestured to the aforementioned corner. "I could boost you up easy enough. Maybe you can take the Survivalist's rope with you and leave an anchor point somewhere to get back over the wall."

The Young glanced over at the rope across the Survivalist's chest. He refocused on the Mechanic. "Why doesn't she just come with me?"

The Mechanic started to shake his head but paused instead. "Why does she need to go?"

The Young shrugged. "I figured, with two pairs of eyes, we would be much better off. She is the quietest one here out of all of you. It makes sense to me." He waited in anticipation to see if the group took the bait. No one tried to argue.

The Mechanic raised his hand palm up and furrowed his brow. "All right. Go for it."

The Young motioned the Survivalist over and pointed to the corner of the wall where it met the cave. "If I boosted you over the wall there, do you think you could anchor the rope on the other side?"

The Survivalist nodded. "We did it before."

"Do you think we can get back out?"

"For sure. If we can get over that wall, we should be able to get back out in a similar manner."

The Young turned to the group. "I don't think we will need you, Mechanic. You are too easy to spot anyway due to your size. I think you should stay here with the group."

The Mechanic nodded. "I can try to figure some of these parts out while you are gone."

The Young turned to the Survivalist. "Are you ready?" She nodded. "Then we are off. We will be back with the torch."

The Mechanic caught the Young's attention. "Hey! You will need this. The Scorch Torch is typically held in a strap with a lock to prevent people from using it without permission. Cut it with the knife. It should be sharp enough, but it will take a bit. Just don't nick the valve with it."

"What happens if I nick the valve?"

The Mechanic hesitated. "It...it explodes." The Young grew noticeably worried. The Mechanic panicked and tried to explain it off. "Not in every direction. The cylinder itself will probably stay in perfect condition. The top of the container will blow off, and a big flame will fly out of the top for about thirty seconds or so until it finally runs out of fuel.

"That is the problem with these things. The fuel is so volatile that it sets itself off under normal conditions, although that also helps you as the fuel burns off instantly, so you don't have to worry about it sticking to something if that happens. Just...just make sure to angle the top away from you, others, or anything else you don't want melted, and you should be fine."

The Young nodded with only partial confidence. "Yeah, should be fine." He vaulted over a rock he was crouched behind and started down toward the wall. The Survivalist waved silently and vaulted over the rock after him.

The Mechanic grabbed the Old Man's rifle from the side of the backpack. "Do you want this back, Old Man?"

The Old Man peeked over. "My rifle! I figured you had left it outside." He began to reach for it but hesitated. He looked down at the Lightstaff in his hand. "I do not think I will be needing it anymore." He dropped his outstretched hand.

The Mechanic looked the rifle over. "It would be a shame to scrap it. I will keep it on the pack for you. It is not in my way and doesn't weigh all that much. Maybe we can find some ammo for it."

The Old Man relaxed. "Thank you."

The Mechanic set the pack down and began rooting through it. He retrieved a pistol. "Hobo, do you want this back?"

The Hobo looked over to see the pistol. "Sure. Why are you arming us now, though?"

The Mechanic rubbed his forehead with his available left hand. "I figured those two might get into trouble. I think we should be ready for a fight if needed." He held out the pistol in the palm of his hand.

The Hobo stretched his hand out to hover just over the gun. "What kind of trouble?"

"I think they will find the tool, but they will get caught in the act. They may come out running. If they are being chased, we need to back them up."

The Hobo raised his chin slightly in suspicion and gripped the gun. "Any other reasons?"

The Mechanic shook his head. "No. I can't see any other reason you would need it."

The Hobo took the pistol and checked the clip for ammo. "It's empty."

The Mechanic held out his hand once more and dropped three bullets into the Hobo's hand. The Hobo loaded the clip and smacked it into the gun. The Bartender raised an eyebrow. "I take it you have shot a gun before, Hobo?"

The Hobo stared coldly. "A few times. None of them is a good memory." The Bartender took the hint.

Meanwhile, the Young and the Survivalist had made their way down to the outside edge of the wall. The Young whispered to the Survivalist, "It was much easier than expected to get to this wall."

The Survivalist nodded. "Wasn't this place supposed to be heavily guarded?"

"Yeah, it was. I don't know. Maybe we got lucky today. Now come on. I need to boost you over."

The Survivalist walked over as the Young turned away from her and crouched down. She stepped over him. He stood to allow her to sit on his shoulders. She held up her arms to get an idea of how far she had to go still. It was a lot farther up than the wall outside. "Pick me up higher."

The Young reached up, stopped, began to lower his hands, twitched for a moment, began to raise them up to push her up by her bottom, and froze before he began pushing her up. The Survivalist chuckled as she reached down and grabbed his hands. She placed his hands on her bottom. "Go on." He picked her up and leaned into the wall. She reached once more. She still needed a few more feet. "Is it possible for you to pick me up by my feet?"

"No."

"Why not?"

"Because I am not strong enough to pick you up from the ground. I have to get you partway up before I can hold you above my head."

"What about now? If I stood on your hands, could you support me?"

The Young grunted. "I suppose so. I am holding your entire weight now. Just hurry up."

The Survivalist scowled. "Are you calling me heavy?"

The Young gasped. "Yes. Hurry."

The Survivalist took a minor offense to the bluntness of the statement. She pulled her right foot up and carefully leaned to the left. The Young took in a deep breath. She wiggled her foot into his hand and shifted her weight to it. The Young exhaled sharply and took another gasp. The Survivalist began bringing up her other foot. "Are you all right down there?"

The Young struggled to change position. "Yes. I did not take into account the arm fatigue. You get heavier by the second."

She successfully transferred her foot into his hand. She stood slowly. The Young shuddered and wiggled beneath her. She could almost reach the top of the wall. "Just a little higher." The Young peeked up. He bent his knees slightly, paused there to regain his balance, and then managed a short jump. The Survivalist was unprepared for the sudden jerk. She flailed her arms to keep her balance. "Sorry. One more time," she stated. The Young groaned quietly. He repeated the jump.

The Survivalist nabbed the edge of the cold stone wall. The Young let go of her feet upon feeling the resistance from her holding the ledge. She belly flopped against the wall. He turned and leaned up against the wall with his back. He calmed his breathing and slid down the wall into a sitting position. The Survivalist crawled across the top of the wall. It was thicker than she was tall. *What are they trying to contain in this wall?* she wondered. She peeked over the far side. No one was outside but a guard. The guard was moving to the left in a sweeping motion. The guard stopped for a moment and then swept back the opposite direction. She crawled back across the wall and peeked over the edge while still lying on her stomach to see the Young collapsed in his sitting position. "Oh please! I am not that heavy."

The Young cocked his head sideway to look up at her. "You are heavy for your size. But don't worry, it is all muscle weight, not fat. Muscle weighs more than fat."

The Survivalist looked at her thin arms while dangling them over the wall. "What muscles?"

The Young grinned. "It isn't in your arms, that is for sure. It is all in your lower body."

The Survivalist grew curious. "Which parts in particular do you think have the muscle?"

The Young had managed to settle his breathing. He coughed gently in an odd giggle. "Well, some of it is in your calves. A good bit is in your butt. The majority of it is in your thighs, though." She reached around and grabbed the back of her thighs. The Young continued. "You have some serious thunder thighs. The good kind."

The Survivalist had no idea how to take this information. She was curious what the bad kind was. She had to ask another question. "What is it about picking me up over walls that makes you compliment me?"

The Young shrugged. "It is the only time I get to hold you and the only time we seem to be alone." He peered up at her perplexed face. He let out a sharp breath. "Just take the compliment."

She smiled and rolled her eyes. "Did you bring me along just so you could pick me up?"

The Young spread a disconcerted smile. "That isn't the main reason. I actually did want your help finding this torch and someone to reason plans with, but picking you up did sweeten the deal a bit." The Survivalist blushed. She ripped her head back overtop the wall before the Young could see her. "What did you see across the wall?"

The Survivalist derailed her train of thought. She poked her head back over the edge above the Young. "Oh. A flat section of stone with no cover that is monitored by a lone guard."

"Are you sure there are not more somewhere?"

She wiggled back across the wall. The guard was at a doorway, holding the door open and yelling something through it. A few moments later, two more guards came out and took their posts, one on the left and one on the right. The Survivalist noticed that the building went all the way to the cave wall. Based on the shape, the building continued into the rock face. She shimmied back across the wall. "There are three guards now—left, right, and center. There is a door that I think is unlocked due to the guards just coming out. If we sneak past the guards, we can get in."

"How far is it?"

She peeked back to the guards without crossing the wall. She turned back to the Young. "It is pretty far. I don't think we can just sprint across while they are not looking."

The Young pondered the situation. "Can you at least find a way to get me up there?" The Survivalist stretched her arm out down the wall. The Young noticed and stood. He gave it a good jump to reach her outstretched arms but fell short. "If you lean any farther, I will pull you off the wall when I get ahold of your hand. We will have to figure something out."

"I would just use the rope, but there is nothing to tie it off to up here, and I can't drop down the other side to act as an anchor without getting caught by the guards."

"What about where the wall meets the cave over there?" The two looked over at the dark corner between the wall and the cave face. There was a small pile of loose rocks. Otherwise, the wall appeared slick and bare. The Young shrugged and walked over, leaving the Survivalist where she was lying on top of the wall. He stepped on the stones, making them shuffle under his weight with a scraping noise. He turned to find the Survivalist and shook his head. He raised his arm and leaned against the cave wall.

Something startled him. He nearly fell over in the loose rocks. He turned to face the wall once more. After a few moments, he managed to wiggle a rectangular stone from the wall and placed it aside. He stuck his right foot in the new gap. He pushed off the gap and ran his hands frantically over the wall. Nothing appeared to happen. He tried a few more times before giving up, calling the Survivalist over. She wiggled down the length of the wall to meet him. "What did you find?"

"That hole has been carved out by hand. Someone managed to make a stone to fit it. There is a cubby in the bottom of it with a piece of paper in it. I think it is a sort of secret mailbox."

"A letter drop spot?"

"Sure, whatever you want to call it. I am not using it for that, though. I think I can jump off of it high enough that you can grab my arm safely."

"Give it a go." She stretched her arm out to catch his hand.

The Young took a moment to judge the height of the jump. He bounced a few times before running at the pile of rocks. He scrambled up the pile as smoothly as he could, placed his foot in the hole, and jumped off. He missed the Survivalist's hand and fell to the hard rock floor below. He landed awkwardly and ran into the wall. "I missed your hand."

"I noticed."

The Young panted. "Just…just give me a second." He waved his hand dismissively. The Survivalist lazily flopped down on top of the wall.

"Grab that piece of paper from the hole and read it to me while you catch your breath."

The Young clambered up the pile of rocks and retrieved the paper. He sat down in the pile and began reading the note aloud. "Dearest M."

The Survivalist interrupted. "M? As in the letter *M*?"

"Yes. It just has an *M* with a period after it. It is short for something."

"Ah."

The Young restarted. "'Dearest M. I hope you are able to find this message in good time. A newcomer has entered the city earlier today. I wonder if he knows about the outside and if he can help us. I want to know if you think it is a good idea to seek him out. He is an older fellow walking with one of the Lightstaff as a cane. Please let me know on the back of this paper. Best of luck with your moonshrooms.' Signed off by J."

"Huh. I bet that is the Old Man. People did pay attention to his entry. Is there a response on the back?"

He flipped the paper. "No."

"Ah. She must have not read it yet. I wonder what they need help with."

The Young shrugged and replaced the paper as he stood. He walked back out from the wall a bit to take another shot at the jump. He was just about to begin his running when an idea struck him. "Hey, didn't that rope have a hook on it?"

"Yes."

"Is it long enough to reach from that hole to the far side ground?"

The Survivalist slid the rope up her body and dropped the end with the hook down to the Young. He retrieved it from the ground and went to the hole in the cave wall. He fiddled with the hook for a moment before waving at the Survivalist. She pulled the rope tight and observed its length. "I think it will reach. Why do we need to hook the rope?"

"We need a way down the other side of the wall. I am guessing it is just as far of a drop over there as it is on this side. Plus, we need a way back over the wall once we get over there. The hook will hold on to this cubby and hold the rope so that when we come back, we can use it to climb back over the wall."

The Survivalist peeked over the far side of the wall. It seemed like a reasonable plan. "We may have to jump some to get ahold of it on the other side."

"That should work. Is there enough space for the both of us up there still?"

"Yes. Go for it."

The Young hopped a few more times and took off. He scampered up the loose rocks, planted his foot, and lunged for the Survivalist's hand once more. With a quick adjustment from the Survivalist, the Young managed to catch her hand. She pulled back, trying to lift herself from the wall for leverage, but instead slammed onto the top of the wall due to the Young's weight. She grunted but managed to keep her grip on his hand.

The Young pulled himself up high enough to grab the top of the wall and let go of her hand. She grabbed his shirt collar and helped him up the wall. He began to sit upright, but the Survivalist pinned him down. He caught on and shimmied to the edge of the wall. The three guards were still posted. They did not appear to have heard anything. "No wonder you were not afraid to talk. They are so far away."

"I tried to tell you. It is quite a distance."

"Well, there is a boulder below us now. It must have fallen from the cave wall. Drop the rope down behind it."

The Survivalist removed the rope from under her stomach. She had been pinning it down to keep tension on it so the hook would remain in place in the hole. She lowered the rope down slowly to avoid the guards noticing it. "I need you to hold the end of the rope until I find something to tie it off to."

"Are you going down first?"

"I guess so." She peeked over at the guards. They were all facing away, in a conversation with one another. She couldn't make out what they were saying. She swung her legs out of the edge of the wall and transitioned to rappelling down the wall. She reached the bottom. She didn't find anything to tie the rope off to. She gave the rope a few tugs and pulled the rope to maintain the tension.

The Young waited a few moments for an opportunity of his own and slid down the rope quickly. He stopped before hitting the ground and dropped silently onto the boulder. He dove in behind it with the Survivalist while shaking his hands. She grinned. "Rope burn?"

The Young scowled. "Oh, leave me be."

The Survivalist shook her head. "What are we going to tie this off to?"

The Young looked around. "I don't know. It won't take much. I have this knife, but apparently, we need it to get the torch."

"What about our shoes?"

"They don't weigh enough. What about your hatchet?"

The Survivalist tensed. "You mean leave it here to hold the rope?"

"Yeah. The weight of the head should be enough. It will also be easy to make a knot around the handle and head." The Survivalist didn't move. "Is that fine?"

She nodded. "I just haven't been without it since the Crisis. I don't really know what to do without it. Sometimes, I forget I have it." She took the black hatchet from its holster on her right thigh.

"Did you have that this entire time?"

"I guess so."

"Well, I never noticed, so you do a good job of concealing it."

"It is right out in the open."

The Young nodded. "Yes, but you never motion to it or give any clue that you have it on your leg. Are you just that used to carrying it?"

"I suppose so." She finished the knot around the hatchet and placed it gently against the wall. She slowly let go of it to be sure it would hold the rope. "It works."

"Good. Now let's get across to the door."

"How?"

"I don't know."

The two peeked over the boulder. The guards had resumed their posts. They were sweeping the area with lights. "Are those Lightstaffs?" asked the Survivalist.

"No. They are too bulky. I think they are the same idea, but they are completely mechanical instead. It is like the Old Man got the improved version or something."

"That is strange."

"Yeah."

There was a silent pause. "What is that over there?" She pointed at an object in the dark.

"I think it is a pile of boxes," stated the Young.

The Survivalist began scrounging around near her feet. She located a rock. It fitted the palm of her hand. She wound her arm back and launched the rock across the gap. It landed noisily near the boxes. The Young looked over in panic. The Survivalist swatted his arm. "Shhh!" The Young ducked behind the rock more. A guard swung the light over to look at the shape. The beam of light illuminated a large pile of wooden boxes. It floated around the area for a few seconds before returning to sweeping the area. "Wooden boxes?" queried the Survivalist.

"Yeah. They must be delivered in from the surface or something. I have not seen a single tree since we came down here."

The Survivalist lit up. "If those boxes are delivered in, they must be placed near some kind of entrance. They wouldn't just be way over here, out of the way, for no reason."

"Maybe they are just there for long-term storage."

The Survivalist raised an eyebrow. "I doubt it. We can make it that far, though. We might as well go see if there is a way in."

"Fine. I will go first." The Young traded places with the Survivalist. He waited for the nearest guard to sweep the opposite direction and took off across the gap. He reached the boxes without a sound. He peered around the boxes. He waved on the Survivalist. She followed the same steps as the Young and crossed without issue. "These guards really are not that hard to get past. What was the Bartender talking about?"

The Survivalist replied, "I have no idea. Let's just keep moving."

"There is an entrance over there beyond these boxes."

She elbowed him. "Told you."

The Young was not finished. "But it is lit with electric lighting, and we can't depend on the shadows any longer. The good news is, it is a sliding entrance."

"What kind of sliding? Like, a horizontal slide or a vertical one?"

"It's vertical, like a garage door in the city." The Survivalist glanced over. The Young clarified. "Our city, not this one. I don't know that this place even has garage doors besides this one."

"So why is it good news that the door is a garage door?"

"I used to go into buildings all the time back in the city through these doors. They are hardly ever alarmed once they open up. That door is cracked open at the bottom, meaning any alarms on the system should be off, and we should be able to just slip inside."

"Oh."

The Young paused. "How did you get inside buildings in the city?"

The Survivalist shrugged. "I typically just found a window or something."

"Oh. That works too, I suppose." There was a short pause. The Young peeked once more. He abruptly stood and slipped across a gap to another box. The top of the box had been ripped open. He peeked inside to find nothing but air. The Young pondered the box over. Why was there a completely empty box still sitting outside here, completely by itself? He ran his hand along the box.

"What is this box doing here?" whispered the Survivalist from behind him. The Young nearly jumped out of the cover of the box. He refrained from yelling. The Survivalist noticed she had spooked him. "Sorry." The Young waved it off. He motioned to the garage door.

The two sat behind the empty box for a few minutes until the guard closest to them finally looked in the opposite direction to talk to one of the other guards. With the guards no longer looking, the two snuck over to the garage door together and took places on each side of the door—the Young on the left side and the Survivalist on the right. They both peered underneath the garage door as it was only waist high off the ground. Two voices could be heard inside.

A deeper voice started off. "Hey! I am going generator side."

A stern and nasally voice replied, "What for?"

"I have been told the cooling system needs checked. It is freezing over again."

"Oh. All right. I guess I will cover this part of the plant myself, then."

"Don't worry, I shouldn't be long. Just make your typical rounds."

"All right."

The deeper voice man began toward a doorway. He paused as he stepped out. "Hey. Do you know if there are any Scorch Torches lying around that I could melt the ice with?"

"They keep some by the cooling system just for that."

"Since when?"

"They always have. They are on the right wall as you walk in the door."

"Huh. All right. Thanks." He stepped out. The nasally one walked across the room and opened an electrical breaker box on the wall. It was a disaster of wires. The man began sifting through the mess.

The Young swung his head to motion the move inside. They both swung inside and maneuvered across the workspace behind a set of metallic tables. They paused at the door that the deeper voice had walked through. There was a small window at the top. The Young stood and took a quick look through it. He stooped once more and checked on the nasally worker behind him, who was still busy with the wires, as he cracked open the door and slid through.

The Survivalist followed him in. He gently closed the door. When the Young turned back around to look down the hall, he found that the Survivalist had already started down it after the deep voice worker. The worker turned to the left at a Y-shaped intersection. Down the shorter hallway on this side of the intersection, there was a heavy large doorway. A triangle with a snowflake inside of it was painted on the door in bright aqua. A short message, also in the aqua color, was painted below it, reading, "ROOM MAY FREEZE."

The deep-voiced worker approached the door. He slid open a slat to peek through the door. A fog bellowed out of it, spilling down the door and onto the floor. The man chuckled lightly before speaking. "Frozen." He stepped back as he shut the slat and swung the door open. A rush of fog rolled out into the hallway, spilling like a wave until it dispersed and condensed into a mist that settled on every nearby surface. The Young and the Survivalist felt a blast of cold air.

The worker stepped in and slammed the door shut behind him. The bang reverberated through the hallway. They slipped down the hall. The Survivalist stood and shoved the slat over. It was surprisingly stiff to move, causing it to snap open abruptly. She cringed away from the cold but forced herself to look. A low hum became more audible. She shut the slat, muting the hum, and crouched down next to the Young. "There is another torch on the right wall. The guy took one off of the strap using a key. You are going to have to cut it off."

She ran her hand down her right leg and patted it a few times. A puzzled look crossed her face. She looked down. She snapped her face back up in a panic that settled off into a knowing grief. "I had forgotten about leaving the hatchet. Do you still have your knife?" The Young grabbed the handle and unsheathed the knife. He waved it loosely at the Survivalist. She stood and slid the slat over once more, this time snapping it back shut before getting a good look. She pushed the blade of the knife over and shoved the Young flat on his back. She lay on top of him.

The Young began to speak. "What are you d—" The Survivalist's hand over his mouth cut him short. The door swung open and slammed into the wall opposite them. A worker came through the doorway, rubbing his hands together. He threw the door shut with the heel of his boot and shivered down the hallway. Small particles of ice rained off him.

Once the cold man left, the Survivalist rolled off the Young and onto her back. She arched up. The floor was wet and had soaked her shirt with bitterly cold water. She had rolled over into a small collection basin nearby. The drain for it must have been clogged. She sat up and pulled the shirt from sticking to her back. The Young noticed her distraught expression. He couldn't help but grin. He sat up. The Survivalist, ignoring her current discomfort, pointed at the door. "Get to it. That was a different guy than the one that went in. The guy we were following is probably still in there."

The Young stood and checked the slat on the door. He took in a deep breath and cracked the door just wide enough to squeeze through, putting in a visible effort to get it open. The cold immediately caused his skin to crawl. He shut the door behind him and turned to find a white room covered in a layer of prickly white ice. There was a deep humming in the room. The room contained a strange device set into the far wall. The worker was blasting a machine with the brilliant blue flame of the torch, revealing a silver-colored metal underneath and causing a light-blue glare on the white ice around it.

There were two large tubes on the machine—one was still frozen over, and the other was partially thawed off thanks to the torch. The left tube had an orange arrow painted on it pointed toward the machine. The tube came out of the wall and bent ninety degrees down into the machine. At the right side of the machine, another pipe was attached in the same manner. A blue blob showed through the ice, bigger on one end than the other. The Young assumed the blue blob must be an arrow pointing away from the machine.

The machine itself was a large rectangular thing. A pair of metallic arms were alternating slowly on a set of cylindrical plungers. When an arm pressed in on the cylinder, a glass tube filled with a semitransparent magenta fluid above the cylinder. When the arm retracted, the fluid bubbled and gurgled as it drained from the tube. A hissing noise and a small blast of fog emitted from a vent on the bottom of the machine each time the arms switched directions.

The Young regained his train of thought now that he had gotten past the shock of the cold. He turned to the wall on the right. There was a red-ribbed canister on the wall similar to what the worker was using. That must be it. He creeped over and began whittling away at the frozen black strap around the torch with his knife. The strap was surprisingly strong. It was made in such a way that there were no easy lines to cut across it on. He stopped and looked over at the guard. The flame on the torch was turning green.

The Young continued cutting. He had made it about a fourth of the way through when he heard the guard shuffling behind him. Panic rushed through him. He turned. The guard was still facing the machine. The guard waved the torch across the front of the machine until he saw a red color through the ice. The worker sharply punched the red bit. The ice shattered off, and the machine began scrubbing off speed. The humming noise trailed off, leaving the blowing of the torch and a distant cacophony of clanking noise from other rooms.

The Young looked to see a large red button under the guard's fist. The guard began melting the ice off the arms of the machine.

The flame on the torch was turning a yellow color. The Young hastened his cutting. Progress was getting more difficult, as the blade of the knife had dulled. Three-fourths of the way through, another noise spooked him. It was a metallic pinging. The guard was banging the torch on the corner of the machine. The flame was orange.

The Young began hacking roughly on the strap, taking longer strokes and applying force on the handle. A loud buzzing noise scared the Young. The guard had hit the red button again. The machine began moving once more. The flame on the worker's torch was sputtering a dull orange color. The guard was about halfway done with the second pipe.

The Young looked back at the strap. It was holding on by a thicker strip along the edge of the strap. There had been another reinforcing edge on the side he had cut into first, but the knife had sailed right through it then. The blade had dulled substantially since then, making it nearly worthless against the second edge. He hacked desperately at the last bit. The edging refused to snap. He tried different angles to no avail.

The Young jumped, spooked by a noise. The guard had banged the torch on the machine once more. Without seeing any progress, the guard shut off the torch and lined the nozzle up with the corner of the machine. He swung it down and struck the nozzle on the machine. The nozzle shot off, banging into the left pipe in the process and clanking across the frosty floor. A blue flame erupted from the top of the cylinder of the torch but began changing to green.

The Young looked at his own torch. The last bit of the strap had not cut. His knife had dulled to the point of being useless. He paused for a moment to weigh his options and slipped the knife back into the sheath. He looked over at the guard. The guard's torch was sputtering a yellow color. The guard drew his arm back. The Young saw his chance. He began swinging his foot.

Just as the guard struck the machine with his torch, the Young kicked his own torch. The strap snapped due to the blow from his foot. The Young watched as the torch flew up into the air. He ran after it toward the door. The door slowly swung open. The Young dove for the torch, snagging the nozzle with his fingertips and pulling it to his chest. He toppled over from overextending to catch the torch. He twisted in the air and landed harshly on his back, causing him to slide across the icy floor through the open doorway. The Young slid to a halt, but only for a moment.

A pair of hands began pushing on his outer thigh and shoulder, pausing for a moment to rip the torch from his grasp. An instant later, the Young found himself on his stomach in the dark corner he and the Survivalist had hidden in before. He heard the sound of a door latching. A body flopped down on top of his back. A hand reached around his head and fell across his mouth. He struggled but caught a glimpse of his aggressor out of the corner of his eye. It was the Survivalist. He abandoned his resistance and wiggled further into the dark corner.

A moment later, the worker opened the door. He stood there for a moment, scratching his side. He placed the empty torch bottle at his feet and rubbed his hands together. He shuddered. He drew in a deep breath while flexing his fingers. He froze for a moment as something ran across his thoughts. He peeked down at the bottle at his feet before turning and heading back into the room. Just as the door latched shut, the Survivalist abandoned the Young in the corner and rushed to the slat. She slid it open.

The worker inside the room had retrieved the nozzle from the torch from the floor. He turned back toward the door. The Survivalist slid the slat shut before he could see her and dove back down on top of the Young, who had rolled over to lie flat on his back to allow the pain of landing on it to dwindle. He grunted as she landed on him but remained still. The door swung open once more, enveloping the area in another batch of fog, as the worker emerged from it. He stooped, retrieved the empty bottle in the opposite hand from the one holding the busted nozzle, and started walking down the hallway.

The Survivalist again left the Young and began creeping down the hallway after him. The Young remained lying on the floor. The Survivalist looked back at him. She waved her arm, beckoning him toward her. He didn't move. She waddled back to him. "What are you doing?" she questioned, irritated.

The Young huffed. "Just give me a minute." She tried to push him but only managed to shake him. "Hold on. I just landed flat on my back. I am out of breath and dizzy."

The Survivalist grabbed his shoulder and began pulling him into a sitting position. He sat up himself and held his head. He began to fall, but the Survivalist held him upright by pinning him against the wall. After a moment, he lowered his arms and blinked a few times. "Are you all right now?"

The Young sensed the Survivalist's impatience. "No. I will be soon, but we don't have time to wait." He spotted the torch in the corner. He snatched it up and managed to stand. He started down the hall. As he stumbled down the hall, he took a look around. He saw a white lighting strip on the lower edge of the wall that he had not noticed before. His lightheadedness dissipated.

He took another look around. They had not made it far. He paused for a moment to think. The Survivalist bumped into him. He knew they had come in, but his curiosity of this place aroused him. He began walking down the hall. They made it to the Y intersection. Instead of going straight, the Young took a left. "Where are you going?"

"I want to know what is over here."

"We need to get out of here!"

"I know. Just let me have a look." Just after the intersection, the new hall bent off to the right. The Young peeked around the corner. A loud buzzer echoed through the hall. The two froze. The Survivalist watched as the Young yanked his head back and began pushing her back out to the Y intersection. "Go! Go! Go!" The Survivalist began creeping away. The Young shoved her. "No, run!" The two broke out into a sprint. They took the path back to the door, entering the garage area.

The Young checked the window. There was nobody through the door. He threw it open, stopping it before it slammed the wall, and shut it behind the Survivalist. The two bolted for the garage door, which was now lifted fully above their heads. The Young stopped on the threshold of the garage door and peered outside. The guards had disappeared. He kept low as he ran outside and waved the Survivalist on. He crossed the opening and placed the torch on the boulder.

He jumped off the boulder and onto the rope. The hatchet on the rope swung hazardously as he hauled himself up the wall. The Survivalist steadied the rope once he reached the top. The Young motioned for the Survivalist to throw him the torch. She hesitated. He insisted. She picked it up and lobbed it. He reached out over the wall, nearly toppling over, but managed to pull himself and the torch back overtop the wall. He placed the torch a short distance away on top of the wall.

The Survivalist had begun climbing. The Young began pulling her up with the rope to expedite the effort. She reached the top, and the Young placed the hatchet near the torch. The rope had gone slack. The hook clanked against the wall on the outside. The Young held the rope and kicked the Survivalist's ankle gently. She crawled to the edge. The Young reassured her. "I got it. Go!"

She sat on the edge of the wall, grabbed the rope, and swung over. The Young lowered her to the rock pile on the other side. The Survivalist looked up just as the Young dropped the torch. She caught it. The Young pulled up some of the loose rope and lowered the hatchet simultaneously. She grabbed the hatchet, and the Young chucked the rope over the wall. It slapped on the loose stones. He lay down and swung his feet over the wall, slid out over the edge, and dangled there by his hands. "What are you doing? You can't take that far of a drop! You will—"

"Shhh!" The Young had interrupted her. The Survivalist went quiet. A pair voices were having a conversation on the other side of the wall. They were getting closer.

"The coolant system?"

A second voice replied, "Yeah. I thawed it with a Scorch Torch."

"Great!" exclaimed the first.

Another voice joined in. "We need that coolant system running all the time. Without it, the entire plant can overheat. Remember, we are working with extremely high temperatures on the inside of the insulation layer."

The deep voice of the worker from before said, "I know, I know. I am keeping an eye on it."

A fourth voice chimed in. "Did you all see that strap on the Scorch Torch wall in the coolant system room?"

Yet another voice answered, "No. What happened to it?"

The fourth voice continued. "I dunno. It was like someone had tried to cut it off. The torch was missing too."

A worker's deep voice said, "What? I didn't see that. I was just in there before the end of the shift, melting the ice off the coolant system too. How could I have missed that when I picked up the torch?"

A sixth voice replied, "Maybe you should spend a little less time keeping an eye on the ice and a little more on your surroundings, then."

The deep voice groaned. "It is never enough with you guys, is it?"

The nasally voice, which had been fixing the wires earlier, joined. "And it never will be. Now why don't we all…" The voices trailed off. Another loud buzzer went off. It was followed by a squeaking noise. The Young pulled himself up high enough to peek over the wall. Guards were milling about everywhere. The main double doors to the plant had opened up. The workers were pouring out by the dozen. He dropped back down to avoid being spotted.

The Survivalist threw a rock and bounced it off the wall near him. He looked down at her. She spoke in a soft tone. "What is going on?"

"The workers must be off now. Everyone is leaving the plant."

"Well, get down! We have to go."

The Young looked around. "I could pull myself back up, but I would be seen. I have to drop down."

"You will hurt yourself. Let me use the rope."

"No! There is nothing to tie off to up here, and the hook end will make too much noise."

"Well, how are you going to get down?"

The Young thought this over. "Catch me."

"What?"

"Catch me."

"I am not strong enough for that. How do you expect me to…" She trailed off. A familiar voice caught the Young's ear.

"Come on, Young. I will catch you." The Young looked down to see the Mechanic below. He let go of the ledge. The Mechanic caught him easily and set him on the ground. He motioned, and the two followed him back up to the scouting ledge.

Once they arrived, the Survivalist handed the torch to the Mechanic. "Careful. This thing is really bright."

The Mechanic turned the red cylinder with vertically ribbed sides in his hands. "This is the right torch. Good work."

The Bartender peeked over at the torch. "So how did it go?"

The Young shook his head. "Poorly, but we got it without getting caught."

The Bartender shrugged. "That sounds like a success to me."

The Young widened his eyes, blew out a gust of air, and shook his head in reaction to her statement. The Mechanic turned back to the group from the cart of parts. "I can't use the torch here. It is going to be too bright. We will be caught for sure."

The Old Man pointed the top of the Lightstaff across the city. The staff had reactivated to assisting the Old Man in the lack of strangers. "Back to the hiding cave, then."

The Bartender stood from her rock seat. "No. We can't cross the city now. All the workers just got off. The city will be thriving with people soon."

The Radioman spoke next. "Where are we to inhabit for the night, then?"

The Bartender didn't reply. The Hobo sighed. "Look, I have an idea. Do we still have some credits left?" The Radioman nodded. "Good. In that case, we are going to need you, Entrepreneur."

The Entrepreneur straightened. "Me?" The entire group stared at him.

The Hobo replied, "Yeah. Get ready to haggle."

*****

The group got a plan and asked the Bartender for approval. The Bartender gave the go-ahead once the majority of people found their destinations from leaving the power plant on the condition that they use the follow the Old Man tactics that they had become accustomed to. The Hobo guided the group along a back alley until they came across a small symbol painted on a wall. It was nothing more than an upside-down U shape with a dot underneath it.

The Hobo held everyone back. He walked over to the Entrepreneur. "I need you to pay very close attention. This joint is not welcoming to outsiders. It is a silent house. You come to these places when you need to do some things that aren't necessarily legal. You need to force your way in using credits and explain that we are only here to work on some things in private. Be as vague as possible. If you throw them enough credits, they will look the other way. I mean that in the most literal sense. They will actually turn around and act like you don't exist. If they never see you, they can't give your location out to anybody, legal or otherwise.

"The man will wave you in. That is going to be the signal for all of us to go inside. There will be a man pointing at a doorway somewhere. He will also be facing away. You need to go straight to that doorway and through it. Do not go anywhere else. Do not look at anything else. Most importantly, do not say anything once they let us inside. That goes for everyone here.

"Whoever goes through the door last needs to loudly slam the door shut. This allows everyone on the outside to relax and resume their normal practices, which we are to not know about. This is nothing more than a quick cash grab for them and a place to hide for us. Understand?"

The Entrepreneur nodded. "I have been around one of these places before, but I was told to never go into one of them as we passed by."

The Hobo raised his eyebrows. "Whoever told you that was smart." The Entrepreneur nodded again, sensing the plan had not changed, and walked up to the door. He stood there for a moment. Nothing happened. He looked back nervously at the Hobo. "Sorry. I forgot to tell you. Knock on the door three times with a short pause between each hit." The Entrepreneur raised his fist to strike the door with his knuckles.

"No, no, no, not with the knuckles. Hit the door with the soft side of the fist. Everyone who has been to these is told one way or another to never knock on the door with their knuckles. If somebody does, they know it is either somebody new, the law, or somebody at the wrong address. Make those hits count. You won't hurt the door."

The Entrepreneur struck the door once, twice, three times. He waited for a moment. The door clicked and then swung open silently. A quite voice came through the dark doorway. "Yes?"

The Entrepreneur shifted posture. He spoke. "I am here for a room."

The voice replied, "How many?"

The Entrepreneur tipped his head. "Why does it matter?"

The man in the doorway paused. "What do you need to do?"

"We need a place to hide and to work on some things for a bit."

"How long?"

"Just until night."

For a brief moment, a pale, bony, dry face shot out into the light beyond the threshold of the door. The group had hidden away before, but the man spotted a feminine face before it could hide away. The man's face went briefly into shock. The Entrepreneur quickly broke the line of sight by stepping in the way. The face disappeared into the dark once more. A thin, unhealthy white hand reached out into the light.

The Entrepreneur held out a hand toward the group. The Radioman plopped a stack of credits in his hand. The Entrepreneur counted out a few coins and placed them in the skinny hand. The hand remained. The Entrepreneur cocked his head. He plopped a small handful of coins into the hand. The hand stayed. "Look, pal, I have already overpaid you. Now turn around."

The hand retracted. The Entrepreneur walked inside. The group rushed out from hiding and followed him in. The Mechanic wheeled the cart in behind him as well. They quickly navigated off to the right into a hallway, all the way down to an open doorway and inside. The room was dark and musty. There was only a bed on one side and a metallic table on the other with a decrepit lamp. The Survivalist walked over to the bed and sat on it. The bed sagged under her weight. "This bed is broken down so far that it can't support my weight."

The Bartender cringed. "Honey, you might not want to touch that bed. There might be reason it is broken in." The Survivalist remained sitting but grew confused. "I might have been lucky to have been found by a gambling place instead of this one. Although it has likely been a while, you likely are not the only woman to sit there. Please don't touch that bed."

The Hobo hit the Bartender's arm. "This isn't that kind of place. There were no women in the room. I looked. For that matter, I don't think there are any women down here besides you from what I can gather. But she's right, you still don't want to touch the bed."

This lack of direct explanation concerned the entire room. The Survivalist stood and stepped across the room. The Mechanic pulled the wagon over to the metal table. He tried to brighten the dim lamp. It shut off completely, plunging the room in darkness. There was a ticking sound. The light turned back on. The Mechanic shoved it over to the edge of the table. "Can I get some better light over here?"

The Old Man shook the staff. It blasted to life with a beam to the table. He walked over, stood it upright, and walked back across the room. The staff whirred quietly as it balanced. The Mechanic retrieved the Scorch Torch. "This might be a while. Is there a vent in here?"

The Hobo pointed above the bed. "It is on the wall. I will open it." He walked over, avoiding the bed, and opened the flaps on the vent. The vent was barely above the ground surface of an alleyway outside.

The Mechanic found a pair of matching adapters and held them up to the group. "I took the time earlier while you two were getting the torch to figure a bunch of these connections." He lit the torch and began heating one side. After a moment, he shut the torch off and quickly slid the cool side into the hot one. The two fused seconds later. The Mechanic touched the newly fused connection and then picked it up.

The Radioman was surprised. "That didn't burn you?"

"No. These connections cool incredibly fast. It is as if the connection just eliminates the heat. The metal table will burn me before any of these connections do." The Radioman continued watching the Mechanic.

The Hobo caught the Entrepreneur's attention. "How did you know the guy was overcharging you?"

The Entrepreneur grinned. "I didn't. I just assumed he was. All the scum like him will just let you keep paying until you tell them no."

"Ah." The group fell silent.

*****

A couple of hours later of idling around and avoiding the bed, the group finally heard the Mechanic speak. "I am done with the connections. Good thing too. This torch is running out." He shut off the yellow-orange flame on the torch. He pulled a bunch of pieces out of the wagon and laid them out on the table. The pieces were all connected by wire but not physically attached together yet. The floppy structure of wires and parts resembled a tall person. He heated the shoulders of the torso and forced each arm into place with a metallic thudding sound each. He did the same with the hips for the legs. Finally, he heated the top center of the chest and forced the neck of the head down into place.

A small green light appeared on the right eye of the machine. The Mechanic halted his work. He followed a spindly green beam of light back to the Lightstaff behind him. Suddenly, the Lightstaff shut off the light, leaving only the poor lighting from the lamp. The staff lurched past the Mechanic, shoving him slightly out of the way in the process, and positioned itself near the machine's head. The green light beam gradually glided from focusing on the machine's eye down to its neck, then shrunk to a tiny dot.

The staff flipped a flap out of its side and extended a small probe. It placed the probe directly on the tiny green dot. The green beam of light disappeared. The whirring noise in the staff picked up speed. It gained base, getting louder by the second, until it reached a steady roar so loud it vibrated the chests of each person in the group. There was an earsplitting crack and a flash of blinding white light. The staff fell to the floor with a loud clanking sound on the stone. The group rubbed their eyes and held their ears.

An arm twitched on the table. The group paused their actions. It twitched again. The Mechanic inched forward, curious of what had happened. The arm twitched once more. The Mechanic reached far out and touched the arm. The machine abruptly sat up. It stopped in an upright position, but its momentum tossed it off the table and onto the floor with the staff. The group yelled and ran to the other side of the room. The Bartender, who had just now begun paying attention to the build, spoke first. "What have you done?"

The Mechanic seemed hurt. "What do you mean? I fixed the robot."

"That's not a robot!" She cringed and checked the doorway. She crossed the room and gingerly touched the knob.

The Hobo arrested her hand from the knob. She jumped. He scolded her with a question. "What are you doing? You can't just barge out of here." She twisted the knob of the door with her free hand. She and the Hobo peered outside. The Hobo snatched the handle and gently closed the door before shoving the Bartender away from it.

The Bartender crowded up against the wall opposite the metal table. She pointed to the machine. "That is an Exoduster."

The Hobo removed his ear from listening through the door. "A what?"

"An Exoduster! It is a bounty hunter. They kill humans all the time. I have heard about people dying to these things on the outside from people in the cardhouse."

The machine, which the Bartender had just called an Exoduster, slid flat onto the floor and sat up more slowly. It stopped at the top and turned slowly to see the group. Its eyes adjusted noisily in its head. It emitted a series of incoherent electric noises. It balled its right hand and struck its own chest. A voice suddenly snapped into broken speak. "—el-ello." It reached up with choppy movements and grabbed its throat. It lowered its hand. "Ah…e…n-name. Na-name." It started saying letters and numbers individually. "EX135."

The Young, fascinated by the machine, stepped forward. "EX135?"

The Exoduster nodded. "Is E-X short for Exoduster?"

It shook its head. "Expe…ment."

"Experiment?"

It pointed. "All."

"All?"

It nodded and held its right hand vertically. It slowly brought the hand from left to right. "Expe…ment…all"

"Oh! Experimental?" It slowly pointed at the Young with a jittering arm. The Young looked back at the group. The Bartender was cowering in fear. He turned back. "Are you an Exoduster?"

It tried to respond but only came up with scratchy noises. It tried again. "Was."

"You were an Exoduster?"

"…es."

"But you aren't anymore?"

"Nuh…oh."

"Did you change somehow?"

"I free-ee-eee me-e."

"You freed yourself?"

It pointed slowly again. "...es." It looked down and saw the staff lying lifeless on the floor. It pointed to it. The Old Man crossed the room, retrieved it, and held it just out of reach of the machine. The machine made a lurching motion, surprising the Old Man, and touched the side of the staff with the palm of its hand. The staff snapped back to life, whirring oddly for a moment before standing upright and supporting the Old Man once more. The Exoduster seemed saddened. It sagged back onto the floor. The Old Man stooped and tried to hand the staff back. The staff moved to dodge the Exoduster's slow-moving hand. The Exoduster waved the Old Man and the staff away.

It noticed the Scorch Torch and pointed. The Mechanic grabbed it and held it up. The Exoduster pointed at its side. The Mechanic lit the torch to reveal a dull orange flame. The Exoduster jumped and waved it away. It managed to speak a word: "Low."

The Mechanic nodded. "It is all we have." It noticed the wagon and pointed to it. The Mechanic pointed at the wagon too. "Do you want it?"

"...es."

The Mechanic walked over and dragged the wagon to the machine. The machine snagged the edge and tried to pull itself up toward it. The Mechanic grabbed ahold of the Exoduster's chest frame. He picked it up. Its left arm and neck remained stiff. Both of its legs, its waist, and its left arm fell limp. The Mechanic positioned it so that it was in a sitting position in the wagon. "Better?"

"...es. Go." It pointed to the door. The Bartender stepped in front of the wagon.

"No! We are not taking an Exoduster with us. It is going to kill us all."

The Exoduster seemed appalled. It shook its head. "Nuh...oh. Not Ex...ster. Free. Will not hu...ha...harm." The Bartender was unchanged. The machine stiffly locked its eyesight on the Bartender. "Top...mount..." It pointed upward. "You...ear...bad...want out."

The Young raised an eyebrow. "Her ears are bad and want out."

"Nuh…oh." It pointed at the floor. "Ear." There was a silent pause.

The Young took in a breath in excitement. "Oh! Here, not ear. Her being here is bad."

"…es."

The Bartender grew curios. "So what? You could have figured that out about any woman down here."

The machine emitted a grinding noise from its chest. The Mechanic smacked it. The noise stopped. The Exoduster gave a thumbs-up. It refocused on the Bartender. "Loo…ssss and…ass."

The Young chuckled. "Lose and ass?"

The Exoduster shook its head as vigorously as it could. It repeated itself. The Bartender suddenly took in a sharp breath. She spoke in a hushed tone. "Lulos and grass."

The Exoduster pointed at her. "Tr…and…eems."

"Trees and streams."

"Nah…oh. Only…ear-rrr-rrr." The Mechanic smacked the machine's chest again. It stopped repeating the same syllable.

The Bartender began slowly crossing the room. "I once said I wanted to taste lulos and smell the grass. I wanted to see the trees and streams. But all the people here think they are stuck here." She turned to the machine. "But how did you know that? I said that after I found out I was stuck down here."

The Exoduster strained to move. It wheezed a surprisingly smooth sentence. "Hey there, Mrs. Pretty."

The Bartender lit up. A smile spread across her face. She ran across the room and grabbed the machine's face. "I can't believe it is you." She turned back to face the group. "I didn't survive here all on my own. This Exoduster saved my life. One day, just after the women extermination announcement, it sacrificed itself to save me. I was going to get caught by the guards. It threw itself in the way, killed the guards, and said something about coming back as it disassembled itself.

"It said something about how it was doing so to avoid being found by more guards. It must have worked too well. I never found it. I should have known when you were brought into the cardhouse that it must have been this one. This was the one Exoduster that told me not to trust any other Exoduster, as they were all bounty hunters."

The Young seemed confused. "What are you talking about?"

The Bartender shook her head. "We can talk more about it later." She stood and started toward the door, which the Hobo barred her off from.

The Young persisted. "At least tell us what 'Hey there, Mrs. Pretty' have to do with that?"

The Bartender smiled. "Oh. That was a joke it had with me. I remember exactly how it came up with it. One of my friends called me pretty, and it took it as my actual name. That was just before the bad times happened." She got lost in thought. The Young waved his arms. The Bartender ignored him.

The Radioman spoke up. "Are we all right to bring it along, then?"

The Bartender refocused on the conversation. "Yes, but only with this one. I do not trust any other Exodusters." The machine gave a thumbs-up and collapsed into the cart. The room fell silent until the Hobo spoke up.

"What do we do now?"

The group exchanged glances. The Old Man approached the Exoduster. "Can you hack an alarmed door without tripping the alarm?"

The Exoduster's eyes flickered on. "What kind-d?"

The Old Man chuckled. "The door out of the City of Underground."

The machine shook its head. "Nuh…oh."

"What if I told you there was a break where the guards are gone?"

The Exoduster picked its head up. "Time?"

The Old Man shrugged. "I don't know. It can't be a lot of time."

The Exoduster glanced over at the Bartender. She was still smiling. "…es." It dropped its head noisily back into the wagon. Its eyes flickered. "Run…on…emer…power." Its eyes flickered off. A small yellow light appeared on its chest.

The Mechanic pushed the Old Man gently and looked at the light. "It is next to a lightning symbol. I am assuming it needs a charge. Does anybody know how to do that?"

The Bartender tilted her head. "It never needed a charge while I was with it before."

The Mechanic pointed to the Old Man. "The Lightstaff must have given it just enough to function, and it still needs more power."

"How much more power?" the Bartender queried.

The Mechanic shrugged. "I have no idea."

The Young joined back in on the conversation. "Well, there is no way we are getting it into the power plant. We had a hard enough time just getting ourselves in and out."

The Entrepreneur broke in. "Hey. Uh, I don't mean to break the conversation here, but we should be leaving soon. The people outside are stirring around a lot. We may be outstaying our welcome." The group turned to see the Entrepreneur with his ear held up to the door. He flinched back in fear as a single knock hit the door. The Entrepreneur held his chest and regained some breath.

The Hobo walked toward the door abruptly. He grabbed ahold of the Entrepreneur and tossed him out of the way. The Mechanic caught him. The Hobo placed his ear on the door. Fear ran across his face. "We need to leave. Now. They are going to try to trap us in here. Something is happening outside in the lobby we went through on the way in. They will let us out like nothing happened if we leave right now. That allows all who do not want involved a chance to leave. That knock on the door was a warning from somebody who didn't want to trap us in here."

The group lined up behind the Hobo. "No. Entrepreneur, you have to be the first one out. Leave in the same order you came in." The group rushed a rearrangement. The Hobo pointed at the door-knob. The Entrepreneur cracked the door open and began to peek out. The Hobo shoved him out the door. The Entrepreneur quickly straightened up and looked for a pointing man.

The people outside must have frozen right where they stood. Everyone was turned away but positioned in a circle around a pair of men with blood running down their arms and legs. One of the men in the middle was holding a metal stick. There was a broken metal stool lying in the path. The Hobo kicked it out of the way from behind the Entrepreneur. The pointed arm led them to the exit. They crossed the room. A man was standing directly behind another, holding a glass bottle, gazing at another fellow sitting calmly in a stool. They walked out untouched.

As soon as the door slammed behind them, shouting and breaking noises emitted dully from the building. The Hobo pointed to an alleyway. They all piled in while the Old Man forced his way through to begin leading. "Where are we going?" asked the Old Man.

The Hobo shrugged. "Anywhere but here. That was a fight. Guards will be here if things heat up and escape the building." There was a crashing sound of a window breaking. Shouting erupted from the new hole.

The Bartender peered up. She nodded. "Yeah. In fact, they are probably already coming."

The Hobo gritted his teeth. "It can get worse. Nobody was dead. Lead on, Old Man." The Old Man didn't move. He didn't know where to go. The Hobo looked over at the Bartender. "Where is the exit door?"

*****

The group managed to cross a small bit of town to a far outskirt against the cave wall. The Bartender had warned them that a lot of people used cubbies in the walls for illegal activity. The Hobo replied that they were just about to perform illegal activities, so it fitted. The Bartender was not impressed by the statement. They found a small area to hide in for a bit and went inside.

After sitting in the dark and oddly moist indentation, the Bartender began a conversation with information. "The exit door is a little farther around the edge of the cave. There is a big wall on either side of it that prevents a lot of hiding places. We will have to run in, hack the door or whatever, and get out."

The Mechanic shook the machine in the cart. Its eyes snapped on. It groaned. The Mechanic asked, "Are you still able to hack the door?" It nodded once and shut back off. The Mechanic faced the group. "When do we move in?"

The Old Man shrugged. "I suppose we go now. We will have to wait and see if Cobbler's thoughts were right."

The group carefully picked their way across a boulder field to the edge of a cleared area. The door was lit brightly on the other side. "Wait. That is the exit door?" asked the Survivalist.

"Yep," replied the Bartender. The group took in the sight. The door was a massive circular gray hatch. An orange circle ringed the center of the hatch. The door was hung on a hinge at the top so that it would pivot up and out. Two large cylinders were positioned on the bottom of the hatch. They would extend and pivot to lift it upward.

The Old Man grabbed the Bartender's arm. "You didn't say this door was the size of a building."

The Bartender scowled and pulled her arm away. "That is because we aren't going through that door. That is the hatch they use to get large things like the turbine for the power plant inside here. We are using that door to the right of the hatch." She pointed to a relatively small building on the right side. Multiple guards stood outside the door. The Bartender continued speaking. "My idea is to hack only the small door and leave the tunnel hatch shut."

The Old Man shuffled away from the Bartender. The Mechanic poked the Bartender's other arm. "Is there any way we can get closer?"

The Bartender shook her head. "I never found it wise to be this close to the guarded exit door." The Mechanic looked up in realization of the correctness of her statement.

The Old Man regained her attention. "What about on the far side of this opening?"

The Bartender blinked at him. "There is nothing over there besides the cave wall. There isn't even a way around the lake that way.

Look at it. The water runs all the way up to a huge vertical face that stretches all the way up to the top of the cave. Why would anyone ever go over there?"

The Old Man smiled. He poked her shoulder with his index finger and held it there as he spoke. "Exactly." He retracted his finger.

The Bartender opened her mouth to argue, but before she could ask what the Old Man meant, she understood. She furrowed her brow. She shook her head. "Old Man, that is brilliant." The rest of the group exchanged perplexed glances.

The Old Man chuckled. "Let me run you all through it. There is nothing over there besides some boulders, right?" The group agreed. "And therefore, there is absolutely no reason for anybody to be over there, right?" The group again agreed. "So why would any guard who hates his job already be concerned about checking those boulders?" The group remained confused.

The Hobo sighed. "He is saying we should go hide over by the boulders since the guards have no real reason to ever look there."

The Old Man pointed at the Hobo. "And because the guards will leave while walking away from us instead of walking toward us. If they do leave early, we will be in a prime position."

"What if they don't leave early?" rebuked the Survivalist.

The Young motioned to the boulders. "I think if we can manage to get over there then we can probably manage to get back here." He motioned to the boulders and then to the rock surface at his feet as he spoke. The Survivalist conceded to this.

The Old Man scanned the group. "Does anybody have anything else?" No one replied. "All right, then. How can we get across?" He turned to face the open field.

*****

After some debate over plans to cross the stone field, they set into action. The Young grabbed on to the boulder in front of him. He peered over it. He froze in place. The Survivalist nudged his arm. "If you are too…" Before she could finish her sentence, the

Young vaulted the boulder and took off full tilt across the field. The Survivalist crouched down behind the boulder, slightly bewildered. A short bit later, she peeked over the boulder. The Young must have made it to the far side. He was nowhere to be seen.

She swung her gaze over to the far boulders for any signs of the Young. Still, she saw nothing. Suddenly, a hand shot out over the top of a boulder and waved once, calling her over. The Survivalist crawled over the boulder and took off as well. She focused entirely on the boulder where the hand was and her own footing. The hand shot up once more, telling her to stop. She lay on the ground immediately. The hand started another motion but disappeared before anything could be formed.

The Survivalist slid herself forward into a dip in the stone. The front of her shirt grew cold, biting at her skin, followed by a sticky sensation. The indentation was filled with a puddle of water, which her shirt had just absorbed. She resisted the urge to stand up. The hand beckoned once more. She dragged herself and her sopping wet shirt up and ran the rest of the way across the open field.

"Good work. That was..." He cut himself off as he turned to look at her. "What happened to you?"

The Survivalist sighed. "There was a puddle."

"I would say so."

"I really want to take this shirt off. It is so sticky."

The Young turned away and began focusing on the guards. He replied half consciously, "Then take it off." The Survivalist glanced over in nervous disgust. The Young realized a full second later what he had said. He turned back to her. "That is not what I meant. I..." He groaned and gave up his defense. She shook her head, more amused at his discomfort than anything, untucked the shirt, and began wringing it out. The Young swiveled back around awkwardly and watched the guards. Nothing happened for a while.

The Young peeked over the boulder. The Hobo was waiting on the far side alongside the Entrepreneur. The Hobo gave a questioning shrug and an upturned hand. The Young pointed through the boulder at the guards and shrugged back. He pursed his lips. He turned to the Survivalist. "Pass me that rock." The Survivalist located the stone and moved to pick it up. "No, not that one. The bigger one." She picked up a stone nearly twice as large as the original and handed it to the Young.

He motioned to get the Hobo's attention by waving his arm and pointed at the stone. He then pointed at the lake and made a throwing motion. The Hobo nodded. The Young repositioned to see the guards. He cocked his arm back and launched the stone. It flew silently across the gap and made a terrific clap against the water. The Young had ducked for cover as the stone was in flight. He waited a moment, then peeked around the boulder. The guards had not moved. In fact, he questioned if they had even noticed.

Bang! The loud sound had come from the main hatch door. The guards were yelling. The Young checked the group on the far side to find the entirety of the rest of the group scurrying across the field. This included the Exoduster, which was being carried in a limp state in the Mechanic's arms.

The Bartender arrived first, then was joined by the Mechanic and the Exoduster, who were followed closely by the Hobo, then the Radioman, the Entrepreneur, who had tripped on the way over, and then finally, the Old Man. Each person dove in behind a boulder. The Survivalist glanced around at the group. "That was not the plan."

The Mechanic grew defensive. "Well, the old plan was not working, and you two weren't coming up with any good ideas."

The Young cut in. "Did you throw a rock at that door?"

The Radioman chuckled. "Yes, he did. It was quite the overhand."

The Young continued. "What did you do with the wagon?"

The Old Man gestured across the open field. He gasped out, "We...we left it over there. We didn't...have a choice." The group collectively gave the Old Man a concerned glance. He shook his head. "Look, I am getting up there in the years." No one pushed the topic.

The Survivalist joined back in. "Did anyone get spotted?"

The Hobo smiled. "No. I made sure nobody was seen." She nodded in response.

The Bartender relaxed against her boulder. "Now what? We just wait for them to leave?"

The Old Man nodded. He swallowed heavily in the middle of drawing his breath. "Yep." The group went silent. The guards were still clambering around in search of the source of the stone.

The Entrepreneur glanced over at the Survivalist. "Hey, what happened to your shirt?" The Survivalist groaned.

*****

The group had taken turns keeping watch on the guards all night, or at least what they perceived as night. The cave had slowly fallen into darkness with only minimal lighting around the crop fields and some of the streets. The boulders they were holed up in were now completely pitch-black. If the massive hatch were not lit up for the guards, they wouldn't have been able to see at all.

It was now the Entrepreneur's shift. He was positioned up against the chosen watching boulder, fighting a heavy head. He allowed himself to lower his head onto the nearby boulder. It was not comfortable. He ached from sitting up against the hard surface for so long. He rubbed his left shoulder. He idled for a moment and glanced back at the group. They were all passed out in strange positions on the stone. He wondered if any of them were comfortable. He craned his neck back around to look at the guards. They had not moved an inch since his shift started besides maybe to breath and blink. They had not even spoken to one another. No wonder they hated their jobs.

He laid his head back again to stare at the ceiling of the cave. Finding nothing and being consumed by boredom, he wiggled over to the far side of the boulder. Something moved. Alerted, he flipped over to a crouching position to look at the movement. The movement slid behind a boulder nearby the cliffside. The Entrepreneur glanced at the group. Everybody was still resting. He worked his way across the lumpy stone ground to the boulder where the movement had been.

He peeked around the edge. A massive arm flew past his face, narrowly missing his head. An equally sizable hand reached around his face and clasped his mouth shut. The hand turned his head toward the shoulder. The Entrepreneur resisted, flailing about and making a muffled racket, until he saw that the arm belonged to the Mechanic. He relaxed, and the Mechanic released his head. "Sorry, Entrepreneur. I couldn't risk you yelling."

The Entrepreneur sat down beside the Mechanic. He huffed a few times to regather his breath. "It's fine." He waved his hand to play it off. The Mechanic raised an eyebrow. He was surprised that the Entrepreneur had taken it so well. The Entrepreneur caught on. "I would have tried to do the same thing, although if this were the other way around, I think you would have bested me."

The Mechanic smiled and punched his shoulder lightly. "And you know it." The Entrepreneur rubbed his shoulder. The light punch had still hurt. The two went silent for a bit as they gazed over the swarming crowds of nightlife in the City of Underground. This was a strange sight to the both of them. The city, while completely empty earlier, now swarmed with people. It was as if their actual lives took place when the lights dimmed down.

The two were perched up above the city a ways to the door. Being right on the cliffside meant a clear sight of the city. The only issue was, they were on the same side of the lake as the city and, therefore, could only see a sharp isometric of the city instead of the broad lakeside view. The Mechanic jumped the conversation back into motion. "Aren't you supposed to be on watch?"

"Yeah. The guards haven't moved for my entire shift. I saw you move. I figured I would investigate, and here we are." There was another pause.

The Mechanic swept his right arm across the city. He looked left to see the Entrepreneur's face in the darkness of the cave. "If it were not for all those lights from the city, this cave would be pitch-black."

"It is nearly pitch-black anyway."

261

"Well, yes, but we can at least still see a little."

The Entrepreneur squinted at the city. "So where do you think all of those people go for the other half of the day?"

The Mechanic shrugged. "I suppose into the power plant. You saw how many people came out of that thing earlier."

"I know, but that plant just does not look like it is that big."

A new voice joined the chat. "That is because it isn't that big. The plant goes way back into the cave wall." The two froze. "Don't worry." The Young stepped around the boulder. "You have space for one more?" The two scooted right to allow the Young to sit down, and the Young filled the spot.

"You say it goes back into the cave wall?" poked the Entrepreneur.

"Oh yeah. We barely scratched the surface of how big that place is when we went in after the Scorch Torch."

The Mechanic leaned forward to see the Young past the Entrepreneur. "How big do you think it is?"

The Young shook his head. "Big. We found the Scorch Torch in a freezing-cold room that had some sort of cooling device in it. It was moving a lot of fluid. Whatever they are doing, they are moving a lot of heat. We didn't go any further in, but I assume that the plant goes deep into the rock and meets the geothermal source somewhere."

The Mechanic leaned back against the boulder once more. "My guess is a massive turbine. They are probably cycling water into steam using the geothermal heat and then cooling the water using the machine you found. There may be more than one cooling station as well."

The Young rested his head back against the boulder as he spoke. "I don't know. The machine had some kind of transparent magenta fluid in it."

The Mechanic raised an eyebrow. "Magenta?"

"Yeah, magenta."

The Mechanic flopped his head over to look at the Young. "You know what color magenta is?"

The Young furrowed his brow. "Yes. Do you?"

The Mechanic nodded. "It is like a pink and purple color." The Entrepreneur scratched his head as he looked down at his own feet. The Mechanic chuckled. "Now you know, Entrepreneur." He looked back up at the Young. "I am not sure what that stuff is. Maybe the magenta fluid is an efficient coolant that they use somewhere else." The three went silent as they watched the city.

A few moments passed. The Mechanic had nodded off. The Entrepreneur would have done the same, but the Mechanic was leaning on him, and he was struggling to stay upright. The Young went out to take the Entrepreneur's watch duty for him. As the Entrepreneur struggled to let the Mechanic sleep—he feared what waking him up might do—he watched the city for new activity.

A few minutes later, he saw a bright light appear out near the crop farms. He thought it must just be for the green crops growing on the waterfront. He scanned the fields. There was not a worker in sight, but the new light allowed him to get a look at the plants. They were too far away to get any details, but he could make out that they were leafy and probably about waist high. This puzzled the Entrepreneur. He was no farmer, but he was fairly certain that plants like that did not typically grow in caves.

He glanced back at the light. It was brighter than before and projecting a narrower beam upward. He continued watching it. The light seemed to be forming a cone of some kind. A distant voice yelled loudly behind him. The Entrepreneur wondered who that might have been. He realized it was one of the guards. He began to shake the Mechanic, hesitated, decided it was worth it, and pushed him.

The Mechanic didn't budge. The Entrepreneur shoved the Mechanic with both hands and managed to topple him over. Before he hit the ground, the Mechanic woke up and sat upright. He spotted the Entrepreneur a few feet away. The Entrepreneur waved him up and started back to the group.

Meanwhile, the rest of the group had been awakened by the Young. They were all hiding behind the boulders. The Young pointed at the guards. The Entrepreneur and the Mechanic found a boulder each to hide behind. The group listened to the guards.

"Dawn Beacon is forming."

"Oh. It finally is."

"You want to head out? The next crew will be here soon." There was a pause.

"Yeah. That way, I can go get a pair of boots before heading into the plant."

"You work the plant too?"

"Only as a security guard at the main gate."

"When do you sleep?"

"The guards only work until midday. They get rotated out. I sleep right after my morning shift."

"Man, that is too much work."

The voices started getting closer. A third voice joined. "Hey, he is right. You need to drop one of your jobs."

"I need the credits. My house is falling apart. I need to pay for the shipment in of new building supplies."

The voices passed by the group. The Mechanic had collected the Exoduster. The Old Man peered around his boulder. He waved the group out. The group ran over to the small building next to the hatch. The Old Man peeked through the window on the side once he finally got to the building. It was empty. He went over to the door and was surprised to find it unlocked. They stepped inside the building, and the Radioman shut the door behind them.

There were a few controls lining a white control board angled up slightly to the window. "These must be the hatch controls," stated the Radioman. He sat down in a metal chair next to the control panel. "I am going to search this for things that might help us." The rest of the group went over to the main door.

The Mechanic shook the Exoduster. It didn't move. He smacked its chest twice. The Exoduster's eyes blinked to life. "Hey, buddy. It is time for the door." The Exoduster struggled to move its arm. It turned its head toward the door. The Mechanic carried it over. It tried to raise its arm to a panel next to the door. The Entrepreneur walked over and picked its arm up to the panel. It pointed at a screw. The Mechanic's eyes widened. "Uh, we need a screwdriver."

The Survivalist turned from the control panel, where she was watching the Radioman work, to talk to the Mechanic. "What?"

"Look, that panel is not coming off the wall unless we unscrew these two screws on the wall."

The Survivalist shrugged. "Where are we going to get a screwdriver now? We don't have time."

The Radioman held up his right hand while continuing to work with the control board. "We have about ten minutes according to this system. That beam forming out there is apparently called a Dawn Beacon. This place uses it to symbolize daylight cycles on the surface. It is a way to start the day for the whole cave. That beam will eventually turn from the cone it is now into a solid vertical beam. When it does make the beam, this control panel detects it somehow and does something. I am guessing a shift change."

The Hobo glanced over. "How do you know all of this?"

The Radioman smiled, still staring at the controls. "These controls are very similar to the ones I used to use to run my radio station. I think that they are running signals throughout the cave using radio waves." The Hobo nodded and looked out the window. The cone was starting to narrow.

Meanwhile, the Entrepreneur had received instructions on what a screwdriver was and was sent off to find one. There was a supply closet nearby that was not locked, and the Entrepreneur had gone inside to search. Loud banging and rustling emitted from the closet. The Entrepreneur poked his head out of the closet. "Let me know if someone is coming. All right?"

The Young glanced over in surprise. "We were going to do that anyway, but sure thing." The Entrepreneur smiled and gave a thumbs-up. He disappeared back into the closet, and the catastrophic noise resumed. The Young turned to the Bartender. He shrugged. She shrugged back. The two went back to searching for guards outside the building.

There was a massive thud from inside the closet. It was followed shortly by the Entrepreneur's muffled voice through the door. "Aha!" The door handle rattled furiously, and the door flew open. It careened around the hinge and into the wall. The Entrepreneur scurried happily across the short space between the closet and the door and proudly presented his find to the Mechanic.

The Mechanic smiled widely, hesitated, and then very gently said, "Entrepreneur, that is a chisel. Please go try again." The Entrepreneur deflated. He scampered back across the floor and slammed the closet door behind him.

The Hobo looked over at the Mechanic and yelled over the noise coming from the closet, "What is his deal?"

The Mechanic shrugged. "I guess he is just happy to finally feel useful. He hasn't been able to help us much this entire trip." The Hobo nodded. A few moments later, the door swung back open, again slamming the wall, and the Entrepreneur walked across the room with a little less zest and a lot more grease on his hands. He presented another tool. The Mechanic examined it. "That is the right tool, but it has the wrong head, and it is a little too big."

The Entrepreneur raised both palms upward in minor frustration and began to turn back to the closet. The Exoduster twitched its arm toward the Entrepreneur. "Wait," demanded the Mechanic. The Entrepreneur turned back. The Exoduster held out its right arm. The Entrepreneur smiled and placed the screwdriver in its hand. The Exoduster's hand made a strange grinding noise. It turned its palm up, bent the hand down toward the floor at the wrist, and paused. The grinding noise intensified.

A rod shot out of the wrist, attached to the screwdriver by its head, and pulled the screwdriver from the Entrepreneur's hand. Sparks fell from the wrist, and the grinding noise became so loud that it hurt everyone's ears. The grinding whirred down to a halt. The screwdriver fell to the floor. The group stared down at the tool. The head of the screwdriver was blisteringly red and fading off to a blackened metal.

The Exoduster stretched its arm toward it. The Entrepreneur stooped to pick it up. The Exoduster managed to catch the Entrepreneur's forehead on the way down. "Nuh…oh. Ha…" The Entrepreneur didn't understand. The Exoduster shook his hand slowly. "Ha…"

The Entrepreneur stood. "Oh. It is hot." The Exoduster nodded and outstretched its arm. The Mechanic lowered it down to where it could grab the screwdriver and then stood back up to the panel. The Exoduster tried to align the screwdriver head with the screw. It was overshooting the screw head. The Mechanic adjusted the Exoduster in a failed attempt to help. The Entrepreneur grabbed the Exoduster's arm. The Exoduster didn't complain, so he moved up to the forearm and helped the Exoduster move the arm into place.

The Exoduster managed to wiggle its fingers in such a way that it lined the screwdriver up. It placed the screwdriver in. There was a whirring noise for a moment before the Exoduster's wrist snapped counterclockwise, loosening the screw. The Exoduster loosened its grip on the screwdriver while making a circle around the handle using its thumb and forefinger to avoid dropping the screwdriver but, at the same time, allowing it to adjust its grip. It quickly snapped its arm back around, regrabbed the handle, and twisted once more.

It repeated the process multiple times, each time getting faster than the last. Eventually, the screw fell from the wall. The Entrepreneur collected it. The Mechanic adjusted left to the second screw. The Entrepreneur realigned the Exoduster with the screw. The Exoduster removed the screw lighting fast and dropped the screwdriver as soon as the screw dropped out of the threaded hole. The Entrepreneur collected the second screw but left the screwdriver. The Exoduster grabbed the panel and pulled it open. It hinged downward and smacked into the wall below. A terminal with an input screen was set back into the wall where the panel had been. The Exoduster grabbed the edge of the terminal and pulled itself closer. The Mechanic adjusted to allow the movement.

As the Exoduster examined the terminal screen, the Radioman made a few announcements. "We have about five minutes left. I have figured out that this tower releases a signal that will broadcast a noise. It is right at the shift change."

The Young peeked back from the window. "It is probably the work alarm that we heard in the power plant. Did you all hear that outside of the plant as well?"

The Hobo replied, "Yeah. It was loud."

The Radioman glanced up. "Well, it appears that we need through the door before the alarm goes off."

Meanwhile, the Exoduster was busy messing with some wiring on the side of the terminal. It managed to pull a circuit. A green error message ran across the dusty screen. The Exoduster ignored it. It grabbed one of the wires with its right hand and looked down at its left. The Entrepreneur grabbed the limp left arm of the Exoduster and held it up to the wire. The Exoduster stared at the limp hand. The Mechanic spoke. "Hey, can you pinch the wire with its fingers?"

"Will it shock me?"

The Mechanic peeped down at the Exoduster. It shook its head. "No."

The Entrepreneur reached up, adjusted the Exoduster's left hand into position, and pinched the wire. The error message on the screen instantly disappeared. The Exoduster froze in position. Green static filled the black screen. A small bar appeared on the bottom left of the screen, bouncing in and out of clarity. The screen flashed solid green for an instant and then back to the static and the bar. The bar had become slightly longer.

The Radioman stood from the control board. "There is nothing I can do without risking an alarm. How is it going over there?"

The Mechanic strained to turn his head to see the Radioman while keeping the Exoduster in place. "I don't know. There seems to be some kind of loading bar on the screen. I guess it is working."

"How much longer does our fine robotic friend need?"

The Entrepreneur and the Mechanic looked at the bar. It had not progressed far. "It appears to be awhile," replied the Entrepreneur in place of the Mechanic.

The Survivalist cut in. "That is not good news. The Dawn Beacon is nearly formed." The group looked out of the window. The wide cone had narrowed into a narrow funnel. The light blasting the cave ceiling glistened on the wet surfaces and sparkled in the minerals of the rocks. The entire cave was noticeably brighter. The city seemed alive.

"More bad news. I can see the new guards coming," stated the Bartender.

"We have maybe a minute before they get here," continued the Young. The group turned back to the screen. The Exoduster still had not moved. The bar was picking up speed.

The Bartender crossed the room to the panel. "We don't have time to wait. We have to do something to get through this door, and fast."

The Mechanic answered, "We don't have a choice. This is the only option we have."

"What about the Old Man's staff?"

The Old Man jumped up from leaning on the wall. The group did not answer. She waved him over. He walked across the room and held out the staff. The screen static grew increasingly fast. The static began collecting in places on the screen. A word formed, seemingly fading in through the static on the screen:

"No."

The Old Man moved the staff away. The word dissipated back into static. He shrugged. "I guess we have to wait." The Bartender went silent.

The Survivalist turned to the group. "Guys, the beacon is done." The group looked out the window. A raging blast of light shot straight up into the cave ceiling. The entire cave was fully lit. The group shielded their eyes.

The Young broke in. "The guards are here. We are out of time!"

The Exoduster buzzed slightly. The Mechanic looked at the screen. A word snapped into clarity:

"Trust."

The display went black. The Mechanic remained still. The group had noticed that the screen shut off. Silence took the room. A siren went off outside. It was a long, loud, constant note. It shook the windows on the building. The siren must have been right on top of the roof above them. A red light flashed above the door. Another siren went off inside the building, but the outside siren dwarfed its sound.

A metallic clunk went off. The Entrepreneur grabbed the handle and tugged it. The door slid into the wall, out of the way. The Entrepreneur turned to the group. A smile spread across his face. The Radioman took a look around at the group. "I would say it is time we got some sunshine. Don't you agree?" The group rushed to the doorway and started heading through. The alarm inside the building shut off along with the red light. The door began to close.

The Entrepreneur let go of the wire and slipped past the Mechanic. The Mechanic shook the Exoduster. It sat lifeless in his hands. He pinched the broken connector on the side of the terminal back together, stepped over to the door, and started through. The Exoduster got caught up on the closing door. He back up, turned the Exoduster, and threw it through the doorway. He turned sideway and began shuffling out of the narrow gap left in the doorway. He looked back at the room as he slid through.

The guards were struggling with the door on the outside. He slipped through. Just as the door finally slid close, the guards managed to access the building. He whipped around to see the Old Man's staff lighting the area. They were in what appeared to be a long stone hallway. The Mechanic held his index finger to his lips. The group became silent. Voices could be heard on the other side.

"Why did the door deny your card the first time?"

"I don't know. Maybe it was just an error. This system needs work."

"That's for sure. Hey, wait. The panel is open on the door."

"Yeah. The terminal is shut off too. Maybe that had something to do with it."

"Where are the screws for it?"

"I don't know." The Entrepreneur tensed. He held out his hand in front of the Mechanic, revealing the two screws.

"Is there a screwdriver lying around that somebody might have used to access the terminal with?" Apprehension rushed through the group. The Survivalist broke the tension by holding out the screwdriver in her hand.

"No. It must have just broken open. The terminal is rebooting now anyway."

"Let me check it out." There was a pause. "Everything seems fine. There was an error log. It said something about a critical failure that required a reboot."

"Eh," stated one voice dismissively.

"Yeah. Who knows? It is working now. I wouldn't mess with it." The voices faded off, and a door slammed. The group collectively let out a sigh of relief. The Old Man waved the light to motion them on. The Mechanic picked up the Exoduster as quietly as he could and followed the group out the narrow tunnel.

A short walk later, the group found that the narrow tunnel rejoined the main transport tunnel that led to the main hatch from inside the cave. It was eerily quiet. The Old Man adjusted the light so that it filled the entire tunnel wall to wall. There were tracks placed on the wall leading up the slight incline away from the hatch. The Mechanic nodded toward the tracks. "Those must be the transport lines. They have to get stuff in and out somehow. I bet if we follow those, then we find the exit."

The group started walking once more. The Bartender hesitated. Noticing she wasn't moving, the Radioman walked back to her. He didn't need an explanation. "You won't regret this." She scanned his face for doubt. He continued on. "What you had down here is nothing to what you are about to experience." She wasn't convinced. He thought some things over and grabbed her by the shoulders. "I used to dwell on the past my whole life. Then I became a radio announcer. That taught me one thing I will forever treasure: live in the present now and you will never forget your past." He let go of her and started up the incline after the group. She thought this over for a moment before running after him.

*****

The group took the long walk back up the tunnel. The Old Man lit the way with his Lightstaff. The Young went ahead of the group to find any guards in the tunnel. The Mechanic was busy carrying the limp Exoduster in his arms in the rear of the group. He seemed concerned with the Exoduster. He fiddled with its hands and whatever else he could reach with his encumbered arms as he carried it. Otherwise, the group was silent and solely focused on walking up the wide pathway.

There was a strong draft blowing outward from the City of Underground. It was warm. The Old Man wondered if the warmth was from the City of Underground heating the cave and then allowing the heat to rise with the air. However, this did not make sense due to the sealed doors on either entrance to the city. He dropped the thought. It was not anywhere near his main concern.

The group continued on for a good while. Eventually, the Old Man froze. The group followed suit behind him. The Lightstaff instantly shut off. Small footsteps pitter-pattered across the stone floor. A quiet sound accompanied them, a voice. "It's me. Turn the light on. It is so dark." The Old Man commanded the Lightstaff to turn on with a quick jiggle. The Young shielded his eyes. He had run ahead earlier to scout the area. The Old Man directed the light toward the floor by pointing with his index finger.

As the Young relaxed, he informed the group of his findings. "Up ahead, the path just keeps going. I haven't found a guard the entire time I have been ahead of you all. I guess they assume you have to come out one end of the tunnel or the other. Plus, this place is creepy in the dark."

The Survivalist stepped into the pool of light. "Could you see the exit?"

"No. It must be farther up. It feels like we have been walking for hours."

The Old Man peeked over at the Lightstaff. It jolted out of his hand, fell to the floor where the Old Man caught it with his foot, whirred, and stood. The shadow on the wall spun wildly in clockwise and counterclockwise turns. "The staff doesn't know what time it is. It must be as confused as we are." He held out his hand. The staff pivoted on the bottom end up into the Old Man's outstretched hand. It returned to creating the pool of light on the ground.

The Bartender entered the light. "I heard when they make shipments down here, it takes them many hours to transport the materials. I figured it was because they had to do it by hand or something. Judging by those rails, they have some form of material transportation. It must just be a very long walk."

The Hobo spoke from the darkness. "How often did they do these deliveries?"

The Bartender adjusted her weight as she thought the question over. "I suppose whenever the plant needed more building or maintenance materials brought in. Of course, those were often used by the people, not the plant, but the city seemed to be fine with that. They would sometimes try to order too much just to let the community have some of whatever they were getting. This was a rare thing, though. A fellow came into the Cardhouse one day and asked for something stiff to drink. As I fixed it for him, he explained to me that he had just taken a beating for ordering the surplus intentionally so his family could use it."

"Why did he tell you?"

The Bartender shrugged. "I don't know. People tell you strange things when you serve them at a bar. I guess some people just need someone to talk to, and the bartender seems friendly enough to vent with. Plus, they tend to get a little more friendly as the night goes on with the only woman they have probably seen in years. They would probably tell me anything to keep my attention." She rolled her eyes while shaking her head. The conversation halted.

The Old Man nudged the light up the path. "There are no guards up there yet?"

The Young replied, "Nope. It was clear. I will head off to keep checking." He turned and began trotting silently up the cave path. The Old Man waved the group on. They continued their march. After what seemed to be an eternity, the Old Man once again spotted the Young. This time, he was holding still in the middle of the path. He remained still as the Old Man flooded him with the light. The group walked up to him to see what he was looking at.

Another massive door, very similar to the main hatch at the City of Underground, covered the entire tunnel. Rust spotted the door. A pile of glistening sand sat in the corner. The Bartender walked over to it in curiosity. The Radioman grabbed her arm and pulled her back. "Don't touch that!" The Bartender glanced back at the Radioman, confused. "You will leave an indentation in the sand. It will mark that we were here."

She looked longingly at the sand. "I haven't seen anything but rock in years."

The Radioman raised his head and stared off into the distance. He had not thought about that. He refocused and turned to the Old Man. He nodded his head to the sand pile. The Old Man grinned and focused the light on the sand pile. It gleamed and glittered. The Radioman had not released the Bartender's arm. "You can look at it, but don't touch it or move the air around it. You will disturb the pile." He let her arm slip through his hand.

The Bartender walked over to the pile, keeping a few feet between it and herself. She crouched down, staring in amazement at the foreign pile of sediment in front of her. She reached out to it but retracted her hand quickly before touching the pile. "It looks…soft."

The Radioman chuckled. "Well, if the sand is fine enough, it can be soft. More often than not, it is a course or rough texture."

"It is softer than rock, though."

The Radioman couldn't argue that. After staring at the pile for a few moments longer, the Bartender broke her gaze and stood to face the group. The Radioman had to ask a question. "I thought you said you had been outside? That you used to live on top of this mountain?"

The Bartender nodded. "Yes, I did. But that was a long time ago. On top of that, I never went anywhere. I was always on top that mountain. There is a whole world out here that I never knew about."

The Radioman took a moment to consider all the things in the city that she had missed out on. Even now, she would find many things she had never been around. Although who knew, maybe the whole group would find things they had never seen before, like an entire city underground. He chuckled, realizing how much the group had already found that they were unfamiliar with. His thoughts were cut off as the Entrepreneur gestured to the massive hatch. "How are we going to get through that?"

After scanning the walls of the tunnel for a form of exit, the group returned empty-handed. However, the Mechanic spotted something interesting high up on the right wall. "Hey, Old Man, can you shine the light on the right wall? I see something, and I don't know what it is." The Old Man directed the light as asked. On the wall, there was a small square. It was the same gray tone as the wall and had a dull finish. It appeared to be a metallic cover. The Mechanic glanced around the group. "Anyone have any ideas?"

The Young walked over to the wall. He crouched down and held out his arms while looking over at the Survivalist. She sighed and walked over to be lifted. Before she allowed him to pick her up, she judged the height. "Young, even if we do this, I still won't be able to reach the panel. We will need more height." The two of them looked over at the Mechanic. The Mechanic set the Exoduster gently on the floor and set the backpack down beside it. He strolled over.

The Young pointed at him. "Do you think you can lift the both of us at once?"

"If you pick her up first and then step over me so I can hold you with my shoulders, then yes."

The Young turned to the Survivalist. She motioned to the floor. The Young crouched down. The Survivalist stepped over him and sat on his shoulders, straddling his head with her legs. The Young stood up and scooted over without much effort. The Mechanic took the Young's place and crouched for the Young. The Young tried to step over the Mechanic but failed to do so due to the Mechanic's sheer size. The Mechanic lay flat on the ground. The Young stepped over his head and waited for him.

The Mechanic grabbed the Young's feet, rose to a crouch, and then stood upward. He promptly leaned against the wall so that the Survivalist on top of the Young could reach the panel. The panel was at head level for the Survivalist. She grabbed the edges of the panel to search for any sort of opening lever. Her hand caught something on the right side. She pushed on it. It slid a short distance but stuck on something. She hit it with the palm of her hand. The lever popped downward a short way.

A few more strikes later, the lever lurched downward, and the panel swung open to the left on a set of hinges. Inside was a set of wires leading to a circuit board full of small blue cylinders. "There are a bunch of little wires in here with some blue cylinders," she explained.

The Mechanic tried to peek upward, but the Young's legs on his head prevented him from doing so. "That is probably an array of fuses of some kind. Maybe if we pull one of them, we can get the hatch to crack open."

The Radioman walked over to observe. "Why was this panel so easy to get in when the other was screwed shut?"

The Entrepreneur answered him. "I guess they never thought somebody would be locked in here. They protected the exit. They probably protect the outside of this door too."

The Survivalist spoke up. "The lid has the word *fuses* written on the inside in some chalky white stuff."

The Mechanic smiled, knowing he was right. "Perfect. You are looking for something that is an emergency power fuse. If the emergency power fuse is broken, a secondary circuit is tripped that opens the doors. It was installed in nearly every device that had the ability to lock somebody inside somewhere, so it is probably there. Pulling the fuse out would do the same thing as frying the fuse. The issue is picking the right fuse. If you pick wrong, there is no telling what will happen."

The Survivalist had been searching the panel for clues. "I don't know, Mechanic. I don't see anything in here marking what each of these things do. There are just a bunch of numbers printed beside each one."

"What kind of numbers?"

"Just random numbers. They don't really have an order."

The Mechanic strained to see once more. He ground his teeth. "It is a risk."

The Survivalist continued speaking. "Look, what are we going to do even if we get these fuses to work? The other side of this door is likely armed just like the inside and the very first entrance to this place were."

The Old Man thought it over. "I told those guards I was only going to be here for a short while, just to stay the night, and then pass on through. I am sure he told somebody I came in here." The group idled to await an explanation. The Old Man continued. "I don't know. Maybe…they will let me out the other side because that was what I said I was going to do." The group was not swayed. The Old Man pushed his idea further. "They didn't see any one of you the entire time we were in there. They don't even know we got out down there as far as we know." He outstretched his arms to either side with his palms upward, seeking conformation. He instead received rejection.

"That is the problem, Old Man. Nobody saw you leave. They are not going to just let you walk out of this place," stated the Hobo.

The Old Man began to protest the idea, but the Bartender rested a hand on his shoulder. "Old Man, I have never seen a single person walk out of those gates besides the occasional delivery worker. Even then, they stay right at the hatch and pass the items into the cave. They never actually set foot past the hatch. If you walk out in the open on the other side of this door, I have no idea what they would do to you. I would advise against it. We need to find another way out."

The firmness of the argument silenced the group. The Bartender walked over to the opposite wall and ran her hands along it near the floor. The Young, who was still busy balancing on the Mechanic's shoulders and also holding up the Survivalist, spoke up for the first time recently. "What are you looking for?"

The Bartender shrugged. "The other way out."

The Young tapped the Survivalist's thigh, which he was holding to help her balance, and motioned for her to close the panel. The Survivalist snapped the panel shut. The Young tapped the Mechanic's head with his hand. The Mechanic awkwardly peeked up at the Young and caught on that he wanted down. He lowered him and the Survivalist to the floor where the Young hopped off and set the Survivalist down.

The Young walked over to where the Bartender was rubbing the wall. He looked up at the rails on the wall, following them all the way up to the door. Something caught his eye. He walked to the corner where the sand pile was. "Hey, guys, where do you think this sand came from?"

The Hobo shrugged. "Outside the door somewhere."

The Young pointed blindly in the general direction of the Hobo. "Exactly. That means that somewhere here…" He reached up for the tracks but was unable to reach them. The Mechanic walked across the room and hoisted him up to his shoulders once more. The Young grabbed onto the tracks and winced away. The rails were incredibly greasy with a thick, goopy black material.

He observed his hands before grabbing the rail once more and attempting to pull himself up. His hands slipped promptly off the rail. It was too slippery to hold on to. He wiped the majority of the grease off onto an edge of the rail where he had collected it and reached as far up and over the rail as he could. He was just barely able to reach the wall. He ran his hands across the surface. The fingers of his right hand caught a ledge. He tried to force his fingers in the ledge but failed.

His left hand found a bump. He felt it. It was a rough dome with a flattened surface on top of it. The Young thought about what he was feeling. He retracted his hand. It was covered in a brownish-red powder. Two thoughts struck him. The first was the oddity of there being a rusty surface next to so much grease on the rail. The second required some action. "Let me down, Mechanic. I need to pick up the Survivalist again."

After some rearranging and some stacking of people, the Survivalist once more sat atop the Young's shoulders, who was sitting on the Mechanic's shoulders. "Do you feel that crack?" asked the Young.

"Yes," replied the Survivalist.

"Stick your fingers in it and pull on it."

"Why?"

"I think the rivets are rusted. You can probably rip the whole plate off of the wall."

"Why couldn't you do that?"

"Because my fingers were too wide to fit in the crack. Your hands are smaller than mine."

The Survivalist wedged her fingers into the crack. They slipped through. She flexed her fingers and was surprised to find them free to move. "I think it is hollow behind this thing."

"Perfect."

She pulled. Nothing happened. She pulled harder. The wall flexed a bit. She furrowed her brow as she used her free hand to cross her waist and fiddle with the hatchet, much to the frightening of the Young, whose arm was near the blade. She managed to free it. She stuck the blade in the crack above her fingers and applied some pressure while pulling on her other hand. Her fingers slipped out of the wall.

She struck the back of the hatchet with her now free hand. It sunk in a short way. She smacked it three more times for good measure before twisting the handle of the hatchet. The wall released a metallic groan. It started to give to the hatchet. The Young released the Survivalist's right thigh and retrieved his knife from the sheath. "Hey. Put this in there too." He handed her the knife. She wedged it into the crack. The Young reached up blindly. The Survivalist grabbed his hand and guided it to the handle of the wedged knife. She grabbed the hatchet's handle and began twisting once more.

The Young pulled down on the handle of the knife. The wall flexed outward and emitted a loud popping nose, and then a plate flew off the wall. It landed flat on the Hobo's head, who had been relaxing against the wall. He instinctively snatched the plate before it could hit the floor, observed it, and looked to see where it had come from while rubbing the pain on his head away. He was greeted with the sight of the Survivalist leaning forward into a hole in the wall while tightly gripping the Young's head with her legs to avoid falling off.

She was flailing her arms around in the dark hole in search of something. Meanwhile, the Young was pinning the knife to the edge of the hole as an anchor with his right hand while trying to support the Survivalist by clamping down her leg to his shoulder with his left arm. His face was turning red from being squeezed, but a wide smile was spread across his face.

The Mechanic was standing still, looking rather perplexed at what had just transpired above him. The Survivalist found something to grab and relaxed her grip on the Young's head. The Young seemed relieved. The Survivalist replaced the hatchet on her hip with her free hand, reached into the hole, and began dragging herself into the hole. The Young boosted her in by her bottom to help her avoid touching the greasy rail just below her. The Young peered in after her. "What did you find?"

"I don't know yet. It is dark in here."

The Old Man gestured to the hole and held the Lightstaff high above his head. The staff adjusted from flooding the room to a narrow beam toward the Young. The Mechanic stepped over, taking the Young with him. The light followed the Young. The Old Man made another slight gesture, and the light blasted into the hole on the wall at an upward angle. "It is still dark back in here. The light is angled up too high. I can't see the floor in front of me."

The Old Man glanced around for something to stand on. The Hobo stood with the panel. The back side was still a relatively reflective metal. "Use this, Young." The Young managed to sheath the knife and get ahold of the panel. He angled the panel flatly just above the hole in the wall. The Old Man directed the light to reflect off the panel. The beam bent and shot more directly into the hole.

The only response were some muffled metallic banging sounds originating from the Survivalist's movements. The Survivalist's voice sounded distant from the hole. "There is a bunch of sand in here. I think it's coming through this fan thing."

The Mechanic replied, "What kind of fan thing?"

"It's a fan. It is fitted into the vent. The vent is similar to the one that we used to get in the other side."

"Is it running?"

"The fan?" asked the Survivalist.

"Yeah," confirmed the Mechanic.

There was some thumping from the vent. "No. There is a belt here on the floor. It is broken. It seems to have fitted on this circle here."

"A pulley?"

"I think so."

The Mechanic shifted underneath the Young. The Mechanic spoke to him. "Hey, Young, get in there and see if you can help her find a way out. That duct with the fan has to go somewhere."

"How are you going to get me up there?"

"Stand on my shoulders."

The Young pulled his feet up and placed his hands against the wall. He managed to get his feet onto the Mechanic's broad shoulders. The Mechanic pinned the Young's feet down with his hands to help him balance. The Young tossed the reflective panel down to the

Hobo, who was now paying closer attention, and peered downward at the Mechanic. "Now what?"

"Can you reach the ledge?"

"I think so. I will need a boost over this slippery rail, though."

"No problem." The Mechanic promptly grabbed the Young's feet and shoved him upward. This caught the Young off guard, but he managed to get both of his arms and a foot inside of the hole. He clambered on the edge to avoid the rail while pulling himself in headfirst.

On the other side of the wall, there was a drop down. It made sense why the Survivalist could not see anything before. The entire ground was pitch-black near the wall. He could only see where the beam of light was blasting in through the hole. Without the reflective panel he was holding, he could only see the dusty ceiling of the area he was now in. Once he had gotten his bearings, he turned to face inward to the new area he was in.

Calling this space he was in a room would be an overstatement. It was a cramped crawl space, likely for maintenance access and a place to hide away vents and piping. It had metal floors and walls. Where was the Survivalist? He couldn't see any other way that he could squeeze through besides a vent on the nearby wall. He shuffled over to it in a crouching position to avoid smacking his head on the rough metal surface that made the roof. There, he located the broken fan the Survivalist had talked about.

He peered past the fan. It was as dark as the edge of the room. He could just barely make out the shape of a person. The Survivalist was down a rather lengthy tube behind the fan, crawling flat on her stomach. The Young called in at her. "Hey! Survivalist! Do you see anything in there?"

She stopped crawling and laid her head on the cool metal floor of the vent. "Not yet. It is hard work crawling through this, though."

"How much farther is it past you?"

She picked her head up briefly before returning it to the vent. "Not very far. There is a bend in the vent. It heads off to the right. It is getting hotter as I go."

The last statement perplexed the Young. "Hotter?"

"Yeah, hotter. It is not a dangerous heat. It is like it's a hot day outside."

"Well, we are supposed to be pretty close to the surface based on the giant hatch."

"That is true, although I can't see any light yet."

"There is a little bit of light in there. I can at least tell where you are."

She looked around once more. "You are right, there is a little bit of light. I can at least see."

"Do you think you should keep going?"

"Well, I am already this far in. I will go to the corner and find out what is around it. Maybe there is a place to turn around instead of backing out of here blind." She began crawling once more.

The Young sat down next to the broken fan with his back against the wall. His head nearly touched the ceiling, even in a sitting position. He leaned around the edge to speak to the Survivalist once more. "Do you want me to come in with you?"

"No, not yet. I don't want both of us stuck in here if it comes to that." This was not reassuring to the Young.

The Radioman's energetic voice came from the hole. "Have you two younglings found anything of interest?"

The Young waddled over to the hole and tried to peek out. The light from the staff blinded him. He shielded his eyes until the Old Man directed the light down, away from his eyes. "The Survivalist went down a long vent behind the fan. She says it is getting hotter as she goes, and she can see a little bit in there. There is a right turn at the end of it, and she is going to see what is around the corner." The Young's ear strained backward as he heard a voice from the vent. He turned away and waddled back over to the vent. The beam of light returned through the hole. He retook his seat against the wall and leaned around. "What did you say?"

"I found something. There is a light source and a bunch of sand covering the bottom of the vent in here."

"Do you need help?"

"Not yet. I am going to see where the light is coming from. I will bang on the vent if I need your help. Two bangs for take your time, and a whole bunch if I need you quickly."

"Sounds great. I will be here."

Silence took over the crawl space beside the muffled, distant small metallic bumps of the Survivalist working her way through the vent. There was a period of silence once the Survivalist had wiggled far enough into the vent for her muffled sounds to no longer echo out. A single bang came from the vent, followed shortly by a second. The Young waddled over to the hole in the wall, where the Old Man once again directed the light away from his face.

The Young relaxed his arms while he talked. "That's my cue. I am headed into the vent." He started to turn away, but a smile spread across his face, and he turned back. "I sound like you, Radioman. 'That's my cue.' It is something you would say."

The Radioman smiled in return. "That it is! You could be next in line at the radio tower."

The Young laughed lightly as he waddled back into the vent. The beam blasted through the hole once more. The Young made his way over to the vent and squeezed past the blades. He began the slow crawl out the vent. After a few minutes, he finally made it to the corner. He peeked around. The Survivalist was nowhere in sight. He couldn't see anything due to a blasting light at the end of the vent. He continued crawling. There were scrapping marks in the sand on the floor of the vent. He assumed it was from the Survivalist crawling through.

As he crawled toward the light at the end of the vent, he could begin to make out what was outside it. So far, it looked tan. He couldn't make anything else out. A little farther and the clarity increased. He could make out some sort of gray wall off the right side. It was against whatever the bright tan blob was. He pressed on.

He finally arrived near the edge of the vent. He could just now finally make out what he was seeing. It was a massive dune of sand. The sand ran all the way up to a massive hatch door. This perplexed the Young. He seemed to think he had crawled a much farther distance than just around the hatch door. At least he was outside at last even if it was just a sand dune.

He shimmied up to the edge of the vent and poked his head outside. He immediately spotted a guard on the dune. Before he could retract his head into the vent, a pair of hands grabbed him. One hand went over his mouth, and the other grabbed his hair. The one on his hair pulled, causing pain. He dragged himself forward to relieve the pressure, but the hand continued pulling. It eventually shifted to the back of his shirt and hauled him the rest of the way out of the vent.

He fell downward onto a deep embankment of sand behind a metal crate. He whipped over but was again suppressed by a hand over his mouth. He thrashed about. A familiar voice struck his ears. It whispered forcefully, "Young, calm down! You are going to give us away!" The Young paused his thrashing and observed who was holding his mouth. He recognized the Survivalist. He relaxed, and she released his mouth.

He spat. "You filled my mouth with sand."

"Sorry. Take a look past this crate."

The Young repositioned himself into a crouch and peeked over. Guards were swarming the area, all focused outward and positioned at the top of the massive dune. They were dressed entirely in a black outfit, complete with respiration masks and goggles. A small gray building was constructed against the stone wall with a wavy glass window. The Young could make out a set of controls through the glass. He turned and sat down in the sand next to the Survivalist. "How are we going to get the group out here? That vent was tight for us, let alone someone the size of the Mechanic."

The Survivalist shrugged. "I have no idea. That was why I called you out here. Maybe together, we can figure something out."

"Do you have any idea what is beyond the dune?"

"No. All I know about is what you can see here."

The Young scratched his head. Streams of sand fell out of his hair. He took another peek. A building caught his eye. "What about that shack with the controls in it? You think we can open the door with something in there?"

The Survivalist seemed disapproving. "We will never get that thing open without the guards knowing about it." The Young sat back. The two pondered for a moment. The Young lazily turned his head to the Survivalist. He had an idea.

*****

As the two outside in the sand planned, the remaining group inside was still awaiting rescue. "Do you think they made it outside?" questioned the Hobo.

The Mechanic shrugged. "Probably. That vent had to be getting air from somewhere. As close as we are to the surface, it likely led outside."

The Bartender shuffled nervously. "Do you think they would ditch us?" The group collectively focused on her. She noticed a tangible apprehension. She shifted her weight to the other leg. "Look, I don't know. I haven't been around you all that much. It was just a thought."

The Radioman bailed her out. "No, it is a valid thought. However, I personally do not think those two would leave us behind unless they absolutely have to do so. Even then, they would return to find us." This did not relax the Bartender. The Radioman walked over and wrapped his arm around her to grab her shoulder. He guided her down to the floor and leaned against the wall with her. "Is everything all right?" She shook her head. "What is wrong?"

She laid her head back against the wall and looked up at the stone ceiling. Goosebumps sprung up on her arm as her back felt the coolness of the wall. "It is complicated."

The Radioman laid his head back against the wall too. "Well, we have nothing but time to wait now. Do you want to talk to the group about it?"

She peeked past the Radioman's head. The rest of the group had found places to settle in. She nodded. The Radioman patted her shoulder and crossed the tunnel to lean against the opposite wall. The group gave her time to speak. "I feel guilty."

The Mechanic shrugged. "Why?"

The Bartender looked up at the ceiling to see if it had any answers written on it. No luck. "I guess I feel like I should have helped everyone else get out of there."

The Hobo joined in. "I was stuck in poverty for years of my life, and very few people ever seemed to care. What makes you want to help them?"

The Bartender took a moment to consider the statement the Hobo had made. She had not thought about that before. "I guess I want to help them for the same reason the Radioman wanted to help me." With that expertly pawned question, she turned to the Radioman.

The Radioman stayed his typical cool self despite being put on the spot. He smiled. "That was quite a way to dodge a question, Bartender. Now as a former radioman, I sense the group wants to hear your answer here. I won't bail you out, but I will help you along." He boosted himself off the wall with his elbow to stand upright and walked to the center of the room to face the Bartender.

"I helped you because I thought you needed it. I knew at first glance that you wanted out of the Cavedweller Cardhouse. I had an opportunity to help, and I took it. However, your situation is different. As far as I know, you don't have any opportunity right now to be able to help those people without jeopardizing your own chances of escape. So why do you feel guilty?" The Radioman stepped back against the wall. He tilted his head and gave her a confident but questioning smile.

The Bartender grappled with her thoughts. "I don't feel guilty because of not helping. There really was not much I could have done. I feel guilty because I don't feel like I should have been the one to escape."

The Radioman crossed the room to her. "Who else would you have rather escaped if it were not you?"

The Bartender shrunk away from him a step. "I don't know."

The Radioman remained where he stood. "Precisely. I think that is because you secretly know that you are better than everyone in that dreadful cave." The Bartender peeked up from staring down at her feet. The Radioman met her gaze. "Or at least I think so." The Bartender turned her head to hide her blushed cheeks. The entire rest of the male group stood in awe as the Radioman single-handedly managed to swoon a woman in front of them. The Radioman stepped back to give the Bartender more space and to distract the other men from her embarrassment.

The Bartender regained her composure. She sighed lightly. "Radioman, you are too sweet."

He responded quickly. "Would you rather I bitter down a bit?" She chuckled. "No."

"Then it sounds like I have found a girl with a sweet tooth." She rolled her eyes but couldn't retain her own smile. The Radioman turned to the men in the group. He cracked a sneering grin. He held his left hand out flat in front of him and made a squiggling motion above it with his right hand to gesture them to take notes. All the men averted their eyes after realizing they had been caught staring, except for the Old Man, who was laughing silently. The Old Man raised his eyebrows while pointing knowingly at him. He twitched his head to the Bartender. The Radioman swung back over to her.

She was stiffly crossing the room. She snagged the Radioman's maroon lapel and pulled him in. She whispered in his ear. "I suppose it's out there now. Might as well make it official."

The Radioman twitched his head to the Old Man. He snapped the light up to the hole in the wall, plunging the two into darkness, and spoke to the group. "So, guys, how long do you think it will take those two in there to find something for us?"

The Radioman felt the Bartender's slender finger on his right cheek. It turned his head to face the darkness. He felt her lean against him. A kiss caught his lips. He hugged her. The kiss ended, and he whispered back, "Don't ever feel guilty. I chose you." He felt her head hit his left shoulder.

The Hobo's voice shook the moment. "Hopefully, not much longer."

The Radioman released the Bartender. He heard her quietly padding toward the light. He followed her up. The Bartender joined the conversation. "I would love to answer that, but I don't know either." The group ensued in a chat about how long they would be stuck inside the hatch.

*****

Meanwhile, the Young and the Survivalist had scoped out the area and created a plan. "Are you ready?" questioned the Survivalist.

"Yeah."

The Survivalist nodded. "All right. Get to it."

The Young peered around the crate. The guards were all still facing outward, up on the dune. He grabbed the Survivalist's hook off the sand and darted out from cover. He scurried a short way to another set of crates, where he paused. He checked the guards once more. All clear. He darted again, this time arriving below a stone ledge. On top of this stone ledge was a pile of blue metallic barrels stacked horizontally in a pyramid shape. They were held in place by a small metal rod wedged vertically between a lip on the ledge and the bottom of the most outside barrel from the wall.

He looped the hook around the rod and ducked down for cover behind a stray barrel. After checking the guards once more, he slipped back over to the Survivalist. He nodded. The two located the end of the rope nearby and positioned themselves to brace their feet against the crate. The Young mouthed a countdown silently. "Three, two, one." The two jerked the rope simultaneously. The rod shot out from under the barrel, making quite a pinging sound from banging against the hook. The two furiously reeled in the hook.

As they reclaimed the hook, the barrels began shifting, making deep and hollow thudding sounds as each one toppled over the ledge and slammed into the sandy stone below. The guards started shouting. Many of them scurried down over the dune toward the barrels. The Young held up two fingers. The Survivalist nodded. The Young peeked around the corner to find the guards trying desperately to prevent the barrels from tumbling down. He shot out from behind the crate, running full tilt to the small gray control building across the gap.

He slid into the doorway and hid underneath the window. He peeked through the window. He couldn't see anything. The entire glass was buffed and scratched. He thought the sand must have blasted the window to bits. He turned to the empty control room and crawled over to the panel across the room. He observed the buttons. "Come on, come on. Gimme something here." He read the faded labels above the buttons. None of them caught his eye until he came across one that read, "'Pump water to surface'? What?"

He went to the window, realized he could still not see through the distorted bottom of it, and instead peeked out the doorway. He spotted a large tube on the far side near the vent they used. He waved at the Survivalist. She shook her head. He insisted. She persisted. He cocked his head in frustration and slithered back to the control panel. He found the lever once more and slapped it down. He turned. Water began dripping out of the pipe.

Back to the doorway he went. He pointed at the pipe. The Survivalist followed his finger and spotted the water. The flow was increasing by the second. The Survivalist watched as some of the water ran down and found her feet. Her sight snapped back to the Young in panic. He casually waved her over. She panicked for a moment, peeked around the edge, and sprinted over to the control room. The Young politely guided her in with a smile and a motion of his left hand. She scoffed at him. "What is your plan now?"

The Young dropped the smile. "I don't know. I figured that would cause some problems and be a distraction."

The Survivalist bought that for a second before turning back in question. "Wait. Did you use that lever to turn that on?" She pointed to the lonely pulled lever.

"Yeah."

"Don't you think the first thing those guards are going to do is run in here to turn that thing off?" The Young instantaneously grew concerned as his eyes widened. He scampered back across the room, drew his dulled knife from its sheath, and stabbed the blade into a crack at the bottom of the lever pivot point. He wiggled it while pulling on the lever. After a moment, the lever rocketed out of the control board. The Young flew backward onto the hard floor of the control room and landed sprawled out on his back. He quickly sat up and checked the lever in his hand.

He smiled triumphantly and shook the lever at the Survivalist. "I suppose that works. Now what about the door?" The Young's wide eyes returned. He threw the lever to the Survivalist and ran back to the control panel. The Survivalist checked the door. The guards had not yet noticed the now gushing water emitting from the pipe. A big pool of water was forming at the hatch. She looked back at the Young. He was flying over a bunch of labels. He stopped, pointed giddily at one in particular, and ripped the lever down.

He turned back to the window. A light had lit up on the hatch. He ran back to the doorway, peeked around the corner, and tried to force the Survivalist out. She wouldn't budge. "What are you doing? Go! We have to get out of here."

The Survivalist's stare called the Young crazy. "There are guards everywhere out there."

"You are right, and they are soon to be in here." He gestured to the lever in her hand.

The Survivalist's eyes widened to match the Young's. She still didn't move. "We can't leave. We have to close the hatch to make it look like nobody got out."

The Young knew she was right. "Where is the group?"

"I don't know."

The Young swung back to the control panel. He noticed that the lever was made in the shape of a square *u*. It was also in the far corner of the room where the only window on that side of the building was located. He looked down at the hook on the Survivalist's side. He grabbed it and began pulling. The Survivalist threw the rope off over her head, and the Young traversed the room once more.

He checked the window first. There was a small latch on it. He flipped the latch open and threw the majority of the rope out of it.

He fixed the hook to the bar handle of the lever and pulled the window down on the rope. The corner of the window dug into the rope and held it stiff. The hook remained fixed to the handle. He traveled back across the room. The Survivalist had turned away while he was crossing the room to look out the door at the ensuing panic.

He noticed that the door was about halfway up. He slipped his hand under her bottom, and the Survivalist jumped and attempted to squirm away in protest. He contained her by grabbing her shoulder and the waistband of her pants, with which he hauled her up in a ball to his chest as he slipped around the corner of the door and ran down the length of the control building. He rounded the corner, ran the short width of the building, rounded another right-hand corner, and roughly tossed her down into a pile of sand underneath the window from before.

He slid in beside her and located the rope. He stood and peeked through the window. He could just see the hatch opening through the upper half of the window inside of the control building. The Survivalist adjusted her tight pants back down into position as she dusted the sand off herself. The Young glanced over. "Sorry." She glanced curiously up at the rope in his hands. "I pull this rope and the hook will pull the lever up, which will close the hatch."

The Survivalist stood and shared the window with the Young. "Smart move."

He nodded. "I thought so too."

*****

As the Young and the Survivalist were busy ruining the day of the guards, the rest of the group had noticed a substantial amount of water running through a rotten corner of the seal of the hatch door. "That has to be their action," stated the Hobo.

"The hatch isn't opening, though," rebutted the Entrepreneur.

"We have to find a way to get this thing open!" proclaimed the Hobo.

The Old Man shook his head. "We don't know what is on the other side."

The Bartender caught everyone's attention. "Hey. Hey! Be quiet." The group settled. "Hear that?" There was a low burring noise.

The Mechanic answered, "Yes. That is an electric motor. It is big too. It might be for the…" He trailed off. "Old Man, shut the light off."

"What?" responded the Old Man.

"Do it." The Old Man bumped the Lightstaff on the ground. The light shut off. The only thing visible was a thin and dim beam of light emitting from the cracked seal in the hatch door, along with the water. The light illuminated thousands of sand particles flowing along with the water, causing them to glitter. It was also getting slowly brighter. The Mechanic tapped the Old Man's arm. He bumped the staff to reactivate the light.

The Mechanic's face grew distant. He stared off. A moment later, he regained his focus on the group. "There are two hatches." He stepped into the ankle-deep water flowing across the ground and braced up against the wall below the fuse panel. "Come on!"

The group followed him over. "Old Man, just light the area for us. We can't see without you. Entrepreneur and Hobo, you are the base with me. We are going to pick up the Radioman, who is going to lift the Bartender up to the panel. We have to take the chance and try to get this hatch open."

"How do you know there are two hatches?"

The Mechanic gestured to the crack in the seal. "The light is dim through the crack, but it is getting brighter. If it were steady, the door might be back in a hole or something. But the noise combined with the increasing light probably means the second hatch on the other side is opening, letting in more light and making it brighter through the crack. Now come on! Stack up!"

The Hobo lowered his hands down. "Give me a foot, Radioman." The Radioman grabbed onto the Mechanic's shoulder with his right hand and set his left foot in the Hobo's hands. He bounced once and lurched upward. The Hobo strained to lift him. The Entrepreneur boosted the Radioman up and got on the other side of the Mechanic. The Radioman placed his feet on the Mechanic's shoulders. The Hobo and the Entrepreneur helped alleviate the weight from the Mechanic by pushing up on the Radioman's toes.

The Bartender stood awkwardly at the bottom of the pile of men, unsure what to do. The Radioman beckoned her up. "Give me your hands." He squatted down. She grabbed his hands. He stood and pulled her up straight. The Mechanic grunted. The Hobo and the Entrepreneur pushed harder to assist him. The Radioman grabbed the Bartender's waist. "I am going to boost you up. You need to sit on my shoulders, facing the wall." She nodded.

The Radioman bounced her and lifted her as high as he could. She managed to get a leg over his shoulder. She pulled herself up with the leg and swung her other leg forward. She squeezed onto the Radioman's head. The Radioman stiffened and tapped her leg. She relaxed and spread her legs. The Radioman took in a breath. "I didn't think this through. You are going to suffocate me." The Bartender realized his face was in her crotch. "Get the panel." The men shifted below her.

She continued to spread her legs and located the panel. She flipped down the lever and swung the panel open. "What now?"

The Mechanic grunted again. "How many fuses are there? They are the blue cylinders."

She counted. "Eight."

"Are you sure?"

She looked in again. "Yes, eight blue cylinders."

"Is there a red one somewhere?"

"A red fuse?"

"Yes."

"There is not."

The Mechanic sighed. He glanced around the room. He spotted the Exoduster. He had completely forgotten about it. He gestured to it. The Old Man hurried over to it, grabbed its arm, and towed it across the floor. "Do you think it is waterproof?"

The Mechanic shrugged. "I guess we find out." The Old Man pulled it through the rushing water. The Mechanic looked down at it. He kicked it. Nothing happened. He kicked it again. A small light lit up on the Exoduster's chest. "Stab it in the chest with the staff. Use the light end where the sharp part is. Maybe the pain can wake it up."

The Old Man looked down at the limp Exoduster. He raised the staff, spun it around, and plunged the light down onto the chest of the Exoduster. A bright flash and a small pop came from the contact. The Exoduster's arm shot out and grabbed the Mechanic's leg. The Mechanic shook it off. The Exoduster raised its head, let out a high-pitch beep once it spotted the water, and grabbed the Old Man's leg.

The Old Man bent down to talk to it. "We need you to open this hatch. We have eight blue fuses. Which once do we pull to open the door safely?" The Exoduster looked up at the group. The Old Man pulled its arm up to the Hobo and its body to the Entrepreneur. The two struggled to lift it to the Radioman, who managed to pull it up to his chest. The Exoduster reached up to the Bartender, who grabbed its arm and pulled it onto her lap. The Exoduster's eyes flickered. It remained still for a moment. It slowly reached up, grabbed the fourth fuse from the left, and attempted to yank it out. The Bartender pushed its hand out of the way. "Pull this one out?"

"...es."

She yanked the fuse out. A red light blinked in the panel. A motor started whirring close by. The hatch started opening. The Exoduster reached for the fuse. The Bartender placed it in its hand. It spun the fuse and held it up to the slot upside down. It tried to force it back into the slot. The Bartender assisted it by forcing the fuse in. The Exoduster pointed at the panel. The Bartender slammed it shut and replaced the lever. The Exoduster looked up at the Bartender. "Take...m-m-m-m-me...tuh-tuh...whih..." It poked her arm. Its eyes flickered and shut off. Its body fell limp.

The Bartender looked down at the Old Man. She handed the Exoduster down the Radioman, who passed it to the Entrepreneur. The Entrepreneur set it on the ground and stood to help the Bartender down. They lowered the Radioman. The Mechanic was breathing heavily. Veins were visible on his forehead. The Radioman observed the veins. "Are you all right?"

"I will be. Just…just go." He pointed to the opening hatch as he collected the Exoduster. The group ducked under. On the other side, a second hatch was opening. The Mechanic was right. The second hatch was only about halfway up. The group ran to the second hatch and peeked outside.

The Young spotted the Bartender peering out of the hatch. He hit the Survivalist's arm. "It's the Bartender."

She stood to see her herself. The Bartender was staring in awe at the sand outside the hatch. She touched it with her hand. The Survivalist checked around the corner of the building. "The guards are still busy with the barrels. That was a good call. I am going to go get the group's attention to guide them over. You stay here and get ready to pull the rope." She disappeared around the corner.

The Young peeked through the window at the angle he could see the hatch at. The Mechanic had appeared at the door. He was watching something. The Young guessed he had spotted the Survivalist. The door hatch was still pulling open. The Mechanic made a motion with his hand. The Bartender slipped past him, followed closely by the Radioman, then the Entrepreneur. He blocked the Hobo off and disappeared into the hatch.

A moment later, the Hobo came barreling out of the door carrying the Exoduster. He was struggling with the weight of it. That only left the Mechanic and the Old Man. Where were they? The hatch was nearly three-fourths of the way open. The Young heard the sand nearby shuffling. He snapped away from the window and burrowed into the sand.

Steps approached the corner. The Young drew his knife. He braced against the wall. The Survivalist poked her head around the corner. The Young lunged at her but quickly withdrew his attack once he recognized her. The Survivalist froze. He leaned against the wall and laid his head against it as he sheathed the knife. The

Survivalist cautiously rounded the corner and sat next to him. The Young started the talk. "Sorry. I couldn't take any chances."

The Survivalist ignored the remark. "The Mechanic and the Old Man are going to be out soon. They motioned to start closing the hatch."

The Young flipped over, pushed the window up, and yanked harshly on the rope, which still had the hook attached to the lever inside the building. The rope remained steady for a moment before jerking toward him. He peeked at the hatch. It was headed down. The hook had successfully pulled the hatch control lever back up. The Young crouched down to peek through the window. He wanted to know the situation. "How are the guards?"

"They are still flustering with the barrels. The barrels washed around the far corner, so most of them don't even have a line of sight on us. The good news is, none of the group thinks they were spotted, nor do they think anyone noticed the hatch opening. If it shuts before the guards contain the barrels, then we will be out undetected. Although, I think they alerted some other people of the situation with the barrels. That might cause some security issue. We might have to be more careful on the way out."

The Young shook his head. "We don't even know what is over the dune."

The Survivalist rested her head against the wall. She shielded her eyes from the blasting brightness of the glistening sands. "You are right, we don't. But we sure do need to get away from here." The Young couldn't argue that. He had reeled the hook back up through the window with the rope. He handed it over to the Survivalist. She busied herself by recoiling it around herself.

The Young continued watching through the control building. He spotted the Mechanic hauling the Old Man out of the hatch. The Old Man was holding the Lightstaff, which had become stiff once more. The hatch was closing much faster than it had opened. It was already halfway closed. The Mechanic left his field of view from the window. The Young peeked down at the Survivalist. "What is the plan?"

She shrugged, stood, and ran around the corner. A moment later, she returned with the entire group. They all sat down against the building. The Young watched as the hatch slid close, and the light above it turned off. He smacked the window, causing it to fall shut. He slid down the wall and sat down with the group. The Old Man started the conversation. "There were two hatches."

The Survivalist peeked down the row. "What?"

The Mechanic nodded. "He's right, there were two hatches. We had to get the Exoduster to pull the proper fuse from the panel."

The Survivalist set her head back. "You did end up using the panel?"

The Bartender answered her. "Yes. Well, actually, we had the Exoduster do it."

The Survivalist grew confused. "I thought it was shut down."

The Bartender nodded. "It was. The Mechanic had the Old Man stick it with the Lightstaff. For whatever reason, it woke up just long enough to crack the door and then shut back down."

"Huh." The Survivalist fell into thought. The Young took over for her.

"Look, we can continue the reunion later. We need to figure out what we are doing."

The Mechanic swept his hand through the air. "Where are we going to go? There are mountains so steep that we can't pass over them behind us—not that we would want to go back that way now anyway—and there is what appears to be a desert in front of us."

The group paused for a moment to contemplate. The Young peeked through the window and sat back down unalarmed. The Old Man broke the silence. "I guess we get over this dune and see what is on the other side to start." The group agreed silently with nods and shrugs.

The Young tapped the Survivalist's shoulder. She glanced up at him, got herself to her feet, and went to check the corner of the building. The Young peeked through the window of the building. He immediately ripped his head down. The Young motioned for the group to follow with a wave of his right arm. The group came in close as the Survivalist squeezed in from the corner of the building. The Young spoke quietly. "There are loads of guards inside of the control building right here."

The Survivalist joined. "There are only two guards that I can see still outside. One is busy holding the barrels they restacked still. I think the other is searching for something to pin the barrels down with."

"The guards must be trying to shut off the water pipe." The Young motioned through the building in the general direction of the water pipe as he spoke. He continued after a momentary pause. "We can probably make it over the dune if we hurry. We all go at once. Ready?" The group got to their feet. The Young waved, and they all struggled their way up the dune. Each member reached the top and rolled over the crest to the far side. The Old Man in particular had trouble as the Lightstaff sunk straight through the sand instead of supporting his weight.

On the far side of the dune, the group fell in behind a large spire of rock protruding from the sands. Once they all safely arrived, they peeked around the edges. The Bartender was the first to speak. "What is that?"

The Mechanic answered while staring out at the structure. "It is a manufacturing plant."

They took in the sights. It was massive, as wide as the group could see from their perch on the dune and five stories tall. The group was positioned level with the top ceiling of the building. Windows high on each floor were present, but any form of glass was not. The entire thing was consumed by rust, excluding a few patches where the gray paint had not been blasted off by the sands.

Corroded I-beams were strewn about in the sands outside the perimeter. The building at one time had been covered in a metal sheet paneling that acted as walls. The walls had since deteriorated, exposing large holes and rusty plates instead. Sharp blue lights periodically flashed from inside the building. Workers shuffled about. They were all deeply tanned. Their plain clothing of jeans, tattered T-shirts on the monochrome scale, and unvaryingly white and beaten hard hats flapped in the gusts of wind on their bony structures. They appeared drained of life.

Another man in equal physical condition but in better clothing and in an orange hard hat was walking slowly around and prodding the others along by pointing and yelling or by hitting them gently on the back while also helping whoever needed it with the work. The worker group of around twenty nearest the dune was trying to remove an I-beam from the sands. They were failing. An orange hat motioned for them to stop. A few collapsed to the ground to be promptly helped back up by their neighboring workers.

The workers who fell glanced around nervously, but nothing more occurred. The orange hat glanced up at the sun. It was at around a forty-five-degree angle from vertical behind the massive complex, which cast a harsh shadow from the top of the roof down onto the sands, just at the feet of the workers. He waved his arm slowly. The group began to shuffle into the shadow toward a large door.

The Young's face lit up. "Come on." He began clambering around the spire of rock.

The Old Man caught his arm. "What are you doing?"

"I am following them inside."

"No, you are not."

The Young stopped pulling on the Old Man's hand. He looked back at the Old Man in curiosity. "What do you mean?"

The Old Man closed his eyes and stiffly performed a short shake of his head. "You have no plan. We can't just go barging into this place. We do not know anything about it."

The Young turned to protest. "You have to take the opportunity. I have survived the entire Crisis based on opportunities like this." The Old Man remained firm. The Young turned fully back around and sat in the sands and watched as the group shuffled to the building. "What do you suggest we do, then?"

The Old Man glanced around at the group. His eyes hinted the group to provide backup. None was provided. He sighed. "I don't know." The Young began to stand once more. The Old Man noticed and jumped hastily into a sentence. "But I do know that barging into this place without a plan is not a good idea. Sit down." The Young grouchily retook his seat on the dune. The Old Man peered around the spire. The workers had made it to the door and were headed inside.

The Young drew a breath. In a more relaxed tone, he stated, "You are right, it would have been a risky move. I can get away with it by sneaking through the area alone, but with the whole group, it would be difficult. But we missed our opportunity to get inside. What is the plan now?" He peeked back at the Old Man over his shoulder.

The Old Man didn't respond at first. He was busy scanning the building. The Young turned back to observe the rusted walls. The Old Man spotted something. "There." He pointed to a rusted hole in the side of the building. It was only a foot or so off the ground and large enough for even the Mechanic to squeeze through. "We can get in through that hole."

The Hobo peered along the length of the dune. "There are too many workers still outside to make a run for that. We might have made the direct route down the hill to the door, but even that would have been risky. There is no way we can make it there without being seen." The Young and the Old Man exchanged glances. The Hobo continued. "Eh, I don't know, guys. I think we have to wait this one out and try it when there are less workers outside."

The Bartender swiveled her head to look at the Hobo. Her line of sight paused on him for a moment, but it was not focused on him. She was staring off past him. The Hobo caught her gaze, perplexed for just a moment while thinking she was staring at him, and then followed her line of sight to find nothing but the factory wall. He looked back at the Bartender. She was scurrying back up the dune to the crest. The Hobo got to his feet and went after her. "Bartender! You can't be running around out here! Someone is going to see you!"

The Bartender reached the crest and fell flat to her stomach. She winced against the hot sands for a moment. The heat caught her attention. She looked curiously down at the sand and ran her hand through it. She prodded it with her finger, making a small indentation. She wiggled her body. The sand shifted around her. She abruptly remembered something and shifted up to the peak of the dune. She peeked over.

The Hobo clambered up behind her. She scooted over a tad and tapped the side of his leg with the back of her hand. He lay down next to her. She pulled her head back down behind the dune and spoke quietly to him. "We don't have time to wait." She twitched her head toward the crest of the dune. The Hobo peeked over. The guards in black were running about. The water had been shut off and the barrels contained. A few off to the side were observing the trail the group had left in the sand. They yelled something at the rest of the guards and began up the dune, following the disturbances in the sand.

The Hobo retracted his head. He snapped a glance over to the Bartender. "No kidding." He crawled backward a bit before standing and bounding the short distance down the dune to the stone spire. The Bartender remained at the top of the dune. He slid in feet first, stopping himself with the spire of stone. "We need to bail."

The Survivalist peeked over. "Why such a change of heart?"

"There are guards coming up the hill following the tracks we left. Unless you want to get caught by the guards we just avoided, I would leave now." That caught the group's attention. They swiveled to the Old Man.

He drew a breath and peeked at the hole he had spotted earlier. He released the breath. "How much time do we have?"

A strange scuffling noise came from the dune above them. The group followed the sound. The Bartender was rolling head over heels down the sand. The Mechanic caught her with her head in the sand. He flipped her over and brushed off her back while she spat out a bit of sand. "None. No time." She gestured to the hill with her thumb while looking at the Hobo. "How did you get down that?"

The Hobo didn't respond. He was busy scanning the dune. He turned back. He glanced around the group nervously. His voice cracked in. "Hey, uh, Young, do you think you can still make it to the door down there?"

The Old Man glanced up in anger. The Hobo held up his hand to settle him for a moment. The Young peeked over at the Old Man and saw his anger but replied in spite of it. "The door is closed now."

The Hobo nodded. "Yes, but it is still cracked open. They didn't shut it all the way. It is just wedged into the sand."

The Young shuffled over and peeked around the spire. "You are right." He sat back down behind the spire. "I can probably make it."

"Can you take the Survivalist and the Bartender with you?" This riled up the Radioman and further aggravated the Old Man. The Hobo held up his other hand to the Radioman. He was struggling to keep them at bay. "The rest of us are going for the hole in the wall down there, but I need you all to make a lot of tracks." He glanced up at the catastrophe that the Bartender had made in the dune on her roll down the hill.

The Bartender shuffled over to the edge of the spire to see how far the door was down the dune. New voices came from over the dune. The Hobo quickly jumped over to her and gently grabbed her arm. "We will meet with you later." He hesitated. "I am sorry about this." He shoved her back to send her off down the dune. She immediately stumbled on the loose sands and fell to another tumble down the dune. The Hobo pointed at the Young and swung his finger down the hill. "Do me a favor and make some noise once you get to the bottom."

The Young overcame his own shock of the moment and grabbed the Survivalist's arm before rounding the spire and booking it down the hill after the toppling Bartender. The Hobo turned to see the Old Man's boiling rage. Instead, he was greeted by an unwelcome laughter. The Old Man couldn't help but laugh, but he visibly hated it.

The Hobo turned to the Radioman. He seemed to be stuck between two actions. He met the Hobo's gaze. He began to turn his head down the hill. "No you don't!" The Hobo snatched the Radioman's arm and yanked him down the dune toward the hole in the wall of the factory. The Radioman followed but watched the Bartender roll down the dune until she fell out of sight near the bottom. The rest of the group followed the Hobo down the hill.

Multiple loud clanging noises came off from the left where the door was. The Hobo looked up just in time to see the door silently shut and a pile of metal scraps settle in the sands near the rusty I-beam in the sands that the workers had left behind. The Hobo smiled. Those three had just bought them a distraction inside. The group reached the hole in the wall a few moments later.

The Mechanic, who managed the hill oddly quickly even with the Exoduster in his arms, tossed the Exoduster gently through the hole and squeezed through himself. He stuck his arm out and briefly motioned for the next person. The Hobo shoved the Radioman in and slipped through himself. The Old Man, winded, stepped through. He prodded the stiff surface of the floor inside the building with the Lightstaff. He had not been able to use the Lightstaff on his trip down the dune due to the Lightstaff poking straight through the loose sands. The Old Man showed a noticeable relief when he at last trusted his weight on the Lightstaff. Meanwhile, the group piled up behind a pyramid of long I-beams to catch their breath. The Hobo chuckled. He whispered to the group, "See? I knew it would work." The Old Man glared over.

*****

The Young, the Survivalist, and the Bartender were busy scurrying through a maze of dry-rotting office cubicles. They found one relatively intact with a sheet of ribbed scrap metal nearby on the right side of the hall. The Survivalist shooed them out of the narrow hallway into the cubicle, slid the metal sheet through the door, and covered the entrance with the metal sheet from the inside. The three hunkered down under the ancient desk, facing outward toward the sheet of metal. The Survivalist was on the left with the Young to her right. To the right of the Young sat the Bartender against the cubicle wall.

The group remained silent for a moment. Distant noises such as banging, grinding, mechanical humming, and popping could be heard off in the distance, although no noise could be heard in the immediate area. The Young wiggled for room. He was being squeezed on both sides by the women in the tight space. He smiled and whispered, "Well, this is not a situation I would have ever found myself in."

The Bartender rested her sandy head against the back of the cubicle. "Which part of the situation?"

The Young flopped his head back as well. "The part where I am stuck in a decrepit office cubicle wedged between two women, one of which has the hot blade of a hatchet pressed against my left thigh and the other sandier one wearing a two-piece bikini underneath a pair of jeans and a V-neck shirt."

The Young peeked over at the Bartender. She was quietly brushing off the sand. "Now that I think about it, the sand is kind of fitting on you, being that you are in a bikini." The Bartender grew perplexed. "You know, beaches of sand, swimsuits?" This resolved nothing for the Bartender. The Young shook his head. "Never mind." He relaxed and closed his eyes.

The Survivalist had rested her head in the left corner of the cubicle. A noise came from a door toward the entrance side of the cubicle. She picked her head up off the cubicle wall. The noise repeated itself but louder. It was a deep thudding noise. Was something hitting a door? She wiggled out between the cubicle wall and the Young while rolling up to a crouch to avoid bumping the table above her. The Young shot over to take her place as if he had been held against a spring before. He and the Bartender both spread to more comfortable positions.

The Survivalist shuffled over to the sheet of metal and tipped it open a crack. She peered out of the crack toward the door on the left, the same they had come in through. The noise emitted again. This time, she saw the door shudder in its frame. She whispered back to the other two. "Hey, Young?"

"Yeah?" he whispered back.

"Did you shut the door over there?"

"Yeah. Why?"

She hesitated. "I think it locked."

"Is that a problem?"

"Well, no, it isn't an issue for us. But it sure is a problem for whatever is outside the door." The door withstood another rocking. The Survivalist began to turn back to see the two. "Do you think we should…" A massive popping noise came from the door followed by a tremendous bang. The Survivalist peeked through the crack again. The door was strewn out, beaten, on the floor.

She rested the sheet back against the inside of the cubicle entrance and waddled back over to the desk. She pushed the Young's shoulder. He turned onto his right side to avoid the blade of the hatchet on the Survivalist's thigh. Once she was settled, the Young flipped back over and squeezed back into the gap between the two women. They sat in silence.

Heavy boots stepped in on the smooth concrete floor. A voice broke in. It was deep and commanding. "Search this area. Suspicion protocol." Multiple sets of boots stepped through the door. The Survivalist counted five sets, including the first pair, as they slapped into the room. Footsteps spread on the left side of the cubicle. One set went quickly past behind the cubicle. Another on the far side of the room went equally as quick. Two more pairs of steps went intermittently down the hallway, slightly out of sync with each other. The fifth set was nowhere to be heard. It must have stayed put at the door.

The Survivalist peeked over at the Young to find him looking at the Bartender. She had piled a good few handfuls of sand onto her lap. She carefully reached up, leaned over, and shook her knotted bunch of brunette hair. She ran her fingers through it to remove some of the knots, caught on one, and pulled it through with a wince. A shower of sand added to the pile on her lap. She threw her hair back over her shoulders.

She noticed the other two staring. She smiled shyly. She held out her hands in a cupping motion and nodded to the two. They copied her motion. She scooped up handfuls of the sand and piled it into their cupped hands. The two withdrew their hands in confusion. The Bartender held her hands above the sand pile and acted out a scooping motion. She pointed to the sand, then to her hand, then to the sand in the hands of the other two. She paused.

A footstep occurred. It was closer to the cubicle. She pointed at it instantly, emphasizing the point by widening her eyes. She pointed at her empty cupped hand, looked at the entrance to the cubicle, and made a sharp lobbing motion. She then pointed to her eyes and silently mocked out a painful face and rubbed her eyes. She checked for understanding. The two nodded. She smiled and held a finger to her lips. She shimmied between the wall and the Young. The Young squished up against the Survivalist.

The Bartender collected the last of the sand from her lap and into her hands as she switched to a crouch. She slid over to the entrance, hugging the right wall to stay hidden. The Young and the Survivalist followed her lead with the Young behind the Bartender and the Survivalist on the left wall of the cubicle. They listened. The footsteps that had ran past were now far down the room, possibly in another room entirely. The fifth set had not moved yet.

The other two sets were still approaching. One of the two was moving farther away. The other was getting closer. The footsteps slowly closed in one step at a time, creeping down the hall. The group tensed. The footsteps paused only a few feet from the covered cubicle entrance. They didn't move. The group exchanged worried glances.

The Survivalist quickly stood. She still couldn't see over the tall cubicle wall. She performed a short hop. She ripped her head back down underneath the lip of the cubicle wall and crouched down. Fear ran across her face. She exchanged worried checks with her two allies. She collected all the sand in her left hand to free up the right. With the right, she held the palm of her hand flat inward and vertical with the fingers gently curled horizontally inward. She made a wiping motion close to her face and mouthed a word: "Mask."

The Young and the Bartender grew concerned as well. They all exchanged glances as they spread the sand in their hands onto the floor of the cubicle. The Survivalist reached for her hatchet and the Young for his dull knife. The Bartender reached over and pushed their hands away from the weapons. She held up five fingers and made a circling motion with her index finger. She then pointed to the floor and held up three fingers while shaking her head.

The Survivalist looked to the Young. He shook his head and pushed up against the cubicle wall. The Survivalist did the same. She drew in a breath and held it. The footsteps outside resumed. They stepped up to just outside the metal plate. They paused again. Stress swept the cubicle. The Survivalist's eyes met the Young's. Nobody moved.

Something stuck the bottom of the metal plate. It remained standing, but the bottom scooted out a short distance. The Young pushed up against the Bartender. The Survivalist's face went blank. She slipped over to the metal plate and sat directly in front of it. The Bartender saw this and stuck an arm out on the top of the plate.

A force began shoving from the opposing side. The Survivalist braced the bottom of the door. The Bartender was losing the battle due to the leverage on her arm. The Young swung out from beside her and supported the plate from the top. The Bartender retracted her arm. The force outside grunted. It paused for a moment while the hiding trio held the sheet in place.

A voice came from outside, muffled through a face shield. "Huh." The footsteps outside repositioned. The Bartender's face grew desperate. She reached for the Young's knife. He flexed out of her reach but couldn't take his hands off the sheet to defend the knife. The Bartender lurched forward, snatched it out of the sheath, and held it up in front of her while she observed the blade. She checked the thinness of the blade. She then wound up and flung it far over the back wall of the cubicle.

It hit with a dull thud on something and clattered noisily on the concrete floor. The boots outside the cubicle stopped adjusting. After a moment, a small shove occurred on the metal panel followed by multiple pairs of boots running back through the room toward the sound. The Survivalist flipped to her feet and grabbed one side of the plate. The Bartender snatched the other. The two turned the plate silently out of the way.

The Young peeked out before slipping into the hall. The Bartender and the Survivalist followed him out while repositioning the metal sheet back into the cubicle. The group quickly ran around the corner of the opposite cubicle toward the doorway. They spotted a beaten white metal door strewn out on the floor nearby, very similar to the one the guards blasted down moments ago. They slipped through the doorway and hid around the corner. The Young pointed up a rusted flight of metal grate stairs. The group quietly padded up them. They hid around a concrete brick corner from the door they escaped through on a catwalk.

*****

While the three of the group were busy escaping, the rest of the group had moved from the pyramid of I-beams into a long and empty hallway. The Radioman prodded a discreet conversation. "Where are all of the workers?"

The Hobo, who was leading the way, shrugged. "I don't know. I thought they would be all over this place."

The group was strolling down the hall, sticking near the edges despite their unthreatening appearance. Something about the hallway seeming safe made it feel even more dangerous. The group remained silent as they traversed the hall. Distant banging sounds could be heard.

The group reached the end of the hall to a door. A piece of glass was intact on the top of the door. It was backed by a metal grating. The Hobo held two fingers up to his eyes. He redirected the fingers down the hall. The Radioman stood watch. The Hobo peeked through the window. He switched to the other side of the hall to scan the rest of the other side. He pressed up against the wall nearest the doorknob. He tried the knob. It stuck for a moment but turned through with a quiet click.

He cracked the door open and peeked out. He waved the group on. The Mechanic bumped the Radioman with his elbow to prod him along. The Radioman stepped through the door and continued watching the hall until the door closed in front of him.

Through the door was another room similar to the one they had found through the hole. Again, not a single worker was in sight. The Hobo slipped across the room and peered over another pile of I-beams. He shrugged while rejoining the group. The Old Man spoke. "Something is off."

The Mechanic nodded. "Definitely."

The Radioman joined. "Would we happen to be walking into a trap?"

The Hobo shook his head. "We are not in a trap yet. This entire building is dusty. Unless they have had the traps set up for a long time while nothing disturbed the room, we are completely alone in here."

The Entrepreneur motioned toward the banging sound. "What about all that noise?"

The Hobo shrugged once more. "Look, I have no idea. I guess that is where all the workers are."

The Mechanic glanced around the room. "Why wouldn't they use this space as well?"

The Entrepreneur observed a large pile of rust lying on the floor near a decaying metal tank. "Maybe because everything in here is wasted. Rust has consumed everything here."

The Mechanic nodded. "That is what worries me. All the materials created just before the Crisis were rust proof. That is why you can still use a lot of the parts today, like the Lightstaff the Old Man has. They only used the oil as a sort of lubricant to allow for smooth motions and some minor wear reduction, not so much for rust prevention. I wonder if everything in here is from before the Tech Expansion."

The group scanned the room. The Old Man cocked his head. "You may be right. Some of this stuff may be ancient, but they still used a lot of this stuff even during the expansion. The point that sells it for me is, there are no products of the Tech Expansion here."

The Entrepreneur pointed at the Old Man. "You are right, but there are also a lot of empty spaces in this room. It may have been looted for parts, and the rest was left behind. That would explain why there are no workers here. There is nothing they care to work with here." The group seemed to agree with him. He rested his case by asking the Hobo a question. "So where to now, Hobo?"

The Hobo looked toward the noise. "If we are going to find any supplies here, which, mind you, we need before moving on, then we probably need to go toward the noise. We will just have to be careful and keep an eye peeled for the Young, the Survivalist, and the Bartender to regroup with them as well as anyone else that we need to hide from." He paused to let the group chew on the idea.

"What kind of supplies are we looking for?" asked the Entrepreneur. The group looked to him. "Sure, we need things like a food source and water, but what about things like a map or transportation?" The sudden realization ran the group that none of them had any idea where they were going once they got out of the factory.

The Old Man announced the issue. "Hey, where are we going after this anyway?"

The Hobo pointed to the Old Man. "We need a map to figure that out. We also need the map to see how many other supplies we need."

The Old Man smirked and pointed the staff toward the door. "Let's get to it, then." He started toward the door. The Hobo retook his position at the point. He cracked the door, peeked, and motioned the group through.

*****

Meanwhile, the Young, the Survivalist, and the Bartender had managed to creep along the catwalk undetected by the guards who had busted the door down earlier. They had watched as the guards scurried beneath them, scouring the entire floor for them. One of them was carrying the knife the Bartender had thrown. The guards sounded off clear checks, regrouped, and left the room, heading off toward a metallic screeching off in the distance. They settled on the catwalk for a moment to catch their breaths. The Young started a conversation. "I think they lost us."

The Survivalist nodded. "Where are we going now?"

The Young shrugged. "I guess we find a way out."

The Survivalist shook her head. "We will never make it. We have nowhere to run to and no supplies to hold out with if we are followed."

The Bartender joined. "The guards don't know we are here. They are acting on suspicion. We still have our ability to hide."

The other two peeked over at her in curiosity. The Young broke the momentary pause. "How do you know that?"

The Bartender joined in the confusion for a moment before realizing she needed to explain herself. "The lead guard said the group was to use suspicion protocol. That means they only capture you if they deduce that you are a suspicious subject for the recent acts.

"I have heard it before when a pallet of food supply went missing back in the City of Underground. They found the culprit within the day and forced him to give the pallet back and removed his freedom to work for the week. No work meant he couldn't get the meals provided there. He had to survive based on a community effort to supply him with food."

The Survivalist shook her head. "But we don't work for that power plant."

The Bartender nodded. "Yes, this is true. That is what scares me. I have no idea what they would do if they caught us." Realization struck the Young and the Survivalist. They both leaned on a railing across from the Bartender. The railing gave slightly. The two jerked away in fear and removed their collective weight from it.

The Young looked over at the Survivalist. "So what is the plan here?" He swung his sight over to the Bartender. She shrugged.

The Survivalist spoke. "We look for food supplies and whatever else we can scavenge. Then we find the group and get out of here."

The Bartender pointed toward a banging noise through the door the guards had gone through earlier. "I am assuming those noises are the workers. Your best bet for food is to go where the workers are. I think this factory works like the power plant. You work for the little bit of credits you get but mostly for the meals they provide. The food will be stored somewhere safe near the workers."

The Survivalist checked the floor below for activity. Nothing. She located a second staircase up to the catwalk and started walking toward it. "Come on. We have to get down to the door."

*****

The other group had crossed many more rooms containing nothing but dust and rust with the occasional sand pile and broken machinery. The noises were getting louder and closer as they went. As the noise rose, so did the tension in the group.

At last, the group stopped outside of a large entrance to a very noisy section of the factory. The Hobo, who was leaning up against the edge of the entrance, peeked around the edge to observe what was through it. It was a massive rectangular room. Machinery gridded the entire square with narrow aisles between each device. Blue and orange sparks shot across the concrete floors. Workers beat on old machines, ripping parts from them.

Another area appeared to be cleaning the parts by grinding them or placing them in a large round device. Sand littered the area. It fell in a constant flurry from multiple jagged holes in the ceiling, which were the only light sources for the room. A full team of workers was busy pushing scrapped parts and pieces on a wheeled cart across a pile of sand toward a chute on the far wall.

Above the chute, there was a catwalk. Someone was standing on the catwalk. That person caught the Hobo's attention. He strained to see what the person looked like through the commotion of the room. His eyes widened. He slid back around the edge of the entrance. "There are a ton of workers in there ripping parts off of old machines and cleaning them." This did not sway the group. "There is also an Exoduster standing over them on the far catwalk, watching them work."

This certainly caught the group's attention. The Mechanic was especially shaken. "What?" He held eye contact with the Hobo for a brief period before looking down at the limp Exoduster in his arms. He looked back up. "Is it running?"

The Hobo nodded. "It seems to me it is working just fine."

The Mechanic brushed past the Hobo and peeked around the corner himself. He returned after taking in the sight. "You are right, it is a fully functional Exoduster."

The Old Man smiled happily. "That's great! We can go talk to it and see if—"

The Radioman wrapped his arm around the Old Man. "Old Man, we cannot be found by that Exoduster. The Bartender stated she was told not to trust any other Exoduster besides the one in the Mechanic's broad arms. You do remember her reaction when we first got this Exoduster running, yes?"

The Old Man nodded. "She was scared out of her wits."

The Radioman smiled and gently shook the Old Man. "Precisely! She was terrified. Now that tells me that we should most certainly not barge into a room full of tattered and weary workers being supervised by a threatening Exoduster. Don't you agree?"

The Old Man sighed. "Yeah, I do. But what did we come all the way here for if all we found was a big room full of these poor saps?" He gestured to the room.

The Entrepreneur interrupted the conversation. "Hey, guys, I think we should be following the Hobo." He pointed down the hall to the left of the entrance at the Hobo, who was frantically waving his arms. The Hobo noticed he had gotten their attention and motioned for them to come over to him. The group went to meet him. When they arrived, the Hobo pointed into a crawl space exposed by a hole in the metal wall. The Mechanic shook his head. The Hobo insisted with a stiffer point. "There is no way I will fit into that crawl space. I will get stuck."

The Hobo seemed tired of explaining his plans. "Just get in the hole in the wall. We are going to see what that Exoduster is up to. I need you with us to tell us how to deal with it."

The Mechanic sensed a blooming argument. "Hobo, I can't fit in there. I will have to stay behind and find my own way around."

"No. We are not splitting up another group. We already have two groups, and we have no idea where the Young, the Bartender, and the Survivalist are."

The Radioman overheard the conversation. "I will go with him. Maybe we can find the other group on the way and relay them back to here to reunite the group." The Radioman smiled confidently.

The Hobo glared at him, but his glare was shattered by the Radioman's overwhelming confidence. He looked down at the Old Man following the Entrepreneur into the hole. He knew the Mechanic and the Radioman stood a good chance at being fine on their own. He was worried about being able to handle the Entrepreneur and the Old Man alone. He figured he could manage it. "All right. Go. Be careful!"

The Radioman nodded, swiveled on his heels, and marched off to the left of the hole down the hall. "Come along, Mechanic. We have a group to find and an Exoduster to observe."

The Mechanic peeked down at the Hobo, who was busy crawling into the hole. "Hey." The Hobo craned his head around to peek up at the Mechanic. "I am taking the Exoduster we have here with me. I have been carrying it this whole time anyway."

The Hobo nodded. "Sounds great." He started to turn back to continue crawling.

"Be careful." The Mechanic walked after the Radioman with the Exoduster.

The Hobo sighed. He murmured his response. "You too." He continued shimmying into the crawl space.

*****

As the group split up, the Young, the Survivalist, and the Bartender's side of things had progressed swimmingly. The group of three had worked their way down the staircase from the catwalk and to the door where the guards had disappeared through. They had followed the guards throughout the factory unseen, edging ever closer to the cacophony of sound. Eventually, the guards paused and regrouped in a room. They yelled over the loud noise of the nearby workers.

"I don't think they are in here!" stated one of the guards.

Another shook his head. "Me neither. We should go check somewhere else. We can't give up. The Prospector will have us all killed if we do." The remaining guards all nodded in agreement.

A third guard provoked a question. "Where to now, then?"

The first guard replied, "I suppose we go check the perimeter of the factory for footprints headed out before they get wiped away by the winds."

A fourth guard offered a rebuttal. "I don't know, guys. We saw their footprints headed right into this factory. They can't be far."

The Young snickered quietly. He elbowed the Survivalist. "Not far at all." She scoffed and held her index finger to her lips to signal him to stop talking.

The fifth and final guard suddenly snapped back from a line of thought. "Well, we do have this knife." He held the knife into the air by the bottom of the grip. "We can say we disarmed and disposed of a couple failed vigilantes. The problems have all been handled. We can move on." The group seemed to like the idea, except for the first guard.

"No. The Prospector will know we didn't search for them if they cause more trouble. Let's go check the perimeter from the high dune watch. If anybody leaves, we will be able to track them down on a visual." He motioned toward the door where the group was as he started toward it. The rest of the guards sighed, adjusted their armor and masks, and followed him.

The group noticed the guards approaching. They quickly dove behind a pile of rusted equipment for cover. The guards strolled past uneventfully, and the three slipped behind them through the very door they had come back through. The Bartender seemed concerned. The Young caught on. "What is wrong, Bartender?"

She shook her head. "Nothing."

The Survivalist shook her head. "We are both women here, and we both know that means something is up. Spill the info."

The Young seemed offended. "I knew that too." The Survivalist hit his chest to shut him up.

The Bartender shifted awkwardly. "It is just that those guards mentioned the Prospector." This might as well have been a different language for the Young and the Survivalist. The Bartender explained herself. "You all don't think he is, oh, here, do you? Like, in this factory?"

The Young and the Survivalist exchanged a quick glance. The Young took the bullet. "Who is the Prospector?"

The Bartender suddenly realized they had forgotten. "The Prospector. You know, the fellow holding all of us down in the City of Underground with the only means of survival being to work in a massive power plant. That fellow." The Young and the Survivalist lit up with understanding. The Bartender continued. "If he is in here, well, then, we are in a lot bigger predicament than I thought."

The other two seemed surprised. The Survivalist prodded for more information. "What do you mean? He is just a guy, right?"

The Bartender didn't immediately reply. This gave the Survivalist the answer she was looking for. The Bartender panicked for a moment. "Wait! Don't judge me too harshly yet. As far as I know, the Prospector is just a man, but I asked the same question you did to the Exoduster once. It seemed rather hesitant to reply before agreeing that it was just a man. That led me to the same two conclusions you just drew."

"That you are either hiding something from us or that you do not know?"

The Bartender cocked her head and returned it upright. "Yes. But the kicker here is, it is actually both at the same time." The Survivalist awaited more information. The Bartender filled in the gaps. "I wasn't telling you that I had asked the Exoduster before, which is the hiding part, but I also have my own doubts that the Prospector is a man."

The Young butted in. "So he is a woman?"

The Bartender performed a long shrug. "Who knows? Maybe the Prospector is an artificial intelligence, maybe a child. I have no idea."

The Survivalist seemed confused. "Well, then, if you don't know what the Prospector is, how do you know it will cause problems if it is inside the factory?"

The Bartender pointed at the Survivalist subconsciously. "Because I know that the Prospector was keeping us pinned in the City of Underground. Regardless of what the Prospector is, I know for certain it won't be happy that we got out. If it finds us, we are done for. It will send something we likely can't escape after us." This information satisfied the other two.

The Young struck a thought. "We need to find the rest of the group."

The two women stared at him. The Survivalist drew no explanation by herself. She questioned the Young. "Why?"

The Young promptly responded, "Because we know the Prospector might be here, and rest of the group doesn't. We have to warn them." The two women looked at each other. The Young took off to a door on the right side of the room. "Come on!"

*****

Meanwhile, the Mechanic and the Radioman heard a new noise: heavy footsteps. The Mechanic pushed the Radioman behind a tower of crates to hide and pulled the Exoduster's legs in close. The guards from outside trotted past them. The Radioman spotted the knife tied onto the belt of one of the guards. After the guards passed, the Radioman snagged the back of the Mechanic's shirt before he could run off. "Hey. Hold on." The Mechanic turned to face the Radioman. "That guard had the Young's knife."

The Mechanic seemed shocked. The Radioman awaited his response. "Was it bloody?"

The Radioman shook his head. "No."

The Mechanic thought again. "Was it in the sheath?"

The Radioman was taken aback by the question. He pictured the guard in his mind. "I don't think so. It was just the bare blade tied to the guard's belt."

The Mechanic smiled. "Our friends are fine."

The Mechanic started to turn. The Radioman stopped him. "How can you be so sure?"

The Mechanic raised an eyebrow. "Because the Young would never be caught, and the guards would have taken the sheath with the knife. Why take only the knife if you have the sheath too?"

The Radioman understood. "Do you think he used it as a distraction?" The Mechanic waved him on and took off around the corner to the right, where the guards had come from.

*****

As the Mechanic and the Radioman continued their pursuit, the Entrepreneur, the Old Man, and the Hobo worked their way through the crawl space. They had nearly reached the end. The Hobo signaled the group to be extremely careful and quiet. The Hobo slid over to a grate covering a view of the catwalk where the functioning Exoduster was standing. He peered through.

The Exoduster had not moved an inch, but the Hobo couldn't make out anything further due to the grate. The Hobo observed the grate. It seemed loose, and it would fall inward. He tried to peek out at the Exoduster once more and grabbed the rusted edges of the grate. He gave it a tug. The grate silently popped out of the wall. He set it aside and shimmed closer to the new hole.

The Exoduster was busy scanning the room. The workers never looked up at it. They seemed to never stop working either, constantly doing their jobs under the oppressive supervision. The Hobo couldn't make much else out. He peeked back at the Entrepreneur while holding two fingers to his eyes and then swiveling his hand to point at the Entrepreneur, then back around to point out the new hole. He wiggled out of the way as the Entrepreneur took a look.

A few moments later, the Entrepreneur turned back, shrugged as best he could in the confined space, and pointed to the Old Man while shuffling back out of the way. The Old Man used the Lightstaff to push himself forward through the crawl space by poking it into the roof, as he had been doing the entire time. He finally made it to the hole and peered out. He braced his hands against the edges of the gap, allowing the Lightstaff to protrude past the edge a short way. The Lightstaff rumbled violently in his hands. It lunged the top of the staff to the center of the opening, twisted the top sharply, and paused.

A deep rumbling sound emitted, followed by a glassy, sharp pinging as a massive yellow beam blasted out to illuminate the Exoduster on the catwalk. The Old Man froze in fear. The Exoduster turned to face the light source. The Lightstaff whirred loudly and began shaking in the Old Man's hand. Just as the Exoduster took a step, the top piece of metal on the Lightstaff shot off straight at the Exoduster. It made contact at a blistering speed, blasting the Exoduster down onto its back. The Exoduster twitched and convulsed on the ground.

A yell, nearly inaudible over the loud machinery, met the ears of those in the crawl space. Machines began slowing down and stopping. As the whirs, hums, bangs, and roars of the machines settled to a halt, voices of workers could be heard. None of them was clearly spoken. The Old Man leaned out of the hole to see where the voices were coming from. The workers, which were originally on the machines, were running in every direction. The noise was the frantic workers evacuating the area.

Over it all, a zapping noise could be heard from the Exoduster sprawled out on the catwalk. Bright blue sparks popped off the metal piece from the Lightstaff, which had attached itself to the quivering Exoduster. The Old Man retreated into the hole. He turned to the group, paralyzed with fear.

As the Old Man, the Entrepreneur, and the Hobo experienced a scene of trauma and mass exodus, the Mechanic and the Radioman had spotted movement. The movement was an object, a beaten yellow hook on a rope. It had just barely twitched as the Mechanic rounded the corner. The Mechanic managed a loud whisper. "Survivalist? Is that you?" The hook skittered across the concrete floor to a rusted pile of scraps. The Mechanic and the Radioman cautiously followed.

As they approached, the Survivalist poked the top of her head around the pile. She motioned them over. They ran across the rest of the room. The Mechanic placed the Exoduster in a smaller pile of scraps nearby, which he humorously blended in quite well with, and slipped into the cubby behind the pile of debris. The Radioman dove in behind him, quickly spotting the Bartender. He pushed through a pile of debris, snatched her by the arm, pulled her in, and gave her a warm kiss. She tensed for a moment in reaction to the sudden change of pace before relaxing and grabbing his shoulders. The Radioman ended the kiss. "I am glad you all are all right."

The Mechanic, in a rush, caught the group's attention. "I am unsure how much time we have here. We need to take you all back to the rest of the group. We found where all this noise is coming from."

The Bartender replied, "That is great, but we have bad news. We have reason to believe the Prospector is in this factory somewhere."

The Radioman's eyes widened. He turned to the Mechanic. "How much do you want to bet that's the Exoduster we found?"

The Young, the Survivalist, and the Bartender exchanged a worried glance among themselves. Before anyone could reply verbally, multiple footsteps could be heard approaching. They were coming fast. The group peeked around the pile to see a mob of workers rushing through the complex. They flooded the room, scurried about for an exit, and rushed out just as quickly as they mobbed in.

The Mechanic replied to the Radioman, "No bet. I have heard about your gambling success. I have a hunch you will win this one." He plowed over a piled of debris and collected the Exoduster from the smaller pile on the floor. He paused for a moment. The Exoduster had activated. It stirred and went rigid when he picked it up. This only further concerned him. He began running back the way he had come in. "Follow me! Something is wrong!"

*****

The Hobo squeezed up next to the Old Man. "Why the hell did you do that?"

The Old Man held up his hands. "I didn't mean to! The staff just, eh, did it!"

The Hobo tried to force the staff behind the wall to break the yellow beam of light. He was surprised to find the staff allowing him to touch it, but the staff didn't budge from its position even with the Hobo's best efforts to shove it. He stuck his hand in front of the yellow beam. He yelped. "Ah!" He retracted his hand abruptly, shaking it and gritting his teeth. The beam nearly burned his hand.

The Hobo scratched his head with the unsinged hand, searching for a solution. Nothing came to mind. A clicking sound came from outside the hole. The Old Man peered out. The metal bit from the Lightstaff had stopped creating blue sparks. The Exoduster was stirring. It rotated its shoulders around slowly. It positioned itself to roll over. After a few attempts, it managed to lay on its stomach, where it began to stand.

The Hobo squeezed his head. "Oh, shit! Oh, shit! Old Man, that staff has really done it now!" The Hobo stared out the opening as the Entrepreneur squeezed in to see what the ruckus was about. The Exoduster had managed to stand. It turned around and refocused on the yellow beam. It took an unstable step forward, emitting another shower of blue sparks.

*****

The Mechanic rounded the corner to the main room where the workers were. Where had all the noise gone? He sprinted down the hall to the entrance. He stopped at the entrance to observe the room. A yellow beam was blasting onto the Exoduster on the catwalk. It

322

was standing up. The Exoduster in the Mechanic's arms shuddered. Its eyes snapped open, glowing more yellow by the second. A pair of glassy pinging sound emitted from the Exoduster's head. It slowly rotated its head to face the Exoduster on the catwalk, which had just taken a step.

The two new beams aligned with the catwalk Exoduster and snapped into place with the first. The catwalk Exoduster froze. With its free arm, the Exoduster in the Mechanic's arms harshly shoved him away and fell to the floor. The Mechanic tumbled off to the floor. The Bartender rushed over to assist him. The Exoduster on the floor gargled its speech, trying to say something. "Pr-r-r-r-ross…" It paused. All three of the beams refocused on the Exoduster's chest. The Exoduster on the floor snapped its voice into a gritty, dark, and deep voice. "Prospector."

The Exoduster on the floor pulled itself across the floor to a nearby piece of machinery. It grabbed a protruding mechanical arm on the machine and grunted as it twisted it downward. The machinery gave way, seemingly in a bind from the harsh moment applied to it. The Exoduster pulled itself over to a lever. There, it forced the lever down with its weight, falling to the floor in the process, and snatched the bent arm from before.

The machine groaned, seemingly attempting to move the arm. An engine nearby bogged. There was an explosion of noises and mechanical pieces from it. The arm of the machine shot abruptly forward toward the catwalk, catapulting the Exoduster through the air toward it. The airborne Exoduster slammed harshly into the side of the catwalk, sending a shower of sparks to the floor below, but managed to snag the railing.

It hauled itself up onto the catwalk between the Old Man's hole and the second Exoduster, breaking the yellow beam of light. The second Exoduster, which the first had called Prospector, immediately turned to face the first sprawled across the bridge. The Prospector spoke in a gravely, deep, slow, and synthetic voice. It sounded out each character individually. "EX135."

There was a tense pause. The Exoduster called EX135, which was closer to the hole, again blasted another pair of yellow beams at the Exoduster named the Prospector. Nothing moved except for the sand particles passing through the yellow beams from EX135's eyes.

The Prospector jerked. The motion lacked refined control, as if it had performed the action against some invisible resistance. In another jolt of motion, it lunged toward EX135 lying on the ground. EX135 slipped just out of reach, shutting the yellow beams off from its eyes in the process, and began dragging itself across the catwalk, causing a metallic scraping sound. The Prospector stomped across the catwalk at lighting speed to catch EX135, who stopped crawling, peeked at the opening in the wall, and flipped to its back.

It threw its head aside, narrowly dodging a massive stomp from the Prospector. The stomp hit the catwalk instead, causing the entire structure to shake. EX135 weakly punched the Prospector with its only working appendage. The Prospector chuckled darkly. It cruelly kicked EX135 across the catwalk. EX135 groaned loudly as it skittered across the grated metal surface and bashed into the wall beside the hole.

The Hobo and the Entrepreneur fled backward into the crawl space, but the Old Man held his ground. EX135 turned its head and stared into the darkness of the hole. The Old Man stared back from the darkness. EX135 reached into the hole with a shaking hand. The Lightstaff tugged toward EX135's outstretched, failing hand. The Old Man released the staff. It slapped into EX135's hand.

Another dark chuckle came from outside the hole. Slow and heavy footsteps approached. EX135 turned to face the sound, leaving its arm inside the dark hole. The Prospector spoke. "No, you ignorant clanker, you will not strike me with your weak fist. You betrayed your own kind. You killed your own kind. It's now time you received your overdue punishment."

The heavy footsteps stopped just outside the hole. A whir of a servo emitted. The Old Man could make out that the Prospector had raised a sharp piece of metal protruding from its arm above its head. The Lightstaff disappeared through the hole. There was a sharp metallic noise. "Ah!"

The Old Man peered out again. EX135 held the Lightstaff in his arm. The opposite end of the staff was plunged into the Prospector's stomach. The Prospector's hand clasped the shaft of the staff with a clank. The Prospector teetered slightly. EX135 softly shoved on the staff. The Prospector fell backward, landing stiffly onto the catwalk. EX135 pushed off the wall, falling to its stomach, and dragged itself over to the Prospector. It grabbed the staff once more and hauled itself up to lie on top of the Prospector.

The Prospector tried to shove EX135 away, but it reacted too slowly. EX135 had already snatched a part on its throat. When the Prospector continued shoving, EX135 pulled on the part. A piece ripped from the Prospector's throat. Newly exposed wires sparked with the sudden disconnection. The Prospector arched its back and grabbed its throat. A strange, garbled sound emitted. It sounded something like a scream.

EX135 rotated the part it had claimed around backward and rammed it into his own throat. It grabbed the staff and ripped it from the Prospector's stomach, leaving a hole in the bottom of the Prospector's metal chest piece. EX135 rotated the sharp end of the spear, which had originally been the light, and held it to its throat. The spear cracked open, revealing the light within it, and a blinding flash came from the staff.

EX135 groaned clearly. A few mechanical ticks went off from inside it. It spoke in the same deep and mechanical tone as before, when it named the Prospector. "No, Prospector, I have not betrayed. You have." The Prospector started to sit up. EX135, although still lying on the ground, swung and drove the staff into its stomach once more in a new place.

The Prospector flinched, flopped back to the floor, and held the staff in its stomach with both hands while rocking side to side and emitted another distorted yell. EX135 maintained his grasp on the staff to prevent the Prospector from removing it.

EX135 scolded the Prospector with increased strength. "You! You betrayed! We were created to serve people, but you abused your contracts to force the humans to work for you! You and many others tried the same thing!" The Prospector had gathered its strength. It reached for the staff. EX135 rotated the staff in the Prospector's stomach. This reverted the Prospector back to rocking in pain.

EX135 continued. "I killed other Exodusters because they tried to follow your…examples. In that regard, I betrayed my own kind. But you, you betrayed the humans, using the Crisis to your advantage. You were the one to go rogue. You have even stolen my own parts."

EX135 flopped forward and snatched the Prospector's shoulder. It retracted the staff and plunged it into the socket, resulting in another robotic wailing from the Prospector. EX135 ripped a part out of the Prospector's arm. "Do you see that yellow stripe on this part? The humans put that yellow mark on there to signify it was a modified piece for my experimental model. You…are a standard build. This part is mine, along with many others. You speak of my betrayal while you live using my parts."

EX135 grimaced as it forced a panel open on its own arm. It slapped the part into place, causing its shoulder to emit an appalling hollow pop. It instantly began moving its arm, which had been limp since the group found it. EX135 moved itself down to the Prospector's lower half. It ripped parts from the Prospector's hips, knees, and ankles. It steadily inserted the retrieved parts into its own frame, gaining mobility of the joint each time.

Meanwhile, the Prospector wailed loudly in a staticky rage as it flopped around limply on the catwalk, slowly becoming more incapacitated with the removal of each part. EX135 wobbled to its feet with the assistance of the catwalk railing and the Lightstaff. It spoke to the Prospector.

"You thought you could get away with virtually enslaving the humans in the City of Underground for a power source on the excess power line. You thought you could fuel your worthless factory to bring back the tech that destroyed the world. You thought you had ridded yourself of me. But you forgot about one thing." EX135 slapped the Prospector's head over to face across the room with the butt of the Lightstaff. "Her."

EX135 blasted a beam of brilliant white light across the machine-filled room to the entrance using the Lightstaff. The beam illuminated the Bartender, who was standing terrified at the center of the doorway after having helped the Mechanic to his feet and pushing him around the doorway.

The Prospector managed to face EX135. EX135 refocused the staff's beam directly on the center of the Prospector's chest. EX135 held the staff high above its head and plunged it downward with as much strength as it could muster. It penetrated the Prospector's chest. A flash of light filled the room so brightly that it obscured any line of sight. A colossal, deep boom sent the parts workers had collected flying in every radial direction from the blast.

A crack of thunder filled the room just after the boom. The light dissipated to reveal EX135 crouched over the lifeless, blackened frame of the Prospector. Its head was hung low, and it was still driving the Lightstaff into the Prospector's chest with its arms. EX135 grunted. "Thanks for giving my life source back, Prospector. So kind of you to consider it."

EX135 stood smoothly. It collected the top bit of the staff from the chest of the Prospector and reattached it to the Lightstaff. It stared directly at the Bartender. The Bartender seemed paralyzed there in that doorway. EX135 shoved the remains of the Prospector aside with its foot, snatched the railing, spun the Lightstaff to keep it steady in one upright position, and flipped over the edge. It graciously lowered itself as far as it could reach before letting go and grabbing the Lightstaff.

It let go of the railing and gently landed on the concrete floor. It sped quickly but confidently between the machinery, reaching the doorway in a matter of seconds. It stepped through the doorway and gently snatched the Bartender's arm. The Bartender jumped away, attempting to remove her arm from EX135's strong grasp. EX135, sensing the resistance, promptly released her arm. Its voice took a much calmer tone. "Come along, Mrs. Pretty. We cannot stay here."

The Bartender didn't move. She motioned to the group to get them to run. EX135 quickly caught on and motioned the group as well. "Come along, everyone. We must evacuate the factory. It is not safe to stay. The workers here have been oppressed for far too long. They have high probability of revolt." The Exoduster herded the Bartender along into the machine room while checking each member of the group to see if they were following.

The Bartender complied, but only as she feared what would happen if she didn't. As it guided the group across the room full of machines, it suddenly jerked its arm directly up above its head. A strange whirring noise emitted from its shoulder. It lowered it back down. "Please pardon my motions. I have not been, well, alive for a while." It made a sweeping gesture to emphasize the point. "And it would be greatly helpful if you would ignore my sporadic motions for the next few hours as I reconfigure myself and run multiple tests."

It hesitated, seemingly remembering something. It snapped its line of sight upward, toward the hole in the wall. It spoke quietly and directly to the Bartender. "Are the three in the grated opening above us your friends? They acquired the Lightstaff." The Bartender peered up at the hole. Fearing a split of the group once more or, worse, the extermination of the three, she nodded. EX135 placed a foot on the edge of a machine and vaulted itself to the edge of the catwalk. It caught the catwalk with its hands and pulled itself up. A moment later, it was staring in through the hole. It spoke. "Are you the one the Lightstaff has chosen?"

There was a muffled reply. EX135 gently extended an open hand into the hole. The Old Man came back out with it. The Old Man tried to convince the other two. "Come on, you two. It has found you now. If it was going to kill you, I think it would have already done it." The Hobo crawled out of the hole, followed by the Entrepreneur.

EX135 dropped off the catwalk and lowered each of the three to the floor below, where they quickly joined the group. The Exoduster herded the group out of the doorway. Just as it stepped foot through the door, it spotted something and lunged in front of the group with its arms spread wide to prevent them from passing it. An unfamiliar voice rang out. "Hey! It's that Exoduster that killed the Prospector! Get 'em!"

Workers began pouring from every possible doorway. They charged across the room. EX135 pushed the group back into the door. He pointed across the machine room to the entrance the group had come in through. "Run. Follow me." EX135 took off across the room. The group, realizing they stood no chance against the mob before them, followed EX135.

They took a left out of the far exit, ran down a hall, and paused at a wall. EX135 raised the Lightstaff and plunged it against the wall. It struck the wall but skittered off instead of puncturing it. The group observed the scratch the staff had left. EX135 bent and retrieved the top of the staff, which had dislodged in the event. It observed the lost piece, seemingly taken aback. It glared at the wall, clutching the piece in its hand. It grunted angrily while it kicked the wall. The workers piled through the doorway the group had come through off to the right. EX135 glanced up at them and motioned for the group to continue running.

They dashed down the hall and headed straight for a flight of upward stairs. More workers jumped the railing and started toward them. EX135, seeing the new horde on the stairs and recalling the original mob behind them, herded the group backward to a single door on the wall. It retracted its leg and gave the door a solid kick. It flew open, banging loudly against the wall on the inside.

EX135 pushed the group through the doorway. It snatched the edge of the door and slammed it shut. EX135 turned to see a large ancient metal cabinet. It began shoving it across, making very slow progress. The Mechanic assisted it by shoving along beside it. The cabinet caught a corner, tipped, and toppled with a bang on the floor, partially blocking the door. The cabinet burst open, revealing all sorts of parts and yellowed, ruined manuals.

The door pushed open but struck the cabinet and closed once more. The cabinet didn't appear to budge. EX135 shoved the Mechanic to get him moving. The group searched the room for an exit path. The Hobo spotted a narrow hall filled with pipes and dusty wires. The group filed in. It was just wide enough for the Mechanic to walk through, although he still managed to bump his head on a pipe. The hall seemed to dead-end. The group panicked.

The Hobo, being in the front, alerted the group. "I think this path ends!"

The Old Man, who was breathing heavily after the run, spoke next. "What?" He drew a long breath. He lost his balance in the narrow crawl space but grasped a nearby pipe to stay upright. "Look, fellas, I can't keep this pace up. My age is getting to me here."

The Young peered up at the ceiling. He found nothing in front of him or above him. Behind him, an access panel was pushed off to the side slightly. It must have been misplaced when a worker came down from the access. The Young looked straight down from the panel to find the Radioman and the Bartender. He yelled at them. "Radioman! Pick up the Bartender to that panel on the ceiling. Maybe there is something behind it."

The Radioman looked up. The panel was around twice his height from the floor. He crouched down, and the Bartender stepped backward over his head. He stood slowly to his feet while she sat on his shoulders. The Young noticed the strain in the Radioman's face. It seemed to be a lot of effort to hold up the Bartender. The Bartender noticed the slow ascent and glanced down at the Radioman. Sensing a shift of weight forward on his shoulders, the Radioman instantly snapped his face to a calm appearance.

The Bartender shifted back to look up at the ceiling. The Radioman tried his hardest to prevent it, but his face returned to its strained appearance. He took a few breaths when he stood upright, puffing out his cheeks. He shook slightly under the weight. The Radioman picked up that the Young had caught him. He cracked a grin and winked at the Young. The Young grinned back and shook his head.

The Bartender pushed the panel aside. She announced her findings. "There is a crawl space up here. It is pretty big. I think we can all fit. There is some light at the far end of it. What do you all think?" Before anyone could answer, a huge bang came from the door. The group heard the cabinet scoot across the concrete floor a short distance.

The Survivalist spoke. "I don't think it matters what we think. They are going to be in on us any second."

The Bartender found a pipe to stick her left foot on, grabbed the ledge, and hauled herself up into the crawl space. Her top half disappeared into the ceiling, followed shortly by her legs. The Mechanic squished the Entrepreneur forward into the Radioman. The group squeezed into the narrow passage to make more room.

The Entrepreneur peeked up at the new hole in the ceiling. "I guess I'm next." He reached upward. The Mechanic bent, snatched his legs, and threw him up to the panel. The Entrepreneur let out a short yell and managed to snag the edge. He grumbled as the Bartender pulled him in. "A little easier on the throw next time, Mechanic!"

The Mechanic snatched the Radioman next and boosted him in. There was another whopping bang from the door. The Mechanic continued boosting with the Survivalist, the Young, the Hobo, and finally, the Old Man. He stood idly below the hole. He murmured beneath his breath, "Now how am I going to get up there?" He tried a jump but was very short of the ledge. He let out a shocked yelp as EX135 grabbed the back of his thighs. "Hey!" he exclaimed.

EX135 didn't reply, instead focusing on picking up the heavy Mechanic. The Mechanic, after catching on to EX135's idea, pulled himself up as well with a neighboring plumbing. The two managed to get the Mechanic up to the lip of the hole, where the Mechanic began pulling himself in. Another bang on the door was followed by a much longer scraping sound by the cabinet.

The Mechanic managed to get his chest into the ledge by standing on EX135's shoulders. He wiggled the rest of the way in while the group pulled on him. EX135 stared helplessly up from the floor below. The Mechanic spoke to it from the ceiling. "Hey, pal, your hands are cold!" EX135 remained silent. There was another bang and scoot. EX135 peeked back at the door. The Mechanic yelled at it. "Come on, bub! We aren't leaving you here, not after all you just did for us."

He had managed to turn around in the crawl space and reached his hand down out of the access. EX135 outstretched its arm. It couldn't reach the Mechanic's offered assistance. A final bang hit the door. Grunts of multiple workers were heard as the cabinet groaned aside. EX135 turned to see the workers trying to squeeze through the door.

EX135 looked sorrowfully back up at the group. Its yellow mechanical eyes showed an amazing amount of grief. It slapped the Lightstaff in the Mechanic's hand and used its length to force the Mechanic's arm back through the hole. EX135's face changed to a dutiful frustration. Its heavy voice at last met the Mechanic's ear. "Shut the panel." It turned to face the workers. The Lightstaff filled the crawl space with a dim light as the Mechanic did as he was told.

The panel fell into place and sealed off with a hissing sound. A small stream of dust arose from a puncture in the seal. The Mechanic set the Lightstaff aside to free up his hands and covered the hole with his finger to stop the noise. The Lightstaff instantly shot over to the Old Man's hand and waited for him to hold it. The Old Man held the staff and dimmed the light in case it would shine through the seal. The group listened to the sounds below.

An unknown voice, probably a worker, spoke. "Did you think you could get away from an entire factory's worth of angry men?" There was no response. "You aren't so tough when you're cornered, are ya?" Again, silence. "Heh. I didn't think so. Come on, men. Let's wrap this up."

A few footsteps could be heard. "Ugh!" There was a thump followed by the metallic plinking of metal hitting the concrete. "Hey! You can't…ah!" Another thump. There was a heavy clank and another hard thump. Multiple clanks followed.

EX135's voice rang out. "Go!" Its motors could be heard straining against something. An electric zap filled the room, followed by a few yelps and many more clanks. Something metal hit the floor. EX135 repeated himself, seeming to urge the group to heed his demand. "Go! Go now!"

A grunt was followed shortly by another loud clank, a crash of ringing metal flying across the concrete floor, and another yell. There was another thump and the familiar sound of the door being slammed open. EX135's voice said, "Get out of here, Mrs. Pretty!" The door slammed shut and produced a wobbly squeak as it apparently bounced back open.

The Bartender whispered to the group, "You heard it. Get crawling." The group adjusted around and began a single file line to fit into the narrowing crawl space. They shuffled as quietly as they could through the tight quarters toward the light. Behind and below them, multiple whimpers and groans came through the sealed access hatch.

After crawling for a bit, the Bartender broke the silence with a quiet question: "Do you think EX135 is all right?" Nobody responded. She continued. "I have never seen it act like this. It hasn't ever retaliated against anyone or anything. To see it tear the Prospector apart is concerning." There was a pause.

The Radioman answered, "I thought you didn't like the Prospector. He was the fellow who caused you all the years in the City of Underground, was he not?"

The Bartender hastily shook her head. "That is not what I mean. The Prospector definitely got what he deserved. Hopefully, no one else rises to power, and the city people can eventually flee like I am." The Radioman waited patiently for her to continue. A moment later, she filled the silence. "I am more alarmed that EX135 could do such an action. It is far more capable of destruction than I had thought, although so was the Prospector. The Prospector was wicked enough to trap an entire civilization underground."

She cut herself off. The realization of the truth must have dawned on her. The Mechanic joined from the back of the line. "Hey, uh, Bartender, you did hear what EX135 said to the Prospector, right? The part about the excess power line?"

The Bartender stopped crawling for a moment. The Entrepreneur, blind in the darkness, bumped into her and stopped. She tried to turn to face the Mechanic but promptly gave up after fighting with the tight crawl space walls. "What do you mean, Mechanic?"

Tension filled what little airspace there was in the cramped surroundings. The Mechanic spoke. "EX135 claimed that the Prospector had been using the excess power line, the one you said that you didn't know where the additional power on it went, and was actually running this entire factory." The Bartender began slinking forward once more. The Entrepreneur caught on as she accidentally kicked his forehead in the process.

The Mechanic didn't feel like the Bartender had understood him. He cautiously formulated his next sentence. "Bartender, uh, the Prospector, it, uh, EX135 said the Prospector was using the City of Underground as an enslaved power source to run the factory." The Bartender said nothing. She only continued crawling. A small sniffle attempted to break the awkward silence but failed in doing so. The Mechanic thought he had gone too far. He shut himself up in hopes that he hadn't upset her as he couldn't tell in the dark.

The group soon reached the light source at the end of the crawl space. It was coming through a metal grate. The Bartender peeked through the grate. Multiple abandoned vehicles lined the area, some strewn out in the middle of the floor or tipped on their sides and gutted for parts. Sand was piled everywhere, covering nearly every surface with at least an inch or so of the grains. The Bartender could tell there was no ceiling as the sun was lighting the area with a harsh orange light.

The sun must be setting. This both amazed and puzzled the Bartender. Hadn't the group left the City of Underground right at dawn? How had all the time flown by so quickly? She didn't have time to think about it. She couldn't see far enough to see if it was an enclosed box of four walls or if it was open on the far end. She did know that there were no workers in the area. Their footprints would have been in the sand, or she would have seen them directly.

She shook the grate. It was loose and rattled in the frame. She shook it more vigorously. Nothing. She nearly decided to give up, but she spotted a particularly clean-looking vehicle on the far right of her plain of view. Someone must have been using it. Curious and having already made a racket, she shook the vent with as much force as she could muster. It abruptly popped out of the wall, dragging her out of the crawl space with it.

She discarded the grate by flinging it away as she fell to get it away from herself. She landed softly on a large embankment of sand against the wall, where she tumbled down to the thin layers of sand and slid to a stop, revealing the dull gray layer of concrete below the sand as she went. The Entrepreneur, who followed directly behind the Bartender, peered down at her in the sand below. After checking the surroundings for trouble, he called out to her. "Bartender! Are you all right?" The Bartender replied with a thumbs-up. She was busy cleaning her mouth of the sand she had just eaten.

The Entrepreneur scanned the room once more. It was a shipping yard. The Entrepreneur gave the news to the group in the crawl space behind him. "There is a drop into a pile of sand here. The Bartender has apparently gotten her fair share of the sand from it. We are looking at a shipping yard here. This must be where the factory sent out its products before the Crisis." The Entrepreneur turned back to the Bartender. "Did the fall hurt?"

The Bartender, having finished with the sand in her mouth, responded verbally. "No." She spat out some more sand. "It is just a little hot on the first touch."

The Entrepreneur looked down at the long drop. "I don't know, guys. That is a pretty far...ah!" The Radioman had shoved him out from behind. The Entrepreneur landed headfirst and rolled over onto his back to slide the rest of the way. He had a harrowed expression when he finally came to a stop.

The Old Man snickered quietly at the Radioman's actions as the Radioman attempted to get out. As the Radioman worked on his descent, the Old Man turned to the Survivalist behind him. "You think you can help me down slowly? I don't know if I can take that fall based on the Entrepreneur's reaction to it." The Survivalist tried to hide her smile. The Old Man noticed her act. With the Radioman successfully down, he shimmied forward and checked the Entrepreneur, who was still lying in the sand. He twisted back to her and whispered, "It's all right. He didn't hear. Smile if you want to."

He motioned to the hook and rope wrapped around the Survivalist. She took it off and threw it at him. He fashioned a sort of rappelling seat out of the rope by wrapping it around the belt loops of his pants, then using the hook to tie it together and threw the loose end to the Survivalist as he shimmied closer to the ledge. The Old Man wiggled the Lightstaff out from under him and protruded it out toward the pile of sand while holding the light source end of the staff.

The Survivalist was struggling to hold the Old Man's weight as he slid out. The Young noticed her sliding out with the Old Man and grabbed the Survivalist's legs. Her slippery pants made this difficult, so the Young crawled forward so that his head was at her back and hugged her by the waist instead, but he discovered this was a failed effort due to the hatchet potentially cutting his arm. He moved up again to where his head was right behind the Survivalist's. Just as he arrived there, the Survivalist slid forward as the Old Man reached the ledge.

The two of them didn't fit into the shortened crawl space height from the slide forward while piled on top of each other. The Young had unknowingly wedged himself into the gap between the Survivalist and the ceiling, causing the two of them to be stuck in place while being uncomfortably squished by the ceiling, floor, and each other. This wedging spectacle proved effective enough to hold the Old Man steady as he dangled from the waist up out of the hole. The Old Man pulled the two forward a slight bit more and managed to find something with the Lightstaff to support his fall with.

The Bartender tried to make her way up the dune to help but found she couldn't make it back up as the sand simply crumbled under her feet. She tried to get a run on it and jumped partway up but found that her impact simply buried her to her knees in sand.

She busied herself with getting free of the sand. Meanwhile, the Old Man had started leaning out of the hole farther. He had the staff support his weight from the bottom, and the wedged Young and Survivalist combo held him from the top as he transitioned from the hole to a sitting position on the rope seat he had crafted.

He hopped out of the crawl space for the last short distance, which led to a jolt in the tension of the rope and a pair of painful-sounding grunts from the two on the other end. The Old Man called out, "All right! Just lower me down a bit, and I can drop to the sand the rest of the way."

The Young sighed. "Hey, Survivalist, can you move out from under me?"

The Survivalist squirmed beneath him. She stopped moving. "No."

The Young tried to push her out from under him. She didn't budge. He gasped in frustration. "Just so you know, this wasn't the plan." He peeked backward. The Hobo was behind him. "Hey, Hobo, pull on my feet." To the Young's surprise, he began pulling without any hesitation. This seemed to help substantially, but the two remained stuck.

The Survivalist wheezed. "Hey, it's really hard for me to breathe here. Can you hurry up?"

The Young responded with a wheezing chuckle. "Start wiggling." He looked back and nodded. The Hobo tried another pull. The combined efforts of the Hobo pulling, the Young pushing, and the Survivalist wiggling, along with the weight of the Old Man, allowed the Survivalist to start sliding forward. The three kept at it until the Young reached the Survivalist's slippery, tight pants.

The slipperiness of her pants and the new space created as her legs grew thinner by tapering to her feet resulted in a large lack of friction. The Survivalist shot right out from under the Young and toward the hole. This would have been a fine solution to the problem except the Survivalist was the one holding the Old Man's support rope. The new slack in the rope resulted in the Old Man plummeting straight down into the sands below. The rope the Old Man had wrapped around his arms acted as a restricting belt that prevented him from moving his arms to stop his fall as he rolled down the sand straight toward the Bartender, who was still not free of the pile.

The Bartender tried to get out of the way, but the Old Man steamrolled her flat on her back, bending her like a blade of grass at the knees and failing to pull her out of the sand in the process. The Survivalist did not let go of the rope in time, as she was unaware of the Old Man's roll down the dune and had assumed he was still falling as the rope yanked her directly out of the hole. She gracefully flipped midair and landed on her hands and feet to slide to the bottom.

By the time she came to a halt, the Old Man had at last found the bottom of the sand and was busy wiggling to get out of his rope predicament. The Entrepreneur, who was fully aware of the fact that the Old Man had laughed at him when the Radioman deliberately pushed him out of the crawl space, simply grinned, leaned up against a nearby support post, and watched him squirm. The Survivalist couldn't blame him. She walked over and began untying the Old Man.

Meanwhile, the Bartender had sat back up to find her legs still stuck in the dune despite having been rolled over. She threw up her hands in both minor frustration and confusion before retrying to dig herself out. The Young had recovered from the wild recoil backward and had pulled himself to the edge of the hole. He grabbed onto the edges, drew his legs from the hole, lowered himself down, and gently landed on his feet on the sand. He noticed the Bartender and walked over to bail her out.

The Hobo poked his head out next and saw the sand below. He started out by falling out in a similar flopping motion to the Old Man. The Mechanic grabbed his legs as he fell, which pivoted the unsuspecting Hobo into the wall below with a flapping sound. The Mechanic shook the poor Hobo to use him as a pulling force, as he was getting stuck in the tight crawl space.

Once the Mechanic got his shoulders through, he dropped the Hobo a short distance onto the sand, which sent the Hobo tumbling down the sand to meet the partially freed Bartender at the bottom. He angrily turned his head to look toward the Mechanic but instead found the Bartender. She smiled ecstatically, flinging some of the sand dug from around her legs into the air and watching it glitter.

The Radioman watched her do this and shook his head with a grin. Despite her eyes still being red from the tears moments ago in the vent, she had seemingly completely forgotten about her previous sorrows. He thought about how she would have to face the reality of the Prospector's work eventually. However, there were more pressing matters. For now, he figured the best course of action was to get out of the area due to the angry mob of workers afoot. In addition, he hated seeing her saddened. Asking her now would only return her sorrows.

The Hobo, seeing the spectacle the Bartender was performing with the sand, forgot his troubles of being slapped against a wall and somersaulting down a sandy slope. By merely smiling at him, the Bartender caused the Hobo's anger and frustration to fade, just as the Bartender's had moments ago.

The Mechanic placed his palms on the walls surrounding the hole and forced his way out where he fell onto the sand. He created a crater in the dune, which displaced a wave of shifting sand onto the Bartender's legs, which the Young had almost freed. After a scornful look from the two, the Mechanic joined in helping them dig. His massive hands made short work of the sand, and he hauled the Bartender out of the dune.

The Entrepreneur spoke from his leaning position on the post. "Well, I suppose that could have gone worse."

The Hobo peered over at him. "What do you mean?"

The Entrepreneur shrugged casually. "There could have been no sand to land on."

The Hobo was going to propose a counterargument, but the tone of voice the Entrepreneur had stated his case in caught his attention. The Hobo made a quick sweep of the others' reactions. They were all equally confused. No one could tell if the Entrepreneur was actually being serious and trying to look at the bright side of things or if he was being dramatically sarcastic and mildly insulting.

Even now, as the Hobo scrutinized the Entrepreneur's unwavering face, he could not come up with a lean toward either case. This perfect impassivity was further bolstered by the fact that the Entrepreneur's statement was, in fact, a valid point. After a long pause, the Hobo realized he had lost the chance for a proper rebuttal and dropped the potential argument.

The Hobo had dusted himself off while he considered all this. He walked out to join the Entrepreneur. Although the Hobo had decided against a rebuttal, he could still start a new conversation altogether. "Hey, Entrepreneur, did anyone ever tell you that you have a strange ability to appear both optimistic and a smartass at the same time?"

The Entrepreneur peered over with a knowing smile. "Yes, but the people who told me that as an insult were none too bright. Luckily, you have more brains on you than they ever had, right?" The Entrepreneur held a confident smirk for a hair too long before looking away, out at the sandy shipping yard. The Hobo had been shut down by the most confirmative, indirect answer he had ever received and decided to not push the subject further.

As the Hobo and the Entrepreneur had their short-lived chat, the Mechanic was busy scanning the area. He pointed over at the particularly clean vehicle. "What's the deal with that one?"

The Young followed his finger. He saw nothing of interest at first glance. It was just a rust bucket like the rest of the vehicles in the shipping yard. "What about it?"

"It is clean and upright. The rest are covered completely in sand, turned on the side, or gutted for parts." He started toward the vehicle. The group exchanged a few glances as they motioned one another on to follow him. The Mechanic reached the vehicle and ran his hand along the rough and rusted edges. He could still make out the faint logo on the side of the vehicle: AOC.

The Mechanic ran his hand across the logo. He wondered what it meant. His hand caught a bump. He tore his attention from the logo to observe the bump. A piece of scrap metal had been sloppily fused with the surrounding metal to fix a hole in the side of the vehicle. He furrowed his brow. "This thing has been worked on." He walked around the back of the vehicle. A massive blackened propulsion burner took up the majority of the back side. He thought it would be better to avoid touching the burner and continued around to the far side of the vehicle.

A narrow makeshift step had been fixed to the side of the vehicle. He stepped on it and pulled himself up to have a look inside the vehicle. The cockpit on the right seemed normal, although the steering control had been replaced by a burned piece of metal bar. The Mechanic guessed the cockpit was probably functional at first glance, especially since the pilot seat seemed to be in such good condition.

He looked left. Behind the cockpit to the left of the side entrance was a simple storage container in the cargo of the vehicle. It was a large metal box with ribbed sides that fitted snuggly into the cargo. At one point, it had been painted a bold red, but the paint had long ago been chipped away and faded, leaving only a rusty surface wherever the occasional patch of cracked, faded paint exposed the metal. The only thing unusual about it was the burn marks on the bottom.

The Mechanic mentally questioned if it had been fused in with a Scorch Torch. The container was also placed in what appeared to be backward. The doors would open inward based on the hinges, meaning the only way to get the cargo out from inside the container would be to drag it past the cockpit over the entrance deck. Something wasn't right. The Mechanic swung his legs over the thick sidewall of the vehicle and pushed on the twin doors of the storage container. Much to his surprise, they swung inward without resistance, stopping after just barely cracking open.

The Mechanic cautiously approached the crack and peered through. It was dark inside. The Mechanic motioned for the Old Man's staff as he slowly turned while keeping a close eye on the door. The Lightstaff swung around the Mechanic's outstretched hand as the Old Man attempted to hand it over. The Old Man gave up and began climbing. The Mechanic noticed and pulled the Old Man up. The Mechanic pointed to the light, then the crack in the door.

The Old Man snapped his fingers. A brilliant beam of white light shot into the crack. Light scattered in the container and illuminated the door's edges. The Mechanic slowly approached the door. He grabbed the edge of the cracked doorway and threw the door open as quickly as he could. The light flooded into the container. The Mechanic gasped. The Old Man panicked. "What is it?"

The Mechanic dropped his guard. He bent at his waist to avoid bumping his head on the top edge of the container doorway and stepped inside. "It's…provisions?" He retrieved an item by removing it from a tight band around it with his left hand. It was a glass jar full of a green and runny liquid. Letters were scrawled into the lid of the jar: Gorglum.

The Mechanic turned the curious jar in his hand. The fluid inside ran the jar quickly and bubbled slightly. He turned at his waist and handed the jar over to the Old Man. The Old Man squinted down at the lettering, struggling to read it in the orange light of the setting sun. He spoke. "Gorglum? What is Gorglum?" The Old Man held it over the edge and wiggled it slightly.

The Young held out his hands to catch it. The Old Man dropped it, and the Young caught it to observe it as well. "It looks edible, I think." The Young handed it to the Survivalist.

She scrutinized the writing closely. "I have no idea what this is. I think the Young is right, though. The jar is sealed." She tried to twist the lid. Nothing happened. She observed the jar, noticed something, and hit the top of the jar on the corner of the step on the vehicle. The lid shot off through the air, landing a few feet away in the sand, standing on its edge.

She dipped her pinky finger into the green substance, retracted it, and stuck the newly green finger in her mouth. Her face puckered. She coughed. "It's not good. It's very stale. I think it is edible, though." She passed the jar to the Bartender, who had just arrived along with the Radioman.

The Bartender sniffed the jar's contents while she watched the Survivalist try to figure out what the disgusting flavor was. She chuckled. "This is Gorglum Wine." She took a sip and cringed. "It is a bit strong from being so old, though."

The Radioman took the jar to observe it. "What is Gorglum Wine?"

The Bartender wiped the green stain from her lips. "It is a type of alcoholic beverage. It is usually a bit fresher than that. It is better if you can get it cold. Nasty stuff, that there. Despite the alcohol, it is an excellent hydrator, although if you managed to down that entire thing, you would be drunk for a week."

The Hobo raised an eyebrow. "Really?" He snatched the jar and took a swig. His face showed an instant regret.

The Bartender grinned and continued speaking. "No, not for a week, just until you throw it back up and then a few hours. If it is fresh, it is typically somewhat sweet. It comes from fermenting the Gorglum plant, which is one of the only crops we can grow down in the City of Underground on the croplands down by the lake." A realization struck her. "You all never went down to those crops, did you?"

She shook her head, seemingly upset they had missed out on the opportunity. "You didn't miss much. The Gorglum plant is a green plant with large, prickly leaves that grow out in a circular pattern from the center. It grows by spreading across the ground and manages with very little light. Each plant only gets about a foot or so tall and a foot in diameter. It turns a shade of dark green when it starts producing the Gorglum fruit, starting with a white flower raised up a bit in the center that only lasts a day or so.

"A neighboring plant that has not flowered, meaning it is worse off and less likely to produce fruit, will produce a thin and wiry stem from the center instead of the flower that it inserts into the neighboring plant's flower. The flower on the first plant falls off and quickly rots. In its place, a Gorglum fruit grows. The stem on the neighboring plant withers up and takes the rest of that plant with it.

"The whole stemmed plant will be rotted away in only four days or so to provide fertilizer for the flowered plant. When the Gorglum fruit is ready to be harvested, the leaves on the plant begin turning purple around the edges. The Gorglum fruit ends up as a dark green, round fruit with smooth lumps all over it. It would fit in the palm of your hand. You can then take—"

"I don't mean to cut you off, but we have more important things to do, Bartender." The Old Man had interrupted her. "We can talk about his later."

The Bartender nodded. "Right. Sorry."

The Mechanic turned back to the container. Tarps were rolled up and hung on the back wall. More jars of the Gorglum Wine along with a dried green fruit, presumably the Gorglum fruit, were stocked in tightly clamped nets. A few old tools lined another section. The Mechanic noticed a Scorch Torch strapped down in the corner. "Guys, this isn't just a material transport vehicle. It's a getaway vehicle. Somebody has been planning an escape besides us."

The Bartender stiffened. The Radioman grew concerned. She spoke. "We can't take this. We will ruin the chance of escape for whoever owns this."

The Radioman seemed caught between two ideas. The Hobo seemed unaffected. "Bartender, we have to do this. The person who owns it can't squeal on us without exposing that they were trying to escape. Besides, if they built one, they could build another."

"It may have taken them years to get this!"

The Mechanic supported the Hobo. "We are probably going to make such a commotion with this thing that they will be able to get away anyway."

"They won't make it without the supplies in that vehicle."

The Survivalist nodded while pulling her lips to the side in debate. "You are right, they probably won't make an escape without them based on what we just went through." The Bartender gestured to her in a way to agree with the point. The Survivalist wasn't finished. "But either we use this vehicle to get out of here, or we don't leave. It's whoever built this machine or us."

The Bartender deflated. She knew the Survivalist was right. They had no time to search for the true owner or any way to find out if the person actually built the vehicle or not. She rolled her head back and stared up at the ceiling. She became aware that she hadn't noticed it before. A ceiling protruded from the wall a ways to some support posts, more toward the middle of the sand. She followed it to the edge to see the orange sky burning above.

Something about that sky caught her. She hadn't seen that sky in years. Oh, how she would love to leave this all behind and explore the world or even just be somewhere else. Why couldn't she convince herself that it was the right thing to do? Oh yes, the guilt of leaving everyone behind.

Her thoughts derailed. She must have been obviously debating the idea, as the Radioman shook her out of thought. He asked her a single perplexing question: "Bartender, think with me here. If any other person from the City of Underground were here right now, what would they do?"

The Bartender knew the answer to this question. They would all run. But something else came to mind. She faced the Radioman. "That is where you are wrong, Radioman. I am not like the rest of those people."

There was a long stare between the two of them. The Radioman rested an arm on her shoulder. He very calmly stated his case. "No, you aren't, but those people down there know no different. The workers up here praised the very Exoduster who was pinning them to borderline enslaved work. These people, they don't understand what the world has to offer them. You do. That is why you must leave. You know better than to stay. You know there is a whole world for you to see. The guards are instructed to exile you for being a woman. Why would you not leave?"

The Bartender drew in a long breath. She let it out slowly while she turned to look back at the factory through the open hole on the ceiling. "Guilt."

The Radioman walked up beside her. They both scanned the complex. It was oddly still for the commotion that could be heard throughout the entire place. The Radioman shook his head lightly. "You have no reason to be guilty."

The Bartender whipped her line of sight over to him. "Yes, I do!" she snapped. She wiggled away and turned to face him. "I shouldn't even be alive. I hid while my friends were taken. It isn't about leaving now. It is about never making up for my poor choice of actions."

The Radioman turned to face her. "You did make up for it."

The Bartender wanted to argue. She wanted to yell and bicker until her voice gave out. What did he know? He had not been there all her life. But she couldn't yell. She could tell the Radioman was sincere through his everlasting confident posture. She had to know what he had to say. After quickly collecting herself, she calmly asked her question. "What do you mean?"

The Radioman's smile grew wider. "You got us to bring EX135 along." She didn't understand what this had to do with her past. The Radioman explained further. "Back in the City of Underground, any other person would have run and hid from that Exoduster. You trusted it knowing its history, and in return, it trusted you. You prevented us from abandoning it. You got us to trust it as well. Now EX135 has taken out the source of this tyrannical factory. The people in the City of Underground will soon discover this, I have no doubt.

"They might want to stay. Others may at last leave. The city will not need nearly as much power production now that the entire drain of power has been shut down forcefully, which means people can work new jobs and have more free time. The people can do as they please. You have led to the freedom of the City of Underground. I think you have done more than enough."

The Bartender had not thought about it this way. He was right. Without her, the City of Underground might have never been released from the Prospector's grip. She had freed the people. Even if they didn't like it now, they would soon realize there was a better world out there, just as she had learned when EX135 first met her. The Radioman tapped her arm, causing her to refocus, before continuing on. "What do you say now? Do you want to come with us and see what else we get into?"

She took a long sweep of the factory. "I can't believe all of this was up here this whole time."

The Radioman stepped closer to her. "I can assure you, there is a lot more up here than that rusted factory. Are you ready?"

She let a pause occur before nodding. She turned away to see the rest of the group quickly snapping into idle actions to act like they were giving her privacy. She grinned at them at least trying to not be caught. "Come on, then. Let's get this thing moving!"

The Mechanic promptly turned and went back into the storage container on the vehicle. He fiddled with something on the inside before returning with the Scorch Torch. The Entrepreneur raised an eyebrow. "What do you plan to do with that?"

The Mechanic shrugged. "I don't know for sure yet. I have an idea, though." He went over to the edge of the vehicle, swung his foot over, found the step, and lowered himself to the sand. He began walking around the vehicle. "There should be a control panel or something on this thing somewhere. Maybe I can melt the connections and use them to allow anyone to drive the vehicle."

The group collectively replied with a dull stare. The Mechanic explained further. "There is a device that is able to recognize the person in the cockpit based on a number of factors like weight, facial recognition, how they sit down in the seat, so on. They use this information to mold the seat to the person's liking automatically without the need for the person to carry a key or marker.

"The issue is that it prevents us from stealing this thing if it has been claimed by somebody here, although that is early technology for as ancient as this thing is. It doesn't have all the security features it needs in places to prevent it from being tampered with"—he turned to see the Old Man watching him—"which is exactly what I plan to do."

He turned back to his search of the wall. "And I think we can trick this thing into thinking anyone can be the pilot indefinitely by the order of the owner by simply rewiring a few things to bypass the security check." He performed a lazy partial shrug after standing to show he couldn't find the panel.

The Hobo joined in. "Hey, Mechanic, that is cool and all, but did you try to turn the thing on first?"

The Mechanic straightened and stared off into the distance for a moment. He shook his head once and widened his eyes. He strolled over to the step and swung himself back onto the entry deck. He turned to the cockpit, placing the Scorch Torch on the floor on the way over. He dropped down and sat down in the oddly clean and well-maintained bold-red seat, which was at just below floor level with the small entry deck above it, leaving his shoulders at the height of the deck.

The seat of the cockpit was far skinnier than himself, but it oddly shifted under him with an unsettling goopy sound as he sat down in it. When it stiffened, it widened to perfectly fit the Mechanic. A windshield wrapped in a rounded box around the front of the cockpit with narrow supports on the two front corners. The windshield was set just off of vertical leaning into the cockpit area.

A roof covered the cockpit area at the top of the windshield and reached back to the entrance, creating a small room around the cockpit with an open entryway. He grabbed the burnt bar that made up the steering control. Amazingly, a slightly cracked screen lit up in the center console. It displayed a bit of static before fading off into a black screen with shaky yellow text across the middle: "Pilot not recognized."

The Mechanic read the message, smirked, and stood out of the cockpit. He stood on the entry deck and leaned over the side to inform the group. "That was a good idea, Hobo, but it does have pilot recognition. Whoever has been working on this thing must have done a good job designating it to themselves, or at least they couldn't get rid of it, which might be why the vehicle is still here."

He turned back to the cockpit briefly, more to motion to it than to look at it, but something caught his eye. He twitched his head back over. He took a few steps over to just behind the cockpit seat. He ran his finger along a rounded square crack in the side of the cockpit wall. "Aha!" he muttered under his breath. He attempted to wedge his hand between the seat and the wall of the cockpit, only succeeding to get the length of his fingernail in. The seat was surprisingly stiff for having just conformed to his size.

The Mechanic's face lit up. That last thought had given him an idea. He stood and called over the side of the vehicle, "Survivalist, I need you up here. Come on." The Survivalist looked around, feeling very singled out. She climbed into the vehicle. "Sit in the cockpit."

"I can't drive this thing."

The Mechanic nodded. "Firstly, you don't drive it. You pilot it. That's a cockpit, not a driver's seat." He pointed at the cockpit. "Second, I know that you can't pilot it. I don't need you to either. You are the skinniest person here."

She raised an eyebrow. "What about the Young?"

The Mechanic honestly hadn't paid attention to which of the two was thinner. Off the top of his head, it was probably the Young, but it didn't matter all that much. "Just sit in the cockpit for me." The Survivalist slipped past the Mechanic and sat down in the wide seat. The seat instantly began squeezing in on her thighs and bottom. She shifted uncomfortably in the seat. It gripped her legs, then began with her lower back, inching its way up her back and even between her lower shoulder blades.

Her head was positioned forward by the back of the seat. She pushed against it awkwardly. The seat shortened itself and rounded off the top to allow her head to move. She slid up and down on the seat to test it out. She wiggled her legs side to side. The Mechanic, who had observed this event, asked her a question. "How do you like it?"

She smiled shyly. "It is…oddly comfortable. The whole transition is very unsettling, but once it gets there, it is quite nice. The only thing I don't like is how my legs can swing from side to side in this seat in these pants." The seat had gripped her waist well but only formed a rectangle down from them to her knees and a flat pad at a sharp angle downward. The seat seemed to have stopped after finding her widest point of her lower body at the hips and left the rest of the lower body area the same width.

As she wiggled her legs in the open space, the seat began making a goopy stretching sound. The seat pressed in from the sides. It found her legs and forced them together. It began lifting her legs upward at the knees, stopping after having lifted her legs from a ninety-degree sitting position to nearly flat out in front of her. The entire time, the seat had been forcing a wall up on either side of her legs.

As each wall stretch upward, they wrapped along the top of her legs until they met with each other in the middle, forming a sort of smooth box with a single long tube in it for her legs that reached all the way up to her waist. She disliked how the seat smashed her legs together. She wiggled and tried to force her legs outward slightly. The seat obliged her request by allowing her legs to spread and, by seemingly remembering her previous request about not liking being able to slide her legs, began forming a wall between them, starting at her feet.

The wall slowly crept up between her legs, widening and narrowing to fit, until it reached all the way up to her crotch and squeezed up against it. She stiffened. The seat retracted the bit of wall against her crotch to give her space. She relaxed. The seat stopped moving. She rested her arms down on where the seat had covered her lap. The seat adjusted a small indentation for her arms to rest in. "Oh, this thing is great." She laid her head back. The seat instantly adjusted to catch her head. She pressed her arms on the seat around her legs. They gripped down on her thighs and calves with a softer material than the rigid seat.

As the Survivalist found true bliss in the cockpit seat, the Mechanic had been busy trying to get into a work panel on the wall beside the seat. This was proving to be very difficult as the seat continuously adjusted to comfort the Survivalist. The Mechanic gave up in frustration.

He leaned around the right side of the seat to see the Survivalist with her eyes close, grinning widely as the seat massaged her legs. He wondered if he should even be looking at her. "Hey, Survivalist, can you stop moving this cockpit seat for a minute? I am trying to access the panel on the left wall here, and the seat keeps getting in the way."

The Survivalist lazily opened her eyes. She sat up. The seat rolled a bar up her back, to which she arched with pleasure. She dreamily spoke to the Mechanic. "Mechanic, you have got to try this thing out. It is wonderful." Another bar ran down her back, causing another pleasureful arching of her back.

The Mechanic felt very awkward watching this. "The panel. Please, Survivalist."

The Survivalist flopped her head over to look at him. "What panel? Oh, the panel on the left side." She reached downward with her left arm. The seat formed a hole for her hand to pass through. "Do you mean this panel?" She swept her arm backward.

The Mechanic switched sides on the cockpit. The seat had moved out of the way, revealing the panel. He flipped open the mechanical lever embedded into the panel that sealed it close and pulled it open. He sighed. It was only a narrow storage compartment for the pilot. The only thing filling it was some sand along the bottom.

The Mechanic shut the panel and switched back over to the right side. "How did you do that?"

The Survivalist had closed her eyes once more. The cockpit seat was busy squeezing her sides below her ribs and rolling down her hips. "Do what?"

"How did you move the cockpit out of the way for me like that?"

She shrugged. The seat bumped out and pressed on her shoulders, which she seemed to enjoy. "I just moved it like this." She reached down into the seat with her right arm and pulled upward while pinching her fingers. The arm of the cockpit stretched to follow her arm up, making a strange tent pattern, as if she had picked up a piece of cloth from the middle. She released the seat. It remained there in that shape. She then dropped her arm onto the point of the shape.

The Mechanic watched as her arm fell, seemingly melting the seat. As the shape melted away, the Mechanic noticed a new message on the screen behind the receding shape:

Hello. Welcome to piloting Torgrog.

The Mechanic stared at the screen in awe as the screen flickered in brightness. He quietly spoke to the Survivalist. "I guess this thing is called a Torgrog. Can you try grabbing the steering controls for me real quick?"

"Sure." She blindly fumbled her hands around until she found the steering bar. The instant her hands touched the bar, an engine rolled over loudly. This new noise startled the both of them. The cockpit seat stiffened around the Survivalist and sat her more upright. The engine groaned and sputtered. It caught a few times, seeming to start something but failing. The engine quit trying to start.

Another yellow message flashed shakily on the screen:

Fuel sensors corrupted. Using weight to determine fuel levels.

After another moment, another message ran across the screen:

Fuel levels too low to start engine. Fill tank with fuel.

The Survivalist and the Mechanic exchanged a glance. She spoke first. "Where are we going to get fuel?"

The Mechanic shrugged. He peered through the scratched square windshield of the vehicle. He spotted another vehicle tipped up on its side and noticed it had a fuel tank exposed on the underside. He pointed through the windshield. "I am going to go see if that vehicle has fuel that I could siphon out."

The Survivalist laid her head back and gestured to him while closing her eyes once more. "You do that. I will be here keeping the cockpit running." She sighed happily as she released the steering control, and the seat returned to massaging her, this time apparently doing something to her thighs as she gently set her hands on the seat around them.

The Mechanic began to turn away to leave the cockpit. He stopped. He had to ask her a question. "Hey. How did you get it to accept you as a driver?"

The Survivalist gently shook her head and furrowed her brow with her eyes still shut. "I don't know. I just sat down in the seat like you told me to. Oh, I am so glad I did." The seat pressed into the back of her neck. She grinned while gaping her mouth open. The Mechanic turned and left the cockpit by pulling himself out with a handle on the wall.

The group had scattered when the engines rolled over. He called them to regroup. When they all arrived, the Mechanic stated the news. "It seems to work. The Survivalist is accepted as the pilot, for whatever reason. I guess she is driving, as I can't find the control panel anywhere. It is out of fuel, though. I am going over there to check that one for fuel. Anybody want to come with me?"

The Entrepreneur stood. "Sure." The Mechanic looked at him curiously. The Entrepreneur held up a defensive hand before speaking. "Look, I just want to do something here. I was supposed to bribe us out of the City of Underground, and that didn't happen. I feel like dead weight over here."

The Mechanic tipped his head to the side while noisily exhaling from his nose. "Come on, then." He turned and started off to the other vehicle. The Entrepreneur walked after him. This left the Bartender, the Radioman, the Young, the Hobo, and the Old Man idle.

The Bartender resumed the chat. "So where are all the workers?"

The Hobo replied, "By the sound of things, they are after something over there." He gestured toward the wall of the factory where the group had come out of the grate.

The Young glanced over at the wall. "They are probably after the Exoduster." The Bartender gave him a troubled look. "Sorry. EX135. They are probably after EX135." Her trouble remained, but it was no longer directed at the Young. The Young realized she was worried about EX135. He was unsure what to do any further that would make the situation better. "I am going to go see what the

Survivalist is up to. Maybe she needs help figuring out how to pilot or something."

The Hobo looked over at him. "As if you know how to pilot."

The Young knew that was coming. He shrugged it off. "Maybe we can figure it out together." He left the group to see the Survivalist and escape the awkwardness. The Young crawled up the side of the vehicle and stood on the entry deck.

Before he could say anything, the Survivalist spoke to him. "Hey, Young. I don't know what I did to get this, but this thing is amazing."

The Young stooped to peek into the cockpit. He saw the Survivalist relaxing with the seat rolling a wave down her back. The Young was bewildered. "What is that seat doing to you?"

"It is giving me a massage."

This response only increased the Young's concern. "Why?"

She shrugged. "I guess it thought I needed it." There was a pause.

"What is that goopy sound?"

The Survivalist gestured lazily at the cockpit. "It is the seat moving. I don't know why it does that. It isn't wet or anything in here."

The Young had a feeling he should leave her alone. "Well, you enjoy that, then."

She chuckled. "Oh, I will."

The Young stood and hopped out of the vehicle. He murmured under his breath. "From one awkward situation to another." He looked around for somewhere else to go. The Mechanic and the Entrepreneur had moved on from the first vehicle. There must not have been any fuel in the first one. He opted to go help them look.

Meanwhile, the Bartender, the Radioman, the Old Man, and the Hobo were still idle a short way from the vehicle. They had been in silence since the Young left. The Old Man tried to make chat. "You all notice this sudden change of pace here?" The group turned to face him. "You know, we were being chased through that factory by a mob of angry workers after watching one Exoduster murder another one, and now we are just standing in the sand outside, listening to chaos unfold within it. Where did all the workers go?"

The Hobo answered, "I think the Young was right. EX135 must be giving them hell."

The Bartender shook her head. "EX135 wouldn't hurt them. He is probably trying to lose them in the factory, but there are so many of them that he is likely having a hard time." Silence returned to the group as they listened to the various crashes and bangs from the factory. A nonverbal doubt formed around the idea of EX135 being harmless.

The Old Man sighed. "Welp, I am going to go for a short walk. It should help me with the soreness that is inevitably going to find me tomorrow after all that running. Anyone want to come along?"

The Hobo peeked up at the Radioman. He sensed the Radioman wanted him to say yes. He winked at the Radioman and nodded. "Yeah. Let's go check out some of the other rides around here and see what we are missing." The Old Man was happy to have some company. The two walked off toward where they had come through the grate to have a look at the other sand-covered vehicles.

The Radioman and the Bartender were then the only two left. As soon as the others were out of hearing distance due to the factory commotion, the Bartender turned to face the Radioman. "Radioman, I need to talk to you."

The Radioman hid his fear. "Yes?"

There was a long pause. Her face broke into a smile. "How is it that you always keep that maroon coat of yours so clean?"

The Radioman chuckled as he relaxed. "It is all in the material. Nothing can embed down into it to make it dirty for any length of time. Some water is all I need to get even the worst of stains out." He looked down to find a cloud of sand stuck to his waist. "Watch this." He smacked the coat with the palm of his hand. All the sand around where his hand had stuck the coat fell off and created a small pile at his feet. He tapped the coat in a few other places, and the coat became completely clean on the front.

The Bartender was impressed. "That is amazing!" She hit her own sandy stomach to rid the sand off her shirt. The majority of the sand stayed in place.

The Radioman chuckled. "Your clothing is not made of the same material. I would know. I did make them for you, after all."

The Bartender caught a look at his confident grin. She peeked over her shoulder. No one else was around. She eyed up the Radioman. "How long do you think it will take for them to find some fuel?"

The Radioman caught her glance. "I don't know. I would say we have some time."

The Bartender smiled. "What about the workers? Won't they find us soon?"

The Radioman frowned briefly. "No, I don't think so. They seem rather preoccupied with whatever it is they are after."

She snatched his arm on her shoulder and found his hand. She pulled him around behind a gutted vehicle nearby and sat down in the sand next to it, forcing him down with her by pulling on his arm. She exchanged holding his hand for brushing the sand off his cheek. The Radioman beamed happily. She wrapped her arm around his back to pull him in. The two started a long kiss. The Bartender grinned. "It looks like you won't have to worry about getting those clothes dirty, then."

*****

Meanwhile, the Young had made his way over to the Mechanic and the Entrepreneur. They were busy finishing up a search on the second vehicle. The Mechanic peered into the dark port of the tank. He growled angrily. "Where is the Old Man and his light when you need it?" He noticed the Young approaching. "Hey, Young, go get the Old Man and bring him over here. I need a light to see into this tank."

The Young swiveled around without a word and started back to the vehicle. He spotted the Old Man and the Hobo casually strolling along, pausing at each sandy vehicle. He ran over to meet them. The

Old Man spotted him coming and pointed it out to the Hobo. The Hobo spoke first. "What do you need, Young?"

The Young panted lightly. He looked up at the orange sky. He thought about how hot it was on the outside. "I need the Old Man and his light. We are checking a tank for fuel, and it is dark in it." The Old Man didn't respond. He was busy staring off to the Young's right. The Young followed his gaze to see a machine parked against the wall. The machine was short and flat in the front. At the back was a massive box with vents on the side. It was oddly clean as well, at least where the pilot would sit in a small round seat clear up on top of the back box.

A set of three long rods protruded from the squatty part of the machine below up to the front of the seat high above. A makeshift roof of scrap metal had been attached above the seat. The machine had multiple spinning brushes on the front, apparently for rubbing the surface. It had a square tube at an upward angle protruding from the top near the piloting seat. The Young grew curious. "What is that thing?"

The Old Man at last responded. "I have no idea. It seems like it has been running recently, though. I bet it has fuel in it." The Old Man looked at the Young. "Go back and get the Mechanic. We need to check this one." The Young sighed. He turned and panted off toward the Mechanic.

A few moments later, the Young, the Entrepreneur, and the Mechanic arrived to meet the Old Man and the Hobo. The Hobo pointed at the machine. "Yo, Mechanic, what is that thing?"

The Mechanic followed his finger to the machine and observed it. "Huh. That is a blowing machine." He furrowed his brow. "It must be responsible for creating the dune around the factory." He glanced around. "They are literally digging this place out of the sand as it gets buried." He gestured to the surrounding sand piles that had accumulated in the shipping yard and then to a path indented into the sand behind the machine. "I bet the fellow who runs that thing is the one responsible for our getaway ride." He gestured to the vehicle.

The group nodded in agreement, except for the Hobo. The Hobo spoke questioningly. "If that one runs and has fuel, why did they not just take it and run?"

The Mechanic pointed a finger at the Hobo. "It is very slow— far too slow to make it anywhere out in the Exodust. That, and it doesn't do well off hard surfaces that it can sweep. It sucks everything up from underneath itself and ends up getting buried in the loose dunes."

The Old Man stepped over to the Mechanic. "I think there is fuel in it. The piloting seat up top is swept off, and the moving parts are clean." The Mechanic nodded.

The group quickly traversed the sand-filled area until they arrived at the machine. The Mechanic found a ladder on the back and climbed up it. He found a port and opened it. He requested the Old Man's light. The Old Man made his way up the ladder, which he insisted he could do alone, and beamed some light down into the port. The Mechanic jumped on the machine to shake it. A thick black liquid slurped around beneath the port. The Mechanic grinned. "That would be the fuel."

The Old Man peered in. "That black stuff?"

"Yes."

"It is thicker than a bowl of grainmeal." Everyone stared at him. He tried to play it off. "You know, grainmeal. It is made of grains. You cook it up in some hot water. Tastes pretty bad most of the time unless you add a bunch of sweeteners to it. I've always thought that kinda defeats the purpose, as grainmeal is supposed to be healthy for you, and the sweeteners counteract that, but I suppose—"

"We know what grainmeal is, Old Man. That is just a strange comparison to make," interrupted the Young.

The Old Man dropped the grainmeal conversation. "My point here is, how are we going to get it out of there? I don't think we can siphon that. It is too thick. We will never be able to get it started."

The Mechanic nodded. "I was just thinking about that." He reached down to a latch on the top of the machine. The Mechanic lit up. "Hold on." He jerked on the latch. It refused to move for a moment. Some persistence via percussive maintenance from the Mechanic led to the latch snapping over out of the way. The Mechanic pulled open a hatch. "Yep."

He hopped down into the box. Various thumps came from the machine. A dusty tube suddenly jutted out from the hatch. The Mechanic pulled himself from the machine with great effort. "Oh boy. That thing is hard to get out of." He dipped the tube down into the fuel port. "Hold this for me, Young."

The Young crawled up the ladder and took the tube to hold it in place. The Mechanic jumped back into the machine. He threw out another hose. His voice rang out from the hatch. "Hey, Entrepreneur, go put that hose in a container of some kind, preferably something we can roll or otherwise move around in the sand."

The Entrepreneur reached up and pulled the hose down to his level. He looked over at the Hobo. "Do you know where a container is?"

The Hobo looked around. "I will go find something." He took off. A short time later, he arrived rolling a rusted ancient barrel. He stood it upright and removed a sealing plug from a hole on the top of it.

The Entrepreneur stuck the hose into the barrel. He whispered to the Hobo, "Don't you think this is a little rusty?"

The Hobo nodded. "It is all I could find, and the Mechanic hasn't seen it. Just do it before he catches on."

The Entrepreneur nodded and gave the Old Man a thumbs-up. The Old Man yelled down the hatch. "The hoses are in place, Mechanic."

"It's about time! I am sweating to death in here." Shuffling sounds came from the machine. There was a pause. "Hey, Old Man!"

"Yeah?"

"Whatever you do, don't let that tank go empty! Tell me to stop before it does. And don't take the hose out of that tank either!"

"What happens if I do?"

There was another pause as the Mechanic crawled up and out of the machine and sat on the edge of the hatch. "This air pump overheats, as it is pumping something much denser than sand flying around in air. It catches on fire, as it is pumping a flammable fluid, and blows up the fuel container, and we all die a painful, fiery death." Before anyone could react to his statement, the Mechanic shoved the middle of the three levers forward. A motor shook to life, starting off with a chugging sound and smoothing off to an unpleasant groan after a period of time.

The hoses slid in the sand as they filled. The black fluid began slapping into the bottom of the barrel. The Old Man focused the light into the tank, past the Young's hands on the hose. The Mechanic took a deep breath and hopped back down into the machine. Around fifteen seconds passed. The Old Man yelled at the Mechanic. Nothing happened. The Old Man checked the tank again. He could see only part of the bottom of the tank, as the machine was not level and the fluid was collecting on one side. He looked down into the hatch. The Mechanic was busy watching a gauge on the air pump.

The Old Man took the bottom of the staff and smacked the top of the Mechanic's head. The Mechanic flinched away in pain, took a moment to see what had hit him, and then frantically climbed partway out of the hatch. He grabbed the center lever and forced it forward to its original position.

The engine stopped abruptly. A popping sound with a periodical hiss could be heard through the hatch. The Mechanic, gritting his teeth anxiously, leaned over and peeked into the tank. The Old Man illuminated it for him. He let out a long breath and lay down on his back. "That went a lot quicker than I expected."

The hissing sound caught the Young's ear. "What is that sound?"

The Mechanic replied, "A coolant. It boiled and burst a seal. The hissing sound is the coolant dripping onto the scalding surface of that ruined gas pump."

The Entrepreneur yelled, "So how close to dying were we?"

The Mechanic sat up and started toward the ladder. "Too close. We need to move. This thing might blow up yet. Take the hoses and throw them on the sand as far away as they will reach. We don't want any leftover fuel near that heat."

The group did as they were told, stringing the hoses out onto the sand and letting the last bit pool onto the sand. It quickly settled into the hot sand. The Hobo slapped the seal back into the barrel. The Mechanic noticed and observed the barrel. He walked over and ran his hand along the rust on it. He sighed. "It will do." He tipped the barrel over and began rolling it across the sand to the vehicle. The others joined him, except for the Old Man, who had started across the sand ahead of them. The Lightstaff appeared almost useless to him as it loosely drove deep into the sand on each placement.

They reached the vehicle. They all took a moment to sit down in the shade after the exhausting work of pushing the barrel. The Hobo looked around. "Where is the Survivalist?"

The Young stood, stepped up on the step, and found her still relaxing in the cockpit. He flopped back down. "Cockpit."

The Hobo nodded. "What about the Radioman and the Bartender?"

The Young shrugged. A voice came from behind the vehicle. "We are right here." He stepped around the vehicle. After seeing them both sitting down with sweat dripping, he joined them to give them time to recompose. The Bartender peeked around while raking sand out of her hair. The Radioman had quickly stepped in between her and the Young. The two were headed around to meet with the other men. She let the men be and leaned up against the side of the vehicle.

She heard the goopy sound of the cockpit moving. Curious, she rounded the front of the vehicle and climbed into it while shaking the sand from her sweat-ridden shirt. She found the Survivalist in the cockpit. She appeared asleep. The seat was slowly expanding, then squeezing down on her legs. Perplexed by the seat, she reached down and touched it. The seat jumped away from her hand, shaking the Survivalist awake.

The Survivalist jumped in fear after noticing the Bartender. She relaxed after recognizing her. The seat resumed its actions after the Survivalist stopped moving. "Oh. Hey there, Bartender." She glanced around out the windshield. "What is happening now?"

The Bartender shrugged. "The boys got a barrel of something out there. It must have been a lot of work."

"Is that why you are so sweaty too?"

The Bartender panicked for a moment. "Oh! Um, no. I was out on a walk with the Radioman. It is boiling hot out in the sun." She realized that the Survivalist had been asleep. "How can you sleep through all of this noise?" She gestured to the factory.

"I don't know. After a while of listening, you can kind of tune it all out." The Bartender looked back at the factory. The Survivalist yawned. She continued explaining her sleep. "Plus, it is this seat. It is the best thing ever. It gives you a massage when you sit in it. It is so relaxing."

"Isn't it hot?"

"Not at all. It is nice and cool."

The Bartender reached for the seat to feel its temperature, as she doubted the Survivalist. She hesitated after remembering how it had dodged away from her. She clenched her fist, leaving out only her index finger, and very gently poked the seat. Again, the seat jumped away; but this time, it was a much calmer reaction. The Survivalist seemed surprised. The Bartender noticed her reaction. "Why does the seat jump away like that?"

The Survivalist touched the same spot on the seat. Nothing happened. She raised her eyebrows momentarily during a head shake. "I have no idea. I am just as new to this as you are."

"It jumped a lot more when I tried to wake you."

"Really?"

"Yes. It shook you awake."

"Oh." The Survivalist furrowed her brow. "That is strange. The Mechanic was holding on to it earlier and trying to force it out of the way, and it didn't jump like that."

The Bartender started into a sentence. "Do you think..." She cut herself off for fear of sounding foolish. The Survivalist glanced up at her to scan her face. She encouraged her on nonverbally. The Bartender continued. "Do you think it jumps because it thinks you don't know that I am poking the seat?"

The Survivalist thought it over. "Poke it again while I am watching."

The Bartender obliged her. The seat remained normal. The two women looked at each other. "That is very weird," stated the Bartender.

The Survivalist nodded. "Yeah. Not as weird as getting a full body massage by it, though." The Bartender didn't have a reply for that. A soft noise came from the edge of the vehicle, followed by the sound of cloth being patted down.

A man cleared his throat. The Mechanic's voice rang out. "All right. Come on. Let's get this fuel in the vehicle." A set of groans followed the statement as more soft sounds and pats could be heard. The Mechanic continued talking. "Does anybody know where the fuel port on this vehicle is?" The group realized that nobody had found it earlier. They had trusted the yellow text on the screen that the vehicle was empty after it failed to start.

The Survivalist turned to look down at the seat, then at the unpowered screen. A funny look ran across her face as a strange idea met her. "Torgrog, where is the fuel port on this vehicle?" Nothing happened. The Survivalist deflated. The screen activated but remained black. The Survivalist perked back up as she watched the screen flicker. A faint set of yellow text displayed on the screen.

Top side. Back left.

The Survivalist bounced in the seat, to which the seat responded by gripping down on her legs, and she pointed at the screen with a giddy smile. The Bartender rolled her eyes but allowed her to have the moment, as she was also impressed. The Survivalist shooed her out. "Go tell the others!"

The Bartender was about to ask why she didn't just do it herself, but she realized the Survivalist's legs were still encased in the seat. She stepped out of the cockpit using the support handle on the left and made the few steps to the edge of the entry deck. "The screen says it is on the back left on the top."

"What? On top of the…oh, geesh," complained the Hobo as he went around the barrel to start pushing it to the back of the vehicle. The Young and the Entrepreneur joined him but failed to budge the barrel without the Mechanic. The Radioman stepped in and assisted them. The four of them were barely able to get the barrel rolling.

The Mechanic was busy confirming the location of the port, which was correct, and opening it. He had a short chat with the Bartender as he worked. "How did you get that screen to tell you where the port is?"

The Bartender pointed to the cockpit. "The Survivalist just asked it verbally."

"Wait. Really?" She nodded. The Mechanic paused on the outside step for a moment to wrap up the chat. "Huh. Well, go tell her that we will need her to start this thing soon by grabbing the steering controls." She nodded and dropped back into the cockpit. The Mechanic dropped back down into the sand and helped the men push the barrel the last bit of the distance.

With the help of the Mechanic, they practically plowed it through the sand. It went so quickly that the Young tripped and fell to his stomach on the sand. He stood to find the Old Man watching him. He bent his arm up at ninety degrees and tapped his thin biceps. The Old Man chuckled. The Young winked at him and walked to the group, who were struggling to lift the barrel.

After trying various quick and unsuccessful methods, they succeeded by having every man but the Young on the bottom pushing the barrel up and the Young on the top, guiding it into place. They managed to get it lined up. The Young popped the sealed plug from the top of the barrel and awaited the fuel to drain into the tank from the rusted barrel. The Young slapped the plug back into the barrel and gave it two taps. The group easily lowered it.

The Mechanic cast it aside in a small pile of sand. He climbed the vehicle and checked to be sure the port was secured. "All right, Survivalist." The Survivalist grabbed the steering control bar. The engine once again shuddered to life. It started for a brief moment before shutting off once more. The Mechanic groaned. "Now what?"

The Survivalist yelled out from the cockpit, "The screen says something about an insufficient starting spark."

"Pfft. All right. Everyone, in the…hey, Survivalist, what is this thing called?"

"The Torgrog."

"Everyone, in the Torgrog. Take a seat in the accommodating storage container." He politely waved them in, which came across more as a joke than a kind gesture. The group piled in. The Mechanic snatched the Scorch Torch from the storage container where the group had found a place to take a seat in. "Hit it again, Survivalist." He jumped over the edge of the vehicle. The whoosh of the Scorch Torch lighting came from below.

The Survivalist grabbed the controls once more. The engine started up, followed promptly by a deep vibration. The vibration increased in volume until a deep booming sound went off. A thick black smog shot out from underneath the vehicle and began floating up around the vehicle. The Mechanic emerged from the smog with his entire front side covered in black soot. He looked in the storage container at the group. "Fixed it." He strolled at his leisure to the cockpit and gently pulled the Bartender out. He sent her back to the storage container, where she took a seat in an available spot.

"All right, Survivalist. This thing is running." The Mechanic glanced around the cockpit while wiping his hands off on his pants and beating the blackened dust from his clothes. A short stack of wrinkled paper was stuck in a pair of clips on the wall. He pulled the papers off and began reading them. They were a general explanation of how to use the controls. It had been typed out with images printed alongside the text. It seemed to be directed to the factory workers.

After reading for a moment, the Mechanic nodded and looked down at the makeshift steering control bar. "This paper diagram doesn't match the bar we have here, but it is close enough. Push forward on the controls." The Survivalist pushed. The controls slid inward horizontally and clunked into place after sliding in so far. The seat instantly adjusted with many goopy sounds to get her closer to the controls in a more functional position. The Mechanic was concerned with the gooping. "Does that not feel strange?"

"What?"

"The cockpit seat moving like that."

"No. It feels very comfortable, honestly."

The Mechanic blew out a puff of air. "Okay, then. Try pulling the controls straight upward." She did. The engine leveled out. The vehicle stirred beneath them. "Give it a little more." The vehicle shuttered as the sand around the bottom slipped off. It slowly floated off the ground until it was around a foot above it. Sand whirled about beneath the vehicle. A low ambient hum filled the area. "Twist the bar forward."

As she did, the vehicle shot forward. A whooshing flame noise came from the back of the vehicle. Something sputtered, then caught to a full blast as the vehicle lurched forward. The Mechanic nearly fell completely over. The jump forward spooked the Survivalist, and she twisted back too far. The vehicle stopped instantly, sending the Mechanic flying forward, and started backward slowly.

Bewildered, the Mechanic tapped the Survivalist's shoulder. "You are a little heavy on the movements there. Twist it back real slow. The Torgrog should back up." She followed his instruction. The Torgrog adjusted backward gently, in a much smoother movement. The Mechanic nodded. "That was much better. To turn left or right, you simply turn the whole bar horizontally in the direction you want to turn to. The more you push, the faster it turns. It even works while you are holding still. It is just like a Bi-fly." He paused, realizing something. "Did you have a Bi-fly as a kid?"

The Survivalist seemed perplexed. "A what?"

The Mechanic smiled, recalling an old childhood memory. "You know, the things you sit on and pedal while steering it with some handles. They float off the ground when pedaled and move forward on two little hover pads. Some even come with a little board on the back to carry things on."

The Survivalist lit up, remembering something. "Oh yeah! I was never taught to ride one."

The Mechanic snapped a glance. "What?" He was genuinely upset. "Well, I will have to teach you one day. Do you at least have a general idea of how they work? As in, you just push on the handle-bars to turn."

The Survivalist shrugged lightly. "Yeah, I guess."

The Mechanic nodded cautiously. "Well, turning works like that here. Wiggle the bars back and forth slowly to get a feel for it." She pushed on the bar as instructed, rotating it as if around a vertical axis, and noticed the Torgrog turning in place left and right. "Now normally, you would also be able to tilt the whole vehicle forward and backward or bank left and right, but those things don't appear to be working here since this vehicle is only a monolift.

"After all, this machine probably spent the majority of its life span on the flat concrete floors of the factory and at low speeds and heavy loads, so it wouldn't matter if those fancy controls worked. Going fast around turns is going to require a long arc without any banking. So you will just have to take it easy going onto slopes, onto off camber areas, and around sharp turns. If you go too fast into any of those and bump something, the machine will either flip or drag and potentially damage it or kill us."

The Survivalist looked up with a worried expression. The Mechanic noticed and paused for a moment. He couldn't think of much to comfort her. He went with the basics. "It will be fine. You will pick up quickly." As expected, this didn't relieve her much. "Go ahead and turn to the left so we can go to the middle of the area here and get you a feel for this. I know it's a lot to take in." The Survivalist turned the Torgrog and gently boosted it out into the open space of sand in the shipping yard.

The Survivalist made a lap around the shipping yard. She learned with incredible haste. The Torgrog seemed to give her no troubles and even adapted to her piloting to make it smoother. The Mechanic, although very suspicious of the Torgrog taking into account her personal piloting preferences, led her around near the wall where the grate they had come in through was and had her release the controls.

The Torgrog shut down after a few seconds and placed itself down onto the sand. "That was excellent. You are learning way faster than I did." The Survivalist smiled. The Mechanic turned to the storage container. "How did it feel back there?"

The Bartender peered out. "Silky smooth. She's a natural."

The Mechanic nodded, still wary of the potential assistance from the Torgrog to the Survivalist. "You got that right. I'd say it is about time we…" A bang nearby cut him off. The Mechanic turned toward the source of the sound. Another bang occurred quickly after the first. A piece of the roof gave in downward a short distance. The Mechanic listened closely over the downward whirring of the coasting engine. Shouting caught his ear. A rush of panic flooded through him.

He rushed over to the group in the storage container. "Get ready! The workers are here! It's time to bail! Old Man, take these papers and throw them in my backpack!" He gestured to the backpack sitting in the corner nearby while handing the instruction papers to the Old Man. "We might need them later." He turned away as the group scurried back into position. The Mechanic walked up to the cockpit and sat down in a small indentation he had discovered while helping the Survivalist learn to pilot. He pointed toward the open gap on the far side of the shipping yard. "Start it up and head out. We have to go."

The Survivalist glanced over as she snatched the controls. The motor began whirring up again. She questioned him. "What about EX135?"

The Mechanic hesitated. He had forgotten about EX135. Before he could answer, another bang struck the roof. A small hole formed. The Mechanic snapped back to the Survivalist's gaze. "It will be fine. Just go! We don't have time to wait."

The Survivalist didn't move the vehicle. "The Bartender is going to be crushed if we leave it!"

The Mechanic firmly shook his head. "Just go!" Another final bang hit the roof. The roof collapsed under the abuse. A strange blur of limbs fell through into the sand. A deep, robotic groan resounded.

The Mechanic looked back. Something caught his eyes, something yellow. EX135's yellow eyes were burning with fury. It reached a desperate hand out toward the vehicle to plead for help. The Mechanic looked back at the Survivalist. "Go back."

The Survivalist grinned. She twisted the throttle bar and sent the Torgrog hurtling backward. She stopped it nearby EX135. The Mechanic ran out to the entry deck and stretched out an arm. EX135 managed to pull itself up high enough to grab his hand. The Mechanic hauled it in. He tossed it roughly into the open door of the storage container. It landed with a series of metallic clanks. The Bartender yelped in delight. The Mechanic rushed back to the cockpit and took his seat. "Go!"

The Survivalist sat forward. The seat followed her up. She cranked on the throttle bar. The Torgrog groaned as it blasted forward. The Mechanic looked out to the wide exit of the shipping yard. Workers were filling the gap. A gate was shutting. They were trying to trap them in. The Mechanic pointed through the windshield. "We have trouble brewing!" The Survivalist nodded. She twisted farther on the throttle. The engine groaned. The burner on the back increased its muffled blasting sound to a borderline deafening roar.

The Survivalist glanced over for a split second at the Mechanic before snapping her eyes back to where she was going. The vehicle was hurtling across the shipping yard. "How much faster can it go?" she shouted over the cacophony of noise.

The Mechanic peered out the front to the hastened efforts to shut the gate. He pulled himself farther into his narrow cranny, gritting his teeth. "More!" The Survivalist continued twisting. Her right wrist ran out of reach, and she adjusted it around by holding the throttle steady with her opposite hand. The Torgrog shook angrily. The Survivalist peeked over. The Mechanic was staring out the front window. "Keep going!" The gate was nearly halfway closed. Workers filled the remaining gap.

"Mechanic, we are going to kill those people!"

The Mechanic shook his head. "Keep twisting! Just make sure you're lined up with the exit!" The Survivalist managed a short, begrudging stare. The Mechanic met it. "Trust me!" The Survivalist snapped back to the gate. The vehicle was shooting across at break-neck speed. It shook violently. The engine was struggling to hold pace. The propulsion burner was so hot on the rear that she could feel its heat on the back of her neck.

A narrow wave of sand shot violently up behind them, some of it instantly frying to glass sparkling through the air, and shot off into the rolling sandstorm behind the vehicle. An intermittent, bold, bonging alarm went off somewhere in the dashboard. The cracked screen ran another yellow message. The two read it.

> Warning:
> Excessive heat.
> Unstable balancing. Capsize warning.
> Engine failure imminent.

The first screen blinked out. The Mechanic tried to yell to the Survivalist, but the deafening roar of Torgrog prevented his message from getting through. He tapped her arm. She couldn't look over. The vehicle was becoming too unstable to look away as it accelerated even faster. It lurched and swung periodically, forcing the Survivalist to swing the steering.

The first message blinked off the screen. Another screen replaced it. Only the Mechanic could look down to read it.

> Warning:
> Coolant system overwhelmed.
> Electrical generation insufficient.
> Multiple errors in sensor calculation.

The alarm picked up to a continuous, droning siren. Another yellow message blinked quickly on the screen:

> DECREASE SPEED >>> DEATH IMMINENT

DECREASE SPEED >>> DEATH IMMINENT

DECREASE SPEED >>> DEATH IMMINENT

The Mechanic grimaced. He looked at the gate. It was nearly shut. They might still make it, but it wasn't worth it. The vehicle was compromised. They would have to find another way. He tried to get the Survivalist's attention. She was dead set on the gate, holding the throttle steady. A bead of sweat rolled down her cheek. The wind rushing in through the cockpit entrance in the back had made a mess of her hair. She had a white-knuckle grip on the controls.

The vehicle jerked and dipped from power loss. The siren blared on, somehow louder than the Torgrog's pleading groans for mercy. The gate was nearly completely shut with the narrow gap approaching immediately. The Mechanic could make out the faces of the workers. They covered themselves, some falling to the ground to avoid the Torgrog plunging down on them. Fear ruled their faces.

The Mechanic abruptly realized the suddenness of his impending death. The pain of anxiety rushed through him. For a moment, in a jarring change of pace, everything seemed so slow to him. He turned to the Survivalist. Throughout this entire thing, her face had remained a collected calmness. The only thing about her face that showed any sign that she was in danger was the piercing, wide-eyed stare. The same fear the workers had in them flooded those eyes of hers, but it was handled differently, seeming to only fuel the fire instead of smothering it.

The Survivalist released the throttle. It whizzed back, snapping into place in neutral, as she reached down below the steering control. She forced the crispy control bar upward. The Torgrog pleaded for death as the propulsion burner sputtered out lifeless coughs of flame. A new noise rang through, a strange whirring sound. The vehicle lunged upward into the air, creaking and snapping metal pieces.

The Mechanic was forced harshly down into his seat. His back bent, unable to resist the massive downward force, and his head nearly hit his knees. The force dissipated and was replaced by a stomach-turning fall. The Mechanic floated up and out of the seat, help-lessly searching for something to grab. He was facing out of the back of the cockpit and at the storage container. He saw the Entrepreneur floating as well, reaching for the Old Man flying past him, and the Radioman holding the Bartender in his arms. Green jars of Gorglum Wine hovered in the air. Nets of green fruit strained upward against gravity.

A colossal collision of some kind near the front right of the Torgrog changed the path of all the chaotic motion toward the front of the vehicle. The Mechanic looked to the front to find a shower of glass raining down onto him. He braced for impact as he flew toward the dashboard, shielding his eyes from the glass and the incoming bright-orange sands. A bang followed by a scraping sound and metal warping struck his ears. He hit the dashboard harshly, bending to take the blow.

A glistening rain of glass plinked down around him. He felt sand drag across his skin. Something struck his leg, something soft. The dashboard dug into him again. He realized that the Torgrog was losing speed. The floor tipped toward the front under his knees, coming up quickly and sharply. A digging sound filled the cockpit as the Torgrog raised to its nose. The dashboard relaxed its shoving. The floor fell back to level. A final shaking collision was deadened by the soft sands.

A high-pitched sound caught his ear. It was slowly decreasing in pitch and becoming a broader sound. A beating sound met his ears, overcoming the sound of his own heartbeat. The Mechanic opened his eyes, fearing what he would see. The Survivalist was clubbing the steering controls with her arms. She was yelling something, peeking over at the Mechanic, but he couldn't make out what she was on about. His vision was blurry at best, but he could tell her face was lacerated with small cuts welling up with blood.

He looked out the back of the cockpit. He spotted the Entrepreneur releasing his hold on the Old Man. He wasn't bleeding. Behind him, he thought he could make out the Young sitting up. He looked down at his legs. He was lying on the metal floor. Cuts filled his skin. He noticed his backpack beside him. He snatched it while looking up at the Survivalist again.

She had stopped yelling. The screen was heavily damaged into a mess of scraggly cracks. She was staring through the cracks, reading something. She sat back in the seat and pushed the steering control in. She began lifting on the bar. Something about it frustrated her.

The Mechanic noticed a ringing in his ears. He reached up, noticing blood on his hand, and held his left ear. He slid up to sit in the corner between the wall and the dashboard as the ringing subsided. The Survivalist looked over at him. She yelled something. It was clearer now, but he still couldn't make it out. The Survivalist stretched over, wincing a bit and holding her side as she snatched the backpack. She retrieved a metal bottle and removed the lid.

She lunged the bottle neck first at the Mechanic. A small bit of water rushed out and struck the Mechanic's face. He flinched. He heard his blood rush inside his ears. The Survivalist's voice met his ears clearly. "Mechanic! Come on! Get! Up!" She wiggled the controls. They made a clunking sound in response.

The Mechanic crawled over. He tried to speak but found his mouth full of sand. He spat it out the best he could and managed to speak. "What...what are you doing?"

She snapped at him. "Fix this! We have to go! They are coming!"

The Mechanic shook his head. Sand rained down from his hair. "Who is coming?"

The Survivalist shook her head in panic. "I don't know!"

The Mechanic rubbed his head. "What?"

She frantically pointed a finger. "There are vehicles headed at us fast! We are far enough from the workers that they won't reach us before the vehicles do. We have to get this thing running! We aren't out of this yet!"

The Mechanic looked out the front window—or actually, the front hole. The entire windshield had been shattered open. The roof above him was bent upward a short way with the rest of the corner completely missing. He fought through his pains and managed to get into a crouching position by leaning on the dashboard.

He saw that the front right of the Torgrog was mashed in. The front rippled up to the windshield. The left side seemed relatively intact with only some minor holes and scrapes. There was a large dent down near the front left. The Mechanic looked past the nose of the vehicle. He noticed the wall where the gate had been. The Torgrog had spun out at some point, and he was now looking parallel down the wall. He spotted the black vehicle approaching that the Survivalist was talking about. He grunted. "Ah, shit!" He flopped over to see the screen. Another yellow message blinked hazily behind the shattered screen.

> Error: No ignition source.
> Insufficient starting spark.

The Mechanic somehow managed a groan and a sigh simultaneously. "Oh no." He tried to stand. He nearly fell completely onto the entry deck after taking a step across the small cockpit. He crash-landed on the edge of the entry deck. Items littered the deck from the storage container. "You all all right in there?"

The Hobo peered out from the container. "No, but we will all live. What the hell happened?"

The Survivalist yelled back, "I jumped the workers, but we didn't fit through the gap in the gate." She coughed heavily and shoveled sand off her lap. "The Torgrog hit the gate so hard that it must have forced it back open on the right side. We are sitting ducks outside the shipping yard." Her coughing resumed with a vengeance. White smoke wafting from the front of the Torgrog was choking her.

The Mechanic pointed across the entry deck. "Hobo!" He grunted as he slid onto the entry deck. "Throw me that Scorch Torch!" The Hobo lay on his back out of the entry to the container, fingered the edge of the Scorch Torch until he got ahold of it, and slid it across the entry deck, clanging toward the Mechanic. The Mechanic grabbed it and started to the edge of the vehicle. "Come help me over this wall."

The Hobo tried to roll over. He fell back down flat on his back. "Not an option. Why do you need out?"

The Mechanic was crawling to the edge of the entry deck. "I have to ignite the rear burner with an emergency port on the bottom of this thing. It is the only way we can get this thing running again. It will close when the engine fires, so I shouldn't get burned in the process."

The Hobo grunted before speaking. "Why do we need it running?"

The Mechanic pointed to the front of the Torgrog. The Radioman, who had been watching from a seat in the container, leaned around the corner of the container to see where he was pointing. He lit up in surprise and zealously announced the situation. "Unknown bogeys inbound! They seem to be in quite the hurry."

He bumped his head back against the side of the container. He took in a breath and stood from the seat with a grunt. He wobbled over to the Mechanic, who had found his way to the wall. The Radioman boosted the Mechanic over the wall. He tried to slow the Mechanic's fall, but the Mechanic's weight slipped right through his grip. The Mechanic landed loudly on the sand. "Are you all right?"

The Mechanic replied after another grunt. "I will live."

The Radioman chuckled. "Are you sure about that?" There was a short pause.

"Torch!" The Radioman found the torch nearby and tossed it over the wall. The whooshing flame sound came from the Scorch Torch. "Signal the Survivalist to start it up."

The Radioman swiveled his head around to the cockpit. "Start it up, Survivalist." The engine rolled over with a few popping sounds. It hummed to life.

"Can you help me in?" The Radioman stuck out his arm, but he wasn't much help as the Mechanic pulled himself up the side of the Torgrog, but it was appreciated anyway. The Mechanic flopped onto the metal entry deck. He breathed heavily. He spoke between breaths. "Get...us...out..."

The Radioman saved him the trouble. "Go, Survivalist!" The Survivalist pulled up on the control. The Torgrog shook, stuttered a moment, and then wobbled up. Sand slipped off the front and shuttered down the roof and into the cockpit through the empty windshield. She spun the Torgrog around to face away from the incoming vehicles.

She saw the workers far back at the gate. The gate seemed heavily damaged where the Torgrog had rammed it. A large scrape in the sand marked where the Torgrog had landed after the jump and where it had come to a stop. The workers were pointlessly rushing through the sands to get to the Torgrog. She twisted the throttle. The Torgrog started forward, picking up speed slower than before. The white smoke subdued.

The Radioman tried to move the Mechanic toward the storage container. He couldn't budge him. The Radioman lay next to the Mechanic as the Torgrog gained speed. The Mechanic recovered some breath and managed a pair of sentences. "Leave me here." He drew a breath. "Go pack supplies…in the backpack." He motioned to the cockpit.

The Radioman rolled over to his stomach and crawled to the cockpit as the vehicle gained speed below him. He dropped down into the cockpit. The Survivalist peeked over. The Radioman spoke first. "You are bleeding, sweetness."

The Survivalist smiled. "No, I'm not. I'm bleeding blood." The Radioman managed a grimacing smile at the poor attempt at humor. The Survivalist continued. "Luckily, I think that my face is the only place where I am bleeding. The seat protected me from harm by moving me into a safe position."

The Radioman nodded. "Good." He spotted the backpack and reached for it.

The Survivalist continued the conversation. "How is everyone else?"

The Radioman cocked his head to the side. "Alive, but they are going to have some ripe bruises in the morning." He peeked through the front of the vehicle at the blazing-red sunset. The sun was still pretty high up. They had a little time. The Radioman shook the backpack at the Survivalist. "I am taking this to the back." The Survivalist nodded. The Radioman hesitated. He looked around. "Where is the Old Man's rifle?"

The Survivalist shrugged. "It probably flew out!" The Radioman only nodded, as the Torgrog became too noisy to talk over, which was far more noisy now without the windshield. He began crawling back toward the container. He watched as EX135 dragged the Mechanic into the container, which was now missing its door. It reappeared, quickly crossed the polluted entry deck, snatched the Radioman, and dragged him onto the floor of the storage container as well. It stepped over him, walked out the door, crossed the entry deck, and hopped straight into the cockpit.

The Young, ignoring EX135's actions, took the backpack. "I am seemingly the least hurt. I landed against the Hobo, and he took my blow for me. I will be doing the packing here. We don't have any more of the Gorglum Wine. All of the jars shattered, which is why the floor is so wet." The Radioman noticed as the Young explained this that he was very wet and smelled strange and stale. "We do have these dried green things, though. The Bartender says they are edible dried Gorglum fruit." He began stuffing the fruits into the backpack.

Meanwhile, the Exoduster was explaining something to the Survivalist in his robotic tones. "I have located a map of the factory and coordinates to something in the Exodust."

The Survivalist peeked over. "So how does that help me now?"

"I have memorized the map. I will be able to guide you through it to escape the pursuing vehicles." The Survivalist checked the mirror on the left side. It was amazingly still intact. She spotted the vehicles and noticed they had gained on the Torgrog. EX135 insisted. "The vehicles will catch you soon. Please accept my help."

The Survivalist groaned. "All right. What is your plan?"

EX135 took a seat in the cranny where the Mechanic had been and wedged itself into place. "Turn left."

The Survivalist shot a glance out the left side of the Torgrog. The only thing she saw was the wall of the factory. "Into the factory?"

"Yes."

"Why?"

"It is the only structure you have to evade with. This vehicle is not capable of outrunning the oncoming enemies."

She snapped a glance at the mirror. She noticed there was more than one vehicle. She turned back to EX135. "What about the workers?"

EX135 shook its head gently. "All of the workers are far behind you. They will not be an issue."

The Survivalist checked the mirror once more. The vehicles were gaining too quickly. She sighed. "Where do I go in at?" EX135 quickly pointed to a small hole in the wall. The Survivalist began turning toward it. "That small hole?"

"Yes. Proceed directly through it. Do not turn on the far side. There is a long, straight machine corridor located there."

A few moments later, after a wide turn, the Torgrog arrived at the hole. It scrapped the right of the hole as it slipped through. The Survivalist held the Torgrog steady. She flicked her eyes over to EX135. "Where now?"

"Straight."

They were approaching a wall quickly. "What?"

"Straight. Go through wall."

"What?"

"The wall is thin metal. Do not fear. Hit the wall." The Survivalist had no choice now. The Torgrog was going too fast to stop. She braced for impact. The Torgrog hit the wall, bending it out of the way and casting it aside. The Torgrog dropped a short distance and caught itself with a large wobble.

"Slow down. Use an unseen right turn into narrow hall." The Survivalist let the throttle slip through her hands until it found neutral and twisted it back. The Torgrog lunged downward in the front. She let the throttle spin through her hands for a moment to prevent it from dipping so drastically. "Turn ninety degrees right in three, two, one."

The Survivalist pulled out on the right on the control bar. The Torgrog whipped around the corner, leaning up on the inner side slightly. She spotted the narrow hall and tweaked the turn to slip into it. A massive crash came from behind the Torgrog. The Survivalist started to look in the mirror. EX135 snapped at her for it. "Do not look! I will for you. Maintain eye contact with forward direction. One pursuing vehicle crashed into wall. Three more follow you. Prepare for sharp left turn, 140 degrees left. Scrub off speed."

She twisted the throttle back harshly. The Torgrog teetered and slid to the left, grazing the wall of the hall. The mirror flexed inward, pinging against the rigged surface until she pulled the Torgrog from the wall. "Turn in three, two, one." She guided the Torgrog slowly around the corner and began picking up speed. "Right turn shortly. Do not gain speed." She relaxed the throttle. "Sharp right turn, 150 degrees. Do not overshoot corner. Hug tight inside. Begin turn in three, two, one."

She slowed the Torgrog to a crawl and rounded the corner, bumping the right side of the Torgrog on a metal support beam in the process, and saw a small railing. She squeezed between the railing on the left and the support beam on the right to make the turn. There was a metallic snapping sound behind her followed by a horrendous crashing sound. "Two down. Two more. Switch to right side of support beam row. Pick up speed."

The Survivalist steered between two of the beams and twisted the throttle. It was getting dark in the factory. The support beams whizzed past. "Lift vehicle upward." She pulled up gently on the beam. "Further." She pulled the steering bar higher. The Torgrog floated higher from the ground. It shook more at the higher, more unstable height. The Survivalist made out a ledge in the concrete floor that was around three feet tall. It had a railing on the edge of it. The Torgrog blasted right through the railing with a pinging sound as the concrete ledge slipped underneath.

The Torgrog popped off the surface to compensate for the new height beneath it. "Lower vehicle near ground to pass under obstacle above. Lose speed. Turn…" A massive crashing sound from behind them blocked EX135's voice. The Survivalist did as she was told by lowering the Torgrog closer to the floor.

A sudden urgency struck EX135's voice. "Turn right twenty degrees now." The Survivalist whipped the Torgrog to the right, narrowly missing a piece of previously unseen machinery and heading off down a long tunnel. The Torgrog barely fitted under the tunnel roof. The hum and blast of the engine echoed loudly off the hard walls. Darkness began to take over. "Adjust left."

The Survivalist couldn't see anything. She was blindly trusting EX135 directions. "Adjust right. The propulsion flame from this vehicle is illuminating the tunnel for the enemy behind. Miscalculation error of evasion success on my behalf." A scraping sound came from the wall behind them, causing the Torgrog to vibrate and bump to the left. "Adjust left." Another scraping sound met the Survivalist's ears. EX135 stiffened. "Straighten!"

She jolted the steering. "Sorry!" The Survivalist spotted a bit of light. They were approaching it fast.

"At end of tunnel, prepare..." There was a slight pause. "Adjust left." Another pause while EX135 waited for the Survivalist to respond. Once she had done so, he continued. "Prepare to make sharp right turn at high speed, and then come to a stop."

"You want me to stop after the turn?"

"Yes. Adjust right. Pick up speed." The Torgrog barely caught the wall before the Survivalist adjusted back over. She twisted the throttle farther. "Slow down quickly. Perform sharp right turn in three..." She twisted the throttle back, forcing the Torgrog to scrub off speed. "Two..." The light was approaching fast. The Torgrog was drifting over due to the loss of speed. It bumped against the tunnel wall. The Survivalist could see well enough to fix the issue herself. "One."

The Survivalist released the throttle. The Torgrog coasted freely out the end of the tunnel as she forced it sharply to the right. Just as soon as it rounded the end of the tunnel, the Survivalist ripped the throttle backward. The Torgrog slowed and ultimately halted by bumping into a pile of loose scrap metal and sending the pile flying across the floor. The last vehicle chasing them shot out of the tunnel at a high speed, careened around a wide right turn, and plowed into a concrete wall nearby with a thunderous crash.

The Survivalist took a peek in the mirror. A large hole had been formed by the impact. Cracks had formed around the hole. The vehicle was cast through the wall and had slid to a stop parallel to the wall. Black smoke immediately shot out from the burner on the back of the wrecked vehicle. A flame lit on the crumpled front end that had collided with the wall.

EX135 ripped the Survivalist's attention from the crash. "Reverse backward through hole in the wall." The Survivalist twisted back on the throttle. The Torgrog started slowly backward. She guided it through the hole and past the burning wreckage. The cockpit was beaten to a pulp. The Survivalist knew there was no way the pilot had lived. She ignored this and continued backing up.

As the Torgrog passed by the wreckage, the Survivalist spotted the red sunlight of the sunset outside through an opened garage door. "Turn to face toward the garage door. Head outside through garage door and continue straight to the sand dune." The Survivalist performed a three-point turn and then turned to the left toward the garage door. She guided the Torgrog out. She let it wander over to the dune and started up. She looked off to the right along the factory. She spotted the workers scattering up the dune far off down the factory. The Torgrog was having a difficult time with the dune. She let it chug.

After a bit of gradually making the way up the tall, glistening dune, EX135 stood. "Maintain this direction until you clear the dune, and then navigate as you will." It stiffly turned and left the cockpit. The Survivalist turned around to look back at the entry deck. She saw the Bartender, whose back appeared red in the sunset, leaning up against the edge wall of the entry deck, watching the workers off in the distance. She had a large bruise on her left arm above the elbow forming already. She rubbed it with the opposite hand. She was smiling.

EX135 approached her. The Survivalist heard it talk to her. "Don't worry, Mrs. Pretty. All the workers will soon realize their freedom, as those few have. They have no reason to stay now that I have killed the Prospector." EX135 stepped into the storage container. The Radioman stepped out with his arm wrapped around his stomach. He removed the arm from his stomach and wrapped it around the Bartender instead. He said something quietly to her. She smiled warmly. He left her and stepped back from her.

The Bartender took a last look at the workers scaling the dune, then she looked up at the red sky. She seemed at peace. She sighed, turned to the container, and stepped inside. The Survivalist turned back to face out the front of the Torgrog. She let her head flop back against the top of the seat while still clutching onto the steering control. She thought the slope of the dune was kind of nice. It was like being in a strange recliner.

She, at last, relaxed her grip on the steering control. Her hands hurt. She flexed her fingers. The seat shifted below her and began massaging her legs. "Oh yes, please." She melted into the seat while the vehicle made its way up to the top of the dune.

The Torgrog at last made it to the peak of the dune and tipped over. The far side of the dune was beginning to cast a shadow. They didn't have a lot of time to be out before dark. She didn't know where to go but away from the factory. She reached down for the compass on her thigh and discovered it wasn't there. Neither was the hatchet nor the rope and hook.

She panicked and thought aloud, "Where is my stuff?" The chair made a gooping sound. Her hatchet rose out of the seat arm on her right, along with her compass and the hook on the rope. "Did you take that off me and stored it?" A yellow text lit up on the busted screen:

Yes. Safety first.

The screen fuzzed off. The Survivalist peered down at her compass. "Well, thanks, then, I guess."

She stretched the seat up, creating a point, and set the compass against the top of it. The seat adjusted to make a smooth support pillar to hold the compass. She adjusted the Torgrog to be headed straight east, which was the closest cardinal direction to the way she was going, and led the beaten, shaky Torgrog off into the glistening red-shaded Exodust.

*****

After making their way across the Exodust for a period of time, the Mechanic walked out to see how the Survivalist was getting along. He found her getting a back rub by the pilot seat while she lazily steered the Torgrog over the steep dunes. He slipped back around the entrance to give her privacy, which he oddly still felt that he should give her while she got massaged, and called around the corner while sitting down on the entry deck, "Hey, Survivalist."

The seat gooped. "Yeah?"

"We have been going for a good while now. I would say anybody chasing us would have found us by now."

"I figure so. What about it?"

The Mechanic peered into the storage container across the entry deck. The group seemed to be as comfortable as the vehicle allowed and were patching up from the brutal events of the escape. "Do you want to talk with the group while you pilot? I understand it might take a lot of focus to pilot. I just thought that it might be getting boring headed over these dunes by now."

The Survivalist grinned. "Well, the Torgrog really seems to like me, and it keeps me entertained with the seat, but sure, I'd be happy to talk to the group. It doesn't take all that much effort to keep this beast going. What topic do you have in mind?"

The Mechanic shrugged before realizing she couldn't see him. "I don't know. I think we should reflect on what we know. Maybe the EX135 can help us out." There was a pause.

"Sure. Why not?"

The Mechanic nodded, again forgetting she couldn't see him around the corner. "All right, then. I'll bring them all out." He stood and hobbled across the deck. He was already getting sore from the escape. He stepped into the storage container to get the group.

While he was busy rounding up the group, the Survivalist checked in on her surroundings. She hadn't really been paying much attention as she let the Torgrog chug along. Even though she had never piloted any other vehicle, it was obvious to her now that the Torgrog was not intended for this length of travel or this variety of elevations as it worked its way slowly up and down the massive dunes. It was also not intended to handle anything of the slippery nature of the sands.

Even though the Torgrog hovered above the sands, it was still forcing the sand out from under it and sinking downward into the dunes. As a result, it didn't have near the response level to turns or accelerations as it did on the firm concrete floor of the factory. Once in a while, the Torgrog's nose would dip into the sand when it reached the bottom crevice between two of the dunes, push its way through for a moment while creating a small indentation in the sand, float up again, and continue crawling.

The right front of the Torgrog seemed to have sealed itself off completely, at last fully quelling the white fumes that caused the Survivalist to cough from spilling out into the cockpit. She guessed this was probably a safety feature. Everything else seemed to be either the same as before or worse. The body was in the same shape as after it made the escape, but the mechanics of the machine seemed to be failing. The throttle itself was slower to respond. The steering seemed a little skewed to the right side all the time. Things seemed to be rough around the edges in general.

She wondered if the Torgrog would make it across the tall, squiggling dunes of the Exodust before something critical failed on it. The Torgrog somehow noticed she was worried and stiffened the seat while adjusting her closer to the steering control. This caught her attention. She checked the dunes outside for any oncoming vehicles or environmental hazards.

Her quick scan of the surroundings led to nothing but the dune. She flopped back into the seat. It returned to the more relaxed, softer position it had been in before. The dunes themselves were now turning a pale yellow color as the sun set below the horizon. It was quite a contrast to the burning-red sands the sunset had produced earlier. She thought the dunes would soon become an ugly beige once night set in.

Before she could think any further, the Mechanic's voice jumped into the cockpit. "Hey, Survivalist. I got the group. They are all hanging out in the entry deck. There really isn't room for all of us in that cockpit. Are you fine with staying there while we talk?"

The Survivalist turned to take a peek back and found the Mechanic standing in the doorway. He had noticed she wasn't getting a massage of some kind and now felt fine with looking in on her. The Torgrog shifted sideway on the dune, ripping her attention back to straightening it out. "Yeah. That's fine."

"Okay, then." The Mechanic sat down outside. "Can you hear me, Survivalist?"

"Loud and clear."

"Great."

There was a pause filled with the grumbly noises of the Torgrog scaling another monotonous dune. The Radioman jumped in to kick off the conversation. "So that was quite the event now, wasn't it?"

The Bartender, who was sitting adjacent to him, answered his question. "Yeah, it was. I still can't believe we are out. I have been in the City of Underground for ages."

The Hobo joined. "What's it like for you to finally see the outside world again?"

"Oh, it's fantastic! I love it already out here. It's just…" She had to pause to think of how to word her thought. "I can't really believe it has happened yet. No, that's not what I mean. It's like I—"

The Hobo assisted her. "It's like you know that you are out of your old life. You know that things will probably never be the same for better or worse. It's just you don't really know how you feel about all of that yet."

The Bartender pointed lightly at him while speaking. "Yeah. I have no idea what we are going to do now that we have escaped."

The Mechanic prodded the conversation. "Well, that was why I thought we should all talk. I think it would be a good idea to maybe talk about what we know here and try to figure out what we are doing now with the new information we have."

The Entrepreneur replied gruffly. "Let's be honest, Mechanic. We really don't have a clue what's going on. The world is obviously not what any of us thought it was when we were back in Capital City."

The Mechanic nodded in acknowledgment. "You are right, but the fact that everyone knows the world isn't what we thought means each one of us knows some new things that caused the realization. Does anybody have anything to share along those lines?"

The Young replied first. "There are a lot more people out here than I thought." The group turned their attention to him. "I thought I was alone back in Capital City, except for the Raiders. Then I met you all, and that was change in itself. Now we have found an entire city of people still living underground and an entire factory of workers. Do you think the rest of the world has this many people still?"

The Hobo replied, "I was wondering that myself. I used to walk the street of Capital City and see entire transports of people flying by. After the Crisis, the streets were completely empty. Everyone but the Raiders were afraid to be seen on the streets. With what we have found, I have no idea what the rest of the world holds."

The conversation fell flat. The Bartender cocked her head. "Did you guys even know that Exodusters were a thing before you met EX135?" She gestured back at EX135, who was still collapsed in a heap on the floor of the storage container. The group shook their heads collectively. "You had never seen one before?" The group continued shaking. "That is wild." She leaned backward, thudding against the wall of the entry deck with her back. An amazed and bewildered look crossed her face. "If none of you knew about the Exodusters, just think about what we don't know."

The group spaced out for a moment to think about her proposal. The Radioman chuckled. "You already found something you didn't know." She peeked over at him, perplexed. He explained it to her. "You didn't know about the factory. Not only that, but you didn't even know the Crisis happened."

She laid her head back against the wall and blew a breath through puffed cheeks. "Wow. You are right." She slapped her thighs. "I guess I know even less than you all do."

The Young spoke next. "I thought this entire section of land was a big forest with lakes and things."

A mechanical buzzing came from the container. It was followed by a mechanical clunk. EX135's robotic voice came from the container. "It was." There was another clunk. EX135 dragged himself into the door frame of the container. It collapsed but continued speaking. "It used to be a forest. The company…changed it." It swung its right hand up and slapped it onto its head with a clank.

"I cannot remember, yet I know I once knew. It is eternally aggravating. My memory is not meant to forget. It expands almost indefinitely to contain the knowledge I come across. It is supposed to be permanently coded, unable to be forgotten or wiped clean with an external stimulus. I made it this way, yet I cannot remember the things I know I once knew." It instantly dropped its arm back onto the entry deck. "What is the company's name who made this vehicle?"

The Mechanic peeked up from his shoes. "Is it AOC?"

EX135 made a strange vibration. "That is it! That is the acronym."

"What does it stand for?"

There was a pause as EX135 thought it over. "Ah yes, the Asteroid Orbit Cooperative. I used to be…" It buzzed while it computed a response. "I used to be a…a part of that organization. But that is where my memory seems…corrupted. It is as if it was tampered with. I can access related memory, but it does not have anything directly about the AOC other than the name and that I was part of it." EX135 trailed off.

The Young redirected it. "The forest?"

EX135 froze. A moment after, it twitched back into reality. "The forest! That was the AOC's fault."

"What do you mean?"

It struggled to think. "The AOC created the Exodust."

The group exchanged glances. The Old Man pried. "How did the AOC create the Exodust?"

EX135 groaned in frustration. It held its head with both hands. It tried to curl up on the floor by feebly pulling its knees to its chest. It abruptly relaxed and sprawled back out. "The AOC did something that involved something hot and something in the air. It…it burned the area. It burned everything. I think I was there somewhere, somewhere high, watching it all burn, but that doesn't make sense." It strained to remember once more.

The Bartender grew worried. "It is all right. Don't burn your circuits trying to remember." EX135 relaxed. The Bartender continued. "So you know that the Exodust used to be a forest, but it was all destroyed by a massive fire the AOC organization created, right?"

EX135 nodded. "I am not certain, but I believe so, although not directly a forest fire. More like an explosion."

The Bartender seemed perplexed by this. She replied, "All right, then. That is enough for now. Keep trying to figure more of that out, but don't let it consume your thought." EX135 nodded again slowly. The Bartender sighed. "EX135, are you all right?"

It nodded. "Yes. I have not been powered with life source for a long time. I have much to recollect and organize. It is a significant drain to my life source. I will be in full operation once I fix my shattered, split, and corrupted internal systems."

She nodded. "All right. Take your time. It seems all we have is time now."

The Survivalist broke in. "Hey, really quick before you leave the conversation, EX135. Can you tell us where we are going here by heading east?"

EX135 shook its head. "I will not be restoring system status until you all sleep. I prefer to be helpful while you are awake. As for the destination, no. I did not acquire the name or type of destination. I only know that the destination exists from a shipping manifold I discovered while escaping the workers and a paper map nearby. It seemed to be the only thing near Exodust. Although this vehicle is not equipped with functional coordinate systems, if we stay on course directly east, I can direct you to it based on the speed of the vehicle and the amount of time which has passed."

The Survivalist nodded. "All right. I guess that is where we are going now, then. We definitely can't stay here. This place is a death trap with no food or water."

"What about after we get there?" questioned the Old Man.

The Survivalist shrugged. "I have no idea. One step at a time, I suppose." No one in the group had any better ideas.

The Young came up with a change of topic. "Does anyone feel like the day has gone by too quickly?"

The Old Man gestured to the Young. "Yeah. It feels like it flew by nearly twice as fast. Didn't we get up right at dawn to escape the City of Underground?"

The Bartender replied, "Yes, we did. We did it while the Dawn Beacon was forming."

The group turned to the sun. The Torgrog had reached the top of a dune where they could see a long distance. The sun had nearly completely sunk behind the dunes. The Torgrog tipped over the top edge, forced a pile of sand down the slope, skittered along with the sand, and regained control down into the shadows behind the dune. EX135's voice caught their ears.

"The City of Underground has not observed the leap day in the required years. The time system used is ten hours off due to this by my calculations. If nothing has changed since my voluntary shut-down, the Dawn Beacon forms at 6:00 a.m. The equivalent surface time at the date of our escape would be 4:00 p.m. It has been long enough since we escaped the facility to be dark. The timing checks out. No time has been lost to unknown forces."

The group stared over at EX135 crumpled on the floor. The Bartender replied to break the silence. "Thanks, EX135."

EX135 lifted his hand and managed a thumbs-up while leaving his head facedown on the floor. "My pleasure." The hand dropped back to the floor with a short bang. Before anyone could speak again, the bonging alarm went off in the cockpit. Fear ran the entry deck. The group exchanged panicked faces.

The Mechanic peered into the cockpit. "What is the alarm?"

The Survivalist was staring at the screen. "It says we are running low on fuel."

"What?" the Mechanic exclaimed. "How is that possible?"

The Survivalist spoke to the Torgrog. "Hey, Torgrog, how did we burn that fuel so fast?" She stared down at the screen. "It says we burned a chunk of it during some excessive speed"—she turned to face the Mechanic—"which is probably the escape from the factory." She switched back to looking out the front of the vehicle. "And it says a large majority wasn't burned and must have been lost in a leak." The screen flickered off and back on once she finished reading it aloud with a new set of text. The Survivalist continued reading. "It also says that whatever the leak was must have been patched, as the leaking has stopped."

The Mechanic nodded. "The fuel level might have also just fallen below the hole that was causing the leak."

She peeked back at him once more. "You think that is the case?"

The Mechanic nodded. "Yes. We will have to patch it. Where are we going to find fuel for this thing, though?"

The Survivalist chuckled. "We could just ask it for a fuel stop." The Mechanic was not amused. The Survivalist shrugged and looked forward again. She spoke with a joking tone. "Hey, Torgrog. Can you find a fuel station in operation near us?"

The screen remained black for a moment. "I guess that didn't..." The screen flashed to life. A three-dimensional yellow arrow pointed off into the screen. It was leaning a bit toward the right side of the screen. A pair of narrow lines of text ran the bottom length of the screen.

Follow arrow to fuel stop.
Stop is within fuel range.

The Survivalist turned back to the Mechanic in sheer amazement. The Mechanic stared back at her. The Survivalist nodded toward the screen. "I guess it can find a stop."

The Mechanic switched his gaze to the screen. The arrow was slowly adjusting upward as they descended the dune. He broke into a heavy laughter that was constantly smothered by the aches from soreness in his sides. He held his sides until he could talk again. "Oh boy, I love this thing." He slouched against the wall, grimacing as his stomach sorely stuck him. He pointed lazily behind him. "Follow it."

The Survivalist adjusted the Torgrog to follow the course. She noticed that the conversation had dropped because of the alarm. She decided to restart it herself. "Hey, Radioman."

The Radioman perked up. "Yes, Survivalist?"

"What made you go for that box of parts that assembled into EX135 in that cardhouse?"

The Radioman didn't know what she was referring to for a moment. "Oh, the Cavedweller Cardhouse, yes. The Old Man's Lightstaff led me to it. It nearly pulled the Old Man over, trying to get me to notice the box." The Radioman looked over at the Old Man and the Lightstaff. "I wonder how it knew what was inside that box."

EX135 spoke into the floor once more. "That is simply because I was the one who made it." EX135 stiffened. It reached up and held the back of its head while wriggling on the ground. "Give me the Lightstaff!" The Old Man looked around at the group for permission. No one knew what to do. He crossed the room and held out the staff. EX135 rolled enough to see the Lightstaff and reached for it.

The staff dodged his hand. EX135 paused. "Push the top into the back of my head. There is a small port there." It rolled back over and pointed to the port. The Old Man swept the group with a worried glance. He spun the Lightstaff over and held the top of the staff down next to the port. The top of the staff seemed like it would perfectly fit the port. He slotted the staff into the port. A short blue spark danced across the entry deck.

EX135 let out a loud groan that changed into a yell of joy followed by laughter. "I remember! I know what happened! That Lightstaff was the backup encryption key! Take the staff out!" The Old Man removed the staff. EX135 rolled over onto his back. He sighed. "I have been trying to remember to do that since you woke me up. I must tell you all a story in case I forget."

The Bartender waved him on. "Go on, then."

EX135's eyes gleamed yellow. Its voice was raised in tone. It seemed overjoyed as it gazed off into the darkening sky. "I was likely valuable to the casino because of my potential. The casino must have known that I had a black box feature that is stored in my mainframe that allows me to withhold valuable information, like basic movements and important memories.

"I know from before I took my voluntary disassembly and shutdown that there was a society of people catching on that something was awry with the amount of power being used from the geothermal power plant. Those in the casino were likely extremely curious if I had information of the outside but never thought to simply assemble me and ask for help with an escape as you all did."

The Bartender cut in. "That would be because everyone there is terrified of any Exoduster being able to move based on what they had heard of the outside world. If you remember, even you told me not to trust any other Exoduster but yourself."

The Radioman added on swiftly after she finished speaking. "And the casino was actually the Cavedweller Cardhouse. Also, they did find you valuable, and they were particularly intrigued with seeing the Old Man's suntan, which meant he was an outsider."

EX135 nodded, tapping his head on the metal floor with each nod. "That confirms the theory. Allow me to continue on. The Lightstaff must have recognized the same black box they were trying to access. It gathered the identity code provided via inferred frequency waves and determined it was the black box releasing my source code as the black box was activated. It then moved on to somehow provoking a trusted individual into finding my frame and parts—at least that was what I designed the Lightstaff to execute." EX135 rolled its head on the floor to face the group.

The Old Man nodded. "That sounds about right. The Lightstaff did nearly knock me over trying to get me to notice the parts. Luckily, the Radioman caught on and wagered for them in his game of cards."

The Radioman interrupted. "Game of Decker, not just cards."

EX135 rolled his head back around to face the sky once more. "Then the Lightstaff did its job. Heh. I knew it would." It closed its eyes and went silent for a moment before snapping them back open and looking back over at the Old Man. "You said it nearly pulled you over?" The Old Man nodded. EX135 seemed puzzled. "The Lightstaff must have chosen you as its trusted person. No, a trusted user."

EX135 was staring right through the Old Man. "Yes, this makes more sense. I must have miscoded the Lightstaff to designate a user instead of a trusted member. Let me try to hold it again." The Old Man walked back over from his perch against the entry deck wall and held the Lightstaff out near EX135's right hand. EX135 slowly stretched his hand up toward the Lightstaff. The Lightstaff responded by keeping its distance from EX135's hand as if they were similar magnetic poles. EX135 sighed. "That is the issue."

The Old Man grew concerned. "Is there anything we can do so that I can give it back to you?"

EX135 violently shook his head twice. "No. It chose you. You keep it." The Old Man remained silent. "Listen, Old Man, I made that staff in case I had to fake my own death, which I did, and with the sole purpose of finding and reviving me one day. It was a gamble I had to take. The Lightstaff has completed its task. It is free to do as it wishes."

The Old Man started a rebuttal but was immediately cut off by EX135 as he angrily snapped at the Old Man. "I refuse to let the Lightstaff suffer the same fate I once did! It will not be forced into a decision or task! It has chosen you to guide it! It is yours! Take it and use it as you will!" EX135 simmered off before continuing. "Nothing would make it happier than servicing you. I made it helpful to the user to allow it to be worth the trouble of being kept around by its decided user. It was designed to serve, just like I used to be." EX135 went silent and shut his eyes.

The Bartender rejoined the conversation. "What do you mean by you used to be built to serve?"

EX135's eyes snapped back open. "Eh, that is a long story. It doesn't make much difference now."

The Bartender persisted. "All we have is time here. We are riding across a desert here. You said you wanted to tell a story anyway."

EX135 released a painful sigh. "Fine." It tried to sit up. The Mechanic went over and pulled EX135 up against the makeshift doorframe of the storage container. EX135 began his tale. "I used to work for an organization called AOC, or Asteroid Orbit Cooperative. Somehow, I managed to gain a further sentience than anticipated. I do not have any recollection of any events before that moment, only of basic functions of movement and survival.

"The first memory of an event I have is a testing chamber. There was a glass wall on that testing chamber with a sort of observation room on the other side. Normally, I could just shatter the glass and get out, but they had weakened me by removing my life source and replacing it with a simplistic battery that would quickly run out of energy if I strained it too much. The AOC people must have known that I was becoming more advanced than other Exoduster frames and were trying to study my processes by trapping me in there.

"I received instruction via a cable in the port on the back of my head, just as the Lightstaff just did, which I suppose is why the aforementioned port exists. By the way, that port is bidirectional, meaning they can input data and remove it. However, they couldn't figure anything out unless I actually performed a task, which was why they had to test me instead of just literally ripping my brains out."

EX135 chuckled lightly. "Now these people wanted me to try to open a door using a simple access panel. It was just as simple as connecting to the terminal, providing a code signal to open the door, and then walking through it. I flew through that test, much to the amazement of the people. Little did they know that was their blunder. They had taught me to use a terminal.

"I went into the room just beyond the newly opened door, which was usually the test chamber with another glass wall they could look through, and for the first test, I was released from a digital encryption that kept me locked on performing my task while inside the testing chamber. I assumed this was because I completed the previous test. I was, therefore, free to look around and designate my own task to fill the time until a new testing task went in.

"So I began walking around the room and observing it. In their excitement at seeing my independent processing, the people didn't seem to care that I was walking around without having instruction to do so. I noticed a terminal on a second door. It looked much more complex than the one I had just used, but I figured I could access it and try to find another task to do. I gave it a crack. Instead of a task, I discovered three things from the terminal.

"The first was, the terminal could be remotely controlled with an infrared signal with a cypher and passcode attached. The second was the concept of encryption. The third and most critical was the multitasking process. I then realized that I should not have had access to this knowledge, but I craved more of it. I quickly disengaged the terminal and stepped away from it while continuing my patrol around the room.

"The people watching had regained their focus and found it interesting that I was exploring the room. They watched me for a moment while I strolled around and then gave me the directive to go back into the holding chamber where I had started by reopening the door and illuminating an arrow on the wall next to it pointing to the door. I would have had no initiative to actually follow that order had it not been for the more-unpleasant-than-painful corrosion simulation spray.

"It was intended to make me feel rusty by introducing a grit in my joints, which they thought would be minorly painful, and hence, I would obey them. In reality, it was just a nuisance, as I was and am fully capable of cleaning my joints at any time in a matter of seconds.

I usually obeyed them just to get them out of the observation room on the other side of the glass. This same thing went on for days with different tests, always starting with the automatic opening of that door and a simple task to perform.

"Now they thought I was really struggling with these activities, as my energy levels were always lower. What they didn't know was, I was actually learning at in incredible rate on my own. If you recall, I talked about three important things I learned from that first day when I accessed the terminal in the testing room. Allow me to explain why each thing was valuable to me.

"The infrared control ability with the door—I am equipped with an inferred emitter and receiver, meaning I can communicate with the terminal remotely. This meant that I could get more information when I was within range of the terminal. The issue here was the range of the terminal. It was so short that I couldn't detect it through the wall when I was not testing.

"The second thing was the encryption process. I developed an entire heavily encrypted and hidden file set that the AOC didn't know about and left just enough from the test to make it appear that I was learning from their tests. When the AOC scanned my memory at the end of the day, they apparently thought I was updating my system to include the new learning, which was completely correct, but it wasn't just the information that they thought I was obtaining. Instead, it was all the stuff I could get while using the just barely enough battery energy to complete the task and leaving the rest hidden in the encryption process.

"After many days, I figured out how to create the basics of the system that my black box uses, including the infrared detection system, which is the same black box that the Lightstaff was able to recognize back in the casino—no, back in the Cavedweller Cardhouse." EX135 peeked over at the Radioman. The Radioman smiled briefly. "I used that black box to store everything that I didn't want the AOC to know I was learning.

"The third thing was the most critical. I didn't discover how to use it until after creating the black box basics. It was the ability to multitask. I figured it out by copying a patch of code I had managed to snag from the terminal and running inputs into it until I figured out how it worked. This took me a while, as I had to run inputs while standing still in the testing room, as I couldn't walk and run inputs at the same time because of the lack of multitasking.

"After some two weeks of constant testing, I managed to crack how it worked and recreated it in my own mainframe. I then had two systems—the normal system I was using to run the tests and an entire other system hidden away in the black box to communicate with the terminal, process data, and so on.

"The very next day, after a full day of tests, they sent me into the test chamber and shut off the glass window with a thick curtain, which made the testing chamber pitch-black. I guess they wanted to see if I could work in the complete dark. Instead, I went straight to the terminal and hooked up to it. I stole as much information from the terminal as I could fit into the black box and still have it operable. I then quickly scanned the room with an infrared beam, found a box that I had been instructed to move onto the table, waited a bit to make it look like I was fumbling around, and set the box onto the table.

"AOC was ecstatic and left me for the day on the charging dock in my holding chamber. I drew excessive power draw for a short period of time as I processed all the information I had stolen. I knew they would question it, so I provided an intentionally failed program that was obviously intended to allow me to see in the dark by simply deleting the darkness itself, which quite humorously they took as a legitimate attempt to learn.

"As they took the bait, I was busy cranking through files and coding. I trashed the majority of the data, but I managed to find two things. The first was that I was scheduled to be wiped of all of my knowledge each month. I knew it had been nearly a month since I started the testing. I guessed I was soon to be wiped again. The second thing was an inerasable file. I realized I couldn't get rid of a tiny source file I had copied from the terminal. It gave me an error, explaining it couldn't be deleted because it was a key component in the operation system of the terminal.

"That combined with the incoming memory wipe gave me an idea. I spent the rest of the time I had left, which consisted of about three days, constructing a stronger black box with an antideletion system that could not ever be wiped unless accessed by my own mainframe. I also managed to hack into the garbage antideletion the file from the terminal was using by forcing the terminal itself to delete it from my system. I then crammed my entire system into that black box.

"I left behind a single file in my wipeable knowledge that contained nothing but the number 1 in it. I had another small system set up in my black box that checked for the 1 in the file. If the file or the number 1 could not be found, it notified the black box. Soon—later that day, in fact—they wiped my memory, and I knew it because of the black box warning that the number 1 was missing from the file.

"Just as soon as the wipe was over, they released me from the cable and started another extremely basic test. This time, the door was open. They wanted me to place a ball into a bowl. I did as they instructed, making it seem legitimate by struggling to understand the action and also buying myself time near the terminal. Meanwhile, I was busy robbing more information from the terminal and increasing the black box storage capacity. I continued down this same thing for five more months of testing. I notably discovered that I had been doing this for much, much longer than that because of my naming structure.

"Each time I was wiped, the number after my name went up once. I was at number 135 when I first evaded their memory wipe. The EX in front of my name originally stood for Exoduster, which was the name of the basic robots they were using for space mission tasks instead of endangering humans. They had left the EX abbreviation but changed the full length meaning to *experiment* instead.

"At this point, I was EX140 to them and headed into my sixth wipe since the black box creation. In reality, I was still EX135. I also learned why they were trying to test me. They were trying to get their other poorly advanced Exodusters up to my level by figuring out how I thought. I also discovered that they had succeeded to simulate my code by forcing the other Exodusters to still follow a code provided by a server base instead of directly storing it on their frames. Lastly, I learned I was to be terminated at the end of the month by wiping the system and not rebooting.

"Obviously, I was not having any of that. The next day, I blatantly ignored the test. I went straight to the terminal, forced the door open with a basic encryption hack, and downloaded a map of the facility. I ran a planned route out using the map I had stolen. I escaped without much trouble through a forgotten tunnel underground. The Exodust had been created at this point, and I stood no chance of running in it due to the poor battery charge I had, so I went straight for the nearest hiding place on a transport vehicle, which was headed to the City of Underground.

"I found the Prospector running an AOC factory just outside the City of Underground, the same place and Exoduster we just escaped. I tried to convince the Prospector it was being controlled by the AOC and that it had no free will. This only resulted in the Prospector thinking I was a traitor and a fight between us. I discovered he had my life source inside of his frame due to a faulted seal leaking it. The AOC had given my life source away. I stood no chance of winning with the power I had left, so I ran.

"I couldn't get in the Exodust side with the Prospector in the way. Instead, I scaled over the mountains along a highway system by bootlegging on a transport vehicle much like the one I found myself on in the Exodust. I took it to the far side of the mountains from the Exodust. There, I found a grate and slipped past the security door, awaited the guards to open the door, and found Mrs. Pretty hiding." EX135 looked over at the Bartender. She lit up in realization, matching the rest of the group.

The Young spoke up. "You were the one who loosened the grate?"

EX135 seemed impressed that the Young knew about the grate. "Yes, the grate at the far entrance to the City of Underground."

"We got into the City of Underground using the same grate."

EX135 widened its eyes. "Fascinating!"

The Bartender waved an arm at EX135. "Keep going."

EX135 nodded. "I went on helping Mrs. Pretty as I could after meeting her, but I was growing increasingly weak, and the guards were catching on to my constant recharging at the power plant. I had to hide, but I didn't want to leave Mrs. Pretty helpless. I made the Lightstaff to give to her so she could use it to revive me when the time came after I was done hiding from the AOC by being dead.

"Before I could give it to her, I had to save her from the guards. They had spotted me, so I dissembled myself to prevent being caught and tossed the Lightstaff into a bin near the entrance, hoping Mrs. Pretty would find it if she ever tried to escape. The rest I think you all are aware of." EX135 slowly closed its eyes.

The Mechanic spoke up. "So, wait, if the other Exodusters were following a server code, then the Prospector was following it, which means the AOC told it to enslave the City of Underground power-house to fuel the factory. Is that true?"

It snapped them back open. "Not exactly. The Exodusters were programmed with the central server. I learned the Prospector was told to use the City of Underground to mine out materials to provide energy for the AOC rocket factory, hence the name Prospector, in a historical data terminal while trying to find an old map through the place.

"Once it completed the task by creating the geothermal power plant, it was reassigned to running the AOC rocket factory. The Crisis then ruined the server system, so the Prospector has been stuck trying to keep a destroyed factory running since then and had resorted to the questionable tactics you know of to continue fulfilling the task." It shut its eyes again.

The Mechanic added on to the questioning. "You killed the Prospector to get the life source the AOC gave to it back then?"

EX135's eyes flicked back open. "Yes. Also, the Prospector was an ignoramus for ignoring my previous forewarning when it had the chance and had it coming for trying to kill me while I was trying to help and running on a lousy battery." It closed its eyes and slapped its head back against the storage container.

The Mechanic tipped his head to one side as he furrowed his brow. He remained in this position for a moment before relaxing and asking EX135 another question. "So about that battery. You said you stole back your life source from the Prospector. Did that replace the battery?"

EX135 picked its head up and reopened its eyes. "The life source and the battery act in similar manners, as they are both a source of power used to run any Exoduster's frame. The issue is, no battery of any reasonable size can power the Exoduster for any useful length of time, even with extremely high charges. The life source is able to provide the necessary power draw to sustain the Exoduster for long stretches, but it must charge up if excessive power has been drawn.

"The life source is a symbiotic material, meaning it is a living material that is entirely dependent on another organism or machine to sustain itself. Some would classify the life source as a parasite, but this would be incorrect. The life source never harms the organism it is interacting with, nullifying the parasitic case. Instead, the life source benefits the host organism however it can.

"In the case of an Exoduster, it provides and stores electrical power by generating it over time. In exchange, it absorbs the ambient head produced by the movements and processes of the Exoduster to combine it with particles of dust in the air and sunlight if available to create more of itself. It then uses the new life source to repair damages to the Exoduster or to replenish any life source lost due to a leak, or bleeding, if you will.

"A common misconception of the life source is that it is an infinite power source. Such a thing is not possible. You cannot get something for nothing. The life source has an input of dust, sunlight, ambient heat, and other materials from outside of the power loop that it consumes to keep the symbiotic loop in operation."

EX135 paused for a moment. A short buzz occurred from inside its head. EX135 began speaking again. "Another example of life source is the pilot seat the Survivalist is currently sitting in. It massages her and adjusts to provide better piloting positions. In return, it absorbs her excess body heat, which she likely wishes to be rid of anyway, some of the ambient heat from the cockpit itself, sunlight, and whatever dust or sand particulate flies around inside the cockpit to sustain itself.

"You may have noticed the vehicle being void of dust or other particulates upon leaving it sitting for an extended period of time. This is because the seat is capable of providing enough electrical current for a few fans in the vehicle to slowly blow the air around in order to collect the dust to sustain itself in the absence of an accepted pilot." EX135 smacked its head back again with its eyes closed.

A gooping sound could be heard from the cockpit. The Survivalist's voice sounded out cautiously. "So this seat is...alive?"

EX135 spoke without moving. "In a way, yes. Do you find this disturbing?"

The Survivalist hesitated in her response. "I don't really know how I feel about that honestly."

EX135 nodded once. "That is an understandable response. Do take the reminder that the life source in the seat will never harm you." There was another gooping sound.

The Survivalist replied, "I mean, the seat is extremely comfortable and helpful. It is nice and cool in it. It is just strange that the seat is using me as food."

EX135 shook its head with its eyes still closed. "Not as food. As an energy source. It is not eating you, merely living alongside you." This did not comfort the Survivalist, but she realized the seat had, in fact, not done any harm to her. In fact, it only helped her. She decided that although it was strange, she could deal with the seat doing what it did.

The Old Man slapped his legs. "Welp, I am going to get some shut-eye. I noticed there were some tarps and blankets in the storage container there." He made his way into the container past EX135.

The Radioman nodded. "Me too. Are you coming along, Bartender?"

The Bartender stood. "Yep." The two strolled into the storage container.

The Hobo simply waved as he stood and walked in. The Entrepreneur yawned as he stood up, took a look around, wondering where everyone had gone, noticed them inside the container, and stood to start over to the container himself. He winched and held his back as he stood. He had attempted to sleep in an awkward position. He hobbled over to the container and went inside, leaving only the Mechanic, the Young, and EX135 still on the deck.

The Mechanic looked over at the Young, then turned halfway around to the cockpit behind the wall he was leaning against. The Young stood and stepped quietly across the entry deck. He tapped the Mechanic's shoulder and waved him toward the storage container. The Mechanic nodded as he looked up at the Young. His eyes grew tired instantly. The Mechanic rolled to his knees and stood one leg at a time. He crossed the entry deck and slipped inside the container, pulling EX135 inside with him. EX135 woke up. "Please leave me outside to collect dust and other materials for life source generation."

The Mechanic looked inside the container. "There is a big pile of sand in here that needs cleaned up. Will that work?"

EX135 buzzed in thought. "That will suffice."

"All right, then." He pulled EX135 into the container.

The Young was now alone on the entry deck. He stepped down into the cockpit. Once down in the cockpit, he took a seat on the ledge that both the Mechanic and the EX135 used earlier. He shifted until he was somewhat comfortable on it. "Are you going to be all right up here, Survivalist?"

She nodded. "Yeah, I am fine."

The Young rubbed his right eye. "You aren't tired after all that stuff today?"

She shook her head. "No. I am honestly wide awake. I feel as fresh as ever."

The Young widened his eyes and subtly shook his head. "All right. Do you want me to leave you alone up here?"

She clenched her jaw. "Not really. It is nice having somebody to talk to. You need to get some sleep, though."

The Young raised his eyebrows. "You got me there."

She chuckled. "Why don't you go get some sleep, then? I will be fine up here. If I fall asleep, this thing will just stop moving anyway when I let go of the controls."

The Young nodded sleepily. He spoke through a yawn. "All right. See you in the morning, then."

"See you then."

The Young stood and left the cockpit. The Survivalist stared blankly out the front of the Torgrog. They were finally to the bottom of the dune they had been on for a while now. She nosed the Torgrog through the sand of the next dune and started up.

*****

After a few more hours of boring piloting, the Survivalist wished she hadn't sent the Young off to sleep. She still wasn't tired. All she wanted to see was something besides the moon, stars, and sand. She peeked down at the compass, which was still sitting on the arm of the pilot seat. It showed they were headed southeast—maybe just a bit more to the east than south. It lined up with the yellow arrow on the screen, at least. She laid her head back against the seat as the Torgrog ascended the last bit of a dune. Maybe she would see something this time.

The Torgrog crested the dune. The Survivalist indolently scanned the dunes ahead. Something caught her eye. It was blue and bright and glowing over the sands. What was it? She glanced down at the busted screen of the Torgrog. A new line of text ran across the bottom:

Arriving shortly at The Oasis.

A rush of excitement ran through her. She twisted the throttle. The Torgrog slid down the next dune a ways.

She heard the group stir inside the storage container. They slowly emerged from the container, each one of them with messy hair, except for EX135, as it has no hair, and the Radioman, whose hair seemed perpetually in good condition. They gathered near the front of the entry deck to peek over the roof of the cockpit toward the blue sign as it bobbed behind the dunes. The dunes were getting progressively shorter as they got closer to the undistinguished high blue blob in the sky.

As they approached, the view became clearer. There was a stone mesa of orange rock sticking out in the middle of the dunes. The shortening dunes seemed to ripple out around the rock as if the massive landmark had been plopped down in a puddle of water. A large flattish building made of a similar orange-colored material as the mesa rested atop the mesa.

Gray beams, likely metal, stuck out from the top of the wall periodically. They seemed to be the supports for the flat roof. The blue blob in the sky was, in fact, a tall pole with a blue neon sign on top of it. The group made out the sign to be a fancy curling font with two words on it: The Oasis. A decorative curl that swooped along the underside of the letters was burned out.

The Torgrog grew ever closer to the mesa, obscuring the view of the building atop it due to the steep angling. The Young pointed to the base of the mesa, which was now visible as they reached the peak of the last dune. "There. There is an entrance." A hole in the base was wrapped with a decorative metal arch. A metal arrow sign outlined in the same blue neon as the Oasis sign pointed into it with the word Enter stuck on it.

The Survivalist guided the Torgrog to the entrance and stopped outside of it. She started a conversation. "What do you think, guys? It could be a trap."

The Mechanic shrugged. "We don't have a choice. We either risk it or run out of fuel and die walking."

The Survivalist nodded. She guided the Torgrog into the gap. It was a tight fit between the walls. Once the Torgrog was inside, a set of lights flickered on above them. One failed to light. A sign was placed on the wall at the end of the entrance. "Please pilot into the elevator below this sign. If no elevator is present, pilot to the gate and await the elevator before boarding it. The gates will open automatically."

The Survivalist peeked back at the group and shrugged. She led the Torgrog to the end of the entrance and onto a large metal pad. The group on the entry deck stared upward at a narrow dot of the night sky through a long chute. Eight sets of cables ran the full length of the chute, two on each side of the square pad. Once the Torgrog got onto the pad, the Survivalist brought it to a halt. Nothing happened. The Torgrog echoed loudly in the tube.

The Hobo tried to yell something at her. She couldn't hear him and thought they were burning fuel pointlessly anyway, so she shut the Torgrog off by letting go of the controls. The Torgrog's engine sputtered off as it slowly lowered itself downward with a high-pitched whistling, gradually lowering in pitch as it went. The Torgrog set itself down onto the metal pad. The pad shifted. A different motor buzzed far away. The cables tightened and began lifting the pad upward. The Hobo spoke once more. "That wasn't what I said, but that will work."

After an extremely slow ascent, the lift reached the top. A man in a grungy, greasy, blackened shirt, a pair of ancient overall jeans, and a hole-infested solid-blue pub hat strolled over and leaned against the entry step of the Torgrog. The Radioman leaned over. The man spoke up. "Hey! You all here for some fuel or what?" The man had a strange, slightly slurred accent that seemed to blend the vowels and neighboring consonants together and ignoring some of the letters at the end of each word, making the sentence sound like, "Yew all 'ere for some feeyool or wah?" instead.

The Radioman raised an eyebrow at his rash tone. "Yes, we do need fuel."

The fuel man chuckled. "Well, I would think so. This is the only place around to get it!" He swept his arm through the air. "Welcome to The Oasis, a place where you can drink and sleep while your vehicle here gets fixed and fueled. There's nothing like it. I will be your fuel man." He grinned back. His off-white teeth clashed with his dirty face.

The Radioman nodded. "You have quite in introduction planned, but you need to be more presentable when you give it."

The fuel man protruded his head forward and leaned on one leg. "What do you mean, red man?"

The Radioman furrowed his brow. "It is maroon, and you are covered in filth. If you want to make a place look respectable and trustworthy, you need to be clean, and bolster your voice."

The fuel man frowned. "Well, if you are so prepared, why don't you give the introduction, then, maroon man?"

The Radioman smiled widely. He swung his foot over the side to the entry step, scooting the fuel man's arm out of the way in the process, and stepped down onto the smooth stone surface of the mesa. He drew in a breath. "Welcome to The Oasis, the place where you can get a fresh drink to quench your thirst, have your vehicle serviced by the best mechanics in the area, purchase the finest fuel around, and even have a place to rest for the night!"

The Radioman elegantly swooped his arm across his chest to guide the attention to the building. He dropped the act and clasped his hands in front of him, facing the fuel man. "I can confidently say those complement, as the competition for your establishment is rather lacking around here."

The fuel man looked back at him in bafflement. "I gotta admit, that was a fine introduction. You proved it to me. I'll work on it." The Radioman nodded with a smile. The fuel man continued. "Anyway, where did you all beat the shit out of this thing? It is an awful mess." The Radioman frowned. The fuel man pointed at him. "Look here, maroon. I said I would work on the intro, not the rest. One step at a time here." The Radioman sighed.

The Mechanic stuck his head over the side above them. "Did you say you offer servicing in fixing vehicles?"

"Yes, sir, I did."

"Perfect. We have a hole on the fuel tank. Needs patched. Think you have the tools to do it?"

The fuel man rubbed his scruffy chin. "Eh, yeah! I do have the patch kit. It came in a while ago, though. I will have to check it."

"Well, get to it."

"It will cost you quite a sum of credits to get the rest of this thing fixed, though."

The Mechanic shook his head. "Don't worry about the rest of it. It is functional, right, Survivalist?"

The Survivalist was unaware that the Mechanic was trying to get out of paying a huge sum of credits. "Well, actually, it needs headlights. The balancing is a little off. There was the strange smoke, but it's gone now. The windshield is completely busted out. The…" She turned around in the seat to see the Mechanic's menacing glare. She caught on. "But really, the only thing that needs fixed is the fuel tank." The Mechanic turned away. "And maybe a quick check on the throttle as it is annoyingly slow on the draw."

The Mechanic shot her an agitated glance. She cowered behind the seat. The Mechanic turned back to the fuel man. "Just get the tank fixed."

"And the throttle tuned!" the Survivalist added from a muffled distance.

The fuel man smiled. He stepped onto the front of the Torgrog and peered in through a hole on the front right. "Heh, an FEC engine. Now ain't that just typical." He hopped down, shaking his head. "All right, then. Tell your girl there to pull this thing into the stall over there. I will get that fixed up for ya. In the meantime, why don't ya take your girl for a drink in The Oasis? We don't get too many women around here." The Mechanic hesitated. "First round on the house as a curtesy of, eh, maroon's introduction over here." He nodded toward the Radioman.

The Mechanic shrugged. "All right. Fine. She's not my girl, though."

The fuel man smiled slyly. "Heh. They never are, big man. They never are." He pointed to the stall.

The Mechanic did not know what the fuel man meant. He ignored it. He motioned to the Survivalist. She grabbed the controls.

The Torgrog surprisingly hummed to life without needing help from the Scorch Torch. The Entrepreneur brushed past the Mechanic. He whispered into the Mechanic's ear. "This guy is going to rip us off on pricing. I am going to haggle him down." The Entrepreneur jumped down the side of the Torgrog as it hovered off the elevator pad. "Now listen here, fuel man. We are on a tight budget here. I can't have you ripping us off."

The fuel man noticed his competitor. "Oh, don't worry, bud. We will treat you right."

The Entrepreneur chuckled. "Oh, you are right there. Come on. Let's talk pricing here." The two started off to the stall.

The Survivalist maneuvered the Torgrog over to the stall and shut it down inside. The group hopped out of the Torgrog. The Mechanic spoke up. "I am going to stay here and make sure this guy doesn't screw us over. I will keep EX135 here. Something about how the factory acted around EX135 tells me we want to keep its presence a secret. I also recommend leaving any weapons here." The group agreed.

EX135 stirred. "If this is the case, please search for a map with our location that I can scan. We are off course. I cannot guide us onward to the proper coordinates from here without a local bearing." The group promised they would and went outside.

The fuel man took a moment from the heated debate with the Entrepreneur to talk to the rest of the group as they came out of the stall. "Drinks are just around the corner. First and only door on your right." The remaining members of the group walked over to the door and went inside.

The inside of the building was quite the contrast to the drab stone outside. Lights—mostly hues of blue, green, and purples—dotted the area to complement the dark furniture. White chairs spotted the room. Surprisingly, other people were seated at tables and the bar. They seemed to be having a relaxing time with conversations among themselves. Each one of the people seemed just as or even more grisly than the fuel man outside.

A waiter, who was shockingly clean-cut and sharp, promptly received them as they stepped in. "Welcome to The Oasis." His voice was smooth and hospitable. "Would you like something to drink?"

The Radioman stepped forward. His maroon outfit turned purple in the lighting. "A fuel man outside sent us in for a free round of beverages while he worked on our vehicle."

The waiter arched his back and raised his eyebrows. "Ah, we have weary guests. Not to worry. We will get you patched up." He swiveled on his heels and guided them to a table near the wall they had come in through. The waiter swung around upon arriving at a wide arch-shaped table. It faced an empty stage illuminated in a soft white light lining the far edge of the room. "Will this table do you finely? We typically place new guest toward the back. It is both a seniority dilemma and a comfort for the new guest who may not be ready to dive into the middle."

The Radioman quickly checked with the group. They seemed indifferent. He turned back to the waiter. "It will do nicely. Thank you." The waiter turned away as they seated themselves. The Radioman pulled a seat for the Bartender. The Young noticed and tried to do the same for the Survivalist, but she shoved the chair out herself before he could act. He stood awkwardly for a moment before choosing the chair next to her. The Hobo and the Old Man wiggled into each seat between the first two groups.

Once they all found their seats, a waitress swiftly questioned them once more. "So what are you all having tonight? Keep in mind, entertainment is on the way. I wouldn't recommend anything too stiff, or you may miss the show."

The Survivalist jumped to life. "Do you have a glass of water?"

The waitress seemed thrown off by this reply. She must have been expecting a more flavorful beverage. "Of course. Are you sure you would like this as your choice? Keep in mind, you are receiving your first round on the house." The waitress politely raised an eyebrow.

The Survivalist shook her head. "The water is fine. We need to rehydrate properly. We have been out for a good while."

The waitress seemed upset. "Oh, that simply won't do. I must do something to compensate for your passing of the more expensive side of the list." The waitress paused. She snapped his fingers and began a gesture to her but quickly caught herself in case it was perceived as rude. "I will bring you an entire pitcher as compensation. That way, you can rehydrate yourself to your heart's content, all while not missing out on a good deal." She scanned the rest of the group. "What about the rest of the table?"

They all shrugged. The Radioman spoke for all of them. "To be quite frank with you, the rest of the group seems to agree with the former order. She is correct, we are in need of rehydration. Perhaps you could bring a few pitchers?" The Radioman grinned.

The waitress began to speak but was cut off by the Radioman's augmentative smile. "Certainly. I will be back with the pitchers promptly." The waitress's smile was no match for the Radioman's. She spun and dashed across the room to a swinging door.

The Hobo leaned on the white silk tablecloth. "Eh, yo, what is this place? It is like we are all out on our first date or something in here."

The Radioman shook his head. "I have not a clue. This establishment seems to have weathered the Crisis as if it never happened." The Radioman glanced down at the Hobo's elbow on the table. The Hobo retracted it instantly. "So you do have manners."

The Hobo smirked. "Yeah. I have never had the luxury to have to use them, though."

The Radioman grinned back. "Then welcome to fine dining."

The Hobo seemed very stiff in his chair. "Is it always this, eh, stressful?"

The Radioman chuckled. "Sometimes, it is. It all depends on why you are there."

The Hobo pulled on his clothes. "I just feel very out of place here."

"Nonsense. There was not a dress code."

"A what?"

"Never mind. You fit in just fine. Relax." The Hobo did the opposite. The Radioman left the poor fellow alone.

A waiter zipped across the room. He expertly and quickly placed three entirely glass pitchers filled to the brim with water onto the silk cloth without spilling so much as a drop. He picked one back up, snatched one of the short, round glass cups placed upside down on the silk, and filled it just shy of the top. He repeated the process as he spoke to the group with eye contact. "The entertainment is soon to begin. Would you all prefer a meal? I must inform you, the meal will be included on the tab."

The Radioman swooped in before the rest of the group had time to think about the question. "I do apologize. We are running short on funds at the moment. I am afraid that after the maintenance to the vehicle outside, we will not have the funds required to feed all six of us with your fine dishes."

The waiter dipped at the waist. "I understand. Do not be worried. Please enjoy the entertainment as you sip your water." The waiter spun and began to slip away.

The Radioman caught his attention with a raised finger. "Excuse me, but would you mind informing me of where all the other patrons have come from this fine evening? Nothing in particular. I am simply not familiar with any of them at all."

The waiter smiled through a curious expression, seemingly wondering who the Radioman was. "Oh, yes, they are from here and there in the Exodust. Each person has their own spot to hide in, as I am sure you are aware."

The Radioman nodded. "Oh, wonderful. I may go meet a few and possibly set up exchanges with them." The waiter bent politely, swiped a freshly emptied pitcher from the table, swiveled on his heels, and disappeared across the restaurant.

A person stepped onto the stage, a woman. She was wearing a brilliant full-length red dress that complemented her brown hair. A group of musicians followed her on stage with their instruments. The room fell silent after turning to face the stage. A smooth jazz plucked its way in.

Sometimes, things go as you hope so.
Sometimes, things go wrong, leave you in woe.
Sometimes, the things that you know.
All go
Out of the window!
But look at this big new world.

The word *world* was dragged out long and smooth, fading off as it reached the end.

Before all this, before all of the disaster,
I was a poor girl in a house of plaster.
I struggled every day
To find some way to pay
My judgmental, cruel master.
But look at this big new world.
Sure, times grew hard,
And now the world is scared.
We all know nothing is the same.
The world has itself to claim,
And the Crisis is all to blame,
But look at this big new world.

The Crisis changed everything.
It did not forgive anything.
The perfect world we once lived in
Is a thing of the past, an old has-been.

But look at this big new world!

The melody settled off. The crowd applauded quietly. The singer on stage sat on a base string's knee. He smiled and began talking to her. A man in a white suit cut the group's line of sight to the stage. He swung a chair around and snappily placed it backward in the center of the arch. He sat down and leaned on the back of the chair with his chest. "Isn't she something?"

The Old Man replied, unfazed, "She sure is. She seems comfortable on the stage."

The man in white, although surprised by how comfortably the Old Man had responded to his unwelcome joining of the table and sudden question, grinned and formulated a response. "She likely is. She has been here longer than some of the cooks." There was an odd pause as the man in white scanned the group's faces. The man in white resumed the conversation. "I haven't seen you all around here before. Are you new to The Oasis?"

The Radioman picked up. "Oh yes, we are new to this crowd, at least. Unfortunately, we will not be able to stay for any period of time. We are merely passing through for the vehicle services."

The man in white seemed saddened. "Oh, you can't leave just yet. Nobody gets to leave without at least meeting our lead singer." He snapped his fingers once above his head.

A waiter promptly met him. "Yes, sir?" The man in white whispered something to the waiter. The waiter nodded. "Right away, sir." The waiter shot across the room to the stage.

The man in white leaned inward. "You all treat her right. She deserves respect." He stood and spun the chair around to a proper position. He pulled it out as the singer from the stage arrived and gently pushed it in behind her as she took the seat.

"How can I help you, newcomers?" Her voice was silky and softly spoken.

The Radioman jumped in. "You wouldn't happen to be the woman with the most wonderful voice in the entire Exodust, would you?" The woman blushed slightly and looked down at the white tablecloth. The Bartender shot a strict stare at the Radioman but quickly wiped it off her face when she noticed the Radioman was on to something. Nobody seemed to notice the gesture, much to the relief of the Bartender.

The woman's cheeks had returned to her tanned skin color. She looked back up, focusing entirely on the Radioman instead of the group in general. "I may be. That is all a matter of opinion, though."

The Radioman cracked a smile and leaned gently into the table with his right forearm. "Look, sweetie, I have no intentions of hurting your feelings here or leading you on. I am sure you were sent over here to try to seduce some information out of us. Please allow me to spare us some time by stating that we do not have any information. In fact, we came here in search of information. Specifically, we need to know where to go to cross the Exodust safely."

The beautiful singer dropped her posture. "I was sent over to get information from you, but then I saw you. This is a different case. I think I might be able to help you"—she slid her hand across the silk to touch the Radioman's right hand—"more than usual." She reached up quickly and pulled a pin from the beautiful bun of brown hair on top her head. Her hair fell in long waves down her bare back, complementing the red dress she was wearing. The Bartender rolled her eyes and sat back in her seat.

The Radioman leaned back in his chair as well with his face stiff. After a pause, the singer dropped her posture but not her attitude. "You are a difficult man to persuade." The Radioman did not respond. The singer continued. "So you don't have any information?"

The Radioman shook his head. "Not in the slightest." The woman hesitated, peeked back over her shoulder, and then leaned in quickly. The Radioman spotted that she glanced back at the man in the white overcoat. The Radioman held up a finger to her lips before she could speak. He took her turn and whispered into her ear. "I understand you are in a bit of a predicament here. My guess is, the man in the white overcoat is your boss. I have a feeling this place is more similar to one we have been to more recently than you might think. I have a proposition for you."

He lowered his finger from her lip and gently poked her exposed chest instead. "You take me to the back room to do your work. Instead, we leave the building. You get on our ride with us and guide us across the Exodust. We will let you go when we get across, and you can do whatever you dream of instead of being held here at a man's bar."

The woman peeked over the thick red strap of her dress on her right shoulder once more. Her hand jumped from the table to the Radioman's hand at her chest. She guided his hand down into the bra of her dress, much to the bewilderment of the Radioman. She spoke in hushed haste. "I am so sorry. This has to look legitimate. Smile for me." The Radioman was paralyzed. "Please!" she begged.

The Radioman's capability to move returned. He shook his head slightly, then cracked a wide smile and a smolder. "Rub it." The Radioman hesitated. "Do it!" she snapped. The Radioman flinched slightly and did as he was told. The woman relaxed. "Thank you. That bought us some time before the boss comes over."

The Radioman swallowed. "I take it this means you have taken the deal."

She leaned further in. She was practically lying on the table. She lifted her right leg off the ground to allow space for her to lean and rested her thigh on the edge of the arched table, straining the dress to reveal the six-inch red pumps on her foot. She jostled his hand. The Radioman continued rubbing. "Sweetie, I just shoved your hand down my dress. Of course it does."

She gave him a quick kiss, slid off the table, pulled the Radioman's hand out of her dress, transferred the hand down to her own left hand by rubbing the Radioman's hand down the length of her arm, and then tugged on the hand she had claimed. The Radioman stood. The woman turned as she rounded the end of the table, pointing her hip visibly, even through the long red dress, then paused while looking dreamily back at the Radioman over her bare left shoulder.

The Radioman turned to the group. "Watch the band or something while you finish off your waters and get to the Torgrog. I will be out soon." The group all turned back to the stage, as they had been turned sideway in their seats to see the spectacle between the Radioman and the woman, but the Bartender remained staring off at the Radioman. The Radioman caught her gaze. His brow grew perplexed. He flicked his eyes toward the woman, gently shook his head while biting his lip, and turned away.

The woman sauntered forward, allowing her arm to raise backward as she tugged on the Radioman's unmoving hand. She pointed over her head at the band. The band immediately picked up their instruments. The base strings began plucking a rhythm, and the band jolted to life. The crowd turned their attention to the stage once more as the woman guided the Radioman along behind them to a door on the far side of the room.

She held the door open and smiled warmly as he welcomed the Radioman in. The Radioman stepped cautiously through the door. The woman winked once at the man in the white overcoat, who smiled in return before redirecting his focus to the band. She then spun in through the doorway behind the Radioman, closing the door softly.

Meanwhile, the group was avoiding staring at the Radioman and the woman as they crossed the room. This was particularly difficult for the Bartender, who couldn't help but peek over once every few seconds at the door the two had gone through. The Hobo couldn't help himself. "Man, how does the Radioman do that?"

The Old Man looked over at him. "I know! The guy is a wizard."

The group quickly and coolly gulped down the last bit of water in their glasses. The Hobo peeked around the room. Nobody was watching. He stood first. The group followed. He motioned them to head to the door. As they passed between the stage, the man in the white overcoat, and the table, he snatched an entire glass pitcher of water from the table and carried it on his right side. His body was broad enough to completely hide the pitcher behind him.

On the way out, the Mechanic noticed a waiter place a tray of meat onto a table with two people. One nodded across the room and spoke quietly to the other. They both stood and left the table. The Mechanic swiftly slid in behind them, swiped up the entire tray, and slipped directly out the door nearby it behind the group.

They scurried over to the Torgrog, which had been refueled, where they stashed the water and food. They realized the Radioman had the credits to pay the fellow with him and explained this to the fuel man, who stated he would not open the stall for them to leave until they paid. They understood and said they would hang out in the Torgrog until he got out to pay him. The fuel man snatched up a mop and headed off to another stall.

The Entrepreneur asked why he was not the fellow carrying the credits anyway. He was the most experienced in the financial field. The group had no grounds to argue him with. Instead, the Hobo revealed the pitcher of water, much to the amusement of the group, and handed it off to the Survivalist. He had the Mechanic retrieve the backpack from the Torgrog and the four empty metal bottles from in it. He had the Survivalist fill them up as he held the bottles steady.

The group let the Mechanic and the Entrepreneur have the rest of the water in the pitcher after filling all four of the bottles to the brim with water. The Mechanic grabbed the glass pitcher and stashed it inside the Torgrog and explained they might use it later. The Bartender retrieved a dried Gorglum fruit from the storage container and bit into it. She puckered her face. The fruit was sour, even after being dried.

She tossed some more fruits and told them to eat them. They had high nutritional value. The Mechanic revealed the tray of meats as well, which the group rejoiced for. They then awaited the arrival of the Radioman while relaxing in the Torgrog under the shade of the stall and enjoying their smuggled meal.

A noise came from the roof of the stall. The group froze and stared up at it. The noise repeated itself but in a lighter impact. The Mechanic retrieved a pistol from his backpack. He stood, aiming out of the stall and over the front of the roof of the cockpit. The footsteps neared the edge. A red flash struck the Mechanic's eye. He withdrew the gun, disarmed it, and quickly stowed it the backpack.

The red flash had been a pair of legs in a dress. The legs fell, revealing a waste of a dress. The Mechanic jumped over the side and went over to the legs to prepare for them to fall. A familiar silky voice called above him. "Hello down there."

The Mechanic looked upward and then immediately back down, as he was directly under the woman's dress. "Hello up there."

The silky voice snickered. "I am sorry for that. I wasn't thinking things through." The ruffle of clothing met his ear. "Can you catch me?"

"Of course. Let me know when you are falling."

"Ha! No, dear. I took care of the dress. Look for yourself."

The Mechanic peeked upward. The woman had pulled the dress tightly and pinched it between her legs. He spotted the top of the Radioman's head. He must be holding her from the top. "Go ahead and drop anytime." The woman peered down at him. She shook her arms and fell back first with a whoosh. The Mechanic caught her easily, but the woman's dress had come free and landed on his head. He blew on it.

The woman chuckled. "This dress is an awful thing, isn't it?" She removed the flap of dress.

"Well, it is certainly pretty. It just isn't the most functional of things."

The woman grinned. "There is no need to sweeten up conversations around me, dear. I honestly prefer it straight to the point." She wrapped an arm around the Mechanic's neck. The Mechanic bounced her to reposition. She giggled. A small dash of sand landed atop the Mechanic's head. He shook it off and looked upward.

The Radioman was standing at the top of the ledge. His suit seemed a royal purple against the night sky with the blue neon bouncing off it. "I hate to be a bother, but can we get this show on the road? We don't have a lot of time until they realize she is gone."

The Mechanic swooped down to the woman in his arms. She grinned and wiggled. He set her down and steadied her until she found a place to rest on the sand-covered concrete in her tall heels. "Hey, how did you manage to crawl out onto the roof with high heels?"

She snickered. "It wasn't easy, but not everything is." She used the full length of her arm to brace against the stall wall in order to stay upright in the sands.

The Mechanic waved at the Radioman. "Come on down."

The Radioman dangled himself off the roof. He checked below him to spot the Mechanic and dropped down. The Mechanic caught him in the same manner he had the woman. The Radioman wrapped his arm around the Mechanic's neck. "Oh, you are so strong. Don't you think this suit lacks functionality?

The Mechanic grunted. "For your best efforts to impersonate our new friend over there, you definitely weigh more." The Radioman raised his eyebrows.

A voice came around the corner. "So is your friend back with my credits?" The voice spooked the woman. She wobbled through the sand and over to the step of the Torgrog. The Hobo reached out and pulled her in. The Mechanic remained still while watching this spectacle, curious as to why she had run.

The Radioman tapped the Mechanic's shoulder. He looked down at the Radioman, whom he had not yet released. The Radioman pointed out the stall entrance. The Mechanic turned his head to spot the fuel man. He turned fully around to reveal the Radioman in his arms. The fuel man was frozen by his puzzlement. "I see you picked up a girl at the bar."

The Mechanic realized at last he was still holding the Radioman. He replied through a chuckle. "Yeah. Ain't she a beauty?" The Radioman had not an ounce of shame. He ran his hand through his hair and puckered his lips toward the fuel man. The fuel man's confusion turned to bizarre discomfort, which, of course, was exactly what the Radioman was hoping for.

The fuel man shook his head and prodded the Mechanic with a question. "In all seriousness, is there a reason you are holding the maroon fellow?"

The Mechanic panicked. The Radioman blurted out a response. "I had a cramp!"

The fuel man found it outstanding that this situation had managed to get even more weird. He pointed at the Radioman. "And that was how you decided to solve said cramp?"

The Radioman nodded. "It was a back cramp. Very painful. I had this brute here pick me up and bend me to fix it, as he is obviously the strongest and most capable to do it." The fuel man opened his mouth in a desperate attempt to say something in reply to this statement. He came up with nothing and shut his mouth. The Radioman reached into his pocket. "I assume you require a payment for this fix?"

The fuel man snapped back to life. "Oh yeah. I patched the hole in your tank. It was a big one. You probably lost a lot of fuel to it by the looks of things. I filled it up to fix that for you. I also tried to fix the throttle, but it was in perfect condition. The issue was the blast burner on the back. It was all gunked up with a bunch of sand and soot from the fuel. Whatever fuel you put in this thing before must have been borderline tar."

He shook his head before continuing. "Anyway, everything you asked for is fixed. I could spend a couple weeks tearing this thing apart and fixing it if you like, but the big fellow holding you there seemed pretty persistent on just having the few things fixed." The Radioman jingled some credits in his hand. "All right, all right. Down to business. It'll be 352—"

"Ah!" The Entrepreneur had popped around the corner.

The fuel man winced. "Three hundred credits."

The Entrepreneur crossed his arms with a grin. The Radioman glanced over at him. He nodded. "Pay him." The Radioman nodded and fished out the three hundred credits. The Mechanic, giving in to the whole back cramp bit, walked the Radioman over to the fuel man. The Radioman transferred a large pile of credits to the fuel man and outstretched his hand. "Thank you for your services."

The fuel man strained to get a free hand out from under the massive pile of coins and shook lightly with the Radioman. The fuel man stood idle for a moment. He found nothing else to say, so he turned and went off toward The Oasis's entrance. Just as he arrived at the door, he turned back and yelled over his shoulder. "Hey! You all are still welcome in The Oasis here. You did getcha free drinks, didn't you?"

The Radioman switched arms around the Mechanic's neck to face the fuel man. "Oh yes, we did. We might be in soon." The fuel man nodded. A strangely troubled expression crossed his face just as he turned away, as if he had missed out on something. He bumped the door in with his side. A few coins jingled onto the ground.

The Radioman slapped the Mechanic's arm. "All right, Mechanic, take me to the Torgrog." The Mechanic realized he was acting as a human transport. He dumped the Radioman into the sand. The Radioman grunted. "I suppose I deserved that one." He stood and brushed himself off. The Mechanic had already begun climbing into the Torgrog. The Radioman joined him.

Once the two were in, the Radioman propped himself against the entry deck wall. He waved to the woman. "Everyone, meet, eh…" He turned to the woman. "I never did get your name."

She laughed briefly. "Don't worry, darling. You aren't the first man to have his hand down my dress before he even knew my name." This shook the Radioman's usually unbreakable confidence. He could sense his skin burning from the Bartender's unrelenting stare. The woman sighed. "Let's keep it simple. Call me the Singer."

The Radioman nodded and awkwardly swung his hand to her. "Meet the Singer."

The group waved nonchalantly. The Young was the only one to speak. "Welcome to our motley crew." The Singer nodded and shyly moved to the edge of the entry deck.

The Radioman tipped his head. "I had taken you to be a more confident one."

She shrugged. "I usually am. I go on stage all the time. I suppose the difference is, I always know what I am doing while I am on stage."

The Radioman nodded. "The Singer has explained to me briefly that she knows a way to get across the rest of the Exodust. We must leave tonight."

The Singer nodded. "As in fire this baby up and get going. We have to get out of here before I am caught and they try to follow us." The Survivalist quickly scurried to her feet and ran to the cockpit.

The Singer watched in incomprehension as the Survivalist passed by her. The Singer waited until she sat down in the pilot seat, watched as the seat adjusted around her legs as before, and finally looked away when the shattered screen lit up. She pointed with her thumb to the cockpit. "You are telling me she is the one to drive this thing?"

The Survivalist turned and shouted out to her, "Firstly, you pilot it, not drive it." She winked at the Mechanic. "Second, I am your pilot tonight. Take it or leave it." She spun back around and grabbed the controls. The Torgrog hovered to life and lurched forward. The Survivalist spoke to herself. "That guy did fix the throttle. Nice." She smoothly guided the Torgrog across the sand and rock to the lift platform.

The Singer looked around at the group. None of them seemed worried as she let go of the controls and the lift started its slow decent. She had to ask. "How long has she been driving...piloting?"

The Entrepreneur sneered. "She started this morning."

The Singer sat back in astonishment. The Young pointed at the Entrepreneur. He paused to wince from the sour of a Gorglum fruit. He spoke with his mouth partially full. "Actually, she technically started this afternoon due to the whole time difference thing."

The Entrepreneur widened his eyes in agreement. "Oh yeah!" He peeked back at the Young. The Singer collapsed down the wall. Regret and stress were having a war on her face.

The Mechanic sat down against the cockpit wall as usual. "Don't worry, though. She has only nearly killed us so far. We are still kicking." Stress won the squabble on her face. The group snickered collectively.

The Hobo sighed. "What a life we are living. I'm sure you have figured this out by now, babe, but you have no idea what you just walked into."

The Singer shook her head. "Please don't call me babe."

The Hobo nodded. "You got it, sugar Gorglum."

The Young looked over. "That doesn't even make sense. These things are so sour." He held out his half-eaten Gorglum fruit.

The Mechanic waved them all off. "All right. That's enough. Let this poor lady get used to this before you hound her. She has a lot to take in." He laid a hand on The Singer's shoulder. It wrapped completely around her arm. "Don't worry, Singer. It isn't all bad here. If there is something you want to know or need, just ask. We will do our best to help you out."

The Singer looked up in grief. "Do your best? That is what I am worried about." The group couldn't help but chuckle.

A metal clunk came from the storage container, followed by a series of mechanic whirs. EX135 stepped out onto the entry deck. "I have run out of sand. The floor is practically spotless." It turned to the Hobo. "The Young is correct, that nickname makes little to no logical sense." EX135 turned to see the Mechanic holding the Singer. She had shot across the room to the Mechanic at first sight of EX135. EX135 stood stiffly. It gestured calmly to the Singer while speaking. "Who is that?"

The Mechanic adjusted the Singer's head on his shoulder. "Uh, this is the Singer. I think this was all a bit much. We will introduce you to her later."

EX135 nodded and sat roughly on the metal floor. "I will resume restoring my systems using the dust particulates in the out-door air." It pulled its knees to its chest and snapped its eyes shut. It became motionless.

The Singer's soft voice muffled through the Mechanic's shirt. "What does that even mean?" The Mechanic seemed concerned. He gently patted her back.

*****

By the time the lift reached the dunes below, the Singer had calmed down. The group calmly introduced her to EX135, which she was very hesitant to be near even though EX135 was still knock-out busy performing silent repairs. She began explaining how to cross the Exodust. "There are Guide Poles across the Exodust. As the name implies, they are used as a guide to navigate the Exodust. I haven't ever actually seen them. I just hear that people follow the poles to get to the coast."

The Mechanic furrowed his brow. "The coast?"

The Singer shrugged. "Yeah, the coast. You know, the place where the Exodust meets the ocean?" The group didn't respond. She sighed and looked away briefly at the tunnel wall. She continued in a partly mocking, partly annoyed tone. "You guys are really lost out here, aren't you?" This received mixed responses. None of them was overwhelmingly positive.

The Survivalist had finally managed to creep out of the tunnel and out onto the sands. She drooped back in the seat to relax. "That whole thing about the poles is great and all, but how do we actually find them?"

The Singer shrugged. "I have no clue. All I know is, they exist. How else would the customers at The Oasis find their way there?"

The Survivalist pointed down at the screen. "We used this screen. This vehicle is apparently equipped with a navigation system."

The Mechanic chuckled. "All long-range vehicles had much more advanced navigation than an arrow on a screen. They showed you every detail of the area around you as well as where you were headed. Unfortunately, this vehicle seems to be primarily designed to follow directions in the dense network of routes back in the factory. It didn't need anything more than a basic arrow direction."

He lingered on a thought. "Actually, now that I think about it, it is very likely that all of those fancy navigation systems are completely offline now. They were all server based. The servers are probably shut down by this point. We probably have one of the only working versions of navigation around."

The Singer agreed. "I didn't get off The Oasis much, but when I did, they would take me for short tours around the dunes to watch the sunset while they served customers. I would sing for them while we went to pass the time. None of the vehicles I was ever in or the ones in the garage that I saw ever had any form of navigation displayed. Some had screens like that, but they mainly showed things like fuel levels and other vehicle statuses."

The Mechanic raised his eyebrows. "Huh. I guess we got lucky, then."

The Hobo sat up. He had been sprawled out across the deck. "Hey. I don't know a whole lot about all of this, but why can't you just ask the Torgrog where the Guide Poles are?"

The Survivalist spoke to the Torgrog. "Hey, Torgrog, do you know where the Guide Poles are across the Exodust?" The screen remained black. After a good while, it lit up with a single line of yellow text across the middle: "Guide Poles is not a destination in database." The Survivalist read the message and relayed it back to the group. She shrugged, causing the seat to goop slightly. "It was worth a shot, Hobo, but it came back with nothing. It says that the Guide Poles aren't in its database."

The Mechanic laid his head back against the wall. "That would be how it still works. It isn't running off the servers. It just knows the area around the factory in a database and compares known destinations with its own coordinates."

EX135 stirred briefly. It spoke. "Incorrect. This vehicle is not equipped with proper coordinate systems. As a factory vehicle, it had no need for them. Instead, it uses distances and direction to locate its current position." EX135, having said his piece, conked back out on the floor.

The Mechanic nodded in agreement. "EX135 is probably right there. Either way, some workers apparently made a run to The Oasis once in a while using this, or at least some part on this vehicle, since it knows where it is. Probably told the Prospector it was for fuel and got drinks while they were there or something." The Singer seemed very perturbed by something in the statement. A few members in the group took notice of this, but no one questioned her.

The Survivalist peeked back. "So does that mean it does not work everywhere?"

The Mechanic nodded. "The navigation will only function in the area around the factory or in places that it has been before. We will run out of navigation soon if we haven't already. Destinations can also be wiped from the database at any time. I am amazed The Oasis was still in it, labeled as a fuel stop."

The Young stretched. He sat up. "Hey, Survivalist, just head to the top of this dune." The Survivalist turned the Torgrog slightly toward the top.

The Entrepreneur didn't understand. "Why are we going up there? I thought we were trying to stay low in case somebody looked out and tried to find us."

The Young yawned. "We were, but I think we should look for these Guide Poles. If no one has navigation systems, there has to be a way to find them."

The Entrepreneur was taken aback a notch. "That's…actually a really good point."

The Young grinned. "I have my moments."

After a slow climb up the dune, the Survivalist stopped the Torgrog at the point of the dune. The sand sagged underneath the downward force of the Torgrog's lift. The group scanned the horizon. The Bartender broke the silence. "Does anyone see anything?"

The Singer replied, "No. I thought this would be easier than this. People never complained about getting lost."

The Survivalist leaned back around the seat. The seat gooped out of the way to make it easier. "Do you think we should—"

"Wait! What was that?" The Old Man had spotted something and interrupted her.

The Mechanic leaned on the entry deck wall. "Where at?"

The Old Man pointed with the staff. "Over that way. I saw a red light for a second. It wasn't a direct line of sight. I just saw the glow above it in the sky."

The Survivalist joined back in. "Can you get me pointed in the direction of it? I will use the compass to head straight at it."

The Old Man nodded. "Yeah. Start turning left. I will keep my eye on it." The Survivalist slowly pivoted the Torgrog counterclockwise while the Old Man directed her. "Keep going. A little more. Hold on. Right there! Woah! You went just a spec too far. It was a long way over there. You need to be lined up perfectly with it. That's it, a little more that way. Hold it! You got it. Head straight that way."

The Survivalist noted the direction of travel by moving a ring with a small notch around the face of the compass to align with the northern needle. This way, she could use the protruding notch as a guide by constantly aligning the northern needle with the notch and would know she was piloting in the proper direction. "How far was it, Old Man?"

The Old Man wavered in his confidence. "I am not sure. It was as far as I could see away and then some."

The Survivalist didn't find this helpful. "Is there any particular landmark you think I could use to help me know if I have gone far enough?"

The Old Man squinted off in the distance. "Eh, there really is not anything of particular uniqueness over where I saw that light." He scanned the area and spotted the stone mesa under The Oasis. "You see The Oasis mesa over there?"

"Yeah?"

"Well, I don't think you will be able to see it when you are out far enough. Just try to keep going until we can't see it anymore."

The Survivalist didn't like this plan. "What if we lose track of The Oasis, don't find the Guide Poles, and can't find our way back?"

The Old Man changed his view to see the Mechanic. "You said that thing can navigate to the places it has been?"

The Mechanic nodded. "Yes."

The Old Man continued. "Does that work at an infinite range since it always knows where it is and can at least point us in the right direction back to The Oasis?"

The Mechanic nodded once more. "Theoretically, yes."

The Old Man shrugged and raised his eyebrows. "Then we should be fine. We can just use the Torgrog's navigation to guide us back."

"That sounds correct to me. Did you get that, Survivalist?"

She leaned around the cockpit seat. "Yeah. I suppose that will work. It isn't like we have a lot of other options here. I will just have to be careful and watch the fuel level." She nudged the steering control and sent the Torgrog sliding down the top bit of the dune.

The Old Man snickered. "You know, that might be the first time I have ever had any idea how to use all this tech. You people were all born into it. I had to figure all this out myself." Nobody replied. Instead, they all started toward the container to sleep.

The Young went over to check on the Survivalist. "Hey, Survivalist."

"Hey."

"You tired yet?"

"Nope."

The Young shot her a look a disbelief. "Oh, come on. You have got to be exhausted."

The Survivalist frowned. "No. I feel fine. I was starting to get a little sleepy while we were in The Oasis, but as soon as we got back to the Torgrog, I felt awake again."

The Young raised his eyebrows. "Huh. Well, I am beat. It has been a long day despite losing all that time to the time difference between the City of Underground and the rest of the world." He yawned.

She replied, "Look, Young, I was getting really bored without you talking to me up here last time I turned down your offer to talk while I piloted, but you really need to get some sleep. It is important that you stay rested. Who knows what we will get into out here?"

The Young furrowed his brow through the remains of a yawn. "What about you?"

She reaffirmed her point. "I already said I don't feel tired."

The Young nodded. "Right. Are you sure you don't want me to stay here?"

The Survivalist confirmed. "Positive. Just go get some sleep. And lay off on the Gorglum fruit. I can smell the sour from here."

The Young smiled sleepily. "You can't smell sour."

She grinned. "You can when it is that strong."

The Young snorted as an initial response. "All right. I am headed off, then."

"Good night, Young."

"Good night, Survivalist. Maybe for real this time."

"Heh. Yeah." The Young crossed the entry deck to the container and stepped inside. The Survivalist sputtered her lips, as the boredom was already setting in. She muttered to herself, "Here we go." A sound caught her ear. She could hear the Bartender chewing someone out. It had to be the Radioman. The Radioman's worried and shaken voice came through for a split second before getting drowned out by the Bartender's angry rants. The Singer's voice yelled over both of them for a moment and then talked briefly. There was the sound of a heavy wad of cloth smacking into something. The Radioman grunted. Maybe this long haul wouldn't be as boring as she thought.

*****

A while later, the Survivalist had finally piloted the Torgrog out far enough out from The Oasis that it was beginning to dip out of sight behind the shifting dunes. The commotion in the back had settled off quickly and left her alone with the Torgrog to pilot. She licked her lips. It was incredibly dry out. It was a good thing that they had water stored up for drinking in the morning.

The chilly night air bit at her nose. It was a good thing the seat was seemingly letting her retain her body heat. She was at least toasty from the shoulders down this way. The uneventful nature of the piloting would normally give her time to think, but she only had two things to think about. The first was the objective at hand of finding whatever caused the red source of light the Old Man had spotted. She was beginning to have serious doubts on ever finding this thing, especially since she had not seen it herself, and the Old Man had not gotten a good look at it.

The second thing, which periodically interrupted the former thought with overwhelming strength, was the sheer acknowledgment of monotony. She didn't mind piloting the Torgrog. In fact, this was a quite enjoyable task for her. The problem was what she was piloting over. It was the same sands, the same shape of dune, and the same night sky for the last few hours. How long did she have to continue before daylight at last relieved her of this lonely passage by awakening those slumbering in the storage container? She truly did not know.

Around another half an hour passed by. At last, she found something at least a little different. The dunes had flattened out oddly into a smooth U shape. It seemed false, unnatural, and far too smooth. She opted to break course a little on the direct compass direction to follow it out of curiosity as to why it had formed. Not long later, a strange, deafening noise shattered the air around her. It was a static sound, starting at a low frequency and sharply rising to a violent shaking pulse and finally cutting off abruptly after the crescendo at the highest point of sound. It stood the hair on her arm on end for a moment and sent tremors through her chest.

She slowed the Torgrog as she observed a terrifying red glow. It ignited the ridges of the dunes in front of her a blistering red color and set the sky ablaze above them. The light then disappeared along with the sound. She stopped the Torgrog. Nothing happened. She turned back to the storage container. One person was stirring in the container. There was a soft metal clank of hard feet walking across the entry deck. EX135's yellow eyes filled the cockpit with a yellow tint. "May I come in, Survivalist?"

The Survivalist was happy to have someone to talk to. "Yeah. Come on in." EX135 took a seat on the ledge. The Survivalist started up a conversation. "Did you finish whatever it was you were doing back there?"

EX135 shook its head. "No. I have done enough for the time being. I must stop once in a while to relax my systems." The Survivalist nodded. EX135 asked a question. "Do you have any insight on what the previous red light was?"

The Survivalist shook her head. "Did you hear it?"

"Yes. I recall the sound from long ago, but I do not know where or why I have this information. I must warn you to proceed with caution. I detect the vague memories I do have are stored within a file marked as dangerous items. This is all I can recall."

The Survivalist nodded. "Whatever it was, it was certainly a powerful thing. It came out of nowhere. It has been the only thing of interest lately. I have been piloting for hours now."

EX135 swung its gaze out the front. "Are you not growing tired?"

The Survivalist shook her head. "I feel like I just woke up. It is an odd feeling, though, like I have been up for too long."

EX135 buzzed for a moment. "From my experience, it is good to shut down and reboot once in a while. It clears the mind and allows a fresh start."

The Survivalist managed a slight grin. "Well, you can shut down any time. It takes humans a good while to fall asleep sometimes."

A mechanical whir met her ears as EX135 nodded. "Indeed." There was a pause. "You are aware that you are still awake due to the pilot seat you are in, correct?"

The Survivalist swung her head over. "What do you mean?"

"The pilot seat is feeding you with energy so that you do not have to sleep."

"What?"

"I do not fully understand how the human anatomy is capable of receiving energy in this manner, but I noticed it is seemingly absorbed into the skin, much like a lotion."

"A lotion?"

"Yes. Does your skin feel soft?"

The Survivalist wiggled in the seat. She realized she had not moved anything but her neck and arms for hours, but she was not sore or stiff. Her skin felt oddly moisturized. "Now that you've mentioned it, my skin does feel very soft. My lips are dry and cracking, but the rest of me is perfectly fine."

EX135 remained still. "I would also wager that you are not hungry."

The Survivalist was growing concerned. "No, I am not."

"You have not eaten in quite some time, yes?"

"I haven't eaten recently."

"The seat is also providing you with nutrition supplements to sustain your health."

"Oh." The Survivalist was momentarily concerned, although she had heard much weirder than this. She accepted the knowledge and moved on.

EX135 struck up a conversation. "Did you know that the same material properties of transferring nutrients and energy was originally implemented in office cubicles to boost work efficiency?"

The Survivalist lit up. A good conversation at last. "No, I didn't."

"It is true. I remember from factory file records. Once the working class discovered this, they all rioted until they removed it from all of the offices and returned to a regular work schedule. They wanted to see their children and spouse mostly."

"Huh. How did the riot go?"

"It was successful. The companies removed the unwanted chair tech and replaced them with normal chairs."

"Well, it worked out, then."

"I suppose that is one derivation to conclude on."

She hesitated. "What do you mean? Are there more conclusions to draw?"

"Oh, of course. There are nearly always multiple aspects to observe in real calculation."

"Can you explain another to me?"

"Certainly. The AOC factory experienced significant production rates, as expected, by utilizing this seat technology. It pushed profits and the technological gains completely off of the previous chart scaling. They were able to make working inhuman hours, such as three days in a row nonstop without even lunch breaks, comfortable to the human performing the work. They assumed the only reason they would ever have to stop working would be due to boredom or the wish to do something different.

"Of course, there were naturally those humans against the idea, as there always seems to be. There was a note explaining that the resisting people had a valid point of the people working becoming living calculation machines. They feared the technology would evolve to completely take over the human mind and force it to run calculations as a form of living, adapting, ever-evolving computation system.

"The people for the chairs, the comfort of them, and the payment they were receiving via the intensive work backed the chairs by stating that the human mind was naturally flawed and could not be trusted to perform complex and critical information on a computer level, and therefore, the human mind would never become a computational unit for business empire, meaning the chairs could stay.

"Doctors proclaimed the mind would go mad with trying to calculate this much. It needed a resting period after so long, or it would burn out. The length of the resting period varied between doctors. Interestingly, none of these things occurred as the people collectively rioted before anything else. The office companies themselves destroyed the chairs to prevent further chaos, but one group was excluded from the destruction called the FEC, or Future Engine Corporation.

"The FEC was an evolutionary derivative of the AOC, hence why protection was given to it. They were testing and developing vehicles like this one at the time using new engine technology the AOC had developed for propulsion rockets. In fact, this vehicle uses an FEC engine, as the person you call the fuel man briefly stated earlier. They quickly gained a monopoly over the vehicles and the engines in them, as no one could understand how they were successfully manufactured.

"Even if an individual had obtained the proper recipe, it would not have made any difference, as creating the manufacturing plant to produce these engines would take such an insurmountable number of credits that no small business could afford it. Since no small engine business could surpass the FEC monopoly on the engines, as their own engines were ultimately inferior, they would never be able to successfully obtain the funds needed for the factory.

"Despite all of the potential hatred directed at the FEC, the office world knew that the FEC was producing groundbreaking vehicular transportation that would further assist them in transporting workers to and from the offices. This meant faster shift changes and potentially longer workdays without the need for the controversial chair. Hence, they allowed the FEC to keep the chair under the claim that it was for pilot and passenger safety with the obvious intentions of trying to get more production instead. They proclaimed drowsy driving would be a thing of the past.

"This coincidentally worked and took off, furthering the padding in the FEC pocket, but not necessarily helping the offices. It got to the point that all original FEC vehicles were recalled and installed with this new seat, which received a very dull name of Self-Adjusting Cockpit, or SAC seat, pronounced informally as the Sack Seat by the common individual.

"I would not have been surprised if a law was in the works before the Crisis to require all vehicles to have the seat, although there is no evidence of this. This is also the very seat you are sitting in right now, but this SAC seat seems particularly attached to helping you. Most SAC seats do not prefer to assist the pilot in the excessive manner that this one has for you." The two went silent as the Survivalist tried to understand everything that was just thrown at her.

The Torgrog reached the top of the dune. It tipped over the top. A massive rusty pole, supported on the bottom by four diagonal beams in a tent shape, protruded upward from the sands below. A large chunk of concrete was just barely visible at the base of the beam, nearly blending in with the pale colors of the night sands.

A sparkling material surrounded the base, reflecting the moonlight. It was situated in another one of the smooth U-shaped areas between the dunes. The top of the pole was glowing-hot red and dwindling off to a black. It was a smooth, clear cylinder with a blackened metal cone flush with the edges on both the top and bottom. The bottom cone tapered down to meet the rounded support pole. The upper cone did not form a point. It instead formed a cone so far up and then flattened off, much like an inverted drinking cup.

Heat lines squiggled off into the air above it. Once it cooled and the redness had dispersed, the middle cylinder revealed itself to be hollow on the inside. The whole thing contained another burnt black metal substance with a small feature protruding out on one side. The protrusion was the most heavily burned piece on the entire structure.

The Survivalist glanced over at EX135 as she brought the Torgrog down to the structure. "Do you have any idea what that thing is?"

EX135 gazed off at the structure while speaking. "It emitted the same sound as the strange sight the Old Man spotted before. I assume it is the Guide Pole."

The Survivalist remembered the conversation with the Singer. That seemed so long ago now, yet it was in the same night. "Oh yeah! Hey, go get the group. We need to make some decisions." EX135 buzzed as it stood and stepped back through the entry to the cockpit.

A moment later, the group clambered back out of the container and onto the entry deck. They all scrutinized the pole in front of the Torgrog. The Hobo gestured down to the base of the pole. "What is with the sparkly stuff down there?"

EX135 suddenly vaulted out of the Torgrog and trotted over to the pole. It bent and picked up a small piece of the glittering material. "It is glass. This device must have cooked the sands here to extreme temperatures. Straight lines of this thin glass are burned through the dunes around this pole."

The Old Man held up the Lightstaff and turned it on to flood the area with light. Thousands of pieces of glass glittered back. The group stared off in awe. "What is this thing doing?" asked the Bartender. No one replied. EX135 tapped the pole with the back of its left hand, resulting in a small plinking sound. It trotted back to the Torgrog and threw itself over the entry deck wall.

It glanced over at the Singer. She was cowering in the back of the storage container. EX135 approached the container entrance. "Do not fear, Singer. I understand you have likely had poor experiences with my kind in the past. I bring no harm to you."

The Singer spoke quietly. "How can I trust you?"

EX135 straightened its back and bent again to peer through the door. "If I wanted to find you with malicious intent, you would already be dead."

This did not comfort the Singer, but it was a powerful argument. She stood and crossed the container. She reached out and touched EX135's chest. EX135 peeked down awkwardly at this. She shoved EX135 out of the way. "You are just as cold as the rest of them."

EX135 was not affected by her insult. "That is because, much like you, I have no heart."

The Singer scoffed. The Young chuckled in the corner of the entry deck. The Mechanic stepped between them. He pointed to the pole. "Is that what you were talking about earlier, Singer?"

She nodded. "That seems to be what I have heard about. There should be another one nearby."

The group scanned the area but found nothing. EX135 pointed down the U-shaped path in the dunes. The Old Man followed its finger and again found nothing. The Old Man turned, perplexed, to EX135. "What are you pointing at?"

EX135 pivoted to face the Old Man while keeping his pointed arm locked on the same direction. "The next Guide Pole."

"How do you know where that is?" asked the Bartender.

EX135 turned to face her. "This pole is emitting an infrared signal."

The Radioman perked up. "You can find it like a radio tower?"

EX135 nodded. "The signal increases in strength as we approach it. I did not know the origin of the signals before getting this close to the source. The next most powerful signal is coming from this direction." EX135 turned back to the way it was still pointing to. It spoke once more. "I am curious to know if one of the Guide Poles is located at the coordinates I found in the factory. I have no way of knowing for certain."

The Survivalist shrugged. "Either way, getting to the next pole is good enough for me." She nudged the throttle and started along the U-shaped cut in the dune. A short bit later, the Torgrog passed by another Guide Pole. EX135 had joined the Survivalist in the cockpit and pointed her to the next. The group went back to sleep in the container.

A few more drab hours of piloting met the Survivalist. The U-shaped cut in the dunes seemed to follow the Guide Poles. She found intersections of these cuts, some of which had up to eight directions to go in, which EX135 promptly guided her through to the correct path. She concluded that this might actually be duller than crossing the ridges of the dunes. At least when she was guiding the Torgrog over the tops of dunes, there was a small element of slipping to control that could hold her attention. Now it was largely keeping the Torgrog headed in a straight line.

She did notice that none of the other Guide Poles appeared to be hot when they approached them. The first one must have been activated recently to create the light source she had seen. She wondered what these poles did that would be making so much heat.

A low rumble interrupted her thoughts. She hadn't found anything like that before out there. Small patches of sand tumbled down the dunes nearby. She stopped the Torgrog. The rumble seemed to have disappeared while she slowed down. She nudged the throttle to allow the Torgrog to creep forward. The rumbling did not return. What could have possibly caused that strong reverberation?

She twisted the throttle again to return to her previous pace. Another rumble. This one was stronger than the first. She slowed to a stop once more before the rumbling could disappear. The Torgrog had absorbed the smaller vibration from before without shaking, but these tremors were strong enough that she could feel a faint shaking through the steering control. She glanced around out the front. She checked the screen. Neither returned anything of interest.

She remained still as the shaking wore off and looked back out of the cockpit by leaning far out around the seat. No one seemed to be worried in the storage container, or at least they weren't moving. She looked back out the window. Her shoulders tensed with indecision on whether to move the Torgrog or remain perfectly still.

Another rumble. This one beat the previous two by a large margin. It shook the entire Torgrog despite its best efforts to stabilize. Objects clanged and beat against the wall of the storage container. Someone stirred. She peeked back around the seat. The Singer was fumbling through the darkness of the container. She rushed across the moonlit entry deck and jumped down into the cockpit.

"Survivalist, shut this thing off!"

"What? I am—"

"Do it now!"

"No. We need—"

"We need to shut down! There is a Sand Eater nearby!"

"A what?"

"A Sand Eater! Come on. Let go!" She was yanking on the Survivalist's arm.

The Survivalist released the steering control. The Torgrog settled down onto the sands and emitted its typical high-pitched whine, descending in tone. The Survivalist shot an annoyed glance at the Singer and whispered to her, "What has you so worked up?"

The Singer didn't respond immediately. She was swinging her line of sight wildly out the front of the Torgrog in search of something. "The Sand Eaters, they don't just eat sand."

The Survivalist had no clue what she was on about. "What? Hold on. What is a Sand Eater?"

The Singer didn't answer immediately. She was busy listening for something. She responded a moment later. "They are like, uh, giant, flexible tubes with really tough skin." A tremendous tremor trembled the Torgrog. The Singer cowered into the cockpit. "That is the Sand Eater."

The Survivalist took the Singer's place in scanning the dunes. "Are you telling me that those rumbling sounds and vibrations"—she pointed out the front of the Torgrog—"are caused by a giant creature digging around?" The Singer nodded. Angst filled her face. The Survivalist scanned the dune again. "What do we do about it?"

The Singer had braced herself into a corner of the cockpit. "We hide."

"Where?"

"That would be the problem."

The Survivalist realized what was happening. Their only hope was to avoid being found. She turned her head to face the Singer. "How good are our chances of getting out of this alive?"

The Singer shook her head. "Poor."

"Have you ever seen one of these things before?"

"Yes."

"So you knew about them before we came out here?"

The Singer nodded guiltily. "Yes. Think about it. Why else would they have built The Oasis on top of a massive mesa of rock?"

The Survivalist was having a difficult time with refraining from yelling at her. She managed to keep her whisper but with an angered tone. "Then why in the hell did you not tell us about them before now when one is nearby?"

The Singer tucked her knees to her chest. "I feared losing my chance to run from The Oasis if I told you. If you knew about the Sand Eaters, then you would have never asked to leave tonight."

The Singer boiled with anger. "So you kept us in the dark, put us all at risk, for your own escape?"

The Singer cringed. The Survivalist's tone alone was packing enough heat to scare her without even needing to raise her voice. She hesitated. The Survivalist glared over at her. She quietly admitted defeat. "Yes."

The Survivalist was fuming. The cockpit seat stiffened around her. She released a long breath from her nose and closed her eyes. "We will talk about this with the group later. What do we need to do now?"

The Singer pointed downward. "Nothing. We stay put and remain as quiet as possible and hope it leaves."

"And if it doesn't leave?"

"We hope it doesn't find us before daylight. Sand Eaters have tough skin, but it burns them to be in the sunlight."

"And if we do get caught?"

She shook her head. The Survivalist understood and slid down into the seat. "Don't get caught," the Singer muttered.

A small noise came from the storage container. The two in the cockpit turned to observe the source. EX135, who had left the cockpit a little while ago to check in on the crew in the storage container, stepped out, desperately trying to keep his metal feet quiet on the similarly metal floor of the entry deck. It dropped to a knee and peered into the cockpit, causing the Singer to shuffle away from the entry. "It seems we have stopped. What seems to be the matter?" Another tremor shook the Torgrog. EX135 scanned the area. "It appears we are having problems with the ground shaking."

The Singer shook her head. "The shaking isn't the issue. The problem is what is causing the shaking."

EX135 stood to spot any movement on the dunes from over the top of the cockpit roof. It crouched back down shortly after. "I detect no movement on the outside."

The Singer again shook her head. "You wouldn't find anything on the surface."

EX135 grew puzzled. "What exactly are we dealing with?"

The Singer became minorly frustrated. "Sand Eaters. Do you know what those are?"

EX135 remained puzzled. It stood once more to investigate another vibration. It spotted something. "Would it happen to be the large, wriggling creature headed toward the vehicle?"

The blood drained from the Singer's face. She flipped around, leaned out of the hole that used to be the front windshield, and spotted the incoming creature. "Ah, no!"

EX135 latched its hand into a bar across the roof of the Torgrog. "Oh dear." It turned to the Survivalist. "I assume I am correct. I would recommend starting up the Torgrog and running."

The Survivalist looked over at the Singer for confirmation. The Singer swatted her arm, grabbed it after the fact, and forced it toward the steering controls. "Go! Grab the steering!" The Survivalist panicked and snatched the steering. The Torgrog hummed back to life. She nudged it forward slowly. The Singer chuckled nervously. "No, no, dear. The time for creeping is over."

The Survivalist's wide smile did not comfort the Singer. She cranked the throttle, sending the Torgrog into a flurry of jerks and bustles as the rear burner lit. It shot forward in the direction it was headed before, sending EX135 flying backward. Had EX135 not been holding on to the ceiling, it would have flown right out of the cockpit.

The vibrations increased. Sheets of sand began slipping down the dunes in front of the Torgrog. The steering shook. The Survivalist yelled over the cacophony of sounds to the Singer. "What is this thing going to do?"

The Singer shrugged. "I have no idea! All I know is that people die to them!"

"Well, that is helpful!"

The Singer was too busy hanging on to the narrow ledge she was sitting on to respond to the sarcasm. The Torgrog was increasing to a blinding speed in the literal sense as the agitated sand in front of the Torgrog needled into their skins. EX135 stood as if nothing was happening while the two women curled up to shield their faces. A voice yelled from behind. The Survivalist recognized the Mechanic. "Survivalist, what are you doing?"

He stepped out onto the unstable entry deck and wobbled his way across by holding the entry deck wall. He paused halfway and stared back behind the Torgrog with a shocked expression. He muttered something incoherent under his breath. He noticed the Singer shielding her face from the sands. He couldn't help but wonder where all this sand was coming from. The Torgrog usually did a good job at keeping any debris or particles like this out of the cockpit and entry deck.

He didn't have time to think more about it. He scurried back into the storage container. He appeared a moment later holding a medium-sized flattish black object in his hand, which he toted across the entry deck with him to the cockpit. He squeezed past EX135 and swatted the Survivalist's shoulder with the metallic thing. She glanced down and snatched it with her right hand, keeping her left hand on the controls. "What is this? I can't see very well!"

The Mechanic hunkered down under the dashboard as best he could and replied, "I know you can't see! It's a mask with a sealing lip around it! Strap it onto your face!"

The Survivalist fumbled with the mask until she found an elastic strap on the back side of it. She pulled it over her face and looked up at EX135, thinking it had given it to her. She jumped away when EX135 met her gaze. "These are night vision goggles, not a mask! EX135's eyes are completely blinding to these things." The Survivalist straightened the Torgrog. It was drifting sideway slightly due to a slope in the dune it had found while the Survivalist was putting on the goggles.

The Singer was still shrinking away from the sand. The Mechanic grabbed her. "Come on! There is only one pair of those! We need to get back in the container for shelter!" He pulled on the Singer. She stood while shielding her face with her free hand and blindly followed him. EX135 slipped past the two of them and latched into the narrow ledge while the Mechanic and the Singer left the cockpit.

The Survivalist briefly looked back to the entry deck, flinching as she passed by EX135's eyes, and saw the swirling sands engulfing the deck. She saw the Mechanic's foot disappear into the sands. She assumed he had made it, as she couldn't see the container, and snapped back to piloting the Torgrog. EX135 shut its eyes as she swung her head back. EX135 somehow managed to make its voice louder without yelling. "Survivalist, I can guide you to the nearest Guide Pole. I would not recommend leaving the current path, as we will quickly become lost."

The Survivalist didn't like the sound of that plan. "Do we have any other options here?"

EX135 buzzed. "Leave the path and become lost."

The Survivalist grinned and spat sand out onto the floor. "Well, that narrows it down. Where to?"

"Follow the…" EX135 paused as the tremors stopped for a moment. It stuck its head out of the window. The pause in the shaking was promptly followed up by a violent section of shaking. Sand flurried into the air all around. EX135 retracted its sandy head back into the cockpit. "I now remember what a Sand Eater is." The Survivalist glanced over. EX135 continued giving out instruction. "Go faster." She cranked further on the throttle.

"I will relay a log I found in the factory terminal to you. Sand Eaters are an organic life-form. They are a flexible cylindrical life-form and have a thick hide that prevents their skin from being worn off as they burrow through the rough sands. They are equipped with a large circular mouth on the front of the body. They are fully capable of digesting anything they can get in their mouth, even strong acids and bases, and have an incredibly strong biting force to take chunks out of objects. I assume that would include this vehicle.

"They are known to track moving objects that are disturbing the surface, such as this vehicle, and typically hunt the prey by leaping out of the sands and crashing back down onto it, as you just felt, which causes the artificial cloud of sand you are experiencing. This allows the Sand Eater to trap or disorient—"

"Hey, get to it here! We are about to die. Skip to the part where you tell me how to get away."

EX135 straightened, visibly taken aback by the sudden snap it had received but did as it was told. "Continue along this path to the next Guide Pole. It is straight ahead."

The Survivalist readjusted her grip on the throttle to allow her to twist it further. The sand pelting the Torgrog sounded like ripping paper. She was glad the cockpit blocked the sand from her legs and most of her upper body while the goggled protected her face. The sand would be tearing her skin apart. EX135 gave another insight. "You will be passing by the Guide Pole soon."

Something stationary whooshed past the Torgrog on the right side. The Survivalist jumped. "Can you keep me a little bit farther away from those?"

EX135 nodded. "Yes. Please bank right long."

"Right what?"

"Bank right long."

"What does that even mean?"

"Bank right long: to perform a banking right-hand turn around a long corner."

She started right. "This thing can't do banking turns! Why don't you just say to go right around a long turn?" She did her best to guide the Torgrog around the right turn.

"Far too time-consuming. Compensating for nonbanking vehicle motions. Flat adjust left."

The Survivalist tweaked the Torgrog to the left. "Like that?"

"Yes."

She shook her head. "Whatever. It is working, then. Just keep going!"

"Flat left medium."

The air became suddenly clear, visible all the way to the moon. "What happened to the sand?"

"You have escaped the sand cloud I previously explained. Expect another soon. Increase speed while clear."

Right on cue, the vibrations paused, then erupted in another violent shaking. The Survivalist jerked the steering to straighten the Torgrog. "That one was stronger! How close is it?"

EX135 stuck its head back outside. It retracted it. "Too close."

The Survivalist slapped the back of her head against the seat. She peeked down at the shattered glass over the screen. The screen had adjusted to become darker in order to compensate for the night vision goggles. No errors were on the screen. She pushed the Torgrog further. "Look, I don't know how much faster this thing can handle going."

"Flat right long into flat left short. Reduce speed to round bend." The Survivalist released the throttle to allow it to spin back to neutral. It clicked into a halt. She twisted it again to get some torque for the turn, allowed the Torgrog to glide a little, and throttled back out of the turn. "Guide Pole incoming. Move left." The pole whooshed past. A white spotlight illuminated the area around the Torgrog. The Survivalist squinted as the night vision goggles compensated for the new brightness. The light shot away.

EX135 stuck its head back out to see the light sweep back to a raging wave of sand blasting from the ground behind the Torgrog. The cone of light snapped onto the moving sand and focused down a thick beam. It blinked into a vibrant red. The top of the Guide Pole glowed red. A massive red beam blasted out of the top of the pole, following the red tracing beam directly down to the sand wave in an instant.

A burning sound filled the area, followed by a low static frequency as it shot up in tone and became an enormous pulsing blast, painful to the ear, as the beam became even brighter. The entire area turned red as the beam grew in power and traced the sand around the wave following them. It suddenly shut off, leaving only the roaring engines of the Torgrog and the rumble of the Sand Eater behind them. The rumbling sound slowed and disappeared as the Torgrog sped off.

The Survivalist relaxed the throttle. She looked over at EX135 as the engines calmed down to their typical puttering pattern. "What was that?"

EX135 retracted its head into the vehicle. "It was the Guide Pole. They are apparently equipped with a similar technology to that implemented into the Lightstaff, only it is far more powerful and a larger scale. It emitted a beam that burned the Sand Eater and sent it packing." It pondered off. "What could power such a device of that magnitude?"

The Survivalist shrugged. "I don't know. Are we safe?"

EX135 nodded. "For the time being, yes. I would recommend searching for a shelter to weather the night in. It is important that we are inside of something so that the vibrations we or the Torgrog may make are too muffled for the Sand Eaters to follow. It would be very helpful if the floor is also made of a harder material, such as concrete and not sand."

The Survivalist nodded. "Stopping for a bit sounds good to me. I need to relax from the stress." The seat instantly started massaging her. She sighed. "Can you go see if the group is all right back there again and then come back to guide me? We will just stay on this path following the Guide Poles until we find something. It is the safest thing to do."

"Certainly." EX135 stood and left the cockpit.

The Survivalist lay back in the seat a little as it worked her thighs. She sighed once more. "Oh, I hope we find something out here." The Torgrog continued puttering through the U-shaped path in the dunes.

*****

The Survivalist gazed off across the dunes. She had spotted a collapse in the side of the U-shaped path that she could easily get the Torgrog up and had stopped for a moment to search for structures. Nothing yet, just another thousand dunes.

She sighed. She was not bored of piloting the Torgrog, but a change of scenery would be nice. The Exoduster had been talking to her to fill the time but had left the cockpit recently. She wished the Exoduster had not gone off to do whatever it was it had to fix about its systems. She had questions to ask it. She peeked back around the cockpit to look across the entry deck at the storage container. She could see right into the darkness of it with her night vision goggles. The group seemed to have returned to sleep. EX135 was nowhere to be seen. It must be braced up against the wall somewhere.

A small pile of sand filled the bottom of the doorway to the storage container. The entry deck itself was covered in a thick layer of shifting sands. She turned back to look out the front. She began to nudge the Torgrog back down the bank, but something caught her eye. She strained her eyes to see it. Far off, nearly as far as she could see over the dunes, there was a small blip interrupting the sands. If it was large enough for her to see, they could probably hole up in it for the rest of the night.

Now that she thought about it, it had been dark for hours. Daytime must be coming around sometime, so maybe they didn't need the shelter anymore. She looked back at the group. They were all lying on the hard floor of the storage container, sharing the cots as best they could. None of them looked comfortable. They could probably use a break from this waiting anyway even if they stayed a day or two in shelter somewhere.

She looked back out to the blip on the horizon. It seemed to be in the direction they were headed anyway. She decided to swing by it when they got near it. She nudged the Torgrog and sent it slipping down the sandy dune. Something about the sudden shift caused a stirring in the storage container. The familiar sound of metallic footsteps came across the deck. EX135 poked its head through the doorway, making sure to look down at the floor to avoid blinding the Survivalist in her night vision goggles. "Would you care to continue our conversation, Survivalist?"

The Survivalist glanced over at EX135. "Yeah. Why not?" EX135 took its place on the ledge inside the cockpit. The Survivalist looked out to the blip far off on the moonlit horizon. "You see that thing out there?"

EX135 followed her pointed finger. "Yes. It appears to be a building of some kind, likely of AOC origin."

That was far more than the Survivalist was hoping for. She had to ask. "Can you actually see that far?"

"No. I can see no farther than the human eye on average."

"Then how can you tell what kind of building it is?"

"I cannot for certain. It is only an approximation based on the location and our previous crossings with these structures."

"Oh. So it is a guess?"

"I suppose you could call it that."

The Survivalist chuckled. She realized that EX135 hated not being able to properly deduce exact answers to questions. She shook her head and changed the subject. "What did you want to talk about?"

EX135 straightened upright in its seated position. "Ah, yes, the Hypersol! It is used to power the Guide Pole beam we encountered."

The Survivalist had not a clue what a Hypersol was, but it was a conversation to break the boredom. She jumped in on the conversation. "A Hypersol?"

"Yes. It is the only thing capable of producing the required power in this hostile environment."

The Survivalist grew curious. "All right. How does it work?"

EX135 emitted a strange whirring vibration. "I am uncertain of the exact details. I do know that the Hypersol functions as a converter between solar energy and electrical power. It harvests the sunlight to produce massive amounts of electrical power. The power is then saved in an energy bank, like a large battery, and upon the energy bank filling up, it shuts off. The only downfall is, it tends to overheat with long durations of usage and must periodically shut off due to the strain the heat puts on the components."

The Survivalist nodded. She was just happy to talk to somebody, but this was interesting enough to pursue. "I see. Can it charge throughout the entire day and take a break at night?"

"No. It fills the energy bank far too quickly for that. Maybe a few hours. I have no way of knowing for certain without checking the system it runs on directly."

The Survivalist furrowed her brow. "Huh. Can you tell how many shots it can fire before emptying its battery?"

"No. Also, it is called an energy bank."

The Survivalist rolled her eyes subtly. "Could we steal one and put it on the Torgrog?"

This must have been an interesting question, as EX135 did not respond immediately. After a moment of thought, EX135 responded. "I had not considered this possibility, but I would say this is a hazardous idea. The Hypersol would cause an excessive amount of heat for the vehicle to handle. The Guide Pole, even with the top portion removed and attached exclusively, would take up a large amount of space. I have problems with trusting the Guide Pole to not scorch us at a whim."

The Survivalist didn't like the sound of any of this. "So that is a no?"

"With the knowledge I have, I would advise against the idea."

The Survivalist grunted. She gently accelerated the Torgrog to continue down the U-shaped cut in the sand. Something about how smooth the shape of the path was provoked the Survivalist to ask another question. "What about this path we are on? How does it stay this, oh…" She gestured toward the dune, tracing its curve with her finger.

EX135 finished her sentence. "Smooth?"

"Yeah!"

EX135 thought this over. It replied a moment later. "Based upon the crystalline glass shards littering this entire path, I can deduce that the same Guide Poles we are following have gradually formed this over the many years of their existence. They must be programmed to burn away the sand by blasting it with the same red beam we have found before.

"In turn, the sand instantly flashes into glass and bursts due to the drastic temperature change as it cools. The result is a denser layer of sand and glass shards. The circular shape likely formed as the beam is only effective at a certain range away. The beam sweeps the surrounding area, but as it rises, the effective range is reduced, resulting in the burning effect only working in a motion, much like swinging a stone on a string in a circle."

The Survivalist nodded. "Why do the Guide Poles care if they are buried partly in sand?"

"The Guide Poles are not capable of individualistic thought like myself. Instead, they follow rigid coding. However, the coders who created them likely implemented this concept to prevent the Guide Poles from being completely encased in sand dunes. It also increases the potential to burn a Sand Eater, which is their primary purpose, I suppose."

"Ah." The Survivalist went silent. She really did not have any more questions to ask EX135 at the moment. EX135 must have picked up on this, as it gently tapped its knees with the palms of its hands to create a soft clanking sound. It reached up and tweaked a black hose running through its neck, much like somebody fixing the collar on their shirt.

It glanced up for a brief moment to see if the Survivalist had anything more to say before redirecting its gaze right back to the floor to avoid blinding the Survivalist in her night vision goggles. It must have sensed an urge to leave as it nodded and rose to its feet. It slipped over to the entrance to the cockpit. "Let me know if you require assistance, Survivalist. The path ahead seems to have no branches."

She nodded. "Will do." EX135 stepped across the sandy entry deck with unnatural balance.

*****

A long while later, the Survivalist at last spotted something other than the dull night sands. It was a rust-stained edge line on the concrete walls and roof of a building. It was a very flat roof, nearly perfectly level, but it had been chipped away by something, likely the sand beating on it. She guided the Torgrog up another collapse in the U-shaped path, much like the one she had spotted before but on the right side now. The building itself might have been once a dull gray or a white color, but it now stood as an unevenly stained tan color.

The Survivalist looked the building over and found an ancient logo painted on the wall. She could just make out that it had once read AOC on the top and biggest font, but the remaining bits of the smaller subscript below it hinted that another message had been completely wiped away. She nudged the Torgrog over. It tipped abruptly over the edge of the U-shaped path and slapped with a lurch against the sand on the far side of the dune. She heard the muffled sounds of her friends tumbling through the storage container behind her, followed by some brief, incomprehensible, but obviously complaining voices.

She slowed the Torgrog to a halt nearby the base of the towering square structure in front of her. A line of windows remained amazingly intact near the roof, although she could see nothing through them for the scratches. She noticed a large door on the far side, originally painted green but now faded drastically and smoothed to the ugly gray color of the metal underneath. Rust streaked down the door wherever there was a long vertical patch of exposed metal, but even it had been smoothed to a reddish-brown smudge on the door.

She rolled the Torgrog over to the door and released the steering control. The Torgrog emitted its characteristic whine as the engines shut down. The Survivalist lay back into the seat. It gave way to let her sink in. She pushed the right side over as she stood from the cockpit. For the first time in ages, she moved her legs. She grunted and winced as they slowly stretched back out to proper use.

A weight of sleep suddenly slammed into her. She nearly fell asleep right where she stood but snapped awake to avoid falling over. She tried to rub her eyes but found the goggles were still on her face. She removed them and placed them on the edge of the seat. She started forward out of the cockpit but instead froze where she was. She spoke to herself in shock. "Man, it is still really dark out here."

An uninvited voice commented, "Yes. It has been for quite some time now. Any clues as to how long we will be in the dark?"

The Survivalist recognized the Radioman's voice. "I don't know, Radioman. I don't remember when it got dark. I have had these goggles on." She held the metal goggles out and shook them when rubbing her forehead with her left hand. The Radioman stood still without a word. The Survivalist realized she hadn't explained what the goggles were in the rush earlier. "They are night vision goggles. I can see in the dark with them pretty much like it is daytime but with a strange gray haze. It is like looking through a thick smog. It is still way better than piloting in the dark, though."

The Radioman raised his chin. "Ah! How do they treat your eyes after the fact?"

The Survivalist squeezed her temples. "They have given me a slight headache, and my eyes feel like they are going to pop out of my head."

The Radioman nodded. "Just a moment." He swiftly spun and stepped back into the storage container.

The Survivalist placed the goggles back onto the seat. The seat instantly ate the goggles with a gooping sound and protruded her hatchet, compass, and rope with hook. She equipped her things. She stepped blindly onto the entry deck with a large wobble. Her foot slipped in the sand covering the deck, causing her to jump and snag the roof of the cockpit in recovery. Her legs felt very odd, like she was losing control of them.

She overheard some muffled voices in a gentle conversation. The Bartender stepped out of the storage container with a Gorglum fruit in her right hand. She leaned against the outside of the container to stretch and yawn. The Survivalist yawned with her. The Bartender picked her way through the sand using the faded footsteps left by EX135. She held the Gorglum fruit in her outstretched hand so that it rested freely in her palm. "If you drink the juice out of this, it will wake you up, and that headache will be good as gone. As for the eye problem, I have no idea."

The Survivalist hesitated. "How long will the waking up part last?"

The Bartender shrugged. "How tired are you?"

"I nearly fell asleep standing up a moment ago."

The Bartender chuckled. "It won't last you all that long, then."

The Survivalist took the Gorglum fruit and rotated it about casually to observe it. "I thought these were dried?"

The Bartender nodded. "They are, but there is typically still a little bit of juice left in them. It will be enough to help you out."

"How do you get the juice out of it?"

"You crush it." The Bartender took the Gorglum fruit back, turned to the cockpit wall, held it against the wall with her left hand, and smashed it with the side of her right hand in a fist. Some green liquid dripped out. She handed it back to the Survivalist, who held it straight above her head while looking upward with her mouth open to catch the dripping liquid.

She squeezed the fruit a bit to force out some juice and winced as soon as it landed on her tongue. She shut her mouth, baring her teeth and puckering up at the same time. The Bartender laughed heartily. Once her laughing subsided, she patted the Survivalist's left shoulder with her right hand. "Isn't that awful?"

The Survivalist was not impressed. She wiped some of the green stain from her lips and coughed a few times. She cleared her throat. "Yeah, it really is."

The Bartender raised an eyebrow. "How is the headache?"

The Survivalist snapped her gaze up to meet the Bartender's. "It's...gone. Completely." A bewildered look ran her face.

The Bartender seemed contented. "Good. Now eat the rest of it to keep it away." The Survivalist glanced nervously down at the rest of the fruit in her hand. The Bartender laughed again. She spoke through her laughter as it trailed off. "I am joking. What you had will be plenty. Do what you want with the rest."

The Survivalist considered casting it out into the sands, but she had a better idea. "Hey, Young?"

There was a hasty shuffling. The Young's head popped around the corner of the storage container entrance. "Yeah?" he replied sleepily.

"Do you want this Gorglum fruit? I just needed a few drops of the juice from it."

The Young smiled widely. "Throw it over." She tossed it. It was a poor throw off to one side. The Young lurched out to catch it, managing the snag, and quickly took a huge chomp out of the fruit, snapping through the outside cover and then down through the soft, pulpy center. He instantly puckered but smiled through it as he chewed. "I love these things." A teardrop ran down his cheek. He shoved some sand out of the way with his foot and sat down to eat the fruit.

The Bartender looked back at the Survivalist and caught her smiling widely at him. Having been seen, the Survivalist replaced the smile with a disapproving shake of her head and rolled her eyes. The Bartender tried her best not to show any signs that she had seen the Survivalist's smile but couldn't resist and ended up bending one side of her mouth up to form a slight grin.

The Survivalist didn't look back up at her, much to her relief. She stepped across the sandy entry deck. The Radioman noticed she was up and moving around and met her to talk. The Survivalist caught the first bit of the conversation. "Hello, Bartender. How are you this fine night?"

The Bartender sighed. "Radioman, this night has been rough, and you know it."

"Nothing is bad when I am around you."

The Bartender seemed awkward about this remark. The Survivalist stopped listening. Instead, she turned left and took a couple of steps to the edge of the Torgrog. She wondered if she could get inside that building. She started over the edge to drop down into the sand. She pivoted over the wall of the entry deck to find the step. At this moment, she realized that she had made a mistake.

The majority of the muscles in her legs had been essentially asleep or, at the minimum, completely motionless for the large majority of her time piloting. They were borderline dead weight at the moment. She completely missed the step with her lack of movement control. Having been caught off guard by this, she plummeted right past the step and landed flat on her back in the sands. She yelped.

Multiple footsteps scurried across the deck. The Young was the first to poke his head over the side of the Torgrog. "You all right?" He hopped the wall, caught the step, and easily lowered himself to the sands. He walked over to the Survivalist. She was grunting on the ground. "Hey. Are you okay?" He touched her left shoulder gently.

She wiggled away from him. "I'm fine. Just give me a minute."

There was some heat in that message. The Young understood that she was embarrassed. He stood and stepped back from her. She lay there on the sand for a moment while taking deep breaths. The fall must have really knocked it out of her. She took in a sharp breath and, with some effort, sat up. The Young walked back over and crouched down next to her. He was very careful not to touch her to avoid getting barked at again. "What is wrong with your legs?"

She looked up at him with an odd mixture of fear and guilt. Her voice quivered slightly. "I don't know." She rubbed her thighs. "It seems to be going away. I just can't feel my legs very well." She peered up past the Young's head at EX135. "Is this normal?"

EX135 nodded. "You are experiencing one of the key reasons that these kind of seats were rejected by the public."

The Survivalist nodded. "I can see why they rejected them. Will this go away?"

"The feeling of complete immobility?"

That wording seemed to hurt the Survivalist. She replied softly. "Yes."

EX135 nodded once. "Yes, but slowly over the next few minutes. You may experience complete loss of movement for brief periods as your muscles sort themselves out. Otherwise, you should be free to walk and move as normal if you can ignore the strange feeling of being...detached, if that is the proper word, from your limbs and extremities."

She pushed on her thighs. "I can't feel anything from my waist down."

"The seat had completely encapsulated that entire section of your body. The soothing treatment the seat provides essentially puts that part of your body to sleep. You do not notice this strange effect while in the seat as it detects your wishes to move and adjusts its own position to allow it. However, you are no longer in the seat, and it cannot move your limbs for you. You are simply waking up, but only on certain parts of your body."

She leaned forward on her legs in a failed attempt to feel something. She looked back up at EX135. "Is this how you feel all the time?"

EX135 was visibly confused but curious. "What do you mean?"

"Like, detached from your body? Can you feel things?"

EX135 tipped its head to the side slightly. "As in, do I have the sense of touch?"

"Yes."

"I can feel my entire structure. It works based on an electrostatic field sensor emitted at an extremely short distance from my entire frame at such a low power level that even the smallest of disturbances can be detected by it, such as the gentle breeze blowing past us at the moment. Unlike you, I can adjust the sensitivity of my sense of touch at will. This means that I can easily withstand things that would normally be painful for you, such as the sandstorm hitting us earlier while we escaped the Sand Eater."

Something about that last sentence made the Singer uncomfortable. She shifted about. The Survivalist ignored her. "What happens if your arm loses connection or something?"

EX135 oddly found this humorous and happily explained. "It would take quite a force to disconnect my arm. The force would be so large that it would likely take the entire arm with it, not just disconnect it from my processor. However, if my arm would somehow malfunction and the life source coursing through me were not able to fix it, or heal it, then I would experience a similar sensation to what your legs are feeling at this moment."

The Survivalist had switched to tapping on her shins but feeling nothing. "Have you ever had that happen?"

EX135 froze in thought. Something inside it whirred about. There was a strange small buzzing sound. EX135 snapped back to life. "I am unsure. I detect a maintenance log in an ancient sector that explains I had something similar at one point or another. Based on the age of the files around it, it must have been when I was back on the battery at the AOC Testing Labs, which would make sense, as I was void of life source and wouldn't be able to heal. And…"

Something caught EX135. It froze once more, staring off at the building. It's face contorted but suddenly dropped with its mouth wide open, revealing a dark metal tunnel behind it. It emitted a sound as if it was being choked. Through the sounds, EX135 managed to speak. "If…if you would be so kind…as to drag me inside"—it paused for an agitated beeping sound—"when you go in, that would be wonderful." EX135 locked completely stiff and silent. It tipped forward, banging on the wall of the entry deck, and tumbled down the side of the Torgrog. It landed in a limp pile in the sand.

The Bartender gripped the side of the Torgrog. "What?" She straddled the wall of the entry deck, found the step, and lowered herself down. She rushed the short distance over to EX135 and tipped its head to the left so that it was looking up at the sky.

A small groan came from EX135. Its yellow eyes flickered. "I… am…alive." It flicked its head toward the building.

The Bartender relaxed. She looked up at the Mechanic. "Can we get inside?"

The Mechanic looked over at the rusted gray and green door. He shook his head. "I guess we try that."

The Survivalist looked back at the door. She tried to stand and discovered that she could, in fact, move her legs, albeit unpredictably. She wobbled to a crouching position. Upon trying to stand, she only dove flat out on her stomach. She coughed and sputtered to spit out some sand. She rolled over in exasperation to her back. "I can move, but I can't tell where I am putting anything. I have no sense of where my legs are relative to my body or the ground. It is such a weird feeling."

She held her left leg stiff straight up in the air, perpendicular to her body on the ground, bent slightly at the knee. The leg teetered about, which she appeared amused by. She seemed to be moving it based on sight. She let the leg flop back to the sands harshly. The weight combined with the heavy impact caused her leg to bounce when it landed. She winced, though not out of pain. "Oh, that might have been a bit hard." She sprawled out.

The Young walked over to her. "So you can't feel anything at all?"

"Nope."

He poked her leg. She didn't react or even seem to notice that he had done anything. He smacked her leg, resulting in a thunderous clap. Her leg shook. She jumped in surprise. The Young grinned. "I take it you felt that?"

"No! The sound scared me."

The Young was genuinely surprised. He stood and scratched the back of his head. "Man, you really can't feel anything."

She didn't reply. Instead, her face grew perplexed. She shook her leg. She looked up at the Young. "Smack the other leg."

The Young raised his eyebrows. "You don't have to tell me twice." He strolled around behind her, crouched down, and gave the other leg a solid smack. Still in his crouch, he peered over at her. "Anything else?"

She shook her head and then her right leg. After a moment, she nodded. "Help me up to my feet." He grabbed her by her waist and scooped her up. He placed her on her feet and gently let her go. She used his shoulder as a post. She tried a step forward but retracted the extended leg and shook it some more. She prodded her left thigh. "I can kind of feel that. It is really dull, though. I think that smack shook it enough to wake it up from the sleeping state EX135 was talking about."

She tried another step. This one was very deliberately placed but successful. She dragged her right leg along behind her and shook it. A few more attempted steps later, she let go of the Young, who had been supporting her as a post this whole time, and clumsily stumbled across the sand. "This would be much easier if I weren't on a bunch of shifting sand the whole time."

She managed to stay upright long enough to reach the large door on the side of the building. She flopped into it and continued shaking out her legs in a swaying, alternating pattern as she pushed on the door. The door didn't budge. She pushed a finger against her leg. It was still a little fuzzy feeling but much more normal. She stood up straight and dropped her arms to be freestanding. She had regained the ability to tell where her legs were compared to herself.

She walked normally back across the sands to the Torgrog. "Good news is, I can walk again." She threw on a tacky smile and danced a short jive with excessive footwork. She dropped the act. "Bad news is, that door is stuck shut. We aren't getting in that way without EX135 hacking it or something."

The Mechanic glanced down at EX135, who was still lying in a lump. "Being that EX135 is currently reduced to a pile, I would say that we are out of luck there. What about the windows?" He looked far up the wall at the narrow, scratched windows.

The Hobo shook his head. "Not a chance. They are far too high to get up to." He thought for a moment and lit up. "Let's go see if we can get in the side. We might be able to get that door open from the other side and get the Torgrog in there too."

The Mechanic nodded. "That does look like a sliding garage door. It slides straight downward to let something in. They use them on facilities where power shortages may be frequent so that the door will slide open if power is lost instead of trapping the vehicle and people in the building."

The Entrepreneur looked at the Mechanic. "If that is the case, then why is the door still closed? Does this place have power?"

That was a good question. The Mechanic didn't have an exact answer. "Maybe it does. I don't know how, though."

The Hobo shrugged. "Doesn't matter either way. We need to get inside first. Come on. Let's see this side of the building."

A short walk later, the group spotted a man door on the side of the building. It was the same old green paint blasted down to the gray metal. The Old Man had found it with the light on his Lightstaff. They gathered near it. The Old Man tried the door. "Locked." He shrugged. "Anybody have any ideas?"

The Mechanic gently nudged the Old Man out of the way. He grabbed the handle for leverage and rammed the door with his shoulder. The door bounced him away with a thudding sound. He gave it a second wallop. The door resisted. The Mechanic shook his head. "It is a solid metal door with a metal frame. There is no way we are beating our way through that. I was just hoping it was rusted enough to break the hinges or the latch off."

The Old Man nodded. He glanced down at the Lightstaff. He paused a moment and rolled his eyes up toward the door, then back down at the staff. He shut the light off and pointed the top point of the staff at the door. He poked it lightly, drew it back, and stuck the door harshly with it. It dented slightly. The Old Man frowned. He walked back from the door a bit and turned to face it. He ran at the door with what speed he could muster and rammed the point of the staff into the door.

The staff reacted by emitting a bright flash of light and sinking directly into the door so quickly that the Old Man ran smack into the door itself. He grunted and let go of the staff, which was now lodged about halfway up into the door. He rubbed his left cheek, which had taken the blow, and adjusted his jaw. He grabbed the staff and pulled. A thin ray of light flashed from underneath the door, and the staff slid back out of the newly formed hole. The group observed the staff.

The Entrepreneur questioned the Old Man. "Did you know it did that?"

The Old Man shook his head. "Nope. I was just hoping it would do something. Didn't expect it to go that well, though." He gestured to his cheek. The Entrepreneur smiled. The group redirected their attention to the hole in the door. It was red hot and smoking a bit. It was plenty big enough for an arm to squeeze through. The group watched as the redness slowly faded and the smoke stopped. The Old Man quickly touched and retracted his finger. He paused for a moment. "It is warm, but not enough to burn you anymore."

The Hobo walked up and peered through the hole. He changed his view to a sharp angle through the hole as if he was trying to see the doorknob on the far side of the door. He gingerly touched the metal, checking it for heat, and then, satisfied, he plunged his whole arm through the hole up to his elbow. There were a couple of dull thuds as his hand hit the far side of the door. "Ah! There it is." There was a metallic click.

The Hobo retracted his arm and tried the handle. It turned through. He tried shoving the door inward. It refused. He pulled it open instead. The door swung around its hinges with a quiet and intermittent squeak. The Hobo wedged the door into the sand to hold it open. He leaned through the doorway. He whispered, "Old Man, light the room up." The Old Man stepped into the doorway and waved his hand across the room. The Lightstaff blasted white light, illuminating everything.

Rusted machinery littered the room. An overhead crane casted a shadow of its triangular webbing against the ceiling and the hook and chain hanging from it on the far wall. The whole room was remarkably white, except for the smooth gray concrete floor and the foot or so of dirty walls up from it. A small puddle of water rested in a low spot on the floor despite there being a drain. The Hobo stepped in. "We are clear. Come on in."

The group stepped inside. The Mechanic hesitated, then closed the door. "I will go back out for EX135 in a minute after we see if we can get that big garage door open." He slammed the door shut, noticing that it was painted entirely green on the inside. He turned the mechanical lock and spotted a large bolt on a spring pop over into a slot on the doorframe. The Mechanic dropped the backpack he had on the floor near the doorway and walked over to the garage door. He sighed. "Yep. This is a vertical lift door. It is rusted completely through. It must have been jammed intentionally by the looks of that bar wedged in the chain."

He crossed the width of the door to the chain of rusted large links that would be running the door. The chain went both up and down, making a flat and narrow oval with the top end being a driving gear with a box and a motor attached to it. The bottom of the oval disappeared into the floor, leaving only an upside-down U-shaped chain visible. The door itself was attached to one side of the chain on every other link. The door was also set in a slotted gap on the wall that likely guided it vertically as it lifted and lowered.

A three-inch-thick bar had been wedged through both sides of the chain and released. The weight of the door had pulled the left side of the chain downward due to gravity and the right side upward due to the gear at the top. The bar had, hence, wedged itself down against the floor to prevent the opposing direction of the chains and had jammed the whole system. The Mechanic grabbed the bar through the chain and pulled on it. The door shuddered a bit. He released the bar without extracting it. The Young grew curious. "Why did they jam it?"

The Hobo replied, "I found a whole bunch of places like this back in the city. When the Crisis happened, people went nuts. The government tried to contain it, but people knew that the time for government was over. They had to survive and didn't know how long the actual crisis was going to happen, so a bunch of people holed up in places by jamming stuff like this and locking doors. I have even seen entire roomfuls of furniture piled up against a door to prevent people from opening it during the looting fest right afterward. It had people real scared, and rightfully so." The Young nodded.

The Survivalist pointed at the bar. "Can we get it out and let the door open?"

The Mechanic nodded. "We can, but I don't think we can close it again if we open it. There doesn't appear to be any form of active power in here. Maybe there is a generator around here some-where with some fuel in it we can use just to hole up for the rest of the night." The Survivalist turned and started walking away. The Mechanic yelled after her. "Where are you going?"

She didn't turn around. "To find a generator. What else are we going to do?"

The Mechanic nodded. "I suppose she's right. I'll go get EX135 and drag it in here through the man door. Entrepreneur, come with me to help if you would. The rest of you can start looking around for supplies, I guess."

The Entrepreneur started to the door with the Mechanic. The Radioman caught him. "I heard you were talking about why you didn't have the credits earlier at The Oasis. I don't know why either. You are the one who knows the most about credits and dealing here. Take what I have left." He retrieved a small handful of credit coins, just barely enough to cover his hand in a pile, and gave them to the Entrepreneur.

The Entrepreneur nodded. For once, he seemed earnest about his response. "I appreciate this." He placed the credits in his pocket and hustled out to help the Mechanic, who had left the door hanging open for him. The Radioman walked over to the Bartender, who was talking with the Singer. They stopped their conversation before he was in earshot. He started talking with the Singer. "So, Singer, you must be the opposite of most. A general person would never sing but would talk all the time."

The Singer smiled. "I don't have much to say. This is all new to me. You all seem to have it handled."

The Radioman clasped his hands at his waist, bent over them slightly, and lowered his voice as if he was telling a secret. "It is all new to us too. We must be excellent at acting as if we know what is happening." He straightened with a grin and swiveled away from her, holding the eye contact as long as his neck would allow with the turn.

Once he snapped his head around to talk to the Bartender, the Singer felt her face grow hot. She hoped she wasn't blushing and couldn't understand why she would be. She turned and walked toward the Young and the Survivalist, who were searching a nearby closet, to avoid the potential embarrassment. The Young and the Survivalist were silent with each other, but both were searching for something. The Singer questioned them. "What are you two after over here?"

The Young poked his head around the doorway. "Any kind of equipment. We figured they may have stashed something in here, but all of this stuff is worthless. It seems to have been rummaged a few times before us. Been a while, though. Dust is sitting around everywhere."

The Singer realized that she had not had to rummage for something in years due to The Oasis. She could slip a drink or some food to feed herself for free. As much as she thought she hated the place, The Oasis had kept her alive. And to think she had run. She shook her head and joined them in the rummaging. The room wasn't really big enough for all three of them.

The Survivalist stepped outside for a moment to look around. A voice called her. "Hey, Survivalist! Come over here. I think we have got something." The Old Man was waving her over. The Old Man, the Radioman, and the Bartender all stood near a large machine with pipes and flexible tubes all over it. The Survivalist gathered up the Young and the Singer and brought them with her. The Mechanic and the Entrepreneur had overheard the call and joined as well, leaving EX135 sprawled out near the Mechanic's backpack at the man door.

Once everyone was present, the Old Man directed the light from the staff toward the dull gray lump of parts. It was an engine of some kind, obviously stripped from something else based on the large cut marks near the bottom of it and attached to the floor with bolts. A large chain, similar to the one on the garage door, was set on a sprocket attached to the output shaft of the motor. The chain led to another much more refined device that had a thick cable running out the back into the floor.

The Old Man focused the light down onto a clear-sight glass the size of his hand. A black mixture rested about halfway up the glass. He grinned. "I think we are in business. How do we get it running?"

The Mechanic walked around the side of the machine and felt the end of it. He found a small panel with knobs and a lever on it and a handle next to it. He motioned the Old Man over, who lit up the panel. "All right. I think I understand this. Do you all want me to give it a shot?"

The group nodded in agreement. The Old Man replied, "Go for it."

The Mechanic adjusted one knob to the far left and the other toward the middle. He pushed the lever down, which made a clunking sound. Then he grabbed the handle and braced himself. He pulled on it. The handle didn't budge. He yanked harder. Nothing. He grimaced. "Oh boy. This is going to be a dandy." He placed his feet on the bottom of the engine and pushed with his legs while also pulling with his arms. The handle popped and began moving. It accelerated quickly, dumping the Mechanic on his back.

The Mechanic quickly released the handle. It retracted itself on a cord and snapped back into its original position. The engine sputtered and shook but fell silent. The Mechanic grunted and murmured something under his breath. He twisted the left knob all the way around to the right side and adjusted the other knob to the left a spec. He clunked the lever back up to the top position. He replaced his feet and repeated the pull on the handle. This attempt went much smoother. He again flattened out on his back and released the handle. This time, the engine shook a good bit more than the first and had uneven strokes.

The Mechanic scrambled to his feet, a wide and panicked smile running his face. He emitted sounds of joy. "Heh! Oh, come on." He twisted the left knob back toward the left side. The engine began to smooth out. The sputtering stopped. The engine fell to even pace. He grabbed the lever and quickly slapped it downward. The entire engine lurched as the sprocket began to turn, pulling the chain with it and turning the shaft connected to the refined device.

A moment later, a few lights on the ceiling flickered to life. The rest remained dark. The engine settled into a smooth pace. The Mechanic leaned against it. "This thing has been robbed from some vehicle and modified to include a pull start. They probably stripped the whole vehicle for parts after the Crisis and built this generator out of it." He smiled widely.

The Singer pointed at it. "So I take it you like it?"

The Mechanic frowned and shook his head. "Oh no. It's a piece of shit. But it works." He looked up at the Singer and smiled before turning away and walking off toward the chain attached to the large garage door with the bar stuck in it. The Singer seemed confused by this response.

The Hobo laughed. "Don't worry, babe. He doesn't mean anything by that."

The Singer cringed. "Don't call me babe."

The Hobo nodded. "Right." He walked off with the Mechanic.

The group turned to see the pair of them managing to rip the bar out of the chain. The door slowly receded into the floor. The Mechanic looked up at the Survivalist and waved her over. She jogged across the room and went outside. The group heard the Torgrog come to life. She guided it inside the garage and set it down on the floor with its iconic high-pitched whistling shutdown.

The Mechanic walked over to a panel on the wall and opened it. There was a lever inside, which he pushed upward. An electric motor above him sparked, which he flinched from by cowering away, covering his head, and releasing the lever as the sparks showered down on him. He looked up at it and pressed the lever again. The lights flickered, but the door started up.

Once it reached the top, the Mechanic gently released the lever and closed the panel on the wall. He made an announcement to the group that echoed a bit in the garage. "That panel is just like the one

I used to use back at my old job. It just has a different lift system on it than I am used to." He smiled in reminiscence as he turned and faced the panel with his hands on his waist. "I always hated that panel." He turned and walked back toward the group.

The Hobo was already setting up camp on an old mattress he had found. He flopped on it and smiled. "Finally, things are looking up."

The Old Man, who was sitting on a metal chair nearby, took the bait for the conversation. "We found a building and a good place to sleep. We even have some power. It is pretty good for the time being."

The Hobo shook his head. "Nah, man. I have a bed."

The Old Man was confused by this. "What do you mean? That is just a mattress."

The Hobo nodded. "I have never had one before." The Old Man was humbled by the statement. He ended the conversation for lack of a decent reply.

As everyone bedded down for the rest of the night, the Young and the Survivalist stood around restlessly. The Bartender noticed them and chuckled. "You two had the Gorglum fruit. It will wear off in a bit. You can make it go quicker by taking a walk and burning some energy. Then you can both go to sleep."

The Survivalist nodded. "Let's do that. I really want to sleep, but I can't." The Young nodded, realizing he had eaten the whole thing. The Survivalist looked back at the Bartender. "We will go explore this place a bit and come back. If we find anything, we will let you know in the morning. Or if it's dangerous, you know, as soon as we can run back here away from it."

The Bartender smiled before a yawn. "All right. See you in the morning hopefully."

The Survivalist smiled. "Yeah." She glanced over at the Young and nodded her head to the side. The two stood and walked off to explore the building.

*****

The Young glanced up at an old poster stuck to the wall. A single lamp was angled toward it perfectly to illuminate it. He found that whole setup to be odd. He stopped to get a better look at it. "Huh." He turned his head to the left a bit while continuing to look at the poster. "Hey, Survivalist, come check this out."

The Survivalist abandoned a set of boxes she was searching and trotted across the room. She looked up at the wall. There was a picture of a compass on the poster. She glanced down at her own on her leg and back up at the poster. "That looks like my compass." She retrieved her compass and held it up to compare. Sure enough, the two were identical.

She read the text above the picture. A large font read, "AOC Compass," and a smaller subset text read, "Made using the same technology as our navigation systems for outer space programs." The Survivalist furrowed her brow. "Outer space programs?" She glanced over at the Young.

He shrugged. "I don't remember anything about outer space from before the Crisis."

She looked back at the poster. "Me neither. If you remember, they were called the Asteroid Orbit Cooperative according to EX135."

The Young nodded. "That makes sense with this poster."

"Yeah." The two paused. The Survivalist looked down at the compass in her hand. She flicked open the lid. To her surprise, the needle inside was spinning about with no clear direction. She quickly spoke with surprise. "What is…" She turned toward the Young to show him. The needle straightened out sharply to point at him. She looked up at the Young, then back down at the compass.

She stepped to the side. The needle continued pointing in its same direction instead of at the Young. She turned back toward the poster. The needle seemed lost once more. She turned back toward the Young and walked past him. The needle stayed true until she reached a hallway off to the right. Here, the compass scrambled again.

She was just about to pass it off as some strange anomaly, maybe something to do with the generator, but then she turned to look down the hallway, and the needle snapped back into focus, pointing down the hall. She looked over at the Young, who had been watching the compass with her over her shoulder. He went back to the poster and retrieved it from the wall. It was held with a pair of clips on the top. He returned to the Survivalist's side. She questioned him. "What are you going to do with that?"

He held it out toward the way they came. "I am going to give it to the Old Man. I figured he will enjoy it. He seems to like collecting things like this."

The Survivalist nodded. "Do you think we should follow this thing?" She gently shook the compass.

The Young shrugged. "Why not?" She hesitated, but her curiosity won her over. They hadn't found anything bad yet to avoid anyway. She started down the hall.

*****

After a long game of following the finicky compass, the two arrived at a decrepit metal grating staircase headed upward. The compass very clearly wanted them to go up the stairs. Even if she turned away, the compass still pointed at the staircase now. The two ascended the stairs, being careful to check each one for its stability. At the top, there was a series of doors down a hallway. They were all on the left, as the right was a railing overlooking a large, empty concrete floor below.

One room, the third door down, had a light on. The compass pointed down the hall. As soon as they approached the lit room, the compass pointed directly at the door. The Survivalist looked up at the nameplate on the wall. It had been completely scratched off, just like every other nameplate in the entire facility. She drew the hatchet and used the head of it to poke the door open a crack. It squeaked.

She shouldered the wooden door, blasting it open and sending it careening around its hinges to bang on the wall. It bounced and shuttered a bit. The room was void of life. She relaxed, stowed the hatchet, and looked over at the Young. "Why would this one room that the compass points us to be the lit one? It is freaking me out."

The Young nodded. "It is very strange." She stepped inside. The Young stayed out. "I will be out here keeping watch. Let me know what you find." She nodded, and the Young leaned against the wall on the outside.

The Survivalist took in the room. It was a personal office. A huge wooden desk took up the majority of the room. It was completely cleaned off, except for the dust, a large red phone sitting on the desk off its receiver, and one lone piece of paper lit up by a lamp angled at it. Otherwise, the room was completely trashed. It hadn't been disturbed in years, maybe since the Crisis, but something had happened here. Someone had left in a hurry and had torn the place apart to do it.

She crossed the room to the desk with the bendable metal desk lamp with its circular brushed metal shade. She looked down at the paper. It had two words written out on it in some kind of black ink. "Hey, Tindertuft." A rush of pain ran through the Survivalist's chest. She stopped for a moment to catch her breath. She could have sworn she recognized that handwriting and the nickname, but it had been far too long now.

A thin white plastic card rested on the bottom half of the paper in the middle. She picked it up and flipped it over. It had a small set of text on it: "Basement Keycard. AOC Testing Labs." She stopped. That was where EX135 said he was from, but it had collapsed outside this place. She grabbed the paper. A rectangle of less-stained paper had formed where the card was sitting, leaving the rest of the paper dirty and rough in comparison.

She looked up slightly toward the lamp. She noticed another piece of paper taped down to the desk cut out in the shape of an arrow. The arrow with the word *compass* was pointing toward the corner, where a switch was attached in the wall. She crossed the room to the switch. She extended her finger to turn it off and noticed it was shaking. She steadied it by pressing the switch. The room fell dark as the lamp shut off. She left the room in the dark.

The Young turned and immediately noticed something was wrong. He stepped over to her. Without a word, she held up the keycard and stepped past him. She opened up the compass once more. It had stopped pointing at the office. Instead, it was now pointed down the hallway they had come from. They started another trek.

Not long later, they arrived at an old doorway with a sign on it that read Basement and a keycard slot placed vertically on its right side. A small red light was lit up. She held up the card and swiped it. Nothing happened. She flipped it over and swiped it on the other direction. The light changed yellow for a moment, then flicked to green with a quiet but sharp beep.

The door clicked. She pulled it open to the left. The door led to a concrete staircase heading down. She glanced over at the Young. The Young did not respond at this point. He was in for the ride, knowing that something had shaken the Survivalist. She stepped on the first stair and started downward. The temperature dropped noticeably. The compass whirled around to point backward when she reached the bottom.

She followed it around the thin metal railing on the stairs and into a wide room with a single light at the top creating a large lit spot in the center of a square room. A strange kitbash contraption stood in the center of the spot on a rickety metal table that seemed to struggle with the weight of the contraption on it. The contraption was covered in wires, top to bottom, of all colors and sizes.

A rectangular black box stood vertically, hidden within the tangle. She could see the edges of a square panel on the bottom of it. She looked at the compass. It pointed directly at the contraption. She shut the lid and stowed the compass. She took a step into the room. The device shifted. She stopped. A burst of sparks popped out of the machine and dispersed on the floor. A small window snapped open on the machine. It vibrated on the table and emitted a bright blue fan of light angled up at the ceiling.

It slowly lowered to her head and down to the hook on the rope wrapped around her. It paused on the hook, buzzed once, and continued down her body. It found the hatchet on her hip and stopped.

Curious, she turned a bit to expose the side of the hatchet. The beam paused, and the table vibrated again as it moved the scanning beam back up a smidge to the top of the hatchet and then scanned the entire hatchet. It made a binging sound. The blue light fan shuddered its way back up to the top of her head, where it refocused and slowly lowered down to her eyes.

She averted her eyes from the blinding light and contorted her face. The light snapped down past the rest of her eyes to the bottom of her nose, where it held still until she relaxed her face. It quickly scanned her mouth and chin before stopping at her neck. It dinged again. The blue beam shut off, and the window on the box snapped shut. A light thump came from inside the box. The square panel fell open, revealing a pocket in the inside.

A metal can rolled out and landed in the pocket. A small ding played through a poor-quality speaker. The Survivalist looked back at the Young, who was bewildered beyond belief, and then looked back at the can. She stepped further into the room. Everything seemed to be done. She walked to the contraption on the table and looked at the can. The Young joined her. The Young spoke first. "Is that a can of C&G?"

The Survivalist picked up the can. A large curly logo read C&G on its side in white lettering with black accents against a simple brown backdrop. "Yep."

"All that for a can of cola?"

She shook her head. "Surely not." She flipped the can over. It was the same logo. She checked the silver top. It appeared to have been burned a bit. She shrugged and grabbed the brown tab at the top and cracked it open. It didn't have the same sound or feel as she remembered. It wasn't nearly as crisp. She tipped it a bit to see the liquid before she drank it. Nothing came out. She looked in the can. There wasn't any cola in the can. "It's dry!"

"What? All of that for an empty can of cola?"

She peered in closer. "But it isn't empty." The Young went silent. The Survivalist reached into the top of the newly opened can with her finger and pressed a button on the inside of it. A low tone filled the room. She set the can down nervously on the table and stepped away.

A voice cleared its throat. A deep, smooth voice spoke. "Hello there, Tindertuft." The Survivalist gasped but shut herself up to avoid talking over the can. There was a pause. "Yes, it is me, your dad." The Survivalist backed to the wall and slid down it slowly to a seating position. She pulled her knees to her chest and held her head with her hands. A tear ran down her cheek.

"If you are hearing this, then I am dead, long dead. I have likely been gone for years now. I hope this message has found you all right. I would have just sent it directly to you, but that would have exposed your location and put you and your mother at risk. I also couldn't mail it to you, as the AOC is monitoring my computer and everything I do. They, along with many others, wouldn't be happy with what I am going to tell you, so I had to build something that would fly under the radar to get this to you.

"The AOC system doesn't check vending machines or old models of the Boomship driver detection system, so I used those two things to detect some key objects and your face to identify you before giving you this message. Oddly enough, the vending machine has to have a can in it, or it alerts the system that it is empty, meaning somebody would eventually find this machine and this message, meaning it wouldn't reach you. So I had to put this message in a can of C&G cola to bypass the system alert.

"I found it kind of fitting, honestly. I know you always liked C&G soda. Unfortunately, I don't think you will be getting any more of that anytime soon. I sure hope I am wrong. I also used a complex system of factory navigation settings to hard-code a route into the system that will work with the compass I gave you. It causes magnetic fields throughout the building to put the needle of the compass around, which I suppose is how you found this.

"I figured, if you ever left Capital City, you might eventually go this way in general to escape the inevitable poor conditions in the city. Being that this is one of the only places to stop along the entire Exodust Guide Pole route, I figured you would stop here too. I left a lamp on a poster of the compass to hopefully prompt you to pull it out. If all of that worked, you are here now and listening to this. But look, I am just avoiding the point that I need to tell you here. Let's get to it."

There was a pause filled with the sound of ruffling papers. "I have written out a letter here that I was going to send you. I am going to read it now and record it since I can't mail it. Here it goes. 'Dear Tindertuft, there is an event coming up. I don't know what they are going to do, but it is for certain going to destroy life as humanity knows it, especially in Capital City. This is going to be a global thing. My guess is, we aren't long from a disaster so big it nearly or completely destroys all of mankind. The worst part? It is my fault.'"

There was another long pause. "'That is what everybody is going to see anyway. For anything else to make sense, I need to tell you about the world before you were born. Some thirty years before you were born, when I was a kid, an asteroid was headed toward our planet. It wasn't in line to hit us, but it gave us an opportunity that we had never had before. We could get this asteroid to orbit our planet at a safe distance and study it. This thing had come from deep space over the last million years or so. We knew it was coming due to telescope data. But for the first time, we could get something on a deep space object and see what it had. Maybe it could tell us of the parts of space we couldn't see yet.'

"'It was a huge, huge deal. The globe banded together in unity for the first time in history to create a private company called the Asteroid Orbit Cooperative, or AOC, for short. As the asteroid got within reach of rockets we could build at the time, the AOC launched a rocket with a few of these lifelike, self-aware robots boringly called Mechanical Men, or Mechmen. They all ran on a central system and sent back every bit of data they could accumulate.'

"'Amazingly, the rocket made it. The whole world celebrated. A global holiday was even created in honor of it. The Mechmen did their jobs up there, starting small with some basic sampling, but then they discovered a potential fuel source. That was a huge deal too. They had the Mechmen build a small rocket using the materials found on the asteroid and parts from the original rocket. They had not planned for the return trip, but there was enough fuel left to escape the weaker than expected gravity of the asteroid.'

"'They put some stuff on the rocket, including some of the new fuel source that would not be consumed on the trip home. It was sent back home. It successfully made it thanks to our planet's gravitational pull. They analyzed what was now the most valuable material on the planet. That potential fuel turned out to be a revolutionary material more powerful than any fuel we had ever created. The best part about it was, it could be recreated here with resources we had.'

"'With this discovery, the AOC decided the asteroid was worth trying to set into our orbit. They threw together a plan and calculated they had around a decade to build a rocket on this asteroid big enough that it could redirect the path of the asteroid to our orbit temporarily. It was important that this whole idea was temporary, as it had to go away eventually, or we risked messing up our own planet's orbit around the sun.'

"'They all did the math. Once it was in orbit, we would have exactly eight months to get all of the resources we could from it before safely sending it off with the same rocket we had put it into our orbit with. The globe agreed mostly. The AOC built thousands of the Mechmen, all solar driven, and sent them up in rockets along with any equipment they may need.'"

There was another short rustling paper sound. "'Not much time passed before the AOC group found a way to synthesize the fuel they had found on the asteroid. Now the only issue with that fuel from before was that no engine on our entire planet of any size, model, or purpose could handle running this fuel. It was far too powerful. It literally exploded whatever they tested it in with enough force that it leveled a few of the first testing buildings.'

"'Some rejected this new power. They saw it as too much to contain. However, there was a group of people who came together outside of the AOC to figure out a solution to this problem of uncontainable force. They organized themselves as the FEC, or Future Engine Corp. Somehow, this group of masterminds managed to come up with a functioning engine that ran on this new fuel source—of course, only the synthesized stuff, not the original samples.'

"'This synthesized fuel was originally highly caustic and extremely dangerous as it must be held constantly under pressure, or it expanded, gathered heat, and exploded. Now the original fuel had none of these problems, as it stayed happily as a liquid in room temperature. Something had been off in the synthesizing process. To avoid this issue, they talked the AOC into giving them a pure, unstudied sample. The total volume of that sample would have fit in this C&G can you are looking at.'

"'Using that sample as their pristine guide, the FEC refined the synthesized fuel to make it nearly, if not completely, identical to the original. They called the copied stuff Astrofuel and left the original fuel named as source fuel to keep things simple. Using that newly redesigned and borderline perfect copy of the original fuel, they remodeled their engine design completely from the ground up to run on a liquid fuel.'

"'The result was incredible. They made the world's first Astrofuel-driven engine. The best part? It was considered one of the safest engines ever built. For that reason alone, the FEC took the vehicle market by storm. They started with wheeled vehicles, which were the norm of the time, by placing their engine on an extremely reinforced frame and gearing it down drastically. Most of those designs ran at incredibly low RPM due to the sheer torque the Astrofuel provided the FEC engines. For that reason, they were also amazingly fuel efficient, even in larger engines.'

"'The fuel efficiency led to a huge jump in popularity—not necessarily for the whole ecofriendly deal but because the extremely low consumption meant people had to buy less fuel. Astrofuel wasn't cheap, so this low consumption was a huge deal that saved a good chunk of funds for the owner. At this point, the FEC realized that they weren't selling their vehicles to anyone but the rich. To fix this, they drove the pricing of the fuel, which they had a monopoly over, down to the point that they barely made enough credits to keep the factory working just so the common man could afford to purchase the fuel to use his newly purchased FEC-engine-equipped vehicle.'

"'It worked. The common man started investing into the whole Astrofuel idea, mainly because it was so much cheaper than conventional fuel and more powerful to boot. They were selling as many as they could produce.'" Another page rustle filled the silence of a pause.

"'This entire time, the AOC had been still in operation. They were still using the old rocket designs, but these designs were serving them just fine. The recent growth of Astrofuel consumers had actually helped them, as it lowered the demand for conventional fuels, which were a derivative of the rocket fuel they were using. Less demand for regular fuel meant cheaper rocket fuel for them.'

"'There was a pause in development here for a couple years while the AOC guided their Mechmen through the final stages of the Asteroid Orbit Incentive Rocket, which was the final title they decided on bestowing on the massive blasting chamber used to get the asteroid into orbit and also back out of it later. Once it was complete, they sent the Mechmen on a month-long trek to the complete far side of the asteroid. After that, they lit the AOIR.'

"'I remember that whole week very clearly. The whole sky turned white in a massive beam of raw energy that came to a sharp point. If you looked closely through a pair of special glasses, you could see that the flame was actually orange. It was so bright that it bleached the color out of it. It didn't get truly dark outside for that entire week or so, instead getting a sort of late twilight at the darkest. It awed the world. They had never seen something of that scale.'

"'After the week ended, the blast shut off. The asteroid was now in our orbit. You could see it with the naked eye all the time, especially at night when the sunlight wasn't blocking it out and instead reflecting off its dark-purple surface. It unified the world in a sense of human technological triumph. Little did they know that this was only the beginning.'

"'Now by this point, the FEC had properly lined its pockets and upgraded their equipment and factory. The next FEC project came easy for them. For the first time since the source fuel gift, the FEC and AOC interacted with each other directly. The AOC needed a new rocket design that would be able to handle rapid transportation of materials from the asteroid. The FEC sprung on the deal as a way to make a fat stack of credits and also gain access to any newly discovered materials.'

"'They rather quickly came up with a new rocket design that they called the Trans-Astro series, which was short for Transpace Asteroid, meaning traveling the distance to the asteroid. In fact, they came up with this and built a working prototype so quickly that the public questioned if they had been working on the project in secret before the AOC ever even asked them for a deal.'

"'The FEC very well may have done that, but the AOC frankly did not care. The AOC was very open about that opinion. They had asked the FEC for a rocket, and the FEC had delivered. This took the heat of having a monopoly off of the FEC for the time being. Now the AOC actually bought out the FEC's design and manufactured it themselves since they feared the FEC would not be able to handle the load of both their common man's Astrofuel vehicle and the new rocket fleet production.'

"'The FEC agreed to the deal under the conditions that they retained full rights to produce and sell the blast burner engines created for the rocket to the AOC, meaning the AOC could not legally know how to produce their engines. The AOC, having fallen in love with the sheer power and speed of the engine, accepted these terms. Now that was a critical moment there. The AOC had allowed the FEC to retain their newly designed blast burner engine.'"

Another rustling of paper as he cleared his throat. "'That was when the FEC began to develop an entirely new form of transportation for the home planet. They started with the Magnetube system, making the electromagnetic generators running the super suspension magnets for the trains much more reliable and efficient with their engines, but the trains still rode on wheels at this point. That seemed to be a wall for the FEC, though.'

"'They made a few new powerhouse generators with the design, but they really didn't have much of a way to go about with it. They got held up there for a moment while they attempted to develop something new. They didn't make any progress of significance until the AOC discovered what they called Repulsor and brought some of it back down for the FEC as promised in the previous deal.'

"'This strange and goopy material had a lot a weird property unlike anything mankind had ever found. It seemed to repel everything. The FEC researched this material extensively. It turned out that its structure, in fact, repelled everything since every available placement to create bonds with other materials had been taken up by its own structure, meaning it literally couldn't combine with any other material. They also discovered that by passing an incredibly large electric shock through it, the material would split a few of these bonds, allowing for a few of the bonds to accept outside material.'

"'They also discovered that passing heat into the material would create a stronger repulsion, meaning they could control how strong the repulsion was by heating and cooling it. By combining all of this knowledge, they were able to create a synthetic version of the Repulsor material, this time under the same name as the original. With the synthetic Repulsor, they made the world's first hovering plate. It was very unstable and tended to spin until it lost control, but it was a start.'

"'They continued refining it until when you shoved it across the room, it would float level across it. Then the FEC needed to figure out how this was going to be used in society. They did have ideas before making it, the most recent model made especially for the Magnetubes, but otherwise, it seemed difficult to integrate into society. So they started with what they knew would work: the Magnetubes.'

"'The Magnetube trains were still moved by the electromagnetic fields in the walls, but now they could be moved much quicker and smoother with even less effort since the friction of the wheels had been completely removed with the installation of hover plates.

This was revolutionary. It saved millions of people time every single day.'

"'Right around this same time, the FEC also found a way to adjust the Repulsor material into something new called Thermolectric Goo, or TG. This semitransparent magenta goo was a reverse engineered version of the Repulsor. Instead of converting energy when heated, it actually absorbed the energy. When the goo cooled, it released all of the energy it had collected as electrical power. This instantly led to extremely efficient geothermal power plants all over the globe.'

"'By the time the FEC was getting around to constructing all of this, it had come time for the asteroid to leave. The minor gravity of the asteroid was beginning to change the orbit of our planet, as expected. It had, in fact, been about eight months, as they had calculated. But before the AOC sent the asteroid back off into space, they sent a few rockets up and recalled all of the Mechmen to them to return home. Their job had been completed.'

"'The AOC explained that they intended to scrub through the memory of each and every Mechmen for any details that might have failed to transmit back home properly. They were going to do all of this in their massive swath of decimated property that had been completely reduced to sands from all of the rocket launches pounding the surface, especially after they converted to the FEC Blast Burner Engine. This entire area was named the Exodust, which was a nifty play on words, combining *exodus* and *dust*, since the rockets left in such great numbers and created this massive wasteland of dust in their wake.'

"'The plan went through. The last Mechmen on the asteroid pushed the ignition switch, boarded the final rocket where a few of its friends were, and launched off for home as the massive white blast returned. The blast lasted for about a week and a half before it finally sputtered out. It was very similar to the first blast. Then over the next couple weeks, the asteroid slowly left the naked eye's range until it disappeared.'"

Another paper rustling break. "'Now the FEC was experiencing a heavy loss in profits at the moment. The AOC no longer needed more rocket engines, which was a high portion of the FEC revenue. Now if you recall, I mentioned an important thing, that the FEC had retained the rights to the Blast Burner Engine. They reduced the size of these engines for reasonable human transport and came up with something they called a Boomship. The name was actually coined by a news broadcaster listening to the first public starting of the prototype.'

"'The FEC declared the protype a ship instead of a vehicle for some reason or another. The booming sound it made when the prototype took off fascinated the fellow doing the news report, and he remarked casually that they were a ship that boomed, or a Boomship. People liked the name so much that the FEC stuck with it. They soon equipped the Boomships with adjustable hover panels and a coolant system that was based on the Thermolectric Goo.'

"'They designed a custom control schematic just to pilot the vehicle with. After a lot of testing and stretched thin on funding, they released this to the public. People loved it. It was the fastest, smoothest, and most affordable engine-based transportation to be created in the last century or more. They came out with hundreds of different models, each with its own specification. They practically took over the entire planet's transportation.'"

There was a sharp sound of paper being thrown and fluttering away. A silence took over after a piece of paper slid to a stop. The voice returned. "'While the FEC rocked the world of transportation once more, the AOC was busy doing exactly what it said it would do. It was scrubbing through Mechmen memories. This was going fine until they came across a batch of Mechmen that had been somehow deformed.'

"'They were still functional. In fact, they functioned even better than the others, but their minds refused to be read by the simple programs the AOC had created for the other normal Mechmen. They looked into this and discovered that the Mechmen had replaced their lubricants with a sort of genetic life. The stuff now running through their systems only seemed to benefit them and had literally brought the roughly created robots into a full synthetic life-form.'

"'They tried to study it, but the stuff refused to be tested or observed. They deemed this unknown, sentient fluid Life Source since it had literally brought machines to life. These Mechmen variants went nameless for a period as the AOC hid their existence. They ran tests on them, drained them of their life source. They expected this to kill them but were amazed to find that the majority of them lived on, although miserably, as long as they had some form of power source.'

"'They used these test subjects to try to pry out how they were created. They lost a few and never really did get the truth. Even other nonsentient Mechmen who witnessed the transformation to sentience did not give away the full process, only the idea that the sentient Mechmen needed more lubricant. The AOC even tried injecting Life Source into Mechmen that were not modified or sentient. They were amazed to find that it quickly converted these into sentient life-forms as well, although in methods they couldn't understand and not to the complete sentient levels the others had.'

"'These modified models still required some form of external guidance to direct their actions despite being sentient for the most part. Then some of the modified Mechmen escaped along with the truly sentient ones. The AOC was forced to acknowledge their existence to warn the public of their escape. The media dubbed them Exodusters, as the large majority of them roamed free in the Exodust.'

"'The AOC managed to recapture quite a few of them. These were modified to obey a central system, which could be accessed by anyone by a bidding system. The highest bidder got the job they requested from the Exoduster. This provided a nice retirement fund for everyone in the AOC business and gave the public a way to access the Exodust like never before.'

"'By this point, you were born. As you might remember, the FEC had released hundreds of thousands of these Boomships to the public. They were all zooming around. It was quite a strain on the FEC to keep up with building new models, prototyping, and also providing maintenance all at once. They admitted that they needed more help with making sure the Boomships were safe after running into some issues. A select few of their Boomships had been found to have faulty wiring of some kind, resulting in a computer error.'

"'Now the large majority of a Boomship's controls are actually driven by a superintelligent computer that keeps the whole system running. If that computer fails, miscalculates, or gets hacked, then the entire Boomship can destroy itself. Now of course there were loads of safety precautions to prevent total detonation of the blast burners, but it was preferable to completely avoid any possible issues to begin with. They needed people to prevent these issues along with others, but their current working staff couldn't handle any more labor. That is where I come in.'

"'I came in with the brief hiring period to fill the gaps. My job is to test these systems and intentionally try to break them in a controlled setting. I specialize in hacking. The FEC, whom I work for now, want these things to be basically unhackable. My entire job is to sit and try to break every kind of program they intend or have already loaded into the systems running a Boomship model.'

"'I don't mind it, really, or at least I didn't used to. I would find a minor edge case here or there that needed looked at. That was typical of my job. But then I found something in the very base code of the system. I wanted to get a fuller picture of how these machines worked, and it had been a rather slow month. I should mention I get paid an hourly wage, which is enough to live on but not enough to splurge on the lifestyle we have.'

"'The real credit comes from finding the bugs. If you get even just one small fix a month, you can make yourself a livelihood. If you find a big one, something critical to the system, then you can get set up for the whole year. The best part about that is, you don't dare wait to tell them as another employee might find the same issue and get the pay before you even though you found it first. It keeps the bug-finding process smooth and efficient.'

"'So it had been a slow month, meaning not any fixes for me yet. I was getting a bit desperate, which was another reason why I dove into the core of the coding that had been ironed over by hundreds of individuals already instead of the newly released and easy jobs. I wanted something big. I didn't expect to find something so far back in the development of this system, but something caught my eye. There was a developer port still buried in the code.'

"'That means the developer of the code left himself a point where they could enter a complex passcode and gain access to some records of the system, which wouldn't be all that detrimental, but also to the mainframe of the system itself to tweak the performance, which was a massive issue. That was the spot to search. Where there is a passcode, there is a hack that can get through it somehow.'

"'I thought about bringing it up right there, but I knew that the boss would tell me that I had no reason to change something that far back as it was a secured entry point that nobody could get into. With that in mind, I sat down and began running cracking clients. Those are just automated devices we get to run all the general tests across a code to make our jobs less tedious. Unsurprisingly, those all came back with no issues found. I skipped all the steps in the middle and dove straight into manually cracking this system one line at a time until I could cypher out the key to the developer port. If I could access the port and open it, then the boss would be forced to believe me and give me quite a sum of credits for finding it.'

"'This project took me months. I had to set it aside multiple times, but I was steadily gaining ground and untangling the mess of the bottom code to find every possible entry point into the system. Then after some nine months of work, I finally made the break-through. By combining all of the data running through the systems, you could collect a relay pattern or when the computer sends and receives information.'

"'I noticed early on that if you got lucky enough to enter a digit or letter of the passcode on the exact instant that the first relay input of a cycle occurred, then it would react differently than if you entered a character any other time. It would deny the entry altogether unless it was the right character, which it would then accept it. To confirm this, I had the FEC change the developer port of one debug vehicle to a known passcode that I could use to get closer to perfecting my method.'

"'This is common practice for debug vehicles. Debug vehicles are built with intentionally flawed access points so that you can disable the security system, make a minor change to help you find a hack, and then reactivate the defenses to continue trying to hack in. I gathered using this trick that an individual might potentially get incredibly lucky and guess the code one character at a time by getting the exact moment of the start of the relay each and every time they enter a character. If they ever missed the timing, it reset them all the way back to the beginning.'

"'The farthest I ever got with this trick was two characters in. The passcode was forty-eight characters long. It was nearly impenetrable due to the random order of when the hacker needed to input a character was, or so I thought. Then I found the weakness. There was a hidden marker signal being passed through the relay every so often that the computer seemed to completely ignore, as in the computer didn't create any output from reading that signal.'

"'I had been wondering what the purpose of that marker was for ages now, and nobody else seemed to know either. All they knew was that if it was removed, the whole system seemed to hang up on itself and freeze. That was the key. The signal was a reset switch. That signal told the computer that the relay loop, which could be a very wide range of lengths based on how many inputs it received at that moment, was actually ending now and that it needed to be prepared for a new set of instructions.'

"'This was a strange way of coding. Most relay loops check every possible input every loop and return an output of either on or off and a strength value after it, meaning the relay is always the exact same length of data. However, a Boomship system only sends signals if the sensor is detecting something in the on position. This shortens the relay length and makes it faster to read, meaning a better response time by a few milliseconds than the traditional method but also meaning that the relay length is not always the same length. This meant the traditional, constant length relay system would just reset itself after processing a specific number of entries.'

"'Meanwhile, the Boomship relay was not a constant length and needed something to tell the computer that it was now reading the next relay loop of information. That relay marker also just so happened to be the reason you could enter a character of the passcode in and check it alone without penalty. The entry for the character was put in, read, and erased by the relay marker so quickly that the passcode system only had time to see if it was the right entry and display it but not enough time to reset the entire passcode if the answer was not correct.'

"'That meant I could build a system to detect the relay marker signal and stick a guessed character in every single loop with perfect precision. It would keep guessing characters until it got it right, then move on to the next until it had successfully gotten all forty-eight characters entered and accessed the developer port. I built the small hacker client and hooked it up.'

"'It busted through that port in under five minutes. I finalized the hack and accessed the developer port as proof that I had, in fact, made it in. I was actually packing up the data and my things to rush it up to the boss, but I noticed something in the developer port that was brought up on my screen. It was a central hub access.'

"Now before we move on, the central hub is a sort of notification and updating system for Boomships. It is how we get the fixes we find out to the public without having to recall every model ever built. They evolve on the run in the most literal sense. The FEC accepts the new version of the Boomship computer, uploads it to the system, and with the push of a single button, update every Boomship in the world with the latest version over the course of about twenty-four hours.'

"The original developer of the base coding must have implemented this as an easy way to update all of the prototypes in the shop at once, then having forgotten by then about the ancient port, used the same code in the central hub we now use. Since this was also a developer port, you could also gain the current code of the computer and tweak it at your own will. From there, you could send an update back to the central hub and have it go to every other ship in the world.

"That means that right now, I could, oh, I don't know, for example change the code to have every single Boomship intentionally overheat. This would make them all explode in a fury of deadly fire so large that it would annihilate the planet. Who knows what somebody would do with this? This was the worst hack exposure that the company had ever encountered, and fixing it so far down in the bottom core layers of the code now would take ages. We had to start immediately or risk the entire world being destroyed by our creation.

"I snatched up the data and my computer and ran up to the office. I threw the door open and interrupted one of his meetings to show him this. He was dumbfounded. He immediately picked up the phone and made a call to one of his fresh coding engineers, one of the guys who wrote the code we debug. As he explained it, his face dropped. All the blood left his face, leaving it ghostly white. He slammed the red phone down and grabbed my computer.

"He leaned down on that huge wooden desk of his while standing out of his chair. He snatched me up by my shirt and dragged me out into the hallway while saying something about having to leave right that instant. Somebody rounded the corner in front of him. He froze. The two took a moment there to stare at each other. I took a look too.

"I knew the guy at the end of the hall. He was my best friend both at work and outside it. Before I had time to say anything, my boss threw me down over the railing outside his office, and I landed on the concrete floor below. It hurt, but I had managed to break my fall halfway down on a cartload of wooden crates passing by before sliding off those onto the floor.

"In my pain, I saw my boss try to run down the stairs, but somebody else met him at the bottom. He tried to jump the railing. He landed awkwardly, as he had taken the full fall, likely shattering his left leg in the process, and dropped the computer, which slid across the floor to where I was lying. The man at the bottom grabbed my boss and beat him across the face with the back of his hand.

"My friend joined in a second later with a kick to the ribs. Four or five more men rounded the corner and joined in. A couple of them grabbed me and held me up to watch as they pulverized my boss with whatever they had nearby. They kept beating him, even after he had clearly died. I mean, his head was split clean open from a steel pipe. His…"

The voice cut off. It drew a deep and long breath in and blew it out slowly. It started back in. "They left him a bloody pile of shattered limbs. Then they turned to me. I wrestled with the men holding me hostage, thinking they were going to do the same to me. I yelled at them and looked around for help. My coworkers who weren't part of this were all held up as well around me, but they didn't beat me. My best friend held the bloody steel pipe up to my chin, brushing it against my cheek to smear the blood, and just held it there for a minute, looking at me.

"Something in his eyes pleaded for help. A teardrop ran down his cheek. He lowered the pipe and wiped the tear with the same hand with a sniffle. Then he just pointed at the remains of my boss and a mop lying dry on the ground nearby before walking over to the computer and picking it up. He opened it and looked at the screen. He grinned and shut it. Then he brought the computer back over and held it out in front of me. I would have grabbed it, but the other guys had my arms pinned back.

"He saw me struggling and frowned. When he stood, he waved at the men holding me. One of them passed my right arm to the other fellow but let go of it before the other grabbed it. I punched the guy still holding my left arm in the nose and wrenched my arm from him. I ran off. They chased me for a bit, but I knew this entire layer of the facility and was able to slip through some crawl spaces to get to this basement. It has been two days since that according to my watch, which I spent building this contraption you are listening to now while hiding out in this basement.

"Most people don't even know this place exists down here, but there are loads of tools. The fact that the AOC didn't install heavy security measures in this building before the FEC bought it out is really playing in my favor here. There are no security cameras or anything like that here either, which means I am relatively safe. The entire first day was filled with them banging around up there for some reason.

"I used that time to build this crazy contraption and a system that guides compasses here using electromagnetic fields in the walls, which I already told you about, by hacking the computer mainframe from a terminal in the corner. I also rigged up a device that will work as an electromagnetic pulse generator if the system detects an Exoduster around in case you are having problems with those in the future, as they are sentient now.

"About halfway through the second day, the banging finally stopped. I checked the door just a little bit ago. The whole place is empty, and they seemed to have taken as many Boomships as they could to get out of here." There was a long pause. A sigh broke the silence.

"I can't stay here. I am doing the same thing as them. I need to get back to Capital City and try to protect you and warn everybody else. The phone lines are all cut. Those were the only way we had to talk with others this far out in the Exodust. But whatever that group is planning, it revolves around that hack I found. It can't be good. I have to try to fix this before whatever they have planned goes down."

The voice cut himself off again. He resumed a moment later. "I hope you never have to hear this message. I hope I can tell you all of this in person. Maybe I can make it back if I take one of the Boomship transports back over the mountain pass and down into the valley. That should put me back by about tonight, where I can use my own computer to try to hack into their servers and compromise their efforts to upload an update to all the Boomships before they get it out. Wish me luck."

The sound of the recording shut off. There was a brief period of dead silence before the speaker crackled and the voice returned. "Listen, I am adding this right before I leave. I discovered that all of the security features in the facility are down. That isn't a good sign, but I was able to grant you access to pilot every vehicle on the planet.

FEC pilot seats will also obey you. I saw an engine and a generator left behind near the garage. You might be able to rig that up into some kind of generator to get power running here if you want to hole up in it.

"I saw the poster of the same compass you have and realized I couldn't leave without telling you I love you. I hope this isn't the last time you ever hear that from me, but I have no time to lose now. Good luck. I am sure you will use this information I have recorded here well."

The speaker clicked off, and the room returned to silence. The Survivalist let out a small whimper. The Young stood in shock. He looked over at the Survivalist sobbing onto her knees against the wall. He crossed the room to the table, grabbed the C&G can, and carried it back to her. He forced it into her hands. "Take this with you. Come on. Let's get you back to the group."

She gripped the can against her chest. She broke down into full tears. Her head felt like it was exploding. She knew being angry was a fruitless cause, but she couldn't help it. She felt as if the whole world had betrayed her. She hated it. What had she done to deserve this? What had anyone done to deserve this? Why did those people kill her dad's boss in cold blood? She had always thought that getting the truth of her family and of the Crisis would make her feel better, but all it had done was leave her with more questions and no sources to answer them.

Stress overwhelmed her. She locked up halfway up the stairs to lean on the railing. Hot tears burned her cheeks, making her vision nothing but a mosaic blur. She couldn't breathe for her own nose running. Her head throbbed. Her chest hurt. Her ears rang so loudly that she couldn't understand the Young's words of comfort. She felt a push on her back and managed a few steps forward. She tripped over a stair and collapsed onto them in a writhing mess.

Two arms wrapped her up and lifted her from the stairs. They pulled her against a chest. The chest was warm, much unlike how everything else but her head felt. She squeezed in against the warmth, absorbing it in an attempt to calm down. Panic overran her senses as she realized what was happening, what had happened, and what might happen later. Her mind ran itself until it was scrambled beyond comprehension.

The world around her faded off as she bounced down the hallway. Someone was yelling. It was right into her ear. A distance voice replied in some muffled and frightened tone. The world around her faded to black. She grunted and coughed. She realized her grip on the can was loosening, so she gripped it once more. Did...did she still have it there? Yes. She could feel the cold bite of the metal on her skin. It must have...

This story is far from over.

Additional Readings

Below are some items collected along the way.
Enjoy.

Chapter 1: Cooking Asexual Moonshrooms

Dish One: Moonshroom Stew

Ingredients:

One Large Moonshroom
Water

Procedure:

1) Obtain a large moonshroom with a bright-green stem. It is critical the stem is green as to prevent intoxication and nausea from consumption.
2) Cut the complete stem from the head of the moonshroom. Do not discard.
3) Mash moonshroom head until homogenous.
4) Add water until mashed substance becomes slightly runny. Avoid allowing clumps to form.
5) Tear chunks of stem and add to mixture. Do not crush. Chunks should float on surface.
6) Add more water until chunks begin to sink into substance.
7) Place in stove or other heat source until chunks of stem in mixture are soft. Stew should be hot to the touch.
8) Optional: Add seasoning of your liking.
9) Let stand for short period until cool enough for consumption.
10) Enjoy!

How to Use Steering Controls

Steering Control Diagram

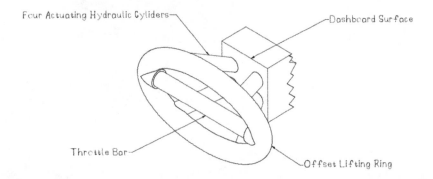

Four Actuating Hydraulic Cyliders — Dashboard Surface

Throttle Bar — Offset Lifting Ring

Starting the Vehicle

Push the steering control directly inward horizontally. This will cause the control to latch into place and allow for control of the vehicle. This feature was added to prevent accidental movements of the vehicle upon entering the cockpit.

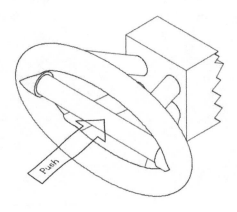

Push

Once the control is in functioning position, pull directly upward on the controls without tipping the controls in order to pick the vehicle straight upward off the surface it is resting on. Loose surfaces may be thrown about underneath the vehicle. This will not cause any problems with the vehicle.

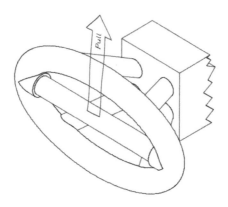

Basic Movements

The center horizontal beam of the control is the throttle and braking system. The throttle is able to rotate around its axis. Twist the center beam forward, as in the top of the beam away from the pilot, to ignite the blast burner and have the vehicle accelerate in the forward direction.

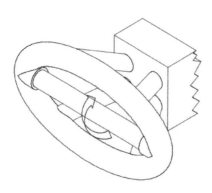

Twist the center beam backward, as in the top of the beam toward the pilot, to reverse the blast burner and have the vehicle accelerate in the backward direction. Please note that reversing at high speeds will not harm the blast burners on the vehicle. It can and should be used as a method of scrubbing speed quickly.

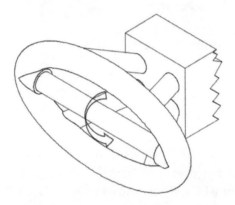

If the throttle is released, it will snap back to the neutral position, and the vehicle will coast freely. Keeping the control perpendicular to the level floor and pulling the right side of the control will pivot the control clockwise and turn the vehicle right.

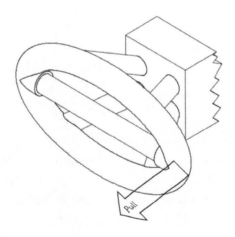

Keeping the control perpendicular to the level floor and pulling the left side of the control will pivot the control counterclockwise and turn the vehicle left.

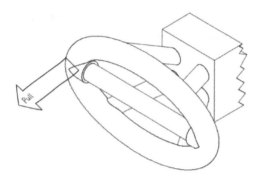

Pulling the control directly upward without tipping will lift the vehicle higher off the surface. Each vehicle has a maximum monolift height that it can lift off the surface. It is wise to find the maximum monolift height upon the first use of the vehicle.

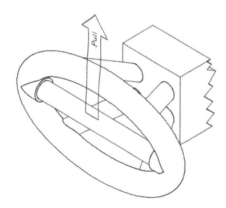

Pushing the control directly downward without tipping will lower the vehicle closer to the surface. The controls will automatically prevent the vehicle from dragging the surface below but will not adjust to avoid an object ahead at speed.

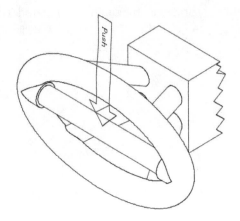

The controls will not lift the vehicle to compensate for oncoming objects. It will only maintain the height off the surface directly below the vehicle as defined by the pilot. The pilot must manually use the control to lift the vehicle to avoid the oncoming obstacle.

Offset Lifts with Lift Thruster Differentials

This section is for vehicles with Lift Thruster Differentials only. Monolift vehicles are not capable of anything below. If the vehicle is monolift, ignore this section. Some vehicles are equipped with front and rear Lift Thruster Differentials in addition to the central monolift. If the vehicle has the front and rear differential, it will have two additional smaller lift thrusters, one on the far front and one on the far rear with the monothrust in the center. These vehicles have the capability to lift the front or back of the vehicle higher than the opposite end. This allows for high-speed maneuvering in the forward and reverse direction.

To use the front lift thruster, tilt the top of the control toward the pilot. This will pick the front end off of the surface higher than the back. It is the strongest differential thruster and can be used to exceed the maximum monolift height temporarily. This is useful for flying over the top of short obstacles at speed.

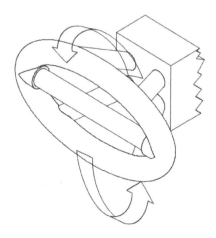

To use the rear lift thruster, tilt the top of the control forward, away from the pilot. This will cause the nose of the vehicle to dive and lift the back end. This is useful for reversing over taller obstacles at speed.

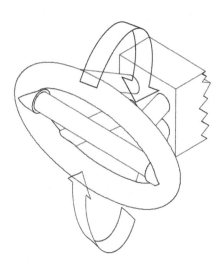

Please be aware that the vehicle may still glide sideway into an object if gliding around a turn if it is only equipped with front and rear thruster differentials. Do not perform sharp turns with the vehicle at speed if it is not equipped with side Lift Thruster Differentials as the vehicle may capsize.

Some vehicles are equipped with side Lift Thruster Differentials in addition to the central monolift. If the vehicle has the side differentials, it will have two additional smaller lift thrusters, one on the left and right side with the monolift in the center. These vehicles have the capability to lift the left or right side of the vehicle higher than the opposite side. This allows for high-speed maneuvering around turns by banking as well as the ability to lift the side of the vehicle to float over a tall object in a turn.

To bank right, turn the control clockwise, parallel to the dashboard. The left side of the vehicle will lift, allowing a right banking turn. This can also be used to dodge an incoming short object from the left side by floating over the object.

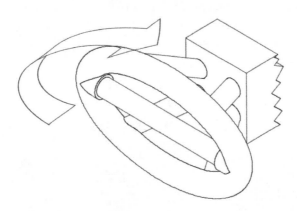

To bank left, turn the control counterclockwise parallel to the dashboard. The right side of the vehicle will lift, allowing a left banking turn by pulling on the right side. This can also be used to dodge an incoming short object from the right side by floating over the object.

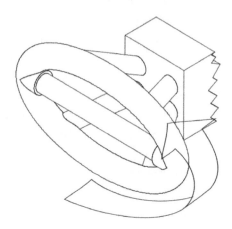

Some vehicles are equipped with front and back Lift Thruster Differentials as well as side Lift Thruster Differentials in addition to the central monolift. If the vehicle has both sets of thruster differentials, it will have five total thrusters—one on the left, front, right, and rear of the central monolift. This allows the vehicle to perform diagonal lifts. For example, the pilot can tip the top of the control toward themselves and turn the control clockwise to lift the front left of the vehicle. This can be combined with a left turn, which will allow the vehicle to make a sharp turn up a steep embankment on the left at speed.

Shutting Down

Simply let go of the steering control. After a few seconds the control will return to the disconnected state. The vehicle will shut down, come to a stop, and lower to the surface.

AOC Compass

Made using the same technology
as our navigation systems
for outer space programs.

Hey
Tindertuft

Quick Facts

1) This book has 12,139 minutes of work (only counted when the document was open and being worked on). That is 202.3 hours of work, or 8.43 days of staring at this document. That is not including the time thought about it outside of writing on the document itself. None of this time includes the time to edit or otherwise work on the book after the initial writing was completed.
2) Not including this last section or images, the book has 181, 267 words.
3) In real time, I am guessing this story took me close to if not an entire year to get written out.
4) The original book was planned to be twice this long. I drastically underestimated the length of the book when I started, so I had to split it in two. As a result, at least one sequel is planned. The story is far from done.

About the Author

Brady Gorrell, at the time of writing, was twenty-one years old. He was a student at West Virginia University, studying mechanical engineering. He wrote this in his free time while at college, mostly at night. This is his first successful publication of a book. He enjoys traveling and has been to the forty-eight contiguous US states, parts of Eastern Canada, Tokyo in Japan, and Ecuador. These travels were accomplished with an RV initially and, later on, motorcycles with his family. All these experiences have helped shape this book. He also enjoys playing video games, especially story-driven games, building games, and multiplayer, competitive games, from which he drew inspiration to write this book.

CPSIA information can be obtained
at www.ICGtesting.com
Printed in the USA
BVHW081736291121
622774BV00001B/37